Also by Hannah Fielding

Burning Embers

Praise for *Burning Embers* and Hannah Fielding:

'*An epic romance like Hollywood used to make...* The setting is Kenya in the 1970s, where Coral Sinclair has come to claim the plantation she has inherited. But the handsome stranger she met on the boat from England turns out to be Rafe, the notorious womanizer. But an unlikely love blossoms against a wild and beautiful backdrop. Ahh!' **Peterborough Evening Telegraph**

'*Five stars to Hannah Fielding and Burning Embers...* Have you ever wished to run away from everyday life and leap into the pages of a mesmerizing book that will embrace you with romance, thrill you with suspense and carry you into a new world filled with exotic fragrances and vivid descriptions that will animate your imagination? Well, *Burning Embers* is all that and then some... Hats rst novel – ar ew

THE ECHOES

OF

LOVE

HANNAH FIELDING

LONDON
WALL
PUBLISHING

First published in hardback and paperback in the UK in 2013
by London Wall Publishing Ltd (LWP)

First published in eBook edition in the UK in 2013 by
London Wall Publishing Ltd (LWP)

Excerpt from Thomas Mann, *Death in Venice* © S. Fischer Verlag, Berlin 1913

Excerpt from 'Burnt Norton' in FOUR QUARTETS by T.S. Eliot. Copyright ©
Estate of T.S. Eliot and 1936 Houghton Mifflin Harcourt Publishing Company;
© renewed 1964 by T.S. Eliot. Reprinted by permission of Faber and Faber Ltd
and Houghton Mifflin Harcourt Publishing Company. All rights reserved.

The moral right of the author has been asserted.

A CIP catalogue record for this book is available from the British Library.

PB ISBN 978-0-9926718-1-5
EB ISBN 978-0-9926718-2-2

1 3 5 7 9 10 8 6 4 2

Printed and bound in the UK by
Berforts Information Press

FSC
www.fsc.org
MIX
Paper from
responsible sources
FSC® C021018

London Wall Publishing Ltd (LWP)
24 Chiswell Street, London EC1Y 4YX

*For my daughter, Alexandra, whose knowledge of Italian art
inspired me and whose loving support is a constant motivation*

Footfalls echo in the memory
Down the passage which we did not take

T.S. ELIOT, *BURNT NORTON* – 'FOUR QUARTETS'

Multitudinous echoes awoke and died in the distance. . .
And, when the echoes had ceased, like a sense of pain was the silence.

HENRY WADSWORTH LONGFELLOW, 'EVANGELINE: A TALE OF ACADIE'

CHAPTER 1

Venice Carnival, 2000

The clock struck midnight just as Venetia went past the grand eighteenth-century mirror hanging over the mantelpiece in the hall. Instinctively she gazed into it and her heart skipped a beat. In the firelight she noticed he was there again, an almost illusory figure, leaning against the wall at the far end of the shadowy room, steady eyes intense, watching her from behind his black mask. An illusory figure indeed, because when Venetia turned around, he was gone.

She shivered. Nanny Horren's voice resounded through her head, reminding her of the strange Celtic superstitions that the Scottish governess used to tell her. One in particular came to mind. *'Turn off the light and look into the mirror by firelight at midnight on Shrove Tuesday,'* the old woman would whisper to the impressionable and imaginative teenage Venetia, *'and if you see a face reflected behind your own, it'll be the face of the love of your life, the man you will someday marry.'*

Was this what had just happened to Venetia? Was this stranger the love of her life?

Rubbish, she remonstrated, laughing at her own reflection, *you're mad! Haven't you learnt your lesson?* Venetia had indulged in such fantasies several years ago and had only managed to get hurt. Now, she knew better. Still, she did not move away. Instead she leant closer to the mirror that reflected her pale, startled face in the flickering light, as tremors of the warm feelings of yester love suddenly flooded her being. For a few moments she seemed to lose all sense of where she was and felt as though she stood inside a globe, watching the wheel of time turning back ten years.

Gareth Jordan Carter. 'Judd'. It was a diminutive of Jordan, chosen by Venetia who hated the name Gareth and didn't much care for the name Jordan either. Judd had been her first love, and as far as Venetia was concerned, her last. She had been young and innocent then; only eighteen. Today, at twenty-eight, she liked to think she was a woman of the world, who would not allow herself to be trapped by the treacherous illusions of passion, however appealing they might seem. She had paid a high price for her naivety and impetuosity.

Venetia tried to shake herself clear of those haunting phantasms and her thoughts ambled back to the masked stranger – well, *almost* a stranger.

Their brief encounter had occurred the evening of the first night of *il Carnevale di Venezia,* ten days before Shrove Tuesday...

*   *   *

It was nearly seven-thirty and the shops were beginning to close for the night. The wind that had blown all day had dropped, and a slight haze veiled the trees, as if gauze had been hung in front of everything that was more than a few feet away. The damp air was soaked in silence.

Venetia tightened the belt of her coat around her slim waist and lifted the fur collar snugly about her neck. The sound of her footsteps echoed off the pavement as she hurried towards the Rialto Bridge from Piazza San Marco, a solitary figure in an almost deserted street. She was on her way to catch the *vaporetto* waterbus that would drop her off at Palazzo Mendicoli, where she had an apartment. A few huddled pedestrians could be seen on the opposite pavement, and there was not much traffic on the great inky stretch of water of the Grand Canal.

Suddenly Venetia saw two figures spring out in front of her from the surrounding darkness. They were enveloped in *carnevale* cloaks, with no visible faces, only a spooky blackness where they should have been. A hand materialised from under the all-encompassing wrap of one of the sinister creatures and grabbed at her bag. Chilled to the bone, Venetia tried to scream but the sound froze in her throat. Struggling, she hung onto the leather pouch that was looped over her shoulder and across her front as she tried to lift her knee to kick him in the groin, but her aggressors were prepared. An arm was thrown around her throat from the back and the second figure produced a knife.

Just as he was about to slash at the strap of her bag, an imposing silhouette emerged from nowhere and with startling speed its owner swung at Venetia's attacker with his fist, knocking him off balance. With a grunt of pain the man fell backwards, tripping over his accomplice, who gave a curse, and they both tumbled to the ground. Then, picking themselves up in a flash, they took to their heels and fled into the hazy gloom.

'*Va tutto bene*, are you all right?' The stranger's light baritone broke through Venetia's disoriented awareness, and he looked down anxiously into her large amber eyes.

'Yes, yes, I think so,' she panted, her hands automatically going to her throat.

'Are you hurt at all?'

'No, no, just a little shaken, thank you.'

'You're shivering. You've had a bad shock and you need a warm drink. Come, there's a *caffetteria* that serves the best hot chocolate in Venice, just a few steps from here. It'll do you good.' Without waiting for a response, he took Venetia's arm and led the way down the narrow street.

Venetia's legs felt like jelly and her teeth were chattering. 'Thanks,' she murmured, still trying to catch her breath, her heart pounding, as she let herself be guided by her tall, broad-shouldered rescuer, who seemed to have taken the situation into his hands.

Thus does Fate cast her thunderbolts into our lives, letting them fall with a feather-like touch, dulling our senses to the storm they would cause should we realise their devastating powers.

They sat in silence at a table in a far-off corner of the crowded *caffetteria*. There was too much noise to talk and Venetia was exhausted, so she concentrated on appraising the man sitting opposite her as she listened to the music playing: Mina's nostalgic 1960 love song, '*Il Cielo in una Stanza*', the unashamedly romantic hit that was so Italian, and therefore still frequently played as a classic all over the country.

Venetia's guardian angel looked more like Lucifer than a celestial being, with his tempestuous blue eyes, curiously bright against the warm tan of his skin, which slanted a fraction upwards under heavy, dark brows when he smiled. They were staring intently at her now with an emotion that puzzled her, and for a few seconds she found herself helplessly staring back into them. It was like gazing into shimmering water.

Strong, masculine features graced his nut-brown face beneath a thick crop of raven-black hair, sleek and shining, swept back from a wide forehead. He wasn't good-looking in the classical sense, his face was too craggy for that immediate impact, but he was a striking man who emanated controlled power, someone used to making decisions who would not be swayed by any argument or sentiment; a hard man. Still, his steeliness was tempered by the enigmatic curve that lifted the corners of his generous mouth into a promise of laughter; this, coupled with the deep cleft in the centre of his chin, gave him a roguish expression that Venetia found appealing.

The waiter brought over a cup of hot chocolate, a double espresso and a plate of *biscotti* which, he said, were offered *con i complimenti della casa*. Her rescuer was obviously a regular customer.

Venetia took a few sips of the thick, warm brew. She felt herself revive as it trickled down her throat, becoming a warm glow in her stomach that reflected on her cheeks.

The stranger smiled at her. 'Feeling better?'

She nodded. 'Thank you, you've been so very kind.'

His smile broadened. 'You are welcome, *signorina*. It is always a pleasure to come to the rescue of a beautiful lady. My name is Paolo Barone, at your service.'

Venetia had been working in Italy for over three years as an architect cum interior designer in her godmother's architectural firm, and was used to the gallant ways and the charm of Italian men. She found their smooth repartee refreshing, and sometimes even amusing, but never took them too seriously. Paolo Barone was different. Maybe it was because she was in shock and felt vulnerable, but nevertheless her heart warmed to this man, who, although not that young, was still in his prime – middle to late thirties perhaps – and she relaxed. Still, even though the circumstances in this case were unusual, Venetia was unaccustomed to accepting invitations from strangers, so she deliberately made no conversation; and to her surprise neither did he.

As she raised the warm cup to her lips with both hands, she was aware of him looking at her directly with unabashed interest. Was he trying to decipher her, she wondered. Relieved that the hot drink's effect on her cheeks was hiding the slight confusion she felt beneath, she sipped a little too quickly and cooled her lip with the tip of her tongue. Then realising what she had done, she glanced up to see his expression deepen into something else, which made her instantly lower her eyes.

When she had finished her chocolate, Paolo smiled at her. '*Andiamo?* Shall we go?' he asked, cocking his head to one side and scrutinising Venetia.

Sparkling hazel eyes flecked with gold smiled back at him through long black lashes that somehow did not belong with her chestnut hair. 'Yes. Thank you for the hot chocolate. It is really the best chocolate I've had in Venice.'

He helped her with her coat, lifting her glorious long locks over the fur collar. At five foot seven inches, Venetia was tall but as he faced her and began buttoning the garment himself, she noticed again how he towered over her. His hands were strong and masculine; she had a curious sensation of warm familiarity, as though he had performed this act with her several times before. Yet mingled with that feeling came one of embarrassment; his touch seemed a rather intimate gesture instead of the impersonal indifference of a stranger, and she drew away with a little nervous laugh.

'Thank you, that won't be necessary.'

He held her gaze intently for a moment, as if surprised at what she had said, and she looked down again, for some reason unable to meet those now midnight-blue eyes and their burning intensity. Then he smiled and held the door open.

'By the way, I don't know your name,' Paolo said as they stepped out into the misty night and began walking towards the Grand Canal.

'Venetia. Venetia Aston-Montagu.'

He quirked a black eyebrow. 'A very romantic name, Venetia, like our beautiful city. But you're not Italian? You speak Italian like a native.'

She laughed. 'Thank you for the compliment! No, I'm actually English, but I was named by my godmother, who is Venetian – she was my mother's best friend and she insisted I learn Italian.'

'So you're on holiday here?'

'No, I live here.'

'Nearby?'

'No, in the Dorsoduro district. I need to catch the *vaporetto*, as the entrance to the building where I live is on the Grand Canal.'

'My launch is moored across the street. Dorsoduro is on my way. It would be a pleasure for me to drop you off.'

'No, thank you. You've already been very kind.'

'It's late and snow has been forecast for tonight. The *vaporetto* is bound to be almost empty. I wouldn't want you to come to any harm, *signorina*. I will give you a lift.' He spoke quietly with an air of command, his hand coming up to her elbow, but she avoided it hastily.

It was very tempting to accept, but Venetia would not allow herself. This stranger was a little too attentive, she thought, and though she had been grateful for his kind invitation to a hot chocolate when she was in distress, and could still recall the feel of his hands buttoning up her coat, she was not in the habit of being picked up by men.

'No, really, thank you very much. I'm used to travelling by *vaporetto*. It's quite safe.'

Paolo did not insist, and for the rest of the way they walked in silence through the narrow, tortuous alleys, Venetia conscious of his nearness in every fibre of her being.

It was bitterly cold. The wind was whistling and a bank of threatening cloud hung over Venice like a white cloak. As they arrived at the waterbus stop, a few snowflakes started to come down. A couple of gondolas, their great steel blades looming dangerously out of the soft velvety mist, glided by swiftly over the gently lapping waters.

'Are you sure you don't want to change your mind? It looks as though there'll be a blizzard and the *vaporetto* may be delayed.' He looked at her with a polite, but guarded smile and she felt a momentary pang of regret at her determination to escape him.

Paolo's pride was spared a new refusal as they heard the croaky purr of the *vaporetto* announcing its lazy approach.

'Here comes my bus,' Venetia said cheerfully. 'I'll be home in no time.'

The boat appeared and presently drew up at the small station, bumping the landing stage as it did so.

'Thanks again for all your help, *signore*,' she went on, smiling as she held out her small, perfectly manicured hand to say goodbye. Paolo took it in his own, which was large and warm, and held it a trifle longer than would be usual. Venetia stood there with waves of heat passing over her, her senses suddenly heightened at this contact. She abruptly withdrew her hand.

His blue hawk eyes gazed down at her, intent though unfathomable, and he paused uncertainly. 'Will you dine with me tomorrow night?' he uttered in a low voice.

It would be exciting to dine with Paolo, she thought, *but you must run from him,* urged the echo of an insistent voice within her; *this man has the power to hurt you.*

'I'm so sorry,' she replied stiffly. 'I'm afraid I'm busy.'

'That's a pity.' He sounded as if he meant it, but did not insist, leaving her feeling curiously disappointed. Silently, he held out his hand again and she took it, also without a word. There was nothing lax or vague in his firm grasp. Like many people, Venetia was swift to gauge character by the quality of a handclasp and had known many apparently vigorous men whose fingers were like limp fish. Once more, she was aware that Paolo's large, sensitive hands held a strength and vitality that stirred her deeply.

She hurried on to the *vaporetto*, suddenly eager to flee, but as the waterbus pulled away from the quay, she watched him go up the stairs and disappear into the snow-white night with a strange sinking of the heart, wondering if she would ever see him again.

*   *   *

As it turned out, in the weeks that followed they had bumped into each other often at Fritelli, a coffee shop on Piazza San Marco where Venetia stopped for a *cappuccino* and *biscotti* every morning on her way to work, and where she met friends at weekends for afternoon tea. Most days, Paolo arrived as she was leaving. Whenever their eyes met fleetingly he had smiled politely, but had never stopped to talk.

And then tonight, on *Martedì Grasso*, at the grand ball that *il Conte* Umberto Palermi di Orellana was giving to celebrate the inauguration of his new home near Piazza San Marco, and the first Carnival of Venice of the twenty-first century, Paolo had been there.

His tight Arlecchino outfit, with bright multi-coloured patches in diamond shapes and a short frilled collar, clung to his muscular body like a second skin, and he wore a white felt beret adorned with a rabbit tail. Almost stopping in her tracks as she entered the vast ballroom, Venetia had recognised him behind the devilish features of his half-face leather black mask, not only because his athletic body towered over most of the guests, but also because of the easy, almost imperious way he moved through the crowd; and then, of course, there was the deep cleft in the middle of his chin that would always give him away.

All evening, Venetia had been aware of the penetrating azure-blue eyes following her around the room, and when occasionally she met their enigmatic gaze she found it hard to tear away from their scrutiny. Neither approached the other; they had merely circled around their mutual awareness, which vibrated heavily in the air no matter how dense the crowd became. And now, as she stood before the mirror, he had once more been there in the dim shadows, the reflection of his powerful silhouette caught in the glass by the leaping light of the fire, devilment sparking from behind the black mask.

A couple of ladies in full carnival dress, their heads clouded in veils of black lace, walked out of the ballroom, interrupting Venetia's reverie. She looked up at the clock. Firelight fell warm on the gold dial. Time had stopped for her. She was amazed at how long she had been standing there reminiscing about her lost life, feeling the echoes of a lost love. She should be returning to the party.

Venetia took off her Columbine mask. She still sensed she was half in the past and paused for a moment with her hand on the door handle, listening to the voices and the people laughing, before turning it and going in.

The long room, flooded with a golden glow from enormous Murano chandeliers, was filled with people mostly hidden behind carnival masks, their disguises rich and colourful, glittering with the splendour of diamonds, rubies, sapphires and emeralds. Transformed by their costumes into stately drifting mountains of Burano lace, with bright trailing peacock skirts of old brocade, the ladies flicked fans before their false faces, their heads adorned with neat, small cockaded *tricorne* hats. The men too wore masks, but with noses protruding like beaks – the famous '*bauta*': the Venetian disguise *par excellence*. For many, the costumes consisted of voluminous black cloaks wrapped high about the neck, and with white stockinged legs they looked much like crows and magpies. Their heads were covered in large black *tricorne* hats with sweeping lines, the edges trimmed with flickering white feathers. There were also costumes inspired by historic court attire, and other fantasy-style masquerade dress. The surreal majesty of the scene reminded Venetia of the dusky painting '*Il Ridotto*' by Venetian artist Pietro Longhi that she had always found so spooky, with its macabre eighteenth-century figures disguised in masks and shrouded in shadows.

The heavy door shut softly behind her and she stood there unnoticed, looking at the guests in their fabulous attire, some masked and others not, all talking and laughing. She felt a little underdressed in her simple, frilled, low-bodice *sobretta* outfit, with its patchwork of red, green and blue diamonds and large white apron and mob cap trimmed with lace. It represented a woman of the people, Colombina, the perky maid in the *Commedia dell'Arte,* the counterpart of Arlecchino, and some-times his wife. The costume had been given to her by her godmother for a New Year's Eve masked ball in London, and it had won first prize; in fact it had been the fancy dress party at which she had met Judd; but that was years ago... so much had happened since... she must not think of all that now. She shook off her darkening mood and moved into the sea of revellers.

Unconsciously searching for him among this pandemonium of masks, Venetia did not see Paolo immediately. When she spotted him, she saw that he had bared his face and was stand-ing at the far end of the room, a glass of champagne in one hand while the other rested on a Corinthian column. He gave an impression of fitness and steadiness, and the other men in the room appeared to Venetia washed out in contrast. Though his body was lithe, there was something almost frightening about his apparent strength and vigour, almost inhuman. She had to admit that Paolo, with his dark head and his deeply tanned face lit by those arresting cobalt eyes, was the most striking-looking man she had ever seen: like a fallen angel.

He was surrounded by other figures of the *Commedia dell'Arte*. There was *il Dottore* wearing a long black tunic with a jacket that reached all the way to the ankles, black shoes, a skull-cap, and an unusual black mask that covered only the nose and the forehead; *il Capitano* in his suit with bright multi-coloured stripes and gilt buttons, a feathered cap and a frightful sword; and *Pulcinella* in a loose linen blouse belted with a rope over thin tights and a huge warped belly, a hat and a half face-mask with a hooked nose giving him a bird-like look.

Paolo was watching Venetia intently, only half listening to the vivacious blonde *cortigiana* in a splendid golden outfit of the courtesan with plunging neckline and a tall conical hat. His head stood out distinctly against the ochre wall, his gold-bronze face beaming now as his host approached. They spoke for a few minutes before threading their way through the crowd towards Venetia.

Il Conte Umberto Palermi di Orellana was a tall, aristocratic, handsome man in his early thirties who was known to be a *bon viveur* and a philanderer. Tonight he was Lelio, the elegant *innamorato*, lover of the *Commedia dell'Arte*, in a sumptuous court dress of the eighteenth century. As was customary for that character, he did not wear a mask. He had met Giovanna Lombardi, Venetia's godmother, at a drinks party. A few weeks later, he had approached Giovanna's firm, Bianchi e Lombardi: Architetti, to take on the refurbishment of Palazzo Palermi, which he had just inherited from his father and which was in need of a total face-lift.

The renovation and redecoration of old historic buildings was Venetia's speciality and the Palazzo Palermi had become her first big project while working in her godmother's firm. After graduating from Cambridge, she had completed a Master's degree in History of Art at The Courtauld Institute of Art in London, and had then spent some time at Istituto per l'Arte e il Restauro 'Palazzo Spinelli' in Florence. Even though she showed great promise in straightforward architecture, Venetia did not feel it was her calling. And so Giovanna had put her in charge of Marmi Storici e Pietra, the department for the restoration of historic buildings, where she was able to develop her talent for restoring mosaics and murals. She had immediately excelled and was beginning to make a name for herself in Venice.

Still, as her first major venture, the job had taken almost a year to realise, during which time Umberto had tried every trick in his book to seduce the young woman. It had been to no avail: his Adonis good looks and his charm left her cold. By the end of the assignment, not only had Venetia managed to carry out the works to completion without falling out with the notorious womaniser, but she had also gained the Count's admiration and respect. So much so, that he had asked her to marry him. She had been careful to turn him down gently. Umberto had taken the rebuff graciously but told her that he would not give up hope and she could be sure he would be asking her again.

'Venetia, *cara*, you look amazing,' Umberto Palermi oozed, taking her hand and bringing it up to his lips, his eyes brilliant with lust. 'I have neglected you all evening. You must forgive me.' Not waiting for her reply, he added: 'Have you met my best friend, *il Signor* Paolo Barone?' and, turning to Arlecchino, he introduced her. '*La Signorina* Aston-Montagu, who waved her magic wand over this place and from a heap of ruins turned it into a *magnifico palazzo*.'

A twinkle lit Paolo's eyes. 'No, I don't think I have had the pleasure of meeting the *signorina*,' he declared, a deep and sexy cadence in his voice.

Venetia felt herself blushing. It was really annoying not to be able to control one's colour. Looking up at Paolo, she was sure he must be aware of the effect he had on her. With luck he would conclude that it was actually Umberto's proximity that was affecting her in this way. His powerfully masculine glance swept over her and she felt an involuntary heat unfurl deep down. Remembering her manners, she put out her hand.

'How do you do?'

Suddenly, there was a violent blast of noise before their hands could make contact.

'Ah, the fireworks have begun,' exclaimed the Count, taking Venetia's arm. 'Come, let's go outside.'

The heavy brocade curtains were drawn back by young pages in eighteenth-century court dress and elegant floor-to-ceiling windows pushed open, inviting guests on to the wide veranda. Venetia was grateful for the interruption that was taking her away from Paolo's silent scrutiny. No man since those far-off days had stirred her as he did, almost from the moment they had met on that strange, dramatic evening. And while Umberto escorted her on to the terrace, although she could not see him, Venetia had no doubt that Paolo's eyes were still dwelling on her with that curious expression she was beginning to know, and which puzzled her so.

Umberto's *palazzo*, only a few streets away from San Marco, had an enviable view over the waterway, where the neck of the Grand Canal joined the broader stretch of water in front of the city's famous square. The wide canal had filled with boats and barges gliding along the dark water like fireflies: each vessel was trimmed with arches of leaves, plume-like clusters of ferns, and festoons of laurels, lit up with hanging paper lanterns and slowly drifting through a swaying mass of gondolas.

From the far end of the Grand Canal, among the docks and shipping, the muffled darkness burst suddenly into a festival of dazzling light as the mysterious night sky became starred with jewels of fire.

The fireworks soared into the air; they broke into raying diamonds of brightness and then floated towards earth, expiring in their downward flight. Other little points of light appeared, followed by tongues of flame rushing up from different places and flowing out large luminous bubbles of silvery-blue and green and sapphire. One after another, the rushing rockets sprang hissing upwards and, towering far above the water, burst with a soft shock into a golden sheaf of fire. They hung uncertain for one moment in the sky, and then came showering down.

Clouds of pearly smoke billowed out from under the trees on the *piazza*, turning from ruby to rose, from yellow to opalescent green – curling mists that enriched everything around and transformed the crowds and buildings into a fabulous, surreal painting soaked in gold.

And then, from out of the obscurity, a crystal waterfall curved up like a wave and streamed down into the darkness, white, noiseless and shimmering; on and on the miraculous river of silver flowed over and melted away, and a great uproar surged from the masses watching from the boats and on the shore.

Venetia was aware of Umberto being called away at this point and relieved that his rather overt attentions next to her were now gone, but Paolo had remained. She could feel his eyes on her, close somewhere, and she shivered slightly though she was transfixed on the scene of great splendour and movement above her. She watched, fascinated, as huge plumes of golden spray tossed high in the sky, looking like dissolving feathers of fire, and wheels of green spun madly to extinction, hurling burning sparks from them and blooming fire flowers.

There was a pause before the spectacular finale. Soft stars of colour shot up, soaring into the night. One after another, bouquets of primrose, coral and lilac rose slowly into the sky, blossomed exotically there, flamed, floated, and then vaguely fell, as if faint with an excess of beauty, into the inky water below, which received them and folded them to itself with a kiss.

It was the first time Venetia had witnessed firework displays on such a magnificent scale from so close, and a strange excitement coursed through her like the blazing colours that had exploded across the dark sky above. 'A dream being born in the night air,' she murmured to herself, as the glimmering wonder ended.

'Just that one moment of insane beauty before they consume themselves and die,' answered Paolo's voice out of the darkness.

Venetia was now even more aware of his disconcerting presence behind her, as Paolo's low voice seemed to caress her provocatively, and she was not sure whether she wanted to welcome his company or flee it.

After a brief moment, she heard him whisper again. 'Life ought to hold that once for everyone.'

'And sometimes it does,' she breathed, without turning round. The evening had taken on a vivid and surreal magic that she did not want to let go of. She did not need to speak to him to know that he was feeling it too, and this connection between them that needed no words intrigued and scared her in equal measure.

The guests were crowding back into the ballroom. Paolo silently took Venetia's arm and guided her away from the crush towards the balustrade that overlooked the canal. Leaning his back against the stone, he took out of his pocket a packet of cigarettes and offered her one. She declined.

'May I?'

'Yes, of course, go ahead.'

He lit the cigarette, drew on it deeply and shook his head. 'Quite a spectacle, don't you think? The last moments of joy before the imminent penance of Lent!' He gave a deep throaty laugh that somehow made her join in.

'It really was a magnificent show. I've never seen anything like it!'

'Only the Venetians know how to celebrate in such an extravagant way, and the dawning of a new millennium just adds to the wildness. It's all part of a long history of revelry and decadence in this city, where prince and subject, rich and poor joined in the festivities, and could move around in complete safety and freedom in the secure knowledge that their identity remained incognito. Carnival fulfils a deep human need for subterfuge, don't you think?' He gazed at her again, his expression unreadable.

She glanced at him sideways. 'I suppose it's an occasion for people to hide beneath a mask and to change a role they have in ordinary life.'

Despite the cold, they remained outside for a while, silently savouring Venice in moonlight. All the lights of the great city were reflected and broken up into countless points of fire, like diamond dust, in the ripples of the Grand Canal; and a velvet canopy of sky, powdered with stars above, sparkled over the distant roofs.

Paolo had turned away to stare at the dazzling view that lay in front of them. 'None of the works of art of man equal the sight of Venice by the Grand Canal when the moon is up,' he murmured, as though to himself, his attention riveted on the endless line of *palazzi*, the ghostly whiteness of their marble fronts rejuvenated by night. 'For a few hours the moon hides the city's frightful rotting façades behind a transparent silver mask, giving her some fairylike quality, a sort of innocence. Looking like this, one would never guess at the decay which gnaws at her core.' And then, facing her again, he added, 'A rude awakening for the unsuspecting tourist when daylight comes, don't you agree?' His voice was passionate, a touch melancholy, and the deep timbre of it once again drew her to him in that curious way she found difficult to fathom.

His words echoed Venetia's thoughts, but not quite. Ever since she could remember, Venice in moonlight had held a strange magical power over her. She didn't see the decay, only the enchantment. The whiteness of Paolo's collar threw the darkness of his tan into relief. She remained silent but was aware of him like never before. For once she held his smoky-blue gaze, fascinated by the changeable colour of his eyes but disturbed by its sad expression and the bitterness in his voice. They stared at each other, a curious feeling quivering inside her, like the vibration of a violin string after it has been played. It was no more than a moment, but it seemed so much longer to Venetia and it left her uneasy.

She glanced at her watch. 'I really must be going.'

'There'll be no *vaporetti* running at this hour,' Paolo remarked, his gaze still intent on her face, 'and even if there are a few, they would not be safe – too many drunken people out tonight looking for a good time. Let me give you a lift. My launch is not far off.'

'I'm sure I'll find a water-taxi without difficulty.'

And then abruptly, his eyes darkened. 'What is a pretty woman like you doing out on the town on her own, on a night like this? I can't believe you have no *fidanzato*, Venetia. Is the man away? Do you have no father? No mother? No brother to care for you?' His outburst was almost angry as he threw down his cigarette, crushing it vigorously beneath his heel.

Venetia bridled with irritation, though it was mixed with an odd thrill at the sound of his using her name for the first time. The questions were rather forward, she thought, choosing to focus on her sense of outrage. The fact that he had rescued her from a robber's assault did not give him the right to be personal. The added vehemence of his reaction was too territorial for her liking. Venetia abhorred a macho stance in men. After all, it was to get away from a domineering father that, when her mother died, she had decided to make her life in Venice.

She forced a stiff smile to her lips. 'Really, I'll be fine. Thank you for your concern.'

Paolo sighed. 'As you wish, *signorina*, but at least let me walk with you until you find a taxi. I don't think you realise what the town will be like on this Carnival Night. Don't forget, it's the first carnival of the new millennium. I dare say the people of Venice will be celebrating tonight with even more enthusiasm than in previous years. The Piazza San Marco, which you must inevitably cross, will be the scene of Babylonian events one can hardly imagine.'

Venetia hesitated. He was probably right; she had already found the journey a little hazardous on her way to the ball. Still, she was uncertain. Sometimes the power of his presence frightened her; she sensed a possessiveness she felt smothered by, even though he sounded really concerned and she knew perfectly well that his suggestions were sensible.

Paolo frowned and his mouth narrowed a little. 'What are you afraid of? You risk much more going through the town on your own than if you ride alone with me in my launch.' His face softened as he tried to suppress a smile. 'I promise you I'm harmless.'

They laughed. He had a point. 'All right, I agree that it would be rather risky for me to walk through the crowds on a night like this,' she admitted meekly. 'I will still insist that you only accompany me until I find a taxi, though, and then we'll part company.'

'Very well then,' he shrugged, but his eyes held amusement. 'You're an exasperatingly stubborn young woman.'

After gathering their cloaks, they went in search of their host to say goodbye and thank him for his hospitality. Venetia sensed that Umberto was slightly put out that they were leaving together; he gave them an acid look but refrained from comment.

The chilly breeze with its tang of salt was invigorating after the smoky atmosphere of Palazzo Palermi. Venice tonight was a city of rapture. It was late, but the carnival was still in full swing. The crowds were surging through the security barriers to sport with each other in mock battles, playfully throwing flowers, and dancing in the streets. The *poliziotti* were good-humouredly trying to keep them back, but it was a gesture doomed to failure as the scrum continued to hurl itself across the streets.

Like a diamond, this magnificent city, Queen of the Adriatic – dubbed *La Serenissima* – seemed to offer a thousand facets. There were stars in the sky and glitter everywhere else: the arcade in Piazza San Marco was brilliantly lit, the shops and rows of alcoves a shimmering crystal grotto, secular and ecclesiastical buildings transformed by lights into something still more glorious. But that was only the stage on which figures seemed to move. They were caricatures of life, on the verge of the unreal, amusing as well as sinister and disturbing. The music was loud and noisy, with blares of sound shooting out from every corner. Vivaldi poured forth through loudspeakers and pre-Lenten celebrants danced by the thousand through the floodlit *piazze*, their faces hidden by expressionless masks with slit eyeholes.

Paolo was right. Everywhere Venetia looked was crowded with masked people singing, embracing without restraint, in a vast, sprawling *commedia*. Hidden behind their disguise, it was as though they were indeed free to act as they wished, uninhibited by custom or convention. She was grateful to have accepted Paolo's invitation to accompany her, at least until she found a taxi. Legions of revellers stood roaring with enjoyment on the quayside of the Punta della Dogana and the Punta della Salute; and in a mass of highly decorated boats, some more spectators waited for the ladies' regatta on the Grand Canal, an unusual and clearly welcome spectacle for many of the male Venetians leaning over the sides and whooping out lusty encouragements.

Paolo walked briskly, holding Venetia's arm protectively, subtly proprietorial, shielding her with his stalwart body against any possible chance contact with those revellers thronging the squares and the bridges. For just a moment she forgot her misgivings, thinking only that this man, who seemed so steady, so self-assured, was different from the usual men she had dated over the last ten years. An intriguing mixture of sophistication and macho maleness, she felt strongly attracted to him.

They had been walking through the crowds for almost half an hour. Venetia had to face facts: there were no taxis for hire; everybody was celebrating.

'*Allora, signorina,* how do you feel? Will you now accept a lift in my launch, or would you prefer us to spend the rest of the night wandering aimlessly in Venice?'

They had reached a quay where a number of luxurious launches were moored. The smile he gave her as she met his piratical gaze lit up his face with a sudden boyishness, lifting from it the lines of bitterness that she had perceived earlier on the veranda.

'To tell the truth, I feel rather irresponsible.' She looked down a little sheepishly.

He placed a hand on her shoulder and gave it a brief squeeze. *'Non ti preoccupare,* don't worry, no harm done. My launch is here.' He signalled towards an elegant boat in beautiful polished mahogany, with her name, *La Serenissima,* written in dark-red letters on the side. 'It'll be no trouble to drop you off at your apartment in Dorsoduro. As I've told you before, it's on my way.'

'Thank you, I really don't know what I would have done without you.'

'We say in Italian, *"la necessità è la madre dell'invenzione",* necessity is the mother of invention.'

'As we do in England, as well as "Don't look a gift horse in the mouth"!' replied Venetia, laughing nervously.

He held out a hand to help her aboard and, as she prepared to step down into the launch, Venetia let go of the big black-and-white striped mooring pole. The boat rocked and she faltered, losing her balance. She would have been sent reeling down into the slimy water had not Paolo, with remarkable deftness, caught her, and she fell against his chest, the breath smashed from her breast.

The hands on her upper arms were iron-hard; the length of his body so close to hers that she was unable to stop her own body's response as once again a heat darted down inside her. Paolo murmured something into her hair that she did not grasp, and she looked up, what seemed an infinite distance, into blue irises so bright that they appeared almost like sapphires. Her mind emptied.

For a long moment they stared at each other, oblivious of everything else. Paolo pulled Venetia a little tighter against him and her hand slipped down to his chest. She could feel the steady thump of his heart beneath her fingers and sensed the warmth of his skin radiating through his clothes. His muscular body was lean and hard, and the spicy fragrance of his aftershave tinged with tobacco went straight to her head. His face was so close now that she could see the deep creases at the side of his eyes and his mouth, and other faint lines, a little lighter, which stood out on his parchment-tanned skin. Up this close, he looked older, with a few stray threads of grey in his thick black hair. Despite the noise and the pandemonium surrounding them, they stood clasped as though alone in the world.

Flames ran through Venetia, and suddenly she wanted quite desperately to move even nearer to him, for his arms to hold her snugly in his embrace, to feel his mouth close over hers, to... She shut her eyes as she felt her need intensifying – the painful yearning for his caresses... This was not only madness, it was dangerous; but it had been a long time since she had felt this stirring inside her, since she had been aroused by the heat of a man's body, since an emotion had possessed her with such violence. She knew what this was and she hated it, but still could not help herself.

'You're tired; you can hardly stand up. Come inside and sit down, you're shivering.' Paolo's voice came to her through the reluctant fog of her desire, as he guided her to one of the soft leather seats inside the cabin. He sat her down, brought her a thimble-size glass of *grappa* and settled himself beside her, after having poured one for himself. 'Here, drink this, it will warm you.'

'*Grazie. Ancora una volta sei venuto in mio soccorso,* once more you've come to my rescue,' she said, a new elation in her voice as she took the glass from Paolo's hand and tried to calm herself. She was thankful that he had been ignorant of the insanity she had been prey to for a few moments, and hoped he had not noticed the deeper colour that throbbed in her cheeks.

The cabin was large with seats upholstered in *Napa*, a soft Italian leather. It was surrounded by windows adorned with royal blue curtains held back with cords. All the fittings were in plated chrome brass. Venetia noted that it was luxurious without being ostentatious and garish, unlike many of the launches. Somehow, she wasn't surprised; Paolo did not seem to be a show-off.

'This *grappa* is quite different to the one I've normally been served,' she told him, as she took a sip of the warm amber liquid. 'Isn't *grappa* supposed to be crystal-clear with a distinctive herbal aroma? This is almost golden in colour, and spicy with...' Venetia hesitated and took another sip, '... hints of liquorice and vanilla, is that right?'

Paolo whistled with admiration. 'You have a very sensitive palate, *signorina*. You're right. This is a *Reserve Grappa* from a vineyard not far from my home in Tuscany. They only produce a thousand bottles a year, for the personal use of the family and local consumption. Do you like it, then?'

'It's got an interesting taste which I admit could become addictive, but I'm afraid it's more potent than I'm used to.'

Paolo flashed her a charming smile. 'I see you're feeling better. Your cheeks have regained some colour. It was a long walk in the cold.' He downed his *grappa* in one go. 'Would you like a little more?'

Now that Venetia had actually accepted the invitation he had pressed on her to ride in his launch, he seemed oddly ill at ease, she thought. Was he perhaps embarrassed by their accidental collision earlier? Had she misread his apparent attentiveness as something more?

'No, thank you – I think we can be on our way now,' she said, her guard back up again. 'I have taken up enough of your time.'

'*Non dirlo neanche per scherzo*, don't give it a thought.' He poured himself another glass, which to Venetia's surprise he drained with equal velocity. 'Would you like to sit outside or stay in the warmth?'

'I'm definitely an outdoor person, so I think I'll sit *alfresco*.'

'You said the other day that the way into your home is on the Canal in Dorsoduro. I know Dorsoduro well and there aren't many buildings with their entrance on the waterfront.'

'My apartment is in Palazzo Mendicoli, a couple of streets away from the church of San Nicolò Dei Mendicoli.'

'*Sì, sì, so bene dov'è il palazzo Mendicoli é*, yes, I know well where that is. I spend a lot of time in Dorsoduro. It's a place of artists, designers and writers, and is one of the most beautiful and charming of Venice's *sestieri*,' he said, his voice soft as he stood looking at her intently again, motioning for her to go up on deck ahead of him. For some inexplicable reason, she found herself blushing, and she hastily climbed the steps, keen to cool her flushed cheeks.

They went back into the open air and Venetia sat on the U-shaped bench, upholstered in blue and white canvas, in the stern of the boat. Silently she watched Paolo's hard, firmly corded figure move around the boat untying the ropes, preparing to exit the mooring basin. Her eyes slid down to his narrow hips as he stood at the helm, tall and relaxed, every contour of his sculped, muscled thighs outlined in his tight Harlequin costume. Once more she was struck by the leanness and power of his body, by his shoulders that were imposing without being heavy. Paolo had a build very similar to that of Judd's, she noticed, and she found herself wondering how it would feel to make love with him.

The waters were still alive with the laughter of masqueraders in gondolas, gliding to and fro, the ripples from their oars making dancing swirls of light as they went by. Still, Paolo was able to skilfully negotiate his launch through the narrow channel. As he came out into the Grand Canal he accelerated suddenly, bringing the beautiful craft to life. Lifting its nose out of the water, it surged forward with a roar.

The moonlight glistened down on the lagoon that surrounded the city, so bright and clear in the velvety blue night, and music came floating over the sea from every corner. The heart of Venice was still throbbing with merriment. The revelry promised to go on until dawn, which was still some time away.

There is magic in the air tonight, Venetia told herself as she watched the rows of stately marble *palazzi* pass by before her eyes, their almost Moorish façades bathed in floods of silver light. She had never found the scenery so enchanting, even though she had been taking this journey twice a day for the past three years. Her gaze fell again on the man at the wheel, his hands guiding the great bulk of teak and mahogany with controlled tension. Paolo stood legs apart to brace himself as they hurried along, creating white waves of foam on either side of the rocking motorboat. He had taken off his cap and his black hair, strewn with its occasional grey, appeared longer than she had at first thought, as it stirred about his face, ruffled by the breeze. His mouth in his well-defined, jagged profile looked severe and hard. He gave the impression of being totally self-sufficient, and yet he carried an aura of loneliness that intrigued her. Paolo was a mass of contradictions and Venetia was suddenly struck that this stranger, to whom she felt so curiously attracted, like Venice itself, might not be all he seemed. She shivered.

Afraid that if she went on staring at him he might turn round and think that she was anxious to make conversation, Venetia concentrated on the scenery. The motorboat had gathered speed and moved swiftly on the waves with a loud swishing sound. The cold light wind blew sea spray against the young woman's skin and tugged gentle fingers at her hair, lifting stray tendrils from her forehead.

Soon the imposing Byzantine *campanile* and elegant fifteenth-century porch of the church of San Nicolò dei Mendicoli came into view. Venetia got up and came to stand next to Paolo. 'There it is,' she said, pointing at the dazzling building.

The engine slowed and the craft nosed its way smoothly towards the Baroque doorway of Palazzo Mendicoli. Its ornate marble façade was lit on either side by elegant electric lamps. The boat stopped within an inch of the tall wooden posts that stood out of the water like giant bulrushes next to the steps of the palace, and Paolo turned off the motor.

'I hope you didn't get wet,' he said with an impish smile. 'When I'm at the wheel I tend to forget myself, and I've been told that I drive rather recklessly.'

'Not at all, I enjoyed the drive as much as I enjoyed the evening. Thank you, you have been very kind.'

Paolo's blue irises gleamed with hidden laughter. Reaching out casually, he caught hold of her wrist and gently drew her towards him. 'So you will have dinner with me tonight.' The phrase was said as if a *fait accompli*, and there was an intensity beneath his playfulness that hit Venetia like a speeding train.

Again, she was aware of that curious pull of the senses that had transfixed her earlier that night when she had fallen against Paolo, a physical magnetism she had thought herself immune to. Her instinct for self-preservation – as well as her irritation at his boldness – made her stiffen. 'It's usual to ask, not command. Anyhow, I'm busy.'

His dark features assumed a wolfish grin. 'Would it help if I got down on my knees?'

Venetia felt unusually nettled. 'No,' she replied coolly, edging away from him.

His mouth twitched with barely concealed amusement. 'And so it will be tomorrow.'

He was pressing her, and she was having none of it. 'No, not today, not tomorrow, nor the day after,' she retorted, allowing herself to be piqued.

'So you are attached, you do have a boyfriend in your life, or maybe he is already your *fidanzato*,' he chided.

Now he was giving her every reason to get angry. How dare he be so personal? He seemed up until now far more restrained and collected. What had happened? The man must be drunk. Come to think of it, she had seen him all evening with a glass in his hand, and then of course there were those shots of *grappa* he'd downed as if drinking water. What if he suddenly decided to drive off with her? And though he gave no sign of the thoughts she ascribed to him, Venetia was quite willingly working herself up. She had the feeling that something was happening to her over which she had no control, and a shiver of apprehension slid down her spine.

Her eyes sparked with anger. 'That's actually none of your business.'

Her indignation seemed to sober Paolo up. He drew in his lower lip, catching it between his teeth, and visibly tensed. 'I apologise, *signorina*, if I have appeared forward. I think I must have been carried away by the exuberance of the Carnival spirit. Please forgive me.'

Extending her hand she forced herself to smile. '*Addio*, *signore*, and thank you again for all your kindness.'

The planes of his face seemed to harden, the armour so exactly like her own slipping back into place. His voice was clipped. 'So it will be *addio* for us rather than *arrivederci*.'

'I'm afraid so,' Venetia whispered, turning away and heading over to the platform. The boat rocked, and Paolo was immediately beside her, his ardent eyes mutely questioning, as if trying to read her mind while he helped her regain her balance and then on to the quay.

Curiously enough, she was less eager to leave now, but she had burned her bridges and it was probably all for the best. As Venetia walked into the *palazzo* without turning, and heard the sound of the motorboat's engine starting up again, she couldn't resist a glance over her shoulder. She felt a moment's regret as she saw *La Serenissima* and her captain move off in a cloud of white foam, but then she regained her senses. Love had already made a painful fool of her. *I have no intention of going through that again,* she repeated to herself as she took the lift up to the third floor.

*   *   *

Palazzo Mendicoli was situated in the western half of the Dorsoduro *sestiere*, the southern peninsula of Venice, on the curve of a small canal. It was a sixteenth-century, three-storey marble façade palace that had been restored in the early nineties and turned into flats, Venetia's being on the top floor. As Dorsoduro was on higher ground than the rest of Venice, one side of the building had the fortune of overlooking the lagoon to the south, and the other faced north-east, with a view over the rest of Venice towards the Grand Canal. Most of the interior's architecture, as well as the paintings and frescos in the rooms, was still intact. Only the part-end of the building, destroyed by fire over the three floors in the nineteenth century, had been totally restructured to create an elegant, old-fashioned lift.

Venetia's apartment was large, with high ceilings carved with lecherous little cherubs pursuing strange-looking winged

animals, and plaster borders embellished within borders. It had
been her godmother's home for the five years that followed
Giovanna's widowhood, until her marriage to Ugo Lombardi.
After this, Giovanna had moved to her new husband's penthouse at the top of the Bella Vista building in the centre of
Venice. It had been the site of an old decaying *palazzo* that Ugo
had bought, on which he had erected a very modern block of
luxury flats where the couple lived during the week. At weekends, they escaped to the Lido, the long sandbar south of
Venice, where Ugo Lombardi had bought his bride the most
fabulous old palace with beautiful views across the lagoon to the
city's medieval towers and ochre rooftops.

The walls of Venetia's apartment were covered in pastel silks,
and the heavy brocade curtains that hung from the tall windows were in deeper but matching tones, held back by thick
cords of the same colour. Each room had a marble fireplace
that was elegantly decorated with scenes of mythological fauna
and flora. The massive pieces of furniture were a mixture of
Baroque and Rococo styles, comfortable and curvy, and also
embellished with motifs such as shells, flowers, and the stars
of the firmament.

Venetia lay back on her cloud of pillows in the sumptuous
four-poster baldachin bed and watched the dance of lights
reflected from the canal below as they chased each other on the
stucco-decorated expanse of white ceiling. The centre of the
plafond was graced with an amber Murano glass *lampadario*,
which hung from a chain of plump, clear glass globules. Lilies
and daisies, their flimsy petals blown in tones of honey-
coloured opaque glass, peered through their delicate green
leaves near the top of the chandelier; and friezes depicting
chromatic birds and butterflies adorned each corner of the
room, enlivening the pale walls.

The bedposts were draped in vanilla-coloured brocade curtains that matched the bedspread. At the foot of it stood a magnificent *cassone*, an opulent gilded and painted chest dating from the sixteenth century, which had been in Giovanna's family since then, and on which were represented winged *amorini*, the infant cupids pulled in chariots by mythical animals representing the Roman gods. It was customary in those days to place these ornate trunks in the bridal suite as a trophy furnishing of Italian aristocrats. A Carrara fireplace jutted forward into the room from between the two tall, narrow windows, topped by an imposing, gilded Rococo mirror. Immediately opposite was a painting by Francesco Zuccarelli of a river landscape with travellers; and underneath it stood a sofa and two gondola-shaped mahogany *bergère* armchairs, upholstered in gold silk fabric with laurel and bee motifs. Facing the bed, beautiful panelling, decorated with *ton-sur-ton* garlands, created a whole wall of built-in cupboards with a secret door into the bathroom, which gave a modern touch to the sumptuous room.

Venetia was unable to sleep. For the first time since she had come to Venice, she found the loneliness and the silence of her room oppressive. Ghosts of the past were crowding in on her. Memories that she thought she had finally banished from her mind, which she had spent years trying to erase, began to drift back. Judd's handsome, smoothly chiselled face swam before her eyes… Judd Carter, the man who had abandoned her just when she had needed him most.

She had been only eighteen when he swept into her life. They had met at a Christmas Snow Ball in London over ten years ago. Venetia was just starting her architecture degree course at Cambridge. Judd was twenty-eight, and though he came from a modest background, he had managed to make his way through scholarships into The Royal Military Academy, Sandhurst, and had become an officer in the Parachute Regiment. Theirs was a case of love at first sight, and a year later Judd had proposed.

Sir William Aston-Montagu, Venetia's father, had violently opposed the marriage, forbidding his daughter to carry on the relationship. Despite the fact that he was ex-army himself, he was an overbearing, old-fashioned kind of man, the type who expected his daughter to marry someone from her own background: 'one of us', as he used to infuriate Venetia by saying. Lorna, her mother, though sweet-natured and kind, was subdued by her husband's overwhelming personality and would never have dreamt of contradicting him. Nonetheless, the young couple had carried on seeing each other discreetly, which wasn't often, as most of the time Judd was called away on duty in Northern Ireland, but they wrote to each other regularly.

And then one day, while Judd was away on manoeuvres in Ireland, Venetia had discovered she was pregnant. She had gone to her parents and told them that whether they accepted it or not she would be marrying Judd Carter, as he was the father of the child she was carrying. Despite his wife's pleading, Sir William had stood his ground, threatening to disinherit his daughter if she did not end the pregnancy immediately. Even now, Venetia could hear her father's harsh voice ringing in anger:

'This young man is a social climber and a gold-digger. He might have wormed his way into Sandhurst, and into your bed, but he's certainly not going to become a member of this family! I will not let you dishonour the Aston-Montagu name, young lady. You get rid of that thing you're carrying, or you are no more my daughter and you'll not see a penny when I'm dead.'

Venetia had then written to Judd with the news, but he had never replied. The string of letters she had sent after that, imploring him to get in touch, had all remained unanswered. If he'd been killed in action, she would have found out very quickly, so even having that morbid reason for his silence was denied her. She was devastated. To her parents' horror, she had moved out of the house and stayed with her best friend, Emma. She was not yet twenty but, despite everything, she had decided to keep the child, too full of her own blind emotions to listen to reason. Three months later, she had fallen headlong down the stairs in a shopping arcade and the injuries to her back had resulted in her losing the baby. Sir William and Lorna had gone to visit her in hospital, where they made their peace, and Venetia had returned home.

She had spent a few months after that in a sort of suspended state, too tired to think coherently, stunned by what she had gone through. But Venetia was not one to be beaten by circumstance and so, with the support of her mother and her friends, she gathered her forces, faced life again, and taken up her studies where she had left them. She had never heard from Judd again.

By now, after a decade, the wound had healed; Venetia had forgiven her father and Judd, but the emotional scars remained, leaving her disenchanted with the whole idea of love and romance. Ever since Judd, she had been wary of relationships, and had never again taken a man to her bed, earning the reputation of being ice-cold among the men in her circle.

Tonight, Venetia allowed her thoughts to turn to Paolo. Her conscience pricked her. Had she been unnecessarily harsh? *'No, not today, not tomorrow, nor the day after...'* Contrarily now, she wished she had not said those words, with their finality, aware that what had prompted such an extreme reaction was her unwillingness to get involved with this man.

Up until now, Venetia brooded, she had always felt in command of the situation when in the company of the opposite sex, despite the fact that some of the young men she had met over the years had been handsome and successful – dream husband material for any other girl but herself. She had built a fortress around her heart, taking a kind of grim satisfaction in not letting anyone past her defences, content to wield her independence and professional dedication like a weapon against her own loneliness.

Suddenly faced with this stranger, Venetia was disconcerted and she was not sure of herself any more; the conflicting emotions he aroused made her feel keyed-up and restless. The courtesy he extended towards her was all part of the Italian tradition. Nevertheless, his repeated invitations to dinner seemed genuine – in fact she had detected a certain sadness in his eyes and in his voice at her desire not to extend their acquaintance. Still, this was not about Paolo, this was about her, and that odd tingling sensation that had come over her suddenly when she had landed unwittingly in his arms on the boat. At this recollection Venetia felt the same sort of delicious tremor run through her, her heartbeat quickened and she found herself secretly hoping that their paths would cross again – a feeling so different to the loathing and dread she usually experienced at the idea of a man's touch. Something she couldn't put a name to, a glimmer of a feeling out of focus, was taking shape inside her, and she was unsure what it meant.

Dawn was breaking and, as Venetia hovered on the edge of sleep, her hazy mind kept interchanging Judd's and Paolo's faces behind her heavy eyelids. A vague sense of guilt pricked at her, almost as if she was somehow being unfaithful to Judd. But Judd had abandoned her and she was alone, haunted by his love. Why could she not forget him? She had the singular impression something was escaping her, something important that she could not immediately pinpoint… it was there, on the tip of her tongue. And then finally fatigue took over and she drifted off into a deep, troubled sleep. Dreams came to her of a dark figure pursuing her through the streets of Venice, cloaked and masked, whispering her name. But each time she turned round, he had gone.

CHAPTER 2

The early morning sun, streaming across the marble balcony through the French windows, settled in a bright bar on the bed. Venetia lay sleeping on her back, one bare arm flung out above her head on the pillow and the other resting on the brocade eiderdown. The golden rays crept upward, touched her breast, her alabaster throat and her fine features in repose. Waves of chestnut hair were scattered on the pillow and tumbled in a cascade down her shoulders, framing her diamond-shaped face with its delicate jawline and dramatically prominent cheekbones. It was an unusual face, with an open and alert expression that made artists want to sculpt and paint it; and the young Englishwoman had experienced no shortage of offers since her time in Italy's most artistic and beauty-obsessed city.

Venetia stirred; the dark heavy lashes lying in two feathery arcs below her closed lids fluttered up as the gold-flecked eyes opened wide. With a languid movement she lifted her head and glanced at the little bedside clock on the night table just as the great bells of the Campanile started to swing and the whole of Venice vibrated with overwhelming, melodious noise. It was nine o'clock; the day had officially begun.

Venetia had barely slept two hours – but she had no work today, apart from meeting with Francesca in the afternoon; she could afford a lie-in. She knew that she would not get much sleep during the coming week as she prepared for the grand exhibition at the much celebrated palace, Ca'Dario. Getting a little extra sleep now would be sensible, but the airy room was filled with light. Her bedroom windows stood wide open all night no matter what the weather, a habit acquired since her boarding-school days in England. Leaning back into the pillows, she pulled the heavy bedspread closer about her shoulders and curled down again.

Snuggled under the quilt, Venetia lay still a few minutes, listening to the familiar sounds of Venice floating on the air: the lap of water against the quayside, the light swish of a gondola racing by, the strident whistling of the *vaporetti*, the distant raucous hoot of a ferry carrying tourists to and from other parts of the world, the cooing of pigeons that came to rest outside her windows on the balcony, and the fluttering gentle thunderstorm of their wings as they flew back into the sky. She loved this district, Dorsoduro. Quiet, and more like an island than the touristy areas of the rest of central Venice, it was full of artists and students, hanging out in bohemian *caffetterias* and bars, talking, reading, discussing life and art over coffee or a glass of wine. She allowed herself to drift off again, enjoying this moment of tranquillity.

Finally she slipped out of bed and ran to the window that overlooked the lagoon. As her apartment was on the third floor, the stretch of shoreline was visible for miles. The waters were very blue under the cloudless sky, sparkling in the sunshine; everything was clear in the crystal air, but it was still very cold. A heavenly morning, too beautiful to stay inside!

Venetia went into the adjoining bathroom and ran herself a bath. She loved its pink mosaic walls and the way the tub had been enthroned beneath the window on a cream-coloured stone platform, reached by a couple of shallow polished steps, so she was able to enjoy the view over Venice as she lay in the warm soapy water. A grand Baroque gilt-framed mirror hung over the sink, and scalloped Murano glass sconces, shaped like shells, were placed on either side of it, diffusing upwards their mellow light. A delicate pink chandelier hung from the domed ceiling, complementing perfectly the warm brass fittings of the elegant room, all of which gave an air of comfortable opulence.

As Venetia lingered in a mass of scented bubbles, thoughts of Paolo fought for supremacy in her mind. She pushed them away determinedly. True, she hoped their paths would cross again, but she was not going to go looking for him. After all, she still didn't feel ready to launch into a relationship, and in her experience men seldom looked for friendship – they usually wanted much more. So what was the point? Better to think of the morning ahead. Perhaps she should use it to go over to Torcello. She never tired of visiting this almost deserted little island, at the northern end of Venice's lagoon, which was so famous for its mosaics; but maybe that would be too ambitious. At this time of year the cathedral might be closed, and the waterbuses going to the island were not that frequent. She stepped out of the bath and, towelling herself, went back into her bedroom.

Venetia loved clothes. She had taken like a duck to water to the traditional Italian way of living, *la bella figura,* which prevailed in Venice more than anywhere else in Italy, and she followed the prevailing fashion that happened to suit her so-called 'stick' figure. Her godmother had told her many times that if one day she tired of being an architect, she could always become a model. Much of her wardrobe was made up of mini-skirts, skinny jeans, jumpers and silk blouses, with a few smart suits for work, some easy morning frocks, and short and long evening dresses.

Casual but smart in tight black jeans, a white cashmere jumper and a short, glossy sable jacket, Venetia went into town to buy a newspaper and stroll the narrow streets of the city.

She had been very busy at the office since Christmas, preparing for the photography exhibition of all the restored *palazzi* that her department, Marmi Storici e Pietra, had been involved in during the past twelve years. Gathering and putting together a collection of the drawings, designs, the plans and snapshots, material samples, building fragments and models of the *palazzi* end products had been a huge job; and she had worked on the project almost single-handedly, helped from time to time by Francesca, the only other specialist in the restoration of historic buildings that worked for the firm.

The models were done by Fabrizio, a brilliant young Venetian who had been with the practice for six years. After studying architecture for over seven years, he had decided that all he liked to do was build models, a passion nurtured since the age of five. But building models was not Fabrizio's only passion. The flamboyant Italian was in love with Venetia and had courted her since the first day she had joined the firm; but, as with other men, her heart had remained tightly closed to his advances. '*Cara*, you break my heart every day, but I forgive you because you are so lovely,' he would gently scold her in his inimitably Italian way.

Venetia spent the morning window shopping, sauntering aimlessly amidst the tourists, just one of the crowd. The city, being so compact, was ideal for strolling down side-streets and picking up an array of strange and wonderful curiosities in Venice's old shops, from exotic fabrics, *objets d'art* and antiques to speciality foods, collectors' books and convex 'witches' mirrors' so particular to the city. She hadn't had any breakfast, so just before one o'clock she ended up at a pretty *trattoria* in Piazza San Marco that had just opened its doors a few weeks ago in honour of the Carnival. Pleasantly exhausted, she sat outside in the winter sun, under its red awning and next to its hedge of potted ferns, sipping her glass of white wine. As Napoleon was reputed to have said of the city's most famous public square, it was 'the drawing room of Europe', and Venetia watched the antics of the people in the *piazza* as though she were in an outdoor parlour. Absorbed in the silence of centuries, she feasted her eyes on the relics of Venice's architecture and art history.

She looked up at the Torre dell' Orologio, representing the three pillars of *La Serenissima*'s power: scientific progress, civic enlightenment and Christian faith; a splendid specimen of Venetian artwork and engineering. Its mystical, pagan influences were no less beautifully depicted in the exquisite representation of the blue and gold zodiac on the clock face. Still, she could never look at the clock without shivering at the thought of the gruesome myth attached to it. According to local legend, the engineers who built the mechanism of the gold and blue *chef d'oeuvre* had their eyes gouged out so as to prevent them from building a similar piece, and ensure that no other city could have such a magnificent clock as Venice.

Stretching alongside the Torre dell' Orologio in front of her were the fifteenth-century Procuratie Vecchie buildings housing an arcade which extended the length of the north side of the *piazza* with its shops and restaurants, round to the west wing of San Marco, constructed by Napoleon. To her right, at the eastern end of the square, St Mark's Basilica stood majestically, a symbol of Venice's history of wealth and power and a famous example of Byzantine architecture with its opulent mosaics, marble decor and huge arches. The four colossal bronze horses set into the façade of the magnificent cathedral looked out over the square like triumphant guardians. Venetia never tired of looking at the five glorious golden domes sitting on top of it, exotically eastern, and in front of it, the freestanding belltower of the Campanile, towering above her. As the waiter glided outside with her lunch on a tray and people began filling up the tables, she decided that she liked this pretty new *trattoria* and would come again.

Venetia tucked in to her grilled *soaso* – a tiny Adriatic turbot taken from the lagoons near Venice – and was just starting on her *gelato al cioccolato all'azteca*, a hot pepper and cinnamon-infused dark chocolate ice-cream, when her heart lurched and her breath caught in her throat. A man and a stunning-looking young woman, who looked scarcely out of her teens, had just arrived at the *trattoria* and were being shown to a table with a reserved card on it, two tables away from hers.

Paolo's tall, imposing frame was clad in close-fitting black cords, a grey jumper and silk scarf under a dark-grey blazer. Sunglasses protected his eyes from the glare, or maybe like most Italian men and women he wore them as an affectation. It was a cultural artifice that still made Venetia smile. There was an impression of nonchalant ease as he stood, broad-shouldered and loose-limbed, waiting for his companion to shed her coat.

The girl was of medium height with a sexy, curvaceous figure that moved provocatively without losing its grace. Enormous, dark, bedroom eyes under thick lashes took up most of her oval face. She wore her loose, luscious curls of raven-black hair pinned half up, half down in a casual tangle, Bardot style. In her snugly tight fuchsia trouser suit, which on some might have seemed too loud, she was dazzling. As she handed her coat to the waiter she gratified him with a languorous come-hither smile that Venetia was sure must have made his day. Paolo helped his date to her seat before sitting himself down opposite her, facing Venetia.

The girl was now talking to him animatedly and laughing, her bejewelled hands gesticulating gracefully in that typical Italian way. Was Paolo listening? Was he amused? Venetia couldn't tell; and although his eyes were hidden by the dark shades, she was sure that he had seen her. There was a stillness about him, a half-smile tugging at that full mouth, which if she didn't know any better seemed just for her. She found it difficult to eat knowing that he might be watching her, but she forced herself to finish her ice-cream, paid the bill and left the restaurant.

Despite feeling a little miffed at Paolo's apparent indifference, Venetia did not let the incident mar her afternoon. She had had no desire to engage in conversation with him, especially as he was accompanied, but she rather expected him to have at least acknowledged her presence, if only with a nod. Still, she was intrigued by the couple. Somehow, she wouldn't have imagined Paolo with that type of woman; they appeared so ill-suited. He was reserved and sophisticated, while his exotic companion seemed earthy, from a different background, and so much younger than him.

Venetia was not in the habit of looking down on others, she had neither racial nor social prejudices, far from it; she had suffered too much from the arrogant snobbery of her dictatorial father. But her sensitive nature made her delve instinctively into the dark underbelly of human relationships to expose the sometimes discordant elements between couples. Perhaps it was the torment of her own abandonment by Judd that made her curious as to what made people tick.

So what was the story behind Paolo and this young woman so at odds with himself? Venetia flinched inwardly as another darker, more destructive emotion pierced her awareness; she didn't want to think about Paolo alone with this girl and what they might be to each other. She was not going to let him get under her skin any more. Shrugging away thoughts of him, she walked quickly from the square, east towards the Castello district.

She was meeting Francesca at four o'clock. That left an hour and a half to kill, and so she went rummaging in one of the old

Venetian palaces that had been turned into a vast antique-
market-cum-workshop, where she often found ideas for the
refurbishment projects in hand, and where she sometimes
picked up *objects de charme* that had delighted her clients.
Though she was totally against buying fake art, Venetia was
unable to remain unmoved by the spectacle and scale of repro-
duction antiques taking place in what had become a warehouse
of beautiful things. Twice she'd had the opportunity to work
there when restoring larger pieces of mosaics, and she had been
delighted by the rather mad-happy atmosphere at the factory,
where furniture was made and pictures painted to the accompaniment of snatches from opera and cheerful old Venetian songs.
Venetia loved the character of this city's people. Their history of
struggle for survival, incredibly building the greatest city in
Europe from a mire of inhospitable mudflats, had bred a strong
sense of community that bound them together in a charismatic
mixture of warmth, fierce pride and joviality.

After sifting through various pieces in the workshop, she was
not disappointed on this occasion either, and was pleased to
find a beautiful glass-relief vase to send back to the office as
inspiration for the Palermi project.

When four o'clock came, Venetia headed back to Piazza San
Marco and met Francesca at their usual haunt, Fritelli. The
caffetteria was teaming with Venetians, the way Venetia liked it
because the rest of the year this *beau monde* retreated into their
homes, taking refuge from the tourist stampede. Being surrounded by these elegant people, listening to their musical
language, was essential to her; without it she felt she was missing
out on a crucial element of life in Venice. To be in Venice without its citizens was to know the city's stones but not its soul.

The Italians in this city were a happy lot and Francesca was
a typical illustration of the spirit of her people. She was a

vivacious, fun-loving redhead with bright-blue eyes and a turned-up freckled nose. A little younger than Venetia, every month she fell in and out of love. 'Get out before it becomes sour,' was her motto when asked about relationships, and consequently she had broken many hearts but had never experienced it herself first hand, even though she had once had a brief but disastrous marriage.

Venetia and Francesca had met at the Institute in Florence where they had become friends. Francesca's devil-may-care attitude to the world, and men, was so very different to Venetia's more serious and self-contained nature that the latter couldn't help but be charmed by the young Italian woman, and welcomed her like a breath of fresh air into her life. After graduation they had stayed in touch and had even holidayed together. From then on, a strong bond of affection and friendship had developed between the two young women. When Venetia had taken on the restoration of Palazzo Palermi, she hadn't much time for other projects and had suggested her godmother hire Francesca, who had just ended an affair with her boss and was looking for a job away from Florence.

The two young women spent an hour gossiping but mostly discussing the up-coming exhibition, while drinking *espressos* and savouring *fritole veneziane*, the authentic Venetian sweet temptation that was very much associated with the Carnival. *Semel in anno licet insanire*, 'Once a year one is allowed to go crazy,' went the saying – though Venetia and Francesca tried these sweet treats at different *caffetterias* every month, and always returned to Fritelli, where the wicked little doughnuts were filled with *Zabaglione* cream. At Fritelli these delicacies were supposedly made according to the original recipe from the eighth century, when they were considered the national cake of the Venetian state, hence the name of the coffee shop.

It was almost half-past five when Venetia and Francesca left the *caffetteria*. The square was very nearly empty. The sun was setting and an intense pink blush in an explosive sky was lighting up the Campanile, the Doge's Palace, and the wonderful group of buildings surrounding the Piazza San Marco. They stood splendidly in that curious half-light, with the last rays of the day slanting in on their rounded sides, and making them cast huge brown shadows on each other. The Grand Canal had the dramatic, blinding brilliance of a purple mirror. Far over it, the golden orb seemed to set in a flood of vaporous colour which appeared to surge up from the land and become reflected in the glimmering pools created by the broken shadows of the buildings. Waves of burning light spread all over the western sky and the boats, the *palazzi*, and the water were dyed a deep rose by the glow.

It was as they came out of Fritelli that Venetia spotted Paolo. He was ambling across the square towards the canal *fondamenta* alone, the warm light of the dying sun blazing over him. He had changed into a black coat and white scarf. Aware of an unwelcome tightening of her stomach muscles, Venetia smothered a gasp as her heart turned over in her breast.

Something in her bemused reaction must have shown in her face because Francesca, quick as a flash, followed her friend's gaze. 'Venetia, what's the matter? You look as if you've seen a ghost.'

Venetia's pulse was beating rather faster than normal. 'Nothing, it was nothing,' she muttered as she felt heat rushing to her face.

Francesca laughed and eyed her sharply. 'You could have fooled me, and you're blushing.'

She turned away and quickened her step. 'I thought I saw someone I knew.'

'Who?'

'It doesn't matter, Francesca, just let it go.'

Francesca's eyes twinkled mischievously. 'There weren't many people in the square. It couldn't have been the old lady walking her dog, nor was it that couple kissing passionately on the bank. It was either the woman pushing a pram with the three children, or else it was that striking-looking man in the black coat.'

'I've told you, let it go, Francesca, I'm not in the mood,' Venetia snapped.

'*Va bene, va bene, ti lascio in pace,* all right, all right, I'll leave you alone, but I know you well enough to realise when something's wrong.'

'Nothing's wrong, trust me.'

'Well, if you feel like telling me about it you know where to find me.'

They walked silently for the remainder of the way. At the church of San Zaccaria above Piazza San Marco, where Francesca was to catch the express line and Venetia her waterbus, they parted company.

'See you in the morning, then. We've got a heavy week in front of us. And don't forget that we're meeting *Signor* Paluzzi at nine o'clock sharp. That man's so punctual. He should be bringing us some slides for the exhibition,' Venetia reminded her friend.

'Don't worry, it's all in hand, and I've ordered some special cakes we'll offer him with coffee to keep him sweet,' Francesca replied cheerfully, and kissed Venetia on both cheeks, still eyeing her with a wry smile as she waved goodbye.

Venetia was still shaken as she sat in the *vaporetto* looking out into the falling night. What was it about Paolo that affected her so much? There was something almost familiar that seemed to grip her every time she looked at him, as if she had known him forever. Nanny Horren used to talk about kindred souls that recognised each other at first glance; but that was what Venetia had thought when she first met Judd, and look how that had turned out. She now wished that she hadn't rebuffed Paolo, even if it all meant nothing to him. But why was she wasting her time thinking of him? He was obviously attached. She needed to dispel this emotion that was taking hold of her before it set in too deeply.

*   *   *

The week before the opening of the exhibition had been nerve-wracking. Days had passed with alarming swiftness for Venetia. She was doing so much – and there was plenty still to be done – that she hardly had time to think about Paolo. Her days were spent darting backward and forward from Ca'Dario, overseeing every detail of the project. She checked lists, and supervised the packers to make sure every photograph and drawing was properly wrapped and labelled. Helped by Francesca and Fabrizio, she mapped out the layout of the exhibition, considering intriguing juxtapositions between the works as she tried to create an interesting dialogue between the art and the audience. 'Your perfectionism never ceases to amaze me, Venetia,' Fabrizio had said with a cheeky grin. 'You've rearranged that presentation three times now… I think we can safely say that our clients will not be complaining of a lack of thought behind it!'

On the day itself, Venetia was strung to high tension. It was the first exhibition she had headed, organising it from start to finish, and many of the items on display were the result of her efforts. Bianchi e Lombardi were expanding their restoration department to encompass the whole of Italy, and an advertising campaign had been put together in the hope of attracting not only a powerful Italian clientele, but also institutions and visiting foreign movers and shakers. In view of this, important people had been invited to the opening night, among them the Mayor of Venice, plus *la Contessa* Rossi-Conteni, a philanthropist whose millions had saved many historic buildings, not only in Venice but the remainder of Italy; and the senior director of the UNESCO team who regularly visited the city. Though the pressure of all this could not fail to impress itself on her, nonetheless Venetia did not betray her nerves by any outward sign; she was controlled, as always.

Only as she was dressing that evening did she allow herself to think of Paolo. It was a fleeting thought, slightly wistful because now she knew – or at least thought – that he wasn't single. She was surprised that this should leave her a little sad and longing but she was aware that seeing him, even thinking about him, troubled her.

Standing in front of her cheval mirror, Venetia studied herself with critical eyes. She wore a blush silk chiffon bustier-gown that showed off the curve of her shoulders and delicate collarbones. From the cleavage of the snug, draped bodice, the petal-thin fabric fell in a cascade of romantic folds to the floor. The internal corset, which consisted of an under-wired bra and boned waist, moulded her to perfection, ensuring a statuesque silhouette.

Venetia had washed her hair with a chamomile shampoo, which always gave her chestnut mane golden overtones. First she thought of letting it fall in long locks at the front and around the back, with thick bangs curled off to the sides; but then she decided to style it up, exposing her long neck. Brushing it back and off her forehead and sides, she pinned the top towards the centre of the back to keep her hair in place, and then she folded the rest of it beneath, up and over the pins, curving the hair under vertically and fastening it with hairpins. It looked soft and feminine and she secured it all with spray, considering the result carefully.

She chose her accessories with equal care, not wanting to overpower the dress. After going through her jewellery box, she finally chose a dainty pair of shoulder-grazing eighteen-carat gold and diamond zigzag earrings, and a matching lightning-bolt gold and diamond bracelet. Just before glancing into the mirror for the last time, she slipped on transparent pin heel sandals – ones she had bought in the eighties and which were still very fashionable – that maximised the floor-sweeping cut of her dress. She took a deep breath; she was ready to go.

Palazzo Dario stood majestically at the water's edge. At its entrance at seven o'clock in the evening, the Grand Canal had become as turbulent as the English Channel, flowing with boats of all sorts going back and forth, dropping off guests. This fifteenth-century Renaissance jewel, built in the Venetian Gothic style, somehow seemed a little incongruous among the other nearby palaces – not very tall, rather narrow and tilted to the right, like a house of cards. With its white-veneered, asymmetrical façade decorated with circular rosettes in green granite and red porphyry, its *Carpaccio* chimney pots, and its unusual flower-shaped windows, Ca'Dario was nevertheless remarkably distinctive and stunningly beautiful.

The building, now sometimes used for art exhibitions, had been lit up by huge flames set in golden torches on either side of the front. The vivid colour of its centuries-old Istria stone and polychrome marble was mirrored in the opal, undulating ripples that lapped its landing.

The interior of the Palazzo was just as dazzling, *'ezuberante'*, as Fabrizio had described it to Venetia before she had seen it for herself. It was a mixture of Baroque and Renaissance styles. Its ceilings and cornices, ablaze with gold and a myriad of colours, incorporated fine carvings with rich stucco designs, and the frescos and murals had been carried out by the hand of masters. The profusion of plush soft furnishings in the vast rooms gave the place an overpowering feel of opulence.

Prestigious guests trooped en masse into the historic palace through a magnificent archway. Artists, curators, critics, journalists and a collection of VIPs mingled on marbled floors under enormous white Murano glass chandeliers. The great reception room with its beautiful arches and tall elegant columns came to life and was filled with noise.

The Bianchi e Lombardi displays were equally fabulous. Animated groups argued over the many exhibits positioned down the centre of the room and along its walls, where Venetia had created a series of curved screens telling the before-and-after story of each one of the firm's projects undertaken during the last twelve years, in a combination of architect's drawings and photographs of the buildings. Down the centre were tables carrying models of whole plazas, demonstrating for city planners how a series of renovated and restored buildings could look.

Venetia stood at the far end of the room, explaining to an eagerly attentive American banker and philanthropist the way in which the mosaics of the small palace pictured on the screen behind her had been moved.

'The rising waters,' she smiled, 'or actually the sinking building I should say, meant the spectacular seventeenth-century floor was permanently under water. We had to seal the room and pump out the water before we could work on the rescue of the mosaic. Technically this part of the job was highly complex as the saturated walls and floor had become unstable.'

Other guests were joining her group as she pointed to the before-and-after photographs, showing how the endangered mosaic had been photographed in situ, then every piece numbered, lifted and repositioned safely and identically on a floor above.

'You'll see,' she continued, finally relaxing and warming to her subject, 'that the mosaic has been shifted and transposed back, but in a tray of inert metal, not cemented into the floor. You see a key part of our restoration approach is to ensure that the building's story is visible. We want people to enjoy the restored building, and of course to feel the ambiance of age. But we also want future generations to understand what we've done, and why. We are not creating a modern pastiche, or pretending the renovated building is in its original form. We wish to deliver delight, but also honesty.' She smiled at her small audience, who were now nodding and talking together earnestly in front of the screen of photographs.

At that moment, Venetia caught sight of her godmother, Giovanna, across the room and gestured politely that she was moving on. Giovanna swept up to her and drew her into a warm hug, kissing her cheek. 'Well done, my dear. Everything looks wonderful!'

Giovanna Lombardi was a slender, upright woman of fifty-five or so, with fine features and blonde hair severely parted and drawn back into a neat roll. There were pearls at her throat and larger pearls in her small, close-set ears. She had delicate hands and feet, and there was an exquisite order in everything about her. Her clothes were trim and tailored, Venetian style, and perfectly cut, with that apparent simplicity which in reality is not simple at all and can only be achieved by spending a great deal of money.

Giovanna had been a beauty in her youth, and was still a very attractive woman, coveted by many men, even though it was known that she was happily married to Ugo. Energetic and known to be a workaholic, she spent as little of her time at home as possible. Sometimes erratic, she nevertheless had startling powers of organisation. No opposition deterred her when she set her mind upon a course; she had complete faith in her powers, and seldom failed to get exactly what she wanted. It was no surprise then that her staff respected, admired and feared her. Venetia, who understood Giovanna instinctively, even though she was not her child, loved her godmother very much and had always enjoyed a close relationship with her.

Venetia beamed at her. 'I'm so glad you think so, *Zia*. Everyone has put in so much work and it does seem to have paid off, judging by the reaction of the guests so far.' Her eyes scanned the room as she spoke, smiling and nodding at a couple of people she recognised.

'But you are the one who has made this happen, *cara*. It's important to the firm to have such an impressive evening to showcase our work, particularly at the dawn of the new millennium. It's a new economic era now we're in the EMU, a chance even for international commissions if we can establish our reputation in Venice. Still, we could really do with a big project for this year nearer to home, and I think I might already have some potential interest.'

'Really? Who from?'

'Well, one in particular – a very interesting character.' She looked up and caught the eye of a client. 'I'll tell you later. I don't want to monopolise you and I need to mingle too.' Giovanna squeezed her arm affectionately. 'Now go and enjoy yourself tonight. I'm very proud of you,' she whispered in Venetia's ear before sweeping off among their guests.

Venetia joined a younger group who were discussing the model of Palazzo Palermi. Fabrizio, who had been describing the works that had been carried out there, turned to his colleague and smiled.

'Ah, *cara*, we're looking at your work on Palazzo Palermi. I've explained that your drawings are your dream of what might be.

These photographs are where we were, and those on the other side,' he pointed at more images, 'show where we've arrived.' Fabrizio turned to the group and grinned broadly. 'You'll agree that it's an exquisite job that *la Signorina* Aston-Montagu has achieved here, *una magnifica opera d'arte.*' He then assumed a mock-serious expression and held a hand to his chest. 'Alas, my poetry is failing me. I am only a model maker, not a wordsmith. Now I'll cede the floor to the specialist so she can tell you more about this project.'

Venetia was about to take her place among the group when, momentarily turning round, her heart lurched as she caught sight of Paolo's elegant towering figure, looking his suave best in black and white, standing among the very people who had clustered around her. His cobalt eyes compelled hers to meet them. He raised a glass to her, a deep alluring smile lighting up his face, and she blushed furiously.

Suddenly she was beset by nerves again, almost losing the capacity to think. Glad to be able to turn to the screen of images behind her, she pointed to the photos of rotted beams and wet plaster in the ballroom of Palazzo Palermi. Her temporarily paralysed brain cells started to function again. 'The core problem for all of these palaces is salt attack that seeps into the walls of the building, and rising damp that rots their exterior cover, as well as subsidence and erosion. As you know, our beautiful city is built on a swamp. Our edifices are constructed on top of oak piles sunk into the mud centuries ago. Sea levels are rising, and Venice will eventually drown. In other words, all these problems are underground.'

Listening to her own speech, Venetia felt like a non-swimmer who had dived into the deep-end of a pool and was floundering around in a sea of words. All the while, Paolo's eyes never left her face, a glint of turbulence trapped in their depths, and she had difficulty avoiding them. She could only hope that he remained unaware of the effect his insistent gaze had on her.

She couldn't afford to pause or she would lose the thread of her thoughts, and so determinedly she soldiered on. 'In our revival of these magnificent *palazzi* we use ventilation, air drains, and blocks cast from smelted waste metal slag which make good impermeable barriers. And though Venice is slowly sinking, we can only tackle the projects clients bring to us,' she said, looking around her audience but studiously avoiding Paolo's gaze. 'The complex engineering and re-engineering of the foundations of our city is the work of other specialists. Here at Bianchi e Lombardi, we do what we can and we cooperate with engineers who bring ideas from all over the world.'

Venetia smiled again, ignoring her uneasiness. 'However, I would like to end this on a note of hope. There are new technologies being developed all the time that will play an essential role in the future of architectural practice. They will open up new links between artifice and environment, between built environment and nature, and will lead to creating positive environmental changes. There is still hope for *La Serenissima* and all the wonderful endangered historic monuments of the world.'

Venetia's words met with thunderous applause. Count Umberto, who had arrived late and had joined their group in the midst of her extensive explanations, raised a glass, first to Giovanna Lombardi and then to Venetia.

'The overwhelming impression of this exhibition is of the enormous impact your work is having on our beautiful city,' he said. 'I have experienced it first hand and am grateful for the impressive work you undertook at Palazzo Palermi and the stunning results you achieved.' The Count smiled pointedly at Venetia, his intent granite-grey eyes conferring all sorts of hidden messages that she preferred to ignore. 'Restoration has always been piecemeal, building by building, room by room, reactive rather than proactive to rising tides. Bianchi e Lombardi, and more specifically Marmi Storici e Pietra, with whom I have worked closely, clearly deliver longer-term plans. I toast your achievements so far and wish you continued success in your endeavours.' He raised a glass again, as did the entire group around him.

As people dispersed, Umberto moved towards Venetia and taking her hand in his, he touched it to his lips. 'You look magnificent and your presentation was brilliant,' he murmured, holding on to her hand. His eyes, raking her from top to toe, made her feel uncomfortable. She looked up and saw Paolo. His back was turned to her, and he was helping himself to some pamphlets.

'You are very kind and very indulgent,' Venetia smiled politely and looked back to the Count, subtly trying to disentangle herself from him, but he was having nothing of it.

'Why do you fight me, *tesoro mio*? Two years I pine over you and still you resist.'

'Umberto, I have been candid with you from the very beginning. I don't deny that you're an attractive man and many women would be flattered by your attentions but I am not someone to indulge in a casual affair.'

'You have misunderstood me, *cara*, and so we must talk.' Without more ado, he put a hand to her waist and propelled her to a far corner of the reception room.

His eyes travelled slowly and appraisingly to her delicate neck and shoulders. '*Cara*, I have proposed to you. *Voglio essere l'uomo che si prenderà cura di te per sempre*, I want to be the man who will take care of you forever. I will give you everything you want: my *palazzi*, my villas by the sea, my estates in the country, jewellery worthy of a queen. We will travel the world together and you will be the envy of every woman. I am not asking you to be my mistress, but my wife.'

Venetia looked back to where Paolo had been, but he wasn't there any more. She donned a fixed smile and said: 'I am very honoured by your proposal, but at this stage in my life I have no desire to get married. There are still many things I want to do before I settle down. My freedom's far too precious to me.'

'But I love you, *tesoro mio*. I have never been interested in a woman the way I have been interested in you.' The Count's voice held the slightest hint of petulance.

This was neither the time nor the place to have such a conversation, and maybe the only way to discourage Umberto was to be blunt. Venetia raised her chin and looked at him directly. 'But I don't love you, and that makes all the difference.'

Umberto arched his eyebrows; it was plain that this sort of treatment was unfamiliar to him. His mouth twitched. 'Once you are mine I will teach you to love me.'

'I find you presumptuous,' Venetia said quietly, 'and also far too confident in yourself.'

Il Conte's features hardened perceptibly, a muscle beating erratically at his jaw. He laughed; it was an angry laugh, which Venetia didn't much care for. 'You disappoint me, *cara*. May I remind you that I'm an influential man and your wounding words have hurt me deeply. I'm sure that *la Signora* Lombardi would not be pleased if, just at the time she's hoping to expand the company, I took away the contracts I have assigned to Bianchi e Lombardi, and advised my friends and acquaintances to do likewise.'

Venetia's heart rose on a wave of passionate resentment. What right had he? Who did he think he was, this egregious, self-satisfied Italian, standing there like a tin god stamping his foot if she didn't fall into line? Her impulse was to fly at this outrageous man, tell him exactly what she thought of him, but Fabrizio appeared next to her just in time to stop the stinging reply that quivered on the edge of her tongue. He first excused himself to the Count and then turned to Venetia, who wasn't sure whether she was relieved or disappointed not to have had it out with Umberto.

'*Signora* Lombardi would like to introduce you to the UNESCO team. They're very keen to meet you – they were very impressed by your presentation.'

Umberto's eyes gleamed almost black as he stared at her and moved aside. 'We'll continue this conversation some other time.' His nostrils flared. 'Yes, *cara*, we will discuss this again, I promise,' Venetia heard him whisper between his teeth as she moved swiftly away, following Fabrizio towards the little group that was awaiting her.

The Count must have left immediately after his skirmish with Venetia because she didn't see him for the rest of the evening. She didn't see Paolo either. The last time she had caught sight of him, Umberto was kissing her hand. After that, her attention had been taken up by the Count and his unwelcome proposal and when she next looked up, hoping for a glimpse of him, he was no longer there.

The evening was long and Venetia, who should have been excited and proud of her success, felt slightly depressed. She had only one wish and that was to get into her bed and sleep for days.

'It's the anti-climax,' Francesca told her when she said she was too tired to join her friend and the other members of the practice who were going to dance the night away. 'A night on the town will do you the world of good.'

Francesca was probably right, the previous week had been so hectic that she'd had no time to think or rest. This hollow in her heart, this feeling of emptiness, was most likely caused by a sudden comedown now that the exhibition was over. Or maybe it was the unpleasant argument with Umberto that had marred her evening. There were plenty of wolves a-prowl in the streets of Venice, and Venetia had had her fair share of fighting them off, but usually they tired and let her alone. This wolf was more tenacious, and by the looks of it a nasty piece of work. Still, she hadn't gone dancing in a long time and it might be just what the doctor ordered, she thought, trying to coax herself out of her gloomy mood.

They went to La Scala, a smallish nightclub set on the island of Giudecca, south of Venice. The interior was lovely: wood floors, soft lighting, earth-tone walls offset by brightly coloured artworks by painters from Venice and the surrounding areas. The scene, cast in flickering light and shadow, was an animated one without being noisy. The music was not too loud – at least you could hear yourself speak – and they played international as well as Italian old favourites, a touch which Venetia loved. The popular Italian hits of Lucio Battisti, Mina, and Adriano Celentano, still mingled with the latest dance music from the US and UK that was all the rage throughout the clubs of Europe.

La Scala catered to an older, more decadently elegant and sophisticated clientele, all local and regulars. Everybody dressed up, good Venetian style – Italians, and more specifically Venetians, were a handsome lot – and the main thing was to be seen. One could dine at the large tables and high-backed wooden banquettes around the edge of the room, where people clustered together over intimate late-night dinners and Prosecco. However, most people sat at one of the smaller tables that surrounded the dance floor, savouring small plates of *antipasti* and the delicious house wine, chatting and getting up from time to time for a dance.

Venetia danced mainly with Fabrizio. She liked him; he was good-looking in an unassuming sort of way, and he was gentle with a great sense of humour. She knew he carried a torch for her – everyone at the office was aware of it and he was often teased about it – but he had never dared to express his feelings openly to her with any seriousness. The only symptom that truly gave him away was when his lazy, cool eyes quickened and warmed when he smiled at her, saying without the need for words that she was lovely and endearing. Venetia was always careful not to lead him on but deep down she enjoyed his harmless attention, knowing that it was no threat to her.

Nearly everyone had been drinking more than was necessary, most of the women were exhilarated and while none of the men could be called drunk, not one of them was thoroughly sober. It was the usual thing among this cheerful crowd – just harmless indulgence. Venetia was used to it and even though she was naturally inclined towards a little more self-restraint, she had occasionally let her hair down too and entered into the spirit of this sort of frivolous party. Tonight, however, she felt out of her element. She danced with various partners, heard herself responding to them, talking and laughing, but all the time her mind was elsewhere.

And then – then Paolo was before her. The crowd seemed to melt away and all she saw were those burning sapphire eyes that never left her face as he moved intently towards her. Venetia caught her breath as a curious lifting sensation blossomed inside her at the sight of him. He gave a formal bow as if she were a great lady and this a ceremonial occasion.

'You're going to dance,' he almost whispered in his low baritone as he took her hand and drew her firmly towards him.

Whatever might be happening inside her, in her rational mind Venetia knew she must never allow him, or any other person, to establish this sort of ascendancy over her. He had done this once before, on his boat, when he had told her he was taking her to dinner, as if it was an undisputable fact. And yet, though part of her rebelled, the other part yearned to be held by this enigmatic man. So although she allowed his pull on her hand to draw her slightly forwards, she looked him straight in the eye and smiled.

'Yes, I probably am going to dance – if someone asks me.'

'But that, *divina*, is exactly what I'm doing.'

Her head went up as a rebellious flame lit the amber irises. 'It's exactly what you are *not* doing. You're telling me – which I thought we'd established I'm allergic to.'

Paolo's eyes still held hers; devilish, amused eyes, showing he was entertained rather than offended by Venetia's remonstrations.

'One does have to be precise with you, I see.'

She was pleased that she had been able to assert her feelings, despite his unnerving effect on her; but also found herself relieved that he hadn't taken umbrage.

'It's advisable, as a rule, to be precise, don't you think?'

He laughed and almost swung her off her feet into his arms, and she surrendered to him, letting him draw her away. He held her close, with his head bent so that his lean, brown cheek was lightly touching hers. Like a knowing reprise, the familiar sound of Mina's '*Il Cielo in una Stanza*' floated around them once more, as it had done the first night they met in the San Marco *caffetteria*. Their steps in perfect accord, moving together as one, they gave themselves up to the nostalgic love song. They danced in silence, their eyes never meeting, lulled by Mina's warm voice, the gently pulsating rhythm and its soaring violins, like two people in a dream. Only Paolo's arms spoke, clasping Venetia closer and closer, and her body responded, yielding to him. His hand scarcely brushed against her bare shoulders, but his feathery touch scorched her to the core and her whole being came alive.

Pressing against the tautly muscled length of him, Venetia felt his need for her and the heat of desire flooded her.

An involuntary sigh floated from her lips and so, slowly, he drew her even further into his embrace. She felt as if she was spinning and falling, and he with her, as if they were both being pulled by a current they could not resist, even if they had tried.

When the music ended, Paolo's head moved so that his lips found the delicate skin of her temple, and though he did not kiss her, she felt his mouth move slightly against her hairline. They stood for a brief moment, still in that entranced silence; and then, without a word, he let Venetia go and took her back to the table. She searched his eyes, wanting to see what they held, wanting to discover if his confusion matched her own, and met with sparkling dark turbulence in his blue gaze.

To her disappointment he made his excuses and left immediately afterwards, and the lights once again went out of Venetia's evening. What had happened between them? What was this strange and heady feeling she was experiencing more and more whenever he was near?

Francesca moved closer to her friend. 'Wasn't that the man we saw crossing the square the other day?'

Venetia stiffened. '*What* man?'

'Come on, Venetia, don't give me that,' the redhead scoffed. 'The man you've just danced with. We saw him the other day crossing Piazza San Marco at sunset. At the time, I even commented on your strange behaviour, if you remember. *Al tuo confessore, medico, avvocato, e amica Francesca, non tener il ver celato*, "To your confessor, doctor, lawyer – and your friend Francesca – do not hide the truth," we say in Italy.'

'I don't recall that,' she answered in a somewhat stilted voice. She did not wish to be pushed into discussing Paolo, afraid of what she might be forced to admit – either to Francesca or to herself.

'Look here, Venetia, if you don't want to tell me about it, that's fine with me, but don't take me for an idiot. I've known

you too long, and anyhow, I'm not blind. He was there at
the exhibition today, devouring you with those fabulous blue
eyes, and he left when he saw you were otherwise engaged
with *il Conte*.'

Venetia sighed. Clearly, Francesca was not going to let go
of this. 'Fine, I'll tell you some other time. This is neither the
time nor the place. Anyhow, I'm tired now and I'm going
home.' She got hold of her clutch bag and was about to get up
but her friend placed a hand on her arm.

'Won't you wait for the others? We've got the office launch
and we'll drop you off. It won't be long now.'

Venetia paused and looked towards the dance floor where
most of her party was now rocking to the psychedelic rhythm of
Madonna's 'Beautiful Stranger'.

'No, look, they're all still dancing. You'll be here until dawn,
I'll bet. I need to get a good night's sleep because I'd like to go to
Torcello tomorrow. I want to examine those mosaics again.'

Francesca eyed her friend with concern. 'You should rest.
You've had a heavy week, and after tonight we'll have work
pouring into the office.'

Venetia pulled a face. 'Not if Count Umberto has anything to
do with it.'

'What do you mean?'

'I told him off,' she chuckled.

Francesca's green eyes widened incredulously. 'You didn't!'

'Yes, I did. But that's another story which will have to wait.'

'Won't you just give me a taster?'

'He was harassing me about his proposal and I told him
where to get off.'

Francesca nudged her and raised her eyebrows. 'You're mad
not to accept his proposal, you know. Half the women of Venice
would sell their soul to *il Conte* Umberto Palermi di Orellana.'

'Well, I'm not Venetian, I'm English,' she retorted.

Francesca laughed. 'But you're living in Italy, and if I remember rightly, you said not so long ago that you would never go back to living in England.'

'True. I love Italy and its people, but I find the machismo of the men here unbearable, and the Count is certainly no exception. And now I really must go or I'll be unable to get up in the morning.'

'Then spend the day in bed!' Francesca rolled her eyes. 'What's the hurry? Torcello will still be there in a couple of weeks, after you've had some rest. You need to relax, Venetia. You've been living on your nerves ever since Giovanna decided to have this exhibition.'

'Look, it'll *be* a relaxation getting away to Torcello, I promise you. The island at this time of year is almost deserted and the weather forecast for tomorrow is good too. I might not get another chance before the end of March, and after that it'll be Easter and the tourist season will have begun.'

Francesca shook her head. 'What shall I say? *Si pu solo portare un cavallo all'acqua ma non puoi costringerlo a bere*, you can lead a horse to water, but you can't make him drink.'

Venetia flicked her friend a teasing little smile. 'Ha, ha! Very funny! And now I really must go,' she said as she kissed Francesca affectionately, got up, waved at Fabrizio who was sitting at the bar, and left.

She picked up a water-taxi from outside Hotel Cipriani a few buildings down. As the boat descended into Byzantine shadows, winding through canal after canal in silence, Venetia's mind turned to Paolo with ambivalent thoughts. He was even trying to break into her daydreams. She still loved her own world, the world where she must be alone, where no one could touch her and where she was touched by nothing. And yet she could not deny it, that man with his quiet, searching eyes, his rather sweet and yet pushy manner – that man had struck a chord in her heart, which had been closed for almost a decade.

She stared into the darkness outside and gave a quivering smile as she recalled the way Paolo's strong arms had slid around her languid body… arms she had not resisted but had welcomed. It had come so naturally, as though their bodies had found each other and were dissolving in the opiate sexual tension that sighed and throbbed between them.

Venetia closed her eyes as her old fears raised their ominous heads. *Danger!* her subconscious shrieked at her. The thought of more disillusionment was terrifying. She resolved that even though her body tonight might have developed a mind of its own, there would be no encores. She must be ruthless and stamp on these feelings, the potency of which she had long forgotten. Relationships brought with them risk, pain and humiliation. Besides, Paolo wasn't a free man. Venetia's heart twisted as she recalled the young woman at the restaurant: whether she was his wife or his mistress, or even a mere girlfriend, clearly there was no place for Venetia in his life; so it was a situation which, one way or another, was a recipe for disaster.

Judd's features floated before her. She hadn't seen him in almost ten years and hadn't thought of him since she had come to Italy; yet suddenly now he was on her mind. In the last weeks she had caught herself reminiscing, wondering if he ever thought of her, wherever he was. The pain had also come back with his memory – the ache, the bitterness and the anger. Venetia opened her eyes and watched the dark labyrinth of the canals slip by, engulfing her in its tenebrous vortex.

*   *   *

Paolo sat on the veranda of his bedroom at the Schiaparelli Hotel, a glass of Rémy Martin VSOP resting on the small enamelled table next to him. He stubbed out the sixth cigarette he'd had since he had come back in after his visit to La Scala. Before lighting his seventh, he took a gulp of the potent cognac.

Venetia's tall, slender, long-limbed silhouette swam in front of him, a mass of golden-brown hair falling in lush ringlets down her shoulders, as it had been when he had initially set eyes on her in the street that first night. He could see her face so clearly: delicately sculpted, with high cheekbones, a mouth that was made to be kissed, and curved eyes a shade lighter than her hair, which betrayed a fiery temperament despite having something disciplined about them.

Paolo was used to women swooning over him, and though he was aware that he did not leave Venetia completely indifferent, she was unlike any other woman he had met. She did not seem to have great experience of men. Though obviously efficient at her job, there was nonetheless something... unworldly... almost pure about her; and yet, paradoxically, he was almost certain she had been hurt by a man. Until he had sat opposite her in the noisy, crowded *caffetteria* on that gloomy wintry night, the only emotion women had been able to awaken in him was animal lust. But Venetia was different: the gold-flecked eyes fringed with thick lashes that met his scrutiny from time to time strangely mirrored a sadness he recognised all too well.

He recalled the warm pressure of her willowy frame blending so easily into his embrace on the dance floor earlier that night. And those small, delicate hands touching his body... it was intoxicating, and also threatened to breach the dam of his self-control. He had tried so hard to stop his attraction to her from overwhelming him.

What was it about this woman that consumed his imagination? Now, tortured by the memory of her body against his, dragging with it an aura of fantasy, he felt his need for her swell, grow and spiral into an emotion deeply buried in himself: the echo of a dream long forgotten. But the alarming feeling came and went, a transient illusion slipping away from him now, in the same way that the memory of her features was fading as he felt the bright star consumed by the darkness around it.

He would dream of her tonight, as he had dreamt of her every night since they had met. Those dreams were always tormented, painful – almost nightmares – from which he invariably woke panting and in a sweat, with at best only a vague recollection of the details. But one thing remained clear: Venetia was always at the heart of them. Was she a danger to him somehow, is that what his subconscious was trying to tell him?

Finishing the cognac in his glass, he stood up abruptly. Paolo's cool blue eyes clouded as they looked into the night. Over the gardens of the hotel in the distance, the ghostly glimmer of the immutable, crumbling Gothic *palazzi* stood guard on the banks of the canal, all a perfect evocation of a city that would one day sink beneath the sea. There was something repellent about it, much like an exotic, heavily scented flower may repel despite its loveliness. Beyond the wall, the lagoon sang its ageless, silent, interminable song. Paolo stood motionless in the moonlight, an impression of fatality resting upon him. He felt claustrophobic, as if *La Serenissima*'s old stones were closing around him. Maybe tomorrow he should get out of Venice for the day. He sighed, glancing up at the stars in the inky canopy above him, as though to find answers to his tormented questions; then slowly he turned and went back into his room.

CHAPTER 3

The sun shone bright and warm. In the clear, still morning there was a velvety quality to the air as the boat to Torcello pushed its way through the dark-blue sea. Venice swayed away southwards, and the quayside and the city became a shadowy blur of vanishing tints. Venetia's spirits lifted, an excited feeling of anticipation coursing through her. Dressed warmly in jeans, a winter-white cashmere roll-neck jumper, boots and a brown leather jacket, she breathed in deeply, letting the tangy sea air fill her lungs. In doing so she thrust Judd, Paolo, Umberto and everything else that had been niggling at her for days out of her mind.

Murano, with its odd lighthouse built of drums of white marble, was quickly reached. Passengers climbed out, and then the *vaporetto* was off again. Gliding past the windless wall of the island's glass factories, they came out into the open lagoon. To the north, hundreds of telephone posts and poles defining the boat channels stuck out of the water, and to the right the ancient cypresses of the tiny Isola del Deserto made a dark-green screen of rich vegetation that seemed somewhat anachronistic in this otherwise stern, industrial environment. Ahead, there was the leaning tower of Burano, while beyond, low on the horizon and scarcely visible, stood the solitary tower of Torcello. The island of Burano was their next stop, with its low-lying gardens, the verges overhanging with broom and tamarisk; but as the station was deserted and Venetia was the only one left on the boat, she signalled to the driver to press on to Torcello.

When they arrived, Venetia got out of the boat and headed for the island's famous cathedral, Basilica di Santa Maria Assunta, a ten-minute walk from the dock. *At last, the smell of clean air and the sight of green grass and trees,* she thought as she made her way along the canal, though it was a pity that it was too early for flowers.

The island was deserted, its marshes and sandy wastes of seaboard fringed with stunted pines, their black trunks bent landwards from long battling with winter storms. None of the few residents of the island seemed to be around; everything was wrapped in a profound melancholy silence, which was how she liked it. In this timeless, desolate landscape it was easy to imagine the first settlers in their wooden houses on stilts, fishing the waters and picking out an existence until driven further into the lagoon by Attila the Hun's barbarians. How incredible it was to think that alongside this struggle for survival had been such an aspiration to create great beauty, and ultimately the building of Venice, she thought.

Passing the lithe fifteenth-century Torcello Bridge, nicknamed '*Il Ponte del Diavolo*', Venetia smiled to herself; she delighted in Italian folklore. There were many bridges all over Italy labelled The Devil's Bridge. The name went back to the legend spread throughout the country during the Middle Ages, according to which many bridges were the work of the Devil, who was building them in exchange for souls.

It was not long before she reached the Basilica di Santa Maria Assunta. One of the most ancient religious buildings in Italy, it was a seventh-century wonder of Venetian-Byzantine architecture, standing like a solemn witness to the birth of its nation.

Venetia loved its stark and strong frame, with its simple *campanile* of rose-pink brick, so different from the rich and elaborate architecture of the majority of Italian churches. Entering, she was always overcome by its extraordinary sense of quiet and dignity – of peace. Perhaps this was because, denuded of the extravagant embellishments usually seen in Italian religious buildings, it echoed in her mind the relative plainness of the Anglican churches back home.

The Virgin and Child mosaic in the central apse was in a precarious state. She wondered how the experts would tackle it without causing large areas of the timeworn gold *tesserae* to break away. In the right apsidal chapel there was still some scaffolding erected over the mosaics being restored. Looking upwards through this frame, Venetia could see great-eyed figures of saints and angels peering down at her, with wonderful, alive expressions.

The only mosaic that seemed in reasonable condition was the vivid representation, in blue, white and gold, of the Last Judgement that took up the whole of the west wall, over the entrance. Not for the first time, Venetia marvelled at the intricate attention to detail in the immense tableau: on the right, the wrathful river of flames pouring over the naked, tormented damned, with worm-eaten skulls below; to the left, the faithful being ushered into heavenly paradise by beautiful angels; and the aged figures of Adam and Eve kneeling at the blowing of the last trumpet. She longed to be able to touch their rough, shining surfaces but even if that were possible, her trained eye, despite the distance, could perceive that there were many loose patches, and the mosaicists would have an immense task keeping the picture intact.

'And so we meet again.'

Venetia caught her breath. She didn't need to look round to recognise the dark, velvety voice that had just made her jump.

She turned to find Paolo standing behind her, an enormous smile lighting up his face and his eyes shining with amused surprise. He looked suitably casual in a pair of blue jeans and a sky-blue jumper over a crisp white shirt. With a Bordeaux polka-dot silk foulard tied around his neck and tucked into the unbuttoned collar of his shirt, he had all the relaxed and natural elegance of a magazine model.

'Forgive me if I startled you.'

She stared at him, her lips parted on an amazed breath, her pupils dilating. She blinked. What on earth was he doing here? The memory of his arms around her the night before, and his body pressed against hers, flooded her mind, taking away her ability to form any words.

Paolo pointed at the mosaic and crossed his arms. 'Hell is horrid, Paradise is splendid, there is no sentimentality here, no softening of the blows, wouldn't you say?'

He continued to look at her directly, clearly enjoying her confusion; but his gaze was also alight with something more, something that was sending warm shivers down Venetia's spine, and somewhere lower, unexplored.

Her heart was pattering hysterically beneath her breast, but somehow her voice managed to emerge cool. '*Ah, buongiorno, Signor Barone.* What brings you to Torcello?'

Paolo beamed. 'The same thing that has brought you here on such a fabulous morning, I suppose: the need to get away from Venice and breathe some fresher air... But to come back to the mosaics you were so engrossed in, I'm curious about your opinion. Don't you agree that it's a formidable illustration of what may await us after death?'

'That's because the incidents of the story are laid in with all the powerful, uncompromising drawing of the period,' Venetia said, looking up at the mosaic as she launched herself into a stream of rhetoric to hide the havoc his sudden appearance had created inside her. 'Though the brilliance of the dramatic vision here is exceptional, and its blend of eastern pre-Islamic artistic traditions with Christian imagery is striking.'

Her pulse was leaping like a mountain stream bounding over rocks, and she hoped he didn't notice the slight tremolo in her voice. 'It was the time of the Inquisition and the fight against heretics, a reaction against the other growing religious movements in the world…' She continued to look up, feeling his eyes still on her. 'The Church used art as a way of ensuring that faith was absolute and crystallised in people's mind for the dogma to reign supreme.'

'You're very knowledgeable, Venetia – you allow me to call you Venetia?' He was smiling at her, admiration and a hint of amusement lurking in his eyes.

She ignored both the compliment and the question, and turned to face him, her brows shooting up. 'Don't you think that we keep bumping into each other a little too often?' Her manner was abrupt, almost unfriendly, but he seemed oblivious to it.

His features relaxed into a soft, musing smile. 'The long arm of Fate, wouldn't you agree?'

Paolo's question caught Venetia by surprise. She was intensely conscious of him standing too close beside her, and it made her feel nervous. All the same, she tried to muster her composure. 'I don't believe in Fate. One forges one's own destiny.'

'I'm afraid that I disagree. I believe there is no flight from Fate. But maybe we could continue this discussion over lunch. It's almost one o'clock and I know of a small restaurant where they serve the most delicious *goh* risotto. It's only frequented by locals, which is usually a good reference.'

'Thank you, but I've brought a sandwich.'

His black brows contracted. 'Thanks, but goodbye?' His tone was gently sardonic.

Venetia looked away. 'I didn't mean to sound rude.'

He made a wry gesture at himself. 'I've never been slapped down so often in my life.'

She met the brooding intensity of his eyes. He suddenly looked tired, as if he hadn't slept for weeks. Her tender heart twisted in unwilling compassion. Was it compassion or perhaps something more potent? Conflicting emotions fluttered through her head. She was almost ready to accept his invitation, but only almost.

'I really need to make some notes about these mosaics. Their condition is very much like a plaque I'm working on at the moment.' Her voice softened. 'So thanks again for the invitation, but maybe some other time.'

Paolo looked down at her from his great height with a glimmer of impatience in his deep-blue irises, his lips tightening in an effort of self-control.

'Very well, it's your choice, of course. Though I cannot understand your obstinacy, please consider the subject closed. I will not importunate you again, *signorina*.' Upon which he nodded politely, turned and walked away, his footsteps echoing softly in the empty basilica.

There was a dreadful finality about his words. And as Venetia heard the door close and the silence return, she felt a cold hand clutch at her heart.

She spent half an hour strolling around the building, trying to concentrate in vain, replaying again and again the conversation that had just taken place. As previously after rebuffing him, she was confused and depressed. Her mind clouded with remorse. How could she be so rude? There really was no harm in accepting his invitation to lunch. Why did he bring out such an acute reaction in her?

Over the years, Venetia had been taken out for lunch and dinner several times; she'd had many dates, and had always welcomed a degree of male attention. She enjoyed flirting innocently, and from time to time had even allowed herself to be kissed but her emotions had never been involved; she had invariably been in control.

Paolo was different. She felt threatened in his presence; not only threatened, but vulnerable. She could sense the ice that she had so carefully wrapped around her heart beginning to thaw. Years of self-control, and the foundations of the fortress she had erected about her were being shaken, putting her emotional and mental state in jeopardy. She needed to protect herself. Even though deep down she believed that the girl with Paolo at the restaurant could have been just a client or a friend, her presence that day had provided a convenient excuse for Venetia to keep him at bay. Now, the current crackling between them was providing a heat that could easily disintegrate her defences.

Still, some part of her yearned to be held once again by a man, to feel her body come alive, as it had the night before on the dance floor in Paolo's arms. Despite the fact that it was faithfully guarding her from love's harm, being celibate naturally had its disadvantages. The need to be loved that had built up in her was occasionally so painful that she found the tension almost unbearable.

Once more Judd's image, which over time had blurred around the edges, grew sharp in her head as if she had seen him only yesterday. With him she had known love, passion and a total fusion of mind and body, and she missed him now almost as acutely as she had missed him all those years back. Judd was probably married with a brood of children by now. He could never be hers, but knowing that didn't end the hopeless ache of longing within her. *Shake yourself out of this glum state, girl,* she remonstrated, *or you'll drive yourself mad.* She glanced at her watch; it was already half-past one. Perhaps she'd find a bench overlooking the lagoon, she thought, or maybe sit on Attila's throne to eat her sandwich. After lunch she would visit the church of Santa Fosca and then head home before dark.

The sun was high when Venetia emerged into the courtyard. The old trees cast shadows upon the ground; the light was tinged with gold. Flanking the lawn, the pink church of Santa Fosca looked impressively lonely with its arcades of stilted arches and its slim, elegant columns of Greek marble with Byzantine-style capitals. Pigeons were circling the columns, perching on the fragile cornices, cooing to each other in their soft, enchanting voices. The ancient little town was her own; she could pause and admire its beauty and its spell to her heart's content. *Impossible to dwell upon a secret grief for long in a place like this,* she told herself as she made for Attila's throne.

She settled herself on the white seat formed by a single piece of rough-hewn stone, which stood on the patch of grass opposite Santa Fosca. As she was taking out the *panino* of salami, mozzarella and rucola from her bag, a voice from behind startled her.

'*Una leggenda locale vuole che chi si siete su questa sedia si sposerà entro un anno,* local legend has it that anyone sitting in this seat will be married within a year.'

She turned sharply and glared, scarcely able to believe that he was still hanging about. 'Do you make it a habit of creeping up on people?'

Paolo's dark features assumed a wolfish grin as he walked round to stand in front of her and folded his arms. 'No, only stubborn beautiful young women who refuse to have lunch with me.'

She looked back up at him, stirring half angrily.

His mock-contrite expression sparkled with mischief. 'What can I say? I simply felt it impossible to take no for an answer.' Resting his elbow in the opposite hand, he touched his forefinger on his lips and gazed at her in contemplation. 'What thoughts are hiding in those honey-dark eyes of yours? Their mystery is intriguing and makes me wonder what I would find if I penetrated their fiery gaze.'

Venetia bristled, fidgeting uneasily on the stone seat. 'Don't flirt with me, *signore*, I promise you are wasting your time.'

'It's *my* time, and I don't mind wasting it if I can just have your company for a while.'

Her eyelids dropped to hide from him a sudden flame of anger. 'If it's an affair you are looking for, *signore*, then you've knocked at the wrong door. I do not indulge in that sort of sport.'

Paolo's brows rose at her vehemence. 'How should I say it...? *"Nothing is more curious and awkward than the relationship of two people who only know each other with their eyes... and who keep up the impression of disinterest either because of morals or because of a mental abnormality. Between them there is the hysteria of an unsatisfied, unnaturally suppressed need for communion..."* Something like that. Thomas Mann, *Death in Venice*.'

He had spoken in English, and shock momentarily cut off Venetia's speech. The deep tonal quality of Paolo's voice struck a haunting chord of recognition. For a split second she could have sworn it was Judd's voice that had just uttered those words, even though Paolo had spoken with an Italian accent.

'I didn't realise that you spoke English,' she breathed through a sudden constriction in her throat.

Paolo shrugged. 'I speak very little of many languages, *cara*.'

Venetia made an effort to carry on her end of the conversation. 'Anyhow, to come back to your quote, Thomas Mann may be right, but I'm not trying to be awkward here, or difficult, and I'm not playing games either. Even if we did know each other better, the only thing I could offer you is friendship.'

His lips quirked in a half-smile. 'In my experience, friendship is a very elastic word.'

'Well, for me the word holds no ambiguity and is not flexible. As defined in the dictionary, it means a person whom one knows, likes and trusts.'

'This is a very interesting conversation which we should continue over lunch. Your *panino* will be stale by now and I have reserved a table for two, on the off-chance that you would change your mind and agree to have lunch with me.'

Venetia felt she was being sapped of the will to fight. 'You don't give up, do you?' she sighed, as she replaced the unwrapped *panino* in her bag and stood up.

'Never.' There was a flash of fierceness in his tone belied by the suave smile he gave her as he gestured the way out across the courtyard.

Trattoria Tonino was a small restaurant on the main drag into Torcello, and opposite The Devil's Bridge. There were no airs and graces about it to attract tourists, merely ten tables in two rows, a bar, and an open-plan kitchen where the three chefs were cooking and singing while flipping pans of risotto up into the air with a wooden ladle, just as if they were performing in a circus. It had cluster-shaped ceiling lamps and a few ceiling fans in use during the summer months. The white walls held shelves decorated with gondoliers' trophies and all sorts of stuffed birds under glass bells.

Paolo explained to Venetia that Tonino, the owner, came from a family of great gondoliers. He was the only one of four brothers not to have followed family tradition, preferring instead to open a restaurant, because, as he often boasted: 'I like my food to be well cooked and you cannot get a decent meal in Venice today. *Inoltre, io sono un cuoco eccellente*, besides, I am an excellent cook.'

To Venetia's surprise the place was packed. Waiters were moving up and down the central aisle and there were far more people coming in than tables to hold them. She had forgotten her apprehension. Paolo's easy manner and the way he seemed to fit in with this charming place were making her feel more relaxed that she had expected.

Tonino, a rotund little man with a mass of black hair and a bushy moustache, greeted Paolo like a long-lost friend. *'Il tavolo è in attesa di lei signore*, your table is waiting for you, *signore*,' he said with an affable business smile as he led the couple to a table next to the window, with a view of the fifteenth-century free-parapet Devil's Bridge. Venetia smiled back at him; she could well imagine this proud man boasting about his cooking.

Venetia let Paolo choose the menu since he seemed to know the place well. He ordered *moeche* soft-shell crab, followed by the traditional *goh* risotto, and a Pino Grigio that the *trattoria* offered in open carafes.

'I love that bridge,' she said, once they were seated. 'I love its lack of parapets. It gives it such an elegant line.'

'Il Ponticello del Diavolo. Do you know why it was named the Devil's Bridge?'

'Something to do with the Devil gathering souls, if I'm not mistaken. Although I don't quite see the connection, but I'm sure there's some kind of illogical superstition behind it.'

'There's a legend about the bridge.'

Venetia laughed. 'Of course there is! In Italy there's a legend for everything. Do you know that one?'

'Naturalmente. Like my compatriots, I'm very superstitious and a great believer in legends.'

She looked at him and it struck her again how well he could pass for the Devil himself.

'So, tell me, what's the legend of *Il Ponticello del Diavolo*?'

Paolo reached for the carafe and offered her some wine. When she nodded, he filled her glass, and she noticed he poured only water for himself. She couldn't help but raise her eyebrows at this but he seemed not to notice.

'During the occupation of Austria, a young Venetian girl fell in love with an Austrian soldier. Her family disapproved of this union and the young man was murdered. The girl was so desperate that she went to a magician who made a pact with the Devil to bring her soldier back to life, in exchange for the souls of seven children. The contract between the Venetian girl and the Devil was signed and their meeting place was the bridge of Torcello. When the sorcerer and the girl went to the meeting, they saw the Devil and the young man on the other side of the bridge. The girl crossed the bridge and both lovers fled. When the time for payment came, the sorcerer and the Devil arranged a new meeting at the bridge, but on the way to the rendezvous the magician died of natural causes before he got there. And from that day onwards, it is said that every night the Devil appears on the bridge waiting for the souls of those seven children.'

'That's a great story. At least the lovers got away – I approve of that.' Venetia's eyes clouded and she added, as though to herself, 'There's nothing worse than meddling parents.'

Paolo cocked his head at her comment but said nothing, and asked: 'Do you often come to Torcello?'

'Not as often as I would like – I never come in the summer because I find it too crowded, and I think it takes away from the island's charm.'

'I also like coming here, but I haven't been for a long time. It's Fate I'm sure that brought us both here today.'

There was more than a smile right now in that sensual mouth and gleaming white teeth, as starkly bright against his tanned skin as his now ultramarine eyes. She wished he didn't look at her in that way. The breeze coming through the window tousled his dark hair so that one lock fell over his forehead, giving him a boyish look that went straight to Venetia's heart.

'I think I've already told you that I don't believe in Fate,' she said, raising her chin. 'Fate is the superstitious mind's way of misinterpreting coincidence.' Though as she spoke, Venetia wasn't sure how much she believed this.

Paolo seemed to ponder for a second, his eyes riveted on Venetia's face. 'Have we met before?' he enquired, barely audibly, the last syllable lifting to a questioning whisper.

'Not that I recall.'

'Have you never heard of the word *maktoub*?'

Venetia shook her head.

'It means *written*. Arabs say that from the day you are born, the name of your sweetheart is invisibly engraved on your forehead. Maybe that explains the flicker of recognition I felt the day we met,' he murmured, not taking his eyes off her as he sipped his water.

Venetia's heart fluttered uncomfortably. She had also experienced that sort of *déjà vu* feeling when she was with Paolo, but she wasn't going to admit it to him. 'Fate is for those too weak to determine their own destiny,' came her bold answer.

He raised his eyebrows. 'You're very lucky if you have always been able to determine your destiny – but you're still young and life is long.' He touched the wooden table.

In all her twenty-eight years, had she been able to determine her own destiny? The thought made Venetia feel slightly tremulous – but she must forget all that for now. Her lunch with Paolo was turning out to be rather interesting, even though she didn't agree with his views.

'Italians are all very superstitious, aren't they?'

'The Moors had a great impact on our country, including their beliefs. Even though there were no caliphates in Italy, there was plenty of Muslim influence, from the Islamic conquest of Sicily onwards. Have you read Omar Khayyám?'

'No, I must admit that though I've heard of him, and of Khalil Gibran and Rumi, I've never read them. Apparently their literature is really beautiful.'

'There is a particular verse of Omar Khayyám that I've always favoured.'

They were interrupted by the waiter bringing the first dish, the deep-fried *moeche* crabs.

'This is delicious,' Venetia said, as she tucked into the crisp crustaceans.

'These small soft-shell crabs are a Venetian speciality. They are found in the lagoon for only a few short weeks at the end of winter and early spring, and at the beginning of autumn, when the crabs are moulting their shells. We're lucky that they're already being served – it's a little early in the year. They must have just come on to the market.'

'I must remember this next time I go to a restaurant.' She watched him lick his finger as he put a piece in his mouth, and then chew it slowly while looking at her. Her stomach clenched and she felt a blush warm her cheeks as her concentration wavered.

'But you were saying?'

'Yes, there's particular verse of Omar Khayyám that I really like and in which I believe firmly:

The Moving Finger writes; and, having writ,
Moves on: not all thy Piety nor Wit

Shall lure it back to cancel half a Line,
Nor all thy Tears wash out a Word of it.'

'It is a rather dark and sad concept, don't you think?'

'Maybe, but it makes a lot of sense to me. Man is not free, Venetia. Our lives are written for us. If what you say is right, and we can control our destinies, why is there so much misery in the world?'

As lunch progressed, they spoke about philosophy, literature, religion and history, neither of them volunteering any personal information. It was as though by tacit accord they had decided to preserve their anonymity, a sort of mysterious halo, afraid to mar the image they thought each had of the other.

Yet, reading between the lines, Venetia sensed a deep unhappiness in Paolo. His smiles were sometimes sad and wistful, and he was easily moved from gentle irony to almost an angry passion about life. From time to time his gaze slid over her through the fringe of his dark eyelashes, intimate as a kiss. Not for the first time, it gave Venetia the impression he was searching for her soul. It lent him an oddly vulnerable expression. Strangely enough, the way he did that reminded her of Judd.

The way he spoke her name seemed like a caress that gave her goosebumps each time he uttered it. She loved the Italian lilt in his voice, and his was very pronounced. No need to wonder why she suddenly felt so light-headed, a peculiar languor coming over her, her throat hot and dry. It couldn't be the wine; she never reacted to alcohol like this, and anyhow, she'd only had a glass of it; the second one Paolo had poured stood almost full in front of her. He was affecting her like a drug and she wasn't sure if she wanted to fight it any longer.

After they had finished their main dish, Venetia declined desert and just ordered a double *espresso* in the hope of sobering up from the strange torpor that had overcome her. Paolo ordered a *caffè Americano*, and then they were on their way. He had not smoked during the meal, and so when they were out in the open he lit a cigarette and they walked for a while along the canal.

There was nothing save the sun, the breeze, the endless sky and the shimmering lagoons. They stood next to each other on the shore, admiring the Venetian fishing-boats being put out to sea. It was a most vibrant and beautiful sight. The colours of the sails were so rich and varied as they shifted and tacked in the changing light, distended against the breeze, the reds and oranges of their canvas in vivid relief against the grey of the lagoon. Crossing and re-crossing each other, they were like coloured shuttles on the leaden water-web.

Venetia glanced at the dark figure of Paolo at her side, and saw him watching her.

'This is a beautiful spot,' he said quietly. 'Don't you think so?'

She found herself caught up in an intensely contemplative gaze. The dark-blue eyes were mesmerising, almost green in this light. He looked more like Lucifer than ever; a curious alien air about him, the tilt of his head, the sensually curved mouth, the deep cleft in his chin. He seemed to be towering over her, his body so near, and a strange excitement began to course through her. She felt lightheaded, filled with a wild chaos of emotions that made her heart beat hard and fast. Her throat tightened, and she dragged her gaze away.

And then she felt his hand on her shoulder, an imperative, possessive hand. Venetia looked up at Paolo again without speaking; in silence she obeyed the unspoken command, the fierce need in those lapis-blue eyes, and let him gather her to him. His arm was about her. She drew in a long breath and went limp against him, just as she had on the dance floor at the nightclub; but this was no dance, instead a desperate embrace. Paolo's face was buried in her neck and she lost all sense of time and place. He held her close – so close it was as though some hidden, unseen power were trying to weld them forcibly from two separate entities into one indissoluble whole. His arms, like a band, strained her to his heart – she could feel it beating through his clothes. From moment to moment it seemed that so strong a clasp must begin to hurt. Yet it did not. Her heart was turning to water, her breath almost to a sigh; it was as if body and spirit were flowing away on a surging tide of... her mind hesitated, afraid to formulate the word... love.

Paolo never spoke, nor did she, but there was no need for speech. He never kissed her and neither did she feel the need for it. The desperate and tragic embrace said all there was to say. It was like something cut out from life, a suspension of time, a poignant, irresistible thing that swept them both up and, Venetia instinctively knew, was never to be acknowledged.

'We should go,' Paolo whispered as he released her. 'It'll soon be dusk. I'll take you back.'

Venetia acquiesced silently as she gazed at the scene in front of them, imprinting it on her heart.

'You like it?' he asked softly.

She smiled. 'How could I not? It's heavenly.'

'Heavenly...' he repeated, almost imperceptibly. Something like doubt and anxiety passed across his expression, but it was gone in a flash and he smiled back at her. His voice, husky and soft, seemed to come from far away as he murmured: 'Thank you, Venetia, thank you for a most heavenly day.'

The sun was a round red ball, making the far, encircling islands appear wild and dark.

Paolo and Venetia wandered slowly back, each with an arm around the other, still enveloped by the luminous aura of what had passed between them, and reached the launch in ten minutes. Scarcely a ripple stirred the sea. As she stepped into it, the boat swayed with a barely perceptible motion. Paolo disappeared into the cabin and came back immediately with a large blanket, which he draped around her shoulders. 'There will be a strong wind on the way back, you mustn't catch cold.'

'Thanks.' She lifted her head and smiled into his face. The expression of bitter pain she read in it snatched away her sense of peace and gripped her heart like claws of ice.

Paolo took the wheel, started the engine, and they set off homeward. The twilight faded into dusk; lights appeared, winking from the tiny lighthouses scattered all over the islands. Paolo was upright and motionless at the helm, silhouetted against the sky. The ache in Venetia's heart deepened; the beauty of the night, the shadowy rocks, the twinkling lights, that tall, strong figure in whose arms she had stood for a short while that afternoon – it was like the climax to some fragrant romance told in a great poem. A shadow had passed over them and she did not understand why. She drew the blanket around her and looked up at the flock of flying birds in the sky, passing like those beautiful fleeting moments of happiness she had felt, as they disappeared into the night.

When they reached Palazzo Mendicoli, and before Venetia stepped out of the launch, Paolo drew her close again, but this time his arms were gentle. His hand caressed the glossy, soft hair that the breeze had disordered, and then with the lightest touch he traced the outline of her cheek with his finger. He kissed her forehead as he might have kissed a child.

'*Addio mio angelo,*' Paolo whispered, gazing into her face with sad, almost desperate eyes.

She lifted a questioning gaze at him and opened her mouth to speak, but he pressed two fingers to her lips and shook his head.

Venetia felt as if a steel door had slammed inside her. The moon glided through the sky, shining her light on his blue, glittering irises and almost handsome face. She stared back at him for a brief moment with a proud, undefeated look and then went up the steps, ignoring the hand he held out to her.

*   *   *

Next day at the office Venetia was distracted, unable to concentrate on her work. She had not slept during the night and had lain staring into the dark, her body burning with a fever of desire, her brain awhirl with confusion.

She had spent a wonderful afternoon with Paolo – 'heavenly' as he had put it – and then he'd uttered those simple words, '*Addio mio angelo.*'

Venetia knew only too well the meaning of that abortive short sentence; its painful echo rang in her ears long after she had buried herself beneath the bedcovers. The message in his serious, sad eyes was unambiguous: however fond of one another we might be, we can only bring each other unhappiness. It had been a passionate interlude and he was ending it before it could go any further. There was only one reason for that which made any sense: Paolo was not free. Paolo was married. And even though the time they had spent together had been fleeting, the thought was almost unbearable and Venetia couldn't help but feel a sense of loss. Just at the point where her defences had been tenderly breached, he had turned away and left her raw and exposed, needing him in a way that she dreaded.

In the morning, she had rushed over to Fritelli for her usual *cappuccino* and *biscotti*, and had stayed on a little longer in the hope of seeing him there. She had to know for sure; she would confront him, even if that meant sacrificing a little pride. But he didn't appear and she finally had to leave to avoid being late at the office.

'You look dreadful,' Francesca told her as they sat in the *trattoria* where they usually went for lunch, close to the office. She broke off a piece of *ciabatta* with her expressive, elegant fingers and gestured with it before popping it into her mouth. 'I told you to stay in bed yesterday, but there's no reasoning with you when you have an idea in your head.'

Venetia sighed and gave her friend a sad smile. 'Well, maybe I should have listened to you.'

Francesca's brows knitted in a deep frown. 'Oh dear, there's something that's gone really wrong that you aren't telling me.'

Venetia's face puckered as a lump formed in her throat. 'I'm very tired, that's all,' she said in a strangulated voice, her eyes threatening to fill with tears.

'Venetia, what have you been up to?'

'I – I've been a fool,' she stammered. 'It's Paolo. You know, the man we saw on the *piazza* with whom I danced the other night.'

'Yes, yes, I suppose you're going to tell *me* about the gossip which I was just going to tell *you*.'

'What gossip? What do you mean?'

'Gossip I heard after you left the nightclub. Paolo Barone is well known in Venice. As Fabrizio put it, the tears that have been poured over him by some of the most beautiful women of this city could fill the lagoons from here to Burano. But tell me first what's wrong with you. Let me guess, you didn't go to Torcello and you saw him again.'

Venetia remained silent. She was feeling too raw to speak about it.

'Talk to me, Venetia.'

Venetia forced a faint smile to her lips over her coffee cup.

'I know what you're going to tell me, Francesca, he's married, isn't he?'

'No, no, I don't think he's married. The story goes that he's in love with a woman whom he can't marry because of his status in society. Some say she's a young girl from the orphanage he sponsors; others allege she's a fallen woman that he picked up from the slums. Anyhow, she's apparently much younger than him and he keeps her tucked away at his home in Tuscany. People have very occasionally seen her accompanying him in Venice. Still, that doesn't stop him from having affairs left, right and centre. His reputation as a womaniser is just as notorious as that of his best friend, the Count.' Francesca leaned forward and tapped the table lightly with the side of her hand for emphasis. 'So, Venetia, *mia cara amica*, whatever you have started with this man must stop immediately.'

Venetia expelled her breath on a sigh of relief. Suddenly a great weight had lifted from her heart. Paolo wasn't married after all – he had some sort of mistress, probably the young girl she had seen him with at the restaurant. He might be dangerous, but in light of what she had just heard, nothing was impossible.

'You mean he's not married?' She thought for a moment. 'A notorious womaniser has never frightened me,' she said, her eyes sparkling.

Francesca gave her a doubtful look. 'Have you seen him again since the other night?'

'Yes, we spent yesterday afternoon together at Torcello.'

'At Torcello?'

'Yes, he just happened to be there.'

Francesca rolled her eyes. 'I can't follow you any more. Why were you almost in tears all morning if you're not bothered about what I've just told you?'

'I thought he was married – the way he acted when we parted yesterday evening made me think that he was seriously attached.'

'He might still be married to this young woman – I'm not sure. I'm only telling you what I've heard.'

'I've seen her, and though she's very young and beautiful, the more I think about it, the more I realise they didn't look like a married couple.'

Francesca shook her head and stared at her friend. 'You've really lost me. How long have you known him?'

'We've met only a few times… and yesterday…' Venetia's eyes took on a dreamy quality as she couldn't stop herself from remembering the way Paolo had held her, 'yesterday was, well… just heavenly.'

'You're mad.' Francesca flung her hands up. '*O, mio dio!* I've just told you that he's dangerous, and you're all "yesterday was heavenly"! *Per favore*, I'm telling you, Venetia, both *il Conte* and this man *sono marci*, are rotten, they make a right pair. Ask Fabrizio, he seems to know plenty about him. He talked to me after you left the club. He was worried, seeing the way you were together on the dance floor.'

Venetia looked suitably horrified. 'Don't you dare breathe a word of this to anyone, and especially not to Fabrizio!'

'Of course I won't, but don't be foolish, *cara*. I have always encouraged you to go out, meet people and make a new life for yourself. Believe me, no one will be happier than I the day you fall in love with the right man and get married. But pursuing this Paolo Barone is pure foolishness, and it's my duty as your friend to guard you from your own folly.'

'Look, don't get on your high horse, Francesca! The way we left it yesterday makes me think I'll probably never see him again anyway.'

'What happened yesterday?'

'We had a perfectly lovely afternoon and then when he dropped me off he used the word *addio* instead of *arrivederci*... and the way he looked into my eyes...' Venetia's heart gave a painful squeeze at the memory.

Francesca scoffed. 'Italian men – they love a little bit of drama. Theatrics are their speciality. Tell me about it, I had a real prima donna for a husband! Even though I'm Italian, I much prefer the phlegmatic behaviour of your English men. I bet you fifty thousand *lire* that you'll hear from him in the next couple of weeks. But that's not the point. You must not have a relationship with this man, Venetia. He's dangerous.'

'A man can never get out of a woman what she isn't prepared to give,' said Venetia, suddenly remembering what her mother used to say. She hoped it was true.

Francesca shook her head vigorously. '*Parole vuote*, empty words, my dear. I can see that you're already infatuated with him and ready for a whirlwind romance. They never work, *cara*, as you well know. If you don't nip this *sentimente nascente* in the bud, you will end up with a broken heart. I've never seen you so, *come dire, turbare,* troubled, upset.'

'Thanks for your concern, Francesca. I do appreciate what you're trying to say.' Venetia sighed and sat back in her chair. 'Rest assured, I'm certain that if I don't go looking for him, I'll never see Paolo again, and my pride will never let me chase after him.'

'*Va bene.*' Francesca gave her friend a sidelong look. 'You'd be much better off giving Fabrizio a chance,' she suggested quietly.

'Come now, Francesca, we've discussed this umpteen times before, and you know my views on that.'

'*Sì, sì,* I know your views, but it's not too late to change them!'

'Okay, subject closed.' Venetia glanced at her watch. 'We'd better get back to work. I was late this morning and I'd prefer not to be late again this afternoon.'

As they went back to the office, Venetia was lost in thought. A new flame burned inside her – she was floating on a cloud, alone with her relief and hope. Still, she knew that Francesca was right, she must be cautious. Italian men were shocking flirts. They said many things under the influence of alcohol or a romantic moment, which they may have meant at the time, but as soon as that instant passed, so too did the feelings and all the good intentions that went with them. Italian women expected a man to make love to them on all occasions; it was a custom of the country. It did no harm unless one was foolish enough to take it seriously.

She would certainly not go looking for Paolo, but if 'Fate', as he called it, put him back on her path, and if he wanted it enough to pursue her... she finally admitted it, she would welcome getting to know him better.

Since Judd, no man had set her mind and her senses in such turmoil. Paolo and Venetia had scarcely touched – a couple of times only, but she could not deny the flame that had smouldered between them, kept in check simply because she had been afraid of its heat, and because he seemed to want it that way too. And yet, whenever they ended up crossing paths, he would not let her go. Even now, at the thought of the way Paolo's arms had held her possessively to his lean hardness, tightening his hold as he pressed himself against her, the warmth of his breath fanning her temple, Venetia felt weak at the knees, craving his lips and his touch.

But it was not only a physical attraction that drew her to him. From time to time when he thought no one was watching, she had read a hint of bitterness and anger in his features, as when driving his launch. Paolo, she believed, was a lonely and unhappy man. The melancholy in his eyes had struck her more than once and she felt an empathy with him that she had not experienced since Judd. Maybe it was true that he was in love with the young woman from the restaurant, and more fool him if he was holding off from marrying her just because of the ridiculous conventional rules enforced by the social circle he moved in. However, Venetia had a presentiment that the sadness in those blue eyes ran much deeper.

From then on, she tried to keep thoughts of Paolo at bay, stifling the voice that urged her to go looking for him, or at least attempt to find out more about him. She and Francesca didn't talk about Paolo again. Instead she drowned herself in work, spending additional hours at her office in the evening and returning home too exhausted to think. She slept soundly at night, as if she had been drugged. She was almost in a state of trance, curiously at peace.

*   *   *

Several weeks had gone by. Venetia had spent a particularly busy afternoon restoring a miniature mosaic on a small panel for a client. She loved working on such *tessellae*, which actually looked more like paintings. This particular *tessella*, dating back to 1282, was especially fine. It depicted a crucifix, with the Virgin Mary and Maria Magdalene kneeling at the base of the cross. The *tessella* was made of gold, lapis lazuli and other semi-precious stones set on to wax on a wooden panel. Venetia's client was an antique dealer and she had promised to drop off her package at his shop in Calle del Paradiso, the most medieval-looking street in Venice, bordered with small old shops and dreary wine bars.

It was six o'clock in the evening and having delivered the mosaic to its owner, she was making her way to Ponte del Paradiso, which stood at the far end of the narrow street. During the day, Calle del Paradiso was quaint, full of amusing nooks and crannies; most of the time it was draped with washing all the way along, so that the light filtered through shirts, bed sheets and underclothing. But on a night like this, when the sun had gone down and evening shadows gathered, and the cramped alley was shrouded in silvery fog, Venetia found the place gloomy and almost sinister.

Although it was March, winter was ceding reluctantly to spring and the weather was still cold, damp and foggy. Clouds had hung like a grey pall over the city for most of the day, and now came a thin drizzle of rain that gave every sign of becoming heavier. The moisture made thin slime of the festering garbage strewn about the sinuous, dimly lit street. Some of the buildings' walls in the semi-shadows seemed to be mouldering and lichen-grown, as if ready to fall to pieces. The streets of Venice in the mist breathed the sadness of faded beauty that waits for the dark veils of night, and the transforming magic of artificial light. As Venetia hurried down the cobbled pavement, she thought of the words Paolo had uttered on the veranda at the carnival ball, *'a rude awakening for the unsuspecting tourist when daylight comes...'*

She had almost reached the impressive Gothic arch spanning the street and opening on to the Ponte del Paradiso when her attention was drawn by a brilliantly lit shop window; so bright that it acted as a floodlight on the pavement and its surroundings. On impulse Venetia went in, without even looking at the display in the *vitrina*.

There was an odd contrast between the dazzling glow of the shop window and the dark room she had just entered, which was laden with the heavy aroma and smoke of incense. This was not the sort of place Venetia was accustomed to visiting and she was about to step out as quickly as she had stepped in when a sing-song voice called out to her in English: 'You have come to right place, young lady.'

Still on the threshold, Venetia turned round abruptly and in the light thrown into the shop by the *vitrina*, she saw a sleek black head, a keen, clear ivory-tinted face, two elongated black eyes, and the frail, tremulous figure of a Chineseman.

He wore the dress of his country: a long silk, green gown with a string of large jade beads ending in a twisted yellow tassel, and a small skull-cap covering his head.

'How did you know I speak English?' Venetia asked, a little wary.

The narrow eyes were filled with a dreamy sort of kindness. Innumerable deep wrinkles formed in his sallow cheeks, and his face brightened up with a slow smile. The Chineseman bowed with enormous dignity, his hands in his wide sleeves. 'I have been waiting for you. Don't be afraid, come and sit down here,' he said cordially, leading the way into the room.

Although the place was dimly lit by a tiny lamp enshrined in an old stone lantern that stood in a far corner, the light was cunningly contrived and the room glowed softly. There reigned a sense of quiet peace and reverence. On the walls, Venetia could make out embroidered silken panels, woodcuts, and scrolls of fine workmanship done on Chinese parchment. She looked up and saw that the ceiling was entirely painted: on one side, the moon, the sun, and the stars depicting heaven; and on the other, beasts, trees, the sea and strange creatures, which she assumed represented Earth. On a wooden stand near the stone lantern were long, thin red and yellow joss sticks burning incense in a large bronze tray filled with sand; and next to it were two low seats made out of big embroidered cushions, facing each other and divided by a red lacquered squat table.

The air was heavy; the woody and spicy fragrance of incense fumes mingling with the acrid scent of opium.

As her eyes got used to the semi-darkness she saw a huge cushion, leaning high against a golden panel, on top of which lay the most enormous coiled-up snake. The creature struck a surreal note in the peaceful room, and Venetia gasped, her hand flying to her throat in fear. She took two steps back.

'Don't be afraid,' said the man softly, with a benign smile. 'This is Nüwa, the goddess who separated the Heaven from the Earth, creating the Divine Land of China. She is the original ancestor of the Chinese people. She does not harm. On the contrary, she creates and she mends.'

Venetia gave a nervous little laugh. 'I'm not very fond of snakes!' *That's the understatement of the year,* she thought. She wanted to flee the place, and everything in her rational mind told her that she was foolish even being here; but she had a strange feeling, as if an invisible, singular power were drawing her more and more into the shop, and something deeper than curiosity compelling her to stay.

'I am Qiqiang Ping Lü, but they call me Ping Lü. Come, sit down. I have been waiting for you.'

'Waiting for *me?*'

'This rain today, it is a good omen. The heavens will speak, and there is so much that is troubling you. Isn't that so?'

Venetia stared back at the fortune teller, slightly bemused at the truth in his words, but didn't answer him. Even though it did occur to her that they were part of a clichéd opening phrase that all fortune tellers used, she had never had her fortune told, and had secretly wondered what it would be like. Why not take advantage of the opportunity? She had nothing to lose.

Ping Lü seated himself on one of the great cushions and signalled for Venetia to do the same. On the other side of him, she noticed a large bowl full of natural objects: shells, stones, crystals, and even small cactus plants. Along the top of the wall behind him was a beautiful scroll coloured in gold, black and brown, depicting a serpent with two human heads.

'This is an old scroll dating back to the Han Dynasty, illustrating Nüwa and Fuxi, her husband, who was the first ruler of the world,' the old man told her, seeing the interest in her face.

'It's beautiful.'

Venetia sat down opposite her host, her eyes straying, despite herself, towards the unpleasant reptile. As the man produced a crystal ball, her attention switched automatically to the glass globe, fascinated. It felt as if the magical sphere reached out to her and caught her up, pulling her into its core. Ping Lü sat very still, eyes shut, apparently in profound meditation.

After a while, that seemed ages to Venetia, he opened his eyes. Reaching out, he took the young woman's hands and placed them underneath his own over the globe. Venetia felt a kind of warm current pass through her.

'Concentrate on what you want to know, keep your mind focused on your questions. The more powerful your concentration, the clearer the message will be.'

Venetia tried to obey, but there were so many thoughts fighting for supremacy in her mind, so much hurt that seemed to be suddenly bubbling to the surface, as though all the pain she had suffered these past years had come to a boil.

'You are not calm. Your heart and your brain are in turmoil. It is hard to hear the whispers of the inner soul in the midst of such turbulence.'

'I know,' she whispered as, to her surprise, tears started to roll uncontrollably down her cheeks.

'Thomas Moore, a poet from your country, said: "*The heart that is soonest awake to the flowers is always the first to be touched by the thorns."* And we have a similar Chinese proverb: *"The rose has thorns only for those who would gather it."* My child, you found love at an early age. You had youth, beauty and love; you were on top of the world, knee-deep in roses... then... the thorns got you, didn't they? And scratched you badly. But though you may not think it now, they didn't do you any lasting damage; the wounds are healing now, and you can still appreciate the flowers, yes?'

Venetia took a deep breath. 'I thought that I was healing, but...' She shrugged, a look of hopelessness clouding her eyes.

Ping Lü blinked slowly and looked at her, his gaze fixed and pensive. 'I know, my child. I can see haze, mist and fog surrounding this man your heart has recognised, this renewed passion, the echo of an old love. I can see youth, and courage, even bravado... a dominating personality, but always honest. Misfortune besieged him: betrayal, lies and prejudice assaulted him of old, and now there is nothing left but loneliness and despair surrounding him among the wreckage.'

'What are his feelings towards me? Will anything come of these few brief moments that we've had together?'

'My dear child, only you can feel such an intimate thing.'

'How will I know?'

'If he is the one for you, if your souls have recognised and chosen each other, then there is no limit to the works of Fate to bring you together.'

'Is there anybody else in his life?'

'The flesh is weak, my child, and the fog around him is a thick, dark and mystifying curtain.'

Venetia was struggling to understand what she was hearing. 'What can I do? Is there any hope for us at all?'

'As long as there is life, there is hope, my child. You must listen to your heart, only to your heart. The stem is long and full of thorns, and there is no shortcut to get to the beautiful flower. Evil forces are at work. I can see jealousy and malice, conflict and chaos. Power abused, and pain, so much pain... But I can also see the stars at the far end of Heaven. After the clouds have passed, they will shine strong and bright in your night, leading the way. The stars represent hope, perception and revelation. Yes, there is hope for a fresh start...'

The Chineseman lifted his eyebrows and looked properly at Venetia this time. 'But you must not doubt, and you must not be obstinate if you want peace and harmony to be realised.'

Her heart beating slightly faster, Venetia listened, fascinated, to Ping Lü's impersonal, sing-song voice that lent an exotic flavour to his words. She felt slightly exulted, knowing suddenly in her heart that all was not lost, that tomorrow may not be as bleak as yesterday, and that she could dream, and her dreams might actually come true.

'I don't know why, and it's absurd because I've only met the man a few times... but I seem to have a deep feeling that Paolo and I are made for each other. I've never been able to put my finger on it but I'm sure that this feeling is reciprocated. Am I wrong? Have years of celibacy clouded my judgement to the extent that the first real yearning I have felt for a man has made me misinterpret it for love?'

Suddenly Venetia was talking, after years of repressing her thoughts and her feelings, years of holding back words that needed to be said. She was pouring her heart out to this stranger, this placid old man from China, a place she had never been to and knew hardly anything about. All the misery and loss she had been through were being laid out on the table in front of her; and Ping Lü listened quietly, an impassive look on his ivory features, his piercing eyes never leaving her face.

'The time for grieving has passed for you, my child. Your wounds have almost healed. Your heart is awakening from a fallow period. I can see a change in the direction of your fate. Every situation, however disturbing in its suggestion, has a reverse facet to it. The future may hold promise unimagined today. It is for you to search for that now.'

'What do I do now? He's gone, and I haven't dared look for him.'

'Believe in Fate. We say in China that what is destined to be yours will always return to you, and when Fate throws a dagger at you, there are only two ways to catch it: by the blade or by the handle.'

'I don't understand. What does it mean?'

'The grief a person goes through causes a change in his perception of himself or his lifestyle, and some sort of adjustment is required to avoid being haunted by the pain. You must choose what to remember from the past, cherish the joys of the present, and prepare for a future – you must look forward, my child. That is the only way.'

Again, Venetia found his placid, dispassionate voice, and his black eyes filled with the unworldly kindliness that had so struck her at first, brought her a sense of calm reassurance. 'I see, I understand. Thank you. Thank you so much.' As if by magic her weariness had left her; her heart brimmed with a new anticipation, half scared, half exultant.

Ping Lü rose and crossed to a small cabinet in the far corner of the room. He opened a drawer and came back with a small red silk bag, which he gave to her. 'This is for you. Open it.'

Venetia pulled apart the two delicate strings ending in tassels and took out a pendant. It was an intricately carved green and white talisman of the part-human, part-serpent goddess, Nüwa.

'The stone is Jade. In China, we call it Ming Jadeite. There is an ancient Chinese proverb that says, *"gold is estimable, but jade is priceless,"* and that is because we believe that this stone protects the wearer, and is a status symbol indicating the dignity, grace and morality of the owner.'

'I will never take it off,' Venetia promised, clasping the jewel about her neck.

As Ping Lü walked her to the door, Venetia turned to him. 'At the risk of being indiscreet, may I ask you a question?'

The gentle, scholarly old man smiled. 'Of course you can.'

'How come you speak such perfect English?'

'I left China as a young man. I was lucky enough to win a scholarship to Oxford. I lived for many years in your beautiful country.' His black, enigmatic eyes dwelled on Venetia's face and he smiled again. 'And to answer the second question which you did not dare formulate, I came to Italy after marrying my lovely Venetian wife. We have been blessed with forty years of happiness.'

'I'm not surprised – there is something very…' she paused, searching for the word, 'restful… yes, there is something very restful and serene about you. I can see that, unlike the rest of us, you're at peace with the world.'

'My bible is Confucius's Analects, a series of books put together by his followers which contain his sayings and teachings. He was a great philosopher.'

'It has been an honour meeting you. You have done me the world of good. Thank you.' Venetia gave a half smile. 'I admit, I was almost in despair.'

'Confucius says: *"By three methods we may learn wisdom: first, by reflection which is the noblest; second, by imitation, which is the easiest; and third by experience, which is the bitterest."'*

At the door, Venetia thanked Ping Lü again and shook hands with him. As she stepped out into the night she turned and waved.

'Remember, my dear child, to follow your heart in all things.'

Venetia smiled at him and nodded. The wind had died down, the mist had dispersed and the night was clear and calm. She glanced at her watch; it was already nine o'clock. She hurried towards the *vaporetto* station, her heart full of dreams and the most wildly impossible schemes. Ping Lü had given her hope; nothing seemed impossible any more. Sober common sense and consideration had just ceased to count, when suddenly it seemed as though mountains could be removed and stars snatched from the sky.

You're building magic castles in the air, a little voice at the back of her mind whispered, *and there are mortgages on castles in the air. You've already been bruised by life,* the voice continued to nag, *do you really want to go there again?*

She must not listen to her fears. Fate would see fit to arrange it otherwise – that 'long arm of Fate' of which Paolo had spoken when they had met so unexpectedly in Torcello. Ping Lü also talked about Fate. Yes, Fate would arrange everything in the end; her heart told her so. She had converted to its power; the only thing she needed to do now was to believe in her lucky star.

CHAPTER 4

Fate did not wait long. It happened two days later, on one of those strange ethereal afternoons which sometimes arrive at the end of winter, sunny and windless with a breath of spring in the air, to be grasped and cherished because tomorrow will bring back the bitter winds and cutting sleet. Venetia was sitting in her studio at Bianchi e Lombardi, struggling with a particularly intricate piece of mosaic. Her mind was still cogitating on Ping Lü's words, as she tried to conjure up some indirect way of finding out Paolo's whereabouts, when Francesca breezed into the room.

The redhead seemed excited, her eyes sparkling with mischief. 'You won't believe who's in the building!'

'Who?' Venetia asked, without looking up.

'I'll give you three guesses.'

Venetia stifled a sigh of irritation. 'Spare me the suspense, Francesca. I've got enough of it in my life at the moment without you adding to it.' She was battling with a set of tweezers, trying to take out a minute piece of corroded mother-of-pearl, deeply embedded in the *tessera* that had been brought in that morning.

'That piece you've been fiddling with for hours belongs to *il tuo dagli occhi blue,* your blue-eyed one. It seems we have a new client.'

Venetia frowned and lifted her face. He was here? For some reason she didn't want to process what her friend was saying. 'Who do you mean?'

Francesca waved her hand in exasperation. 'I can't believe it's been out of sight, out of mind. You haven't mentioned his name since our talk, but I'm sure you've been thinking about him.'

Venetia paled, her nerves jangling. 'Do you mean Paolo?' she said, putting down her work.

'In the flesh, my dear, and looking as dashing as ever.' One hand on her hip, Francesca arched an eyebrow, adding: 'I have to admit, he's even more striking-looking in daylight than he is under sultry nightclub lighting. He's with Giovanna and they're waiting for you in meeting room number five.'

Venetia's hands flew to her hair 'Oh dear, how do I look?'

'You look your usual beautiful self, *cara*. A little pale perhaps – but we could put that down to the filthy weather we've been having the last few days.' Francesca paused and then flicked up her hand with a defeated gesture, smiling wryly at her friend. 'Anyhow, I'd better leave you. Giovanna's ordered coffee, so I think he means business – very welcome at the moment, I must say, as we're looking for this year's next big project.' And with that, Francesca hurried out of the room with a backward wave.

Venetia had been listening to her friend with half an ear, having taken her make-up case from her bag and busily applied some gloss to her lips, before tidying her hair into a ponytail. After Francesca had left the room, she took off the jumpsuit she wore whenever she was doing restoration work and was putting it away when she was aware of a shadow darkening the open doorway. Lifting her head, she drew in a sharp breath.

'Have you missed me?' Paolo enquired in his deep, faintly musical voice, a slight smile hovering on his lips. Propping his shoulder against the door jamb, his eyes skimmed Venetia's exposed slender neck, before moving up to her diamond-shaped face and then down again to her mouth, his black lashes half shading their sparkling depths. He seemed perfectly at ease, as if it was totally acceptable to reappear in her life after weeks of silence, providing no explanation.

Venetia's heart raced. She was torn between a desire to hit him or throw herself into his arms. Warmth stole into her skin and she realised that she was blushing.

'*Buonasera, Signor Barone.*' Her greeting was a little stiff.

Paolo raised dark eyebrows. 'What, we are no more on first name terms?'

He pushed away from the door and stepped into the room, his sombre and powerful figure suddenly crowding the space around Venetia, invading her privacy. *This man has real gall,* she thought, as she looked away from his demanding gaze.

'I'll join you in the meeting room in a few minutes, if you just let me prepare myself.'

Ignoring her words, Paolo sauntered across to her and, capturing one of her quivering hands, smoothed a thumb across the back of it. His eyes were now serious.

'You're cross with me, *cara*, yes?'

Venetia attempted to pull away, but the touch of the firm brown fingers, so dark against her skin, had an absurdly sensuous penetrating warmth. She had dreamt so often of those strong, masculine hands upon her that she couldn't help a suppressed excitement that began to simmer.

'We mustn't keep *Signora* Lombardi waiting,' she argued, turning her head a little to evade his Mephisto stare.

'I've already had my meeting with *Signora* Lombardi.'

'I was told I had a meeting in room number five.'

'Yes, that's so, but I asked the permission of *Signora*

Lombardi to have the meeting with you outside the office over a cup of... hot chocolate?'

'I see,' Venetia said coolly. 'And, as always with you, I suppose I have no say in the matter.'

Paolo ignored the jab. 'You seemed surprised to see me.'

'I was amazed,' she answered stiffly.

He stepped closer. His half smile returned, though his eyes searched hers. 'Are you going to send me away?'

'I should,' she retorted shortly, pulling her hand from his grasp.

With the tips of his finger and thumb, Paolo lightly took hold of Venetia's chin and turned her face towards him. 'I'm sorry, *cara*. I know I behaved badly.' His voice was low and husky, its rich timbre overlaid with a hint of sadness, but sexy nonetheless. '*Mi sei mancato*, I've missed you. You see, *tesoro mio*, I tried, but I couldn't stay away. You've bewitched me with those expressive, fiery eyes of yours,' he murmured, his gaze challenging her before briefly sweeping downwards, '... and your eloquent body has already said so much more than words can tell me.'

They were so close now. He was looking at her with a brooding expression and although Venetia stood as still as a statue, tiny nerves seemed to chase each other over the pit of her stomach. Silence hung between them. Her heart thundered as his brilliant, feverish gaze travelled to her mouth. She felt her stomach clench, sending an urgent heat inside her. *Kiss me, Paolo*, she thought, *kiss me now*. She felt him go tense.

Still holding her chin, staring at her mouth, his other arm closed around her like a vice, and her body was crushed close to masculine muscles and impulses. One hand moved back to cradle her head, while the other held her mercilessly to him. His eyes were now burning into hers, searching her depths, silently provoking her. She leaned back a little and lifted her face, offering her mouth wantonly to him. The all-consuming blue irises held hers a moment longer, and then his raven-black head bent towards her.

Venetia felt the rush of his warm breath across her skin and a cry of relieved surrender escaped her lips as Paolo took them with desperate voracity. A raging thrill coursed through her veins and through her bones like quicksilver as the wild searching caress of his mouth, the raw passion in his wandering hands, ignited flame after flame through every part of her starved body. Venetia's arms moved upwards, encircling his neck. Her lips clung to his as though she would die if he stopped those deep, heated kisses; her breasts, now hard and painful, pressed against the wall of his chest, yearning for his caress. A long-denied hunger was driving her, all her senses aroused; she needed to touch him. From the muscled strength of his nape, her fingers moved over his back, down his ribcage and were then dexterously unbuttoning his shirt, craving the feel of him.

He was murmuring loving words into her ear, his lips moving over her eyelids, her cheeks, and her throat with erotic featheriness. The room was reeling and the nerves beneath Venetia's skin were alive as never before. Her legs felt weak, her flesh dissolving against him with molten languor, her soul trembling inside her burning body like an autumn leaf in the wind, a prisoner of the passion she saw smouldering in his eyes and could feel radiating from his powerful body.

From some dim recess of her mind she was remembering, recognising similar earth-shattering sensations and feelings that now resurfaced and invaded her – the echoes of an old passion once driven to a peak of expectancy, before leaving, shuddering in despair; a love that she had wrenched from her heart and buried in a deep well of oblivion.

'Oh, I'm sorry…! I didn't realise that you were still here. The door was open…' Francesca breathed, before scurrying away.

The redhead's apologetic exclamation jerked the lovers apart. As Paolo released her, Venetia swayed a little on unsteady legs and she automatically put out a hand to grasp the edge of his jacket. Paolo covered it with his, turned it over and gazed at the palm before bringing it to his lips.

'*La mia cara piccola strega*, my treasured little witch. You have breathed life into a body that has been dead for a long time,' he murmured without looking at her, a wistful smile touching the fine outline of his mouth. His eyes, so dark and inscrutable, now vacantly fixed on some point beyond the walls of the room, like a night without hope of stars. Venetia stared at him in astonishment; his words mirrored her own feelings, but she kept her thoughts to herself.

Tidying herself up, Venetia silently watched the back of Paolo's imposing figure. As he moved away from her and across to the window, while doing up his shirt and then adjusting his tie, he appeared to be a million miles away. Once more she was struck by the disconcerting resemblance of his bearing to Judd's. She wondered at the sadness that seemed to dwell so deep in this man – an imposing body with a vulnerable soul. A twinge of jealousy pinched her heart as the image of the beautiful young girl who had accompanied him to the restaurant swam before her, and she recalled the gossip Francesca had related. Still, Paolo had kissed her with a kind of banked-down passionate hunger, as though the obscure tide of feeling that had run like a resurrected, fluid fire through her own veins had touched him too. She pulled on her jacket, suddenly remembering something he said: *I tried, but I couldn't stay away.* So he *had* been avoiding her since Torcello, but why? That strange look in his eyes when they parted had been unmistakeable. What was Paolo about? Why did she feel as if she had known him forever, and yet he was shrouded with so many unanswered questions? Perhaps this was her chance to find out. Once more, he had woven his magic over her, and she felt her anger slip away into curiosity and the dark pull of her attraction.

Paolo turned abruptly and beamed at her. '*Andiamo*, shall we go and find that hot chocolate? Or maybe you'd prefer a glass of wine or a shot of *grappa*? We have some business to discuss.' Gone was the sadness from his eyes, gone were the shadows across his face; the enigmatic, slightly sardonic mask was back, as though those poignant emotions in his distant gaze had been a figment of Venetia's imagination.

They made their way through the deserted office block, and Paolo took her hand in his. Venetia thrilled to the feeling of his strong palm pressed against hers, and ignored the quizzical look the night porter gave them as they left the block. In the three years she had been working at Bianchi e Lombardi, she had made it a rule never to leave the premises after working hours with a man. Venice was a comparatively small place and rumours, true or false, made the rounds of the city in no time.

As they strolled along the waterfront towards Piazza San Marco, hardly a ripple moved the reflections of the *palazzi*, the street lamps and the moon; they hung, drowned and immobile, in the middle of the dark canal. The city's historical buildings seemed to rise to a greater and nobler span, their elegant lines highlighted against the curtain of the purple night. The stars shone like golden pendant balls, so close in appearance that it occurred to Venetia that an outstretched hand could almost pluck them down. Suddenly she was shy and confused, not knowing how to react to the intimacy between them.

'Where are we going?'

Paolo glanced at her as they walked, as if wondering how to take her question, then gave a sideways, wistful smile. 'If I had it my way, I would take you to my palace in the moon, where the stars shine always bright, and the angels sing all night a beautiful lover's hymn.'

She shot him back a playful smile of her own. 'What about the sun? Do the angels also sing there in daytime?'

'Alas, *cara*, my palace in the moon knows only night. Sunshine would be too dazzling and would eclipse the ethereal magic and poetry of the moonlight.'

So why did Venetia get the impression that there was a double entendre of real melancholy behind his words? 'Your palace must be very cold without the rays of the sun.'

'That's why, *amore mio*, I need a passionate queen to warm the shadows and disperse the clouds with the flames of her love.'

He stopped and leaned over suddenly, lifting her face to his, and then his lips were on hers. It was not a demanding kiss, rather a kiss with all his heart in it, she thought; a kiss with a message that she only partly understood.

Paolo released her and Venetia took a breath, half in amazement and half in disbelief. A storm of feelings rioted inside her. This was no game; it wasn't just pretence. With that kiss, Paolo had added another unspoken dimension to his words to bring home his intentions. The imploring intensity of it made her head spin. She couldn't let this go any further… or could she?

As though sensing her troubled thoughts, he put an arm around her shoulders almost in a brotherly fashion, and pulled her gently back into a walk, laughing. 'Come now, *cara*, don't look so serious, it's nice to dream from time to time, to make up stories, no?'

After the heartfelt potency of his kiss, the flippancy of Paolo's tone jarred upon Venetia. It was as if he didn't know on which foot to dance with her. Besides, she was no storyteller and liked to think of herself as a down-to-earth young woman. It was a way of being that she had forged out of necessity. Over the years, she had taught herself not to waste time on empty dreams, a tendency that had been difficult to curb and with which she still struggled sometimes. With Judd, their brief love had been the poetry of two souls in complete accord and she had dreamt of a perfect ending; but she'd learnt the hard way that some poems don't rhyme. She found Paolo's idiosyncrasies, his mercurial presence in her life – his ability to blow hot and cold almost in the same breath – disturbing, and she felt threatened.

Looking up at him, Venetia managed a short laugh. 'I'm too pragmatic for that sort of talk.'

Paolo stopped and stared down at her upturned face in the dimness. He lifted his hand and brushed away a tendril of silky hair from her forehead, his features taut. 'Maybe envisioning things in an ideal form is preparing for disappointment, but don't you ever have a longing for something other than down-to-earth reality, Venetia?'

She coloured. His playfulness was gone again. He had uttered those words as though they had been torn from him. There was a fierce light in his blue eyes that she had never seen before. Her heart misgave her, turning weak and soft in spite of herself. When he spoke like that, when he looked like that…

No words were said and they began to walk again until they came to the Piazza San Marco.

'We're going to take a gondola,' Paolo announced as he steered them towards the Bacino Orseolo, where dozens were bouncing gently in the water.

'Sounds great! I've been living in Venice for over three years, and I've never taken one,' she remarked with a bashful laugh.

'Then we must immediately remedy this considerable oversight on the part of your previous boyfriends.'

Venetia noticed the humorous lift at the corners of Paolo's mouth. She chose not to answer – it would just encourage a conversation that she knew he would leap into with both feet, and which she wanted to avoid at all costs. *Things are already going too quickly,* a voice at the back of her mind nagged. *Do you know what you're getting yourself into?*

Paolo approached a group of gondoliers in striped shirts who were standing around laughing and swapping stories: a habitual event in the evening after they had parked their craft in this wide spot of the canal, cupped by the curving yellow walls of a hotel with red awnings.

Venetia managed to step down into the swaying black cockle-shell boat without faltering, and without Paolo's help. The night was unusually warm and balmy and they reclined upon the inviting plush velvet cushions that lay on the two seats at the far end of the gondola.

'We're going to a small restaurant, La Lanterna. It's one of the best-kept secrets in Venice. I've not been there for a long time, but I think that you'll like it. Tonight, *cara*, I will show you a face of Venice that you'll never forget.' He sounded excited, like a child about to show off his new toys.

Turning her head, Venetia met Paolo's burning gaze and turned swiftly away again. That familiar feeling of confusion stole into her mind once more, as the little voice inside her head started whispering its warnings to pull back from him. And yet she couldn't help herself. His exhilaration was infectious, and he was disturbingly close. She felt the thudding increase of her heartbeat; if she leaned back a fraction she would be resting her head on his arm, which he had stretched out behind her.

The sleek black, slightly crooked boat headed out of the parking lot into the lagoon. There was a kind of breathtaking mystery to the scenery contemplated from this lazily moving romantic boat, differing completely from the experience of watching it from a *vaporetto* or a motorboat. The Grand Canal was floodlit, throwing a dramatic greenish glow over the ancient buildings, making it look like a theatre stage with *palazzi* standing transfixed in the limelight. And as they glided on the glistening canal, neither time nor place held any meaning for Venetia. The romance of the setting, the hour, and the aura of the man sitting beside her all contributed to a wonderful dream, a tremulous, glittering, fragile dream from which she had no desire to awaken. Something opened with a sigh inside her; an obscure chord in her mind was touched and she felt a choking sensation, as though she wanted to cry because of the sheer beauty of it.

'Is anything wrong? You're very quiet, *cara*,' Paolo remarked, leaning his head towards her.

Venetia caught her breath. 'I'm moved by the scenery of your beautiful country. It's the most marvellous sight in the world! It's strange, but looking at the same view from a gondola gives a totally different perspective.'

'The gondola is very special to the Venetians. There are many legends about it.'

Venetia looked up, her amber eyes sparkling with gentle mischief. 'And you're dying to tell me one, aren't you?' she teased.

Paolo threw back his head and burst out laughing. '*Sì, sì cara, stai cominciando a conoscermi*, you're starting to get to know me.'

He looked happy and carefree now. His shifts of mood would never cease to amaze her. Venetia did not understand him, but then she supposed she could hardly expect to do so on such short acquaintance.

She raised her eyebrows expectantly. 'Well? What are you waiting for? I'm all ears.'

'I wouldn't like to bore you.'

'One thing you could never be, Paolo, is boring.'

He hesitated, and then smiled; he looked rather pleased. 'Very well then! The legend says that a crescent moon plunged into the sea to provide a shield of darkness for two young lovers to be alone together. That is the reason for the black colour of the gondola, caused by the abrupt immersion of the phosphorescent body in cold water, and the reason for the silvery lustre of the prow and the stern, which remained out of the water.'

'Wonderful! Our Nordic legends talk about druids, mostly catastrophes. Greek legends are full of revenge of the gods, and death. But Italian legends are always about lovers.' She laughed. 'Italy is definitely the most romantic country in the world.'

Paolo smiled at the look of delight on Venetia's face and stroked her cheek tenderly with the back of his fingers as she gazed out over the dark water.

'I love the rippling sound of the oars, that mysterious music,' she continued. 'It's so soothing. You don't have that when you're roaring along the canal in a motorboat.'

'You're right, there's no sound more peaceful than the sob of oars in the silence, especially at night.'

'But oars don't sob, Paolo. They tickle the water and make it laugh.' Venetia glanced up at him, laughing herself, her whole face illuminated with inner joy. She felt light-hearted and carefree.

He surprised her by answering gravely. 'Only people who grow old in heart hear the oars' sob as they float down the river of years. You must keep your heart young, *tesoro del mio cuore*, and then you'll hear laughter all the way.' Paolo scanned Venetia's face, his eyes blazing with an intensity that looked almost painful for him, and with a muffled oath he pulled her into his arms.

His mouth on hers this time was savage and unrestrained. Like the bursting of a dam too long under pressure, the power of his passion erupted and Venetia gave a small gasp against his lips, allowing his tongue access and feeling it claim her possessively. She was captured, engulfed and drowned by the currents of pleasure that surged through her. She didn't care that their intimacy was in full view of the gondolier and other passing boats; she was in Italy, the land of love.

Venetia was alive to the heat radiating from Paolo, the thunder of his heart beating against her breast. His unintentionally cruel grip caused her rapturous pain, which melted into tenderness as he controlled his initial powerful deluge, turning it into a delicious stream of whispered endearments, caresses and featherlike kisses.

Now he touched her with mesmerising softness, running his fingertips over her eyes, her cheeks and her throat, stirring a range of sensations that flooded Venetia in rippling waves, filling her limbs with a luscious warmth that spread through her whole body.

She smiled dreamily up at him. 'Did you know your hands are like trained magic on me?' she breathed against his mouth.

Paolo stared down at her, eyes glimmering. 'You are the magic that has happened to me, *tesoro mio*. You make me dizzy. And you've given me an ache that has driven me mad since I met you. Beautiful, beautiful Venetia,' he whispered huskily, his hand squeezing her gently against him.

'La Lanterna,' announced the powerful voice of the gondolier who had stood perched at the stern behind them, silently and splendidly like a Florentine statue, moving the craft with skilled ease over the water.

They blinked up at each other, the spell almost broken, still trembling with the power of their emotions. Paolo released Venetia, but the pad of his thumb moved slowly across her full lips, his smouldering eyes fastened to her face; and then reluctantly his hand fell to his side. They sat a short moment in mutual silence, and then Paolo stood up.

'*Andiamo,*' he murmured, reaching a hand down to her. Venetia took it and let him pull her up, reacting instantly again to his touch on her wrist, feeling darts of heat all over her.

Paolo thanked the gondolier, and Venetia noticed he had given him a large tip.

Eyes still bright and faces flushed, the pair went up the elaborately sculpted stone steps to La Lanterna's entrance. A doorman let them into the garden that, except for a cluster of giant sentinel trees, was artfully concealed like a discreet and mysterious jewel, sheltered by high walls and looking out on to the Grand Canal through wrought-iron gates.

The restaurant itself, poised at the centre of its own garden, was much more conspicuous. It was built around a very tall, thick-trunked tree, a pumpkin-shaped building of glass, lit up like a glowing beacon in the night, suspended forty feet above the ground as though floating in the air.

'A restaurant in the clouds,' Venetia breathed. 'How amazing!'

'It's the creation of Mario De Luca's dream, a Venetian young architect who died a couple of years ago at the age of thirty-two – a great loss to the Italian art world. You'll see the interior... it's just as, *come si dice*, fantastic, extravagant, *magnifico.*'

Venetia's eyes clouded. 'Yes, what a terrible waste. I had a friend who died young, not so long ago. He was a brilliant restorer of mosaics. It's frightening when a life is cut off in its prime – it makes you wonder at your own mortality.'

'Indeed,' Paolo murmured, without looking at her.

Hands snugly clasped, they made their way up to the restaurant through an arched loggia walkway, sloping lengthily upwards and overflowing with heavy clusters of wisteria. The delicious fragrance of the purple flowers mingled with the smell of sea breeze. Every now and then, Paolo squeezed Venetia's fingers. 'Just to prove to myself that you're real and not a spirit,' he whispered in that deeply mellow tone which told her he was still emotional.

The dining area was a window on to Venice, a circular room that could seat sixty guests. Here fantasy and reality blended, creating art that, far from being detached from life, was an essential ingredient. With surrounding walls of reinforced glass, the sole décor of the place became the panoramic views over the restaurant's garden, and the life on the Grand Canal and beyond.

Though the restaurant was full, Paolo managed to secure a table next to the window, affording them a breathtaking view over Venice, with the islands of Murano and Burano glowing like brilliant gems in the distance. A further surprise was in store for Venetia as the light in the room switched from calm powder blue to almost dazzling white; she gasped and gave Paolo a puzzled look.

'Didn't I tell you, *cara*, that you'd be just as fascinated by the interior of La Lanterna as you were by the exterior? The lights in the ceiling change every five minutes so that the setting and the mood are continuously different.'

They ordered two Bellinis, which arrived with the menus before Venetia had time to blink. She looked around her while sipping her cocktail. The clientele was elegant, every one of them Venetian. The women were dressed in the latest fashion and the men looked as if they were direct descendants of the Doges. Venetia felt distinctly under-dressed, even though that morning she had put on a black Valentino suit, offset by a chunky gold Cartier brooch and a pair of matching earrings. She had dressed more formally than usual that morning, having been asked to fill in for Giovanna at an important meeting with an American tycoon who had just bought a large panel with a mural of The Last Supper taken from a palazzo that was being pulled down, and had wanted Bianchi e Lombardi's opinion on the matter.

As they studied the menu, the lighting changed again to mellow gold, creating a bubble of intimacy that enhanced the romance of the place. The warm glow gilded Paolo's olive skin and Venetia was conscious, more than ever, of the rugged, darkly charismatic man sitting across from her. Those hawkish, lapis-blue eyes... that full, smooth mouth with its top lip outlined so sensuously. Paolo was a very sexy man to say the least. He was exotic, as were his mannerisms and his accent. Like most Italians, he cared for his appearance – always immaculately turned out; his hair, clean-shaven face and manicured hands were perfectly groomed. The sight of those strong, sun-kissed hands alone was enough to make Venetia go weak at the knees, and she found herself wondering how many women had felt their sensuous touch on their skin.

A waitress came to take their order. The girl was pretty, with the budding promise of an exuberant beauty to come. Paolo gave her his devastatingly charming smile that always made Venetia's own heart beat a little faster, but which, when turned on another woman, made her feel as if a knife was raking her stomach. She thought of the young raven-haired beauty that she had seen with him; had he brought her here too? How many women had he escorted to this place, where, she had the impression, he was well known?

Paolo glanced at Venetia and now turned a special, intimate smile on to her.

'Have you chosen, *cara*?'

'Yes, I think I'll have *Capesante alla Veneziana* to start off with and then the braised Rabbit with Fennel and Herbs. Thank you.'

'Excellent choice! I'll join you with the *Coniglio in Porchetta*. I think I'll have *Arancini con Mozzarella* as an *antipasto*.'

Paolo ordered a bottle of Brunello diMontalcino and, once the young waitress had left, he turned his attention back to Venetia.

The twist of jealousy she had just experienced dampened her feelings and had injected a bittersweet tone into the evening.

'You said earlier on that you wanted to talk to me about some business,' she said, trying to bring some formality into their conversation. Maybe it hadn't been so wise to have dinner with Paolo – neither had it been only dinner, she thought, recalling their passionate interludes.

Paolo laughed deep in his throat. 'You little sorceress, you don't miss a trick! I was going to leave that subject for another day, this place is so romantic it would be a shame to waste it on business, *non siete d'accordo*, don't you agree?'

Venetia felt the intensity of his gaze as he spoke, those sapphire eyes at once casting their familiar spell. Still, she held them defiantly. 'No better time than the present.'

Paolo sighed. 'If you insist, *cara*! There's no use fighting with a woman once she's made up her mind about something... particularly you, Venetia,' he said with amused exasperation. 'I'm in the process of buying five hundred hectares of land in Manciano, which is a little over half an hour away from my home in Tuscany. It's situated in a place of great natural beauty and consists of a very large villa in ruins, a chapel that's also in pretty bad condition, a forest, and much land. I'd like to turn the villa into a luxurious hotel, restore the small church and build a resort.'

'Where do I come in?'

'The chapel is a gem, but all the mosaics and decorations on its walls need to be restored, and I thought...'

'In Tuscany, Paolo? But that's miles away! You can't expect me to commute to Tuscany every day.'

'*Cara*, it was never my intention to have you commute to Tuscany every day. I was hoping that you would agree to be my guest for a month or so.'

What was he talking about? Had Venetia heard right? A distant logic told her it was the rosy shadows from the lighting, which had just turned crimson, that had changed his cobalt-coloured eyes to almost violet; dark and brooding, holding hers in their power. The same shadows softened his cheekbones and touched his mouth with a gentleness she had never seen there before. What was it about this man that could in an instant melt her heart, to the extent that all reasoning, all coherence and all sanity could disappear just like that, at the snap of a finger?

'I'm not sure that Bianchi e Lombardi can spare me for that long. There are only two of us who specialise in mosaics in the department,' she ventured.

They were interrupted by the smiling waiter in a white jacket, bringing their starter.

After the waiter had poured a little of the wine for them to sample, Paolo tasted it and nodded, asking him to leave the bottle with them. He filled Venetia's glass and then topped up his own, waiting until the young man had moved away. His eyes flashed over Venetia, and amusement of a wicked sort leapt into them.

'*Signora* Lombardi has given me the green light.'

Prickles rose on Venetia's back as her old defences started quivering into place.

'*Signora* Lombardi may be my employer and my godmother, but I have my own say in the matter.' Deep inside, Venetia knew this was an empty phrase, but she couldn't bring herself to just accept this mad invitation without some sort of defiant gesture.

Paolo put his elbows on the table and leaned towards her. 'Has anybody ever told you how captivating your amber eyes are when they blaze with such angry golden flames?'

'You always do this to me, Paolo.'

'Do what, *cara*?'

'You spring things on me as though I've no right to have an opinion or a say in the matter. I dislike this dictatorial attitude of yours, I've told you that before. I escaped from it at home and came to Italy to take my life into my own hands – and I'm not prepared to relinquish my freedom for anything, or anybody.'

There was a brief, stunned silence.

Paolo's eyes had narrowed. They were particularly expressive now, ranging from a chilling glitter of reproach to a blaze of white-hot passion, and Venetia could see that his whole body had gone tense.

'The idea of forcing you into anything, Venetia, was furthest from my mind,' he said, leaning back on one elbow and rubbing his chin, his gaze still fixed on her. 'I thought you would be happy to come, that we shared the same feelings… and maybe we would be able to get to know each other better. We Italians are not like you English – we have no half-truths, no subtleties. We are, or we are not.'

Venetia stared back, confounded again by his candour and the look he was giving her. His words made her feel guilty but harsh-ness was her only defence against her fluttering heart and her vulnerability to this curious chemistry between them. Apprehension was pulling at her again. Perhaps it was she who was the mercurial one. She did not know herself any more. Fearful and enthralling emotions seemed to take over her mind and her body in Paolo's presence.

Ping Lü's words came back to her – *follow your heart*, he'd said. She was so mixed up that she couldn't discern what her heart was dictating to her. Still, none of these inner tortuous feelings were a reason for rudeness.

Venetia bit her lip. 'I'm sorry, Paolo,' she apologised. 'All my life, when I was young, I was bossed around by an overpowering father. I resented it bitterly and that's why I decided to leave England. I find it difficult now to... to let go of my control over things.'

Paolo looked at her for a long moment, his expression unreadable. 'You're a creature of surprises, Venetia. You beguile and fascinate me.' His mouth broke into an indulgent smile. '*Ma capisco, cara.*'

She lowered her gaze, her fingers playing with the stem of her glass. 'Neither of us knows anything about the other.'

'Only that there is an undeniable power that is pulling us towards each other,' he said softly. The words seemed to linger in the air between them, equivocal, tantalising, and suggestive of all sorts of possibilities. Venetia felt a blush warm her cheeks and flood her whole body.

The empty plates were cleared away and replaced by the main course. For a while they fell into a companionable silence, concentrating on their rabbit.

Venetia was the first to break it. 'I think I should know a little bit about you before I take this job you're offering me.'

For a moment Paolo's face was blank. Had he paled or was it again the effect of the light, which had switched to green? She watched him light a cigarette and blow out the flame on his Zippo. 'Yes, of course,' he said, after a pause. 'What do you want to know?'

'Did you grow up in Tuscany? Are your parents alive? Do you have brothers and sisters?'

'*Piano piano, cara,* one question at a time!' He cleared his throat. 'My parents are dead, I have no brothers and sisters, and I grew up pretty much all over the place.'

'How come?'

'My father was an ambassador. We travelled every two or three years to a different country.'

'That must have been interesting.'

Paolo's face darkened. 'It was very... unsettling – I don't really belong anywhere.' His words were almost whispered, as though he were talking to himself.

'Did you not have a happy childhood, then?'

'No, not very,' he returned shortly.

'Where did you go to university?'

'In Rome. Actually, at one point, I thought I might become a chef,' he confided, pouring some wine into Venetia's glass, and then for himself.

'So why didn't you?'

He waved a hand dismissively. 'Oh, I suppose it didn't fit with my status. I went to business school instead.' Paolo looked at Venetia across the top of his glass. 'But what about you?' His eyes were alight with curiosity.

She gave a slight shrug. 'My life was very boring until I came to Italy – the life of a poor little rich girl. I went to boarding school, then I read architecture at Cambridge.'

Paolo's gaze was unwavering. 'What about a *fidanzato*? Have you never been engaged?' His blunt question rattled her. The arrogance of Italian men never ceased to amaze her. Venetia shook her head.

'Not even a serious boyfriend?'

'Nope.' She didn't feel inclined to take him into her confidence right now; the last thing she wanted was to go into details about her private life.

Paolo tilted a sceptical eyebrow and took a sip of wine. 'You're a beautiful and passionate woman, Venetia. I'm astonished that, to this day, you've never encountered love en route. You must meet a lot of people in your wide range of work.'

His voice was smoky, soft; Venetia was once more distracted by his perfectly sculpted mouth.

'I guess I haven't been interested in that sort of thing – I love my work… passionately,' she breathed, aware that his blue stare was still on her.

'Work cannot replace the warmth of a person.'

'I suppose not.'

'You've never been in love?'

Venetia looked down to avoid those eyes that were trying to see into her soul. 'Oh, I suppose my heart has beaten sometimes, like any infatuated teenager.'

'Only infatuation, never anything more?' He rubbed his chin again, as if in deep thought.

'If it had been real love, I wouldn't be here today, would I?'

'Are you looking for love then?'

Venetia smiled wryly. 'Isn't everyone?'

They had finished eating and Paolo reached for Venetia's hand and covered it with his own.

The lights had changed to white again, and in the pearly glare she could see that his irises had lost all those violet overtones that had so confused her earlier. There was a little glint of something indefinable in his scrutiny as it rested on her that was electrifying. She felt a tremor run through her and, veiling her eyes with her lashes, she turned away so he couldn't see her confusion. The little warning voice was there again, still wrestling for control. *I must not give in to these feelings*, she kept repeating to herself, but she knew fighting was useless. It was as if his touch and his kisses had branded her.

'You can't deny the magnetism that exists between us,' Paolo whispered, forcing Venetia to turn her face back to him. The intensity of his blue gaze seemed to spring forward to catch hold of hers, searching them in the golden dappled light.

She blinked, feeling like she wanted to give into their power, to fall into them, but such was the turmoil that had stirred up in her again, she didn't know what to say.

'I haven't been able to get you out of my mind since I first saw you – this has never happened to me before,' he continued, a kind of lost expression darkening his face as he raked his other hand through his hair.

Venetia was on the verge of asking him about the beautiful young woman she had seen with him at the restaurant, and the rumours that went around but restrained herself. Her pride did not allow her to show him how insecure she felt. She would take advantage of the next few days to find out more about him.

At that point, the pretty waitress returned to enquire whether they would like some dessert, but they declined and ordered coffee.

'You are not answering me, *cara*,' he pressed, when the waitress had disappeared. 'Why are you denying your feelings? I have invited you to take on this restoration work and to stay in my home because I want to be with you. Venetia, *mia carina*, I'm not a young man, I'm thirty-eight, so I've met and been with many women and I know what I feel for you is… it is not a fad.'

It was the tone that always unmanned her; the incredible tenderness he showed and which turned her heart to liquid. And because Venetia wanted to believe him so much, she was afraid to believe him at all.

Once more, she was about to ask him about the young woman she had seen with him, but again she refrained from it. She didn't want him to see her reaction if his response displeased her; she wanted to hold on to the dream she was living. She hadn't felt normal from the moment Paolo had entered her life. There was something intensely unnerving, almost disturbing, about the manner in which they seemed to click, an affinity that she could not explain. Every part of his body appealed to her as no other man's had since Judd. When they touched, it was as if she was caught up in a crazy fantasy born of the mists of Venice, a fevered dream that had taken place before, in another life.

Venetia was almost certain that Paolo was a loner like herself, and that he, too, had been hurt; she had often noticed a cloud passing over his handsome face. Maybe that was the link between them – an invisible bond connecting two human beings who had been scarred by life. Scarred... Venetia certainly didn't need a second scar. She was quite happy living quietly – never mind if her emotions were stagnating; at least that way she was safe.

Just at that moment, Paolo's mobile phone rang. He reached into his pocket, briefly glanced at it and frowned.

'I'm sorry, Venetia. I'll take this, but I'll be quick.' He regarded her intently as he held the phone to his ear. '*Ciao...*' She watched his expression as he looked away, but it was unreadable. 'Yes, why are you calling me?... Yes, I did say I was busy and couldn't join you.' He lowered his eyes and his voice softened. 'No, of course that's not the reason...'

Venetia looked up sharply and met his eyes. They were dark and impenetrable. It was clearly a woman. Was it the same beautiful girl from the restaurant? There was that knife again, turning in the pit of her stomach, but this time it cut deeper. If he was unsettled by the inconvenience of another woman's phone call at dinner, Paolo didn't show it. She looked away, willing her face not to reveal any emotion.

'*Sì, sì, lo so*, I know... I'll see you when I get back. Now I must go. *Ciao.*' Paolo slipped his phone into his pocket again and turned his attention back to Venetia. He stared at her and frowned slightly as if trying to read her thoughts. 'I'm sorry, *cara*, an unexpected interruption. Now, where were we?'

She was determined not to ask the identity of the mystery caller, but raised her eyebrows. 'Is everything okay?'

Paolo waved his hand dismissively. 'Yes, fine – it's nothing.' He seemed disinclined to discuss it further, and instead his burning blue eyes searched her face.

Was it so easy for him to turn his attentions so freely between the women he juggled? The way he was looking at her now held so many things, it made her head spin with confusion. She stared back at him. What had she got herself into? Yes, this was some kind of fantasy, she thought, but one that would soon turn into a nightmare and consume her. She couldn't go back there again.

The waiter brought the coffees and Paolo lit a cigarette. 'You're very pensive, *cara*.' His voice brought her back to earth.

Venetia smiled at him ruefully. 'It's been an emotional evening,' she whispered, as she sipped her *espresso*.

He took her hand between his own and held it firmly. '*Penso di stare per innamorarmi di te*, I think I might be falling in love with you,' he said gently, in that voice which she found to be one of his greatest charms.

She looked at him in shock and her throat constricted.

'You mustn't, Paolo.'

'Why not, *carina*? Can you deny that you have feelings for me?' His eyes were alight with blue fire and she thought they would burn through her heart.

'I won't deny that I'm very attracted to you,' she said, choosing her words with care, ignoring their treachery, 'but all this has been going too quickly, and as I told you earlier, at the moment I'm totally involved in my career and there's no place for anything else in my life.' She winced inwardly as she felt her defences lock firmly into place. 'We must remain only friends.'

She withdrew her hand. Paolo's face suddenly set itself in grim lines.

'Have you ever heard of friendship between a man and a woman? How naive you are, Venetia, if you think that the passion that consumes me… *yes*, the passion that consumes me – don't look so surprised – can ever become anything else but more passion.'

'I have many men friends, and trust me when I tell you that they are only friends, and the best a person could wish for,' Venetia argued calmly, fighting her own longing to give in to his madness and let Paolo enfold her with the loving tenderness she sensed in him.

His eyes darkened underneath the straight black brows. He was angry now. 'They're only eunuchs, these so-called men you talk about. Emasculated, cold-blooded men,' he burst out.

Venetia didn't answer. She felt the quiet anguish inside her, but she had to put an end to this whirlwind she had embarked on. She had been playing with fire and now she must stop or she would get burned again. With time, she told herself, Paolo's image would dim, but deep down she knew that nothing would eradicate his memory – there was something about him that would be forever engraved upon her heart, and the knowledge nearly tore her apart.

'So this afternoon was just a masquerade?' Paolo's tone was flint, his eyes level, hard as glass.

Her voice trembled, almost choked, her heart so heavy she could scarcely breathe. 'No, Paolo,' she said slowly. 'It was a time of enchantment, an interlude to which I succumbed against my better judgement. Let's just say that I was drugged with the Venetian air, the scent of the sea, the romance of moonlight… and your eyes, Paolo, that caress me with such tenderness that sometimes I feel I could drown in them.' Her gaze held his for a moment and then dropped.

He leaned towards Venetia, mesmerising her, and she felt as if she was falling again. 'You say such beautiful words, *cara*, and the fire in *your* eyes reflects the passion in your soul, so why are you denying us simple happiness? What is it that you're not telling me?'

'This is also very hard for me,' Venetia whispered, her eyes fixed on her empty cup of coffee. 'Please, Paolo, don't make things more difficult.'

His eyes widened. 'I don't want to make things difficult for you. This should be easy.'

'Well, it's not. Not for me. I can't give you what you want, Paolo.'

She felt him stare at her long and hard, as if her words had struck him.

'That means that you have turned down my proposition – I must look for another restorer for my project?'

'I'm already involved with another project which will take me until the beginning of summer,' she said, evading his question.

He stiffened and then closed his eyes. When he reopened them, his expression was impenetrable. 'Very well, Venetia, the subject is closed, I will not importunate you again,' he said dryly.

In response to his signal, the head waiter brought the bill.

Venetia let him help her on with her coat and felt like a tendril of anguish had wound itself tightly round her heart. They went back down the vaulted walkway smothered in wisteria, but this time without holding hands.

*　　*　　*

It was two o'clock in the morning. The blue-lacquered Ferrari 550 Maranello sped through the night towards San Stefano in Tuscany. Attuned to the darkness surrounding him, his sombre mood overwhelming, Paolo drove the sleek, powerful sports car as though he was entering the 24 Hours of Le Mans race. Driving always relieved his stress. But tonight it wasn't stress that was invading his body and his mind; it was the shadowy memory of a woman – Venetia. Vulnerable, bewitching Venetia, who haunted every hour of his days and nights.

Questions and more questions flickered in his eyes. Why Venetia? Granted, she was ravishing, but Paolo was used to beautiful women, not to mention ones who threw themselves at him. As far as he could remember, he had never needed to chase a woman. Still, there was something other than physical attraction that drew him to her. They were barely more than strangers, but he read her moods as if recovering her from another time, another place; somewhere known only to the two of them. Why? He knew almost nothing about her, yet when she had revealed a little about herself, for some reason he had not been surprised. Holding her, their bodies were so attuned that it seemed he had known it all his life.

… All his life? Paolo's face twisted and he laughed aloud, a bitter, angry laugh that echoed like a lonely half-sob in the silence of the car. His hands grasped the steering wheel so tightly that the knuckles showed white. Damn this miserable situation! Damn this 'life' of his!

Still, so much of Venetia remained a mystery. It was the sadness he read in her eyes, whenever she thought she was not being watched, that got to him and puzzled him most. He had almost felt the struggle going on in her as she tried to pull back from him, both physically and emotionally; the pondering, the hesitation… the fear. He had not missed the tremors in her voice when she finally had the courage to rebuff him. Yes, she was afraid, deeply afraid: a fear that bordered on panic. What could have happened in her life to make her build such a protective fortress around her world? She had denied having known true love, but he doubted she was telling the truth; her words might have been deceitful, but her doleful, amber eyes were unable to lie.

Was he being fanciful? Paolo asked himself. Was Venetia only fleeing because she, like him, had felt the strange spell that seemed to weave itself around them, holding them prisoners of their caged, fiery passion? After all, hadn't he too tried to subjugate the rush of feelings that had so overwhelmed him that afternoon at Torcello? Like Venetia, confused and unable to think straight, he had pronounced words of such finality at the end of the day, running away from the enormity of what was happening between them.

Venetia's image swam out of the darkness, a picture of innocence and sensuality. He recalled the way they had kissed – the exquisite tenderness of that kiss had seemed to him to be opening a door into a strange world of beauty: wonderful and unnerving. Holding Venetia in his arms, feeling the rich fullness of her lips had been like a bloom from which he drew an intoxicating sweetness of joy. When her soft, yielding lips trembled beneath his own, more than ever he had been conscious of his own vast hunger for a woman's love, and the dangerous promise of those moments he had spent with Venetia. The intensity of this remembrance was so strong that Paolo felt his body ache with agonising need. He yearned for Venetia with a deep craving of his soul that was alarming. The thought that he might never see her again, hold her to him, smell the scent that filled his senses whenever he brushed against her, was unthinkable. But still the question kept coming back, like a haunting refrain. *Why Venetia? Why Venetia? Could he really be falling in love?*

He tried to tell himself that she had done him a favour, that it was better this way. There was no point in pursuing this passion the way things stood with him – it would be madness. He was not into love and promises and happily-ever-afters, how could he be? *With the heavy baggage you're carrying, how could you ever make a woman happy?* Light entered his life on one side, and darkness on the other. Dreaming of life with a woman, *any* woman, was something he had long put behind him and it had to remain that way. But since he had met Venetia, his life had turned upside down. Nothing made sense any more. He had almost succeeded in hiding the extent of his feelings – until tonight. If only Allegra hadn't called him at the restaurant. It had broken the spell and he had seen the look in Venetia's eye afterwards. He had been so close to telling her what was going on inside him. He felt like an unanchored boat that was being dashed against the rocks in a stormy sea.

As he drove on, the moon shone over the countryside where there were vineyards, and beyond, a belt of olive trees. Paolo was not far now from his destination. He could see Miraggio, the home he had known for the past eight years, perched high on a crag in the far-off distance, outlined against the moonlit sky. The turreted building stood on a bluff overlooking the sea, and, though quite small in size, it towered above the valley on the other side: his sanctuary.

Paolo's heart filled with pride, as it always did whenever he approached Miraggio. He had seen its elegant silhouette bathed in golden light at dawn, drenched in shades of purple and bright pink at sunset, and shrouded in mist and silver shadows as it was tonight; and every time, his breath caught in his throat with the same sense of gratification.

His thoughts roamed back to that first time he had set eyes on it. It was named La Torretta in those days. One stormy afternoon, as he was driving aimlessly around the countryside, the damaged turret of the house had loomed out of the clouds in the distance like a mirage. Curious, he had gone in search of the house and had found it without great difficulty. The dwelling, which he could see had been partly destroyed by fire, was almost a ruin and was set in about twenty-five hectares of untended land. The property stood in solitary desolation, four miles away from the first house in Cala Piccola, with a large 'For Sale' sign posted on its rusty gates.

The estate agent in charge of the sale was only too pleased to get La Torretta off his books. It was going for less than a quarter of the price it would have sold for in its original condition. '*The market is slow and it's been left to rot ever since the tragedy three years ago,*' he had told Paolo. '*Because it overlooks the sea, it's been battered by the winds and the salt. Most of the walls are corroded… And, of course, as with all these types of old properties, there are rumours that the house is haunted, but what house doesn't have its harmless ghosts?*' he'd added with a shrug.

Paolo had gathered, from talking to various *caffetteria* owners and shopkeepers in the village of Cala Piccola, that La Torretta once belonged to a famous opera singer who had retired there when his fame started to dwindle. He was not a very likeable person and rumour had it orgies and other kinds of strange parties took place at his home. The notorious tenor and his guests had perished in the fire set by one of his vengeful mistresses. It was a gruesome story and locals said that on stormy nights as you approached the turreted house, you could hear the tenor singing the aria '*Addio, fiorito asil*' from Puccini's *Madama Butterfly*.

Paolo had bought La Torretta without hesitation, but had changed its name to Miraggio, because of his first impression of the dwelling when it had appeared to him suddenly in the distance, as though suspended in the clouds; and also because the word reflected more or less the way he felt about himself in those days. He saw the opportunity as an optimistic sign – a new beginning after the bad fortune life had dealt him. He would rebuild the grand house, together with his life, which at that time seemed to him a great black hole, with only the unknown to look forward to.

The first years were hard. Paolo had set himself a heavy task, but he had been lucky. In the 1980s, the economy had enjoyed a period of growth, but in the early 1990s, Italy was going through another economic slump. Unemployment was still rife, especially among the under twenty-fives, and high inflation and escalating public debt meant that the whole country was feeling the pinch. Work became increasingly hard to find. Ever the idealist and businessman, Paolo saw the chance to boost local employment in the rebuilding of Miraggio. Young men and women came forward to help, happy to be given a job even if the remuneration was low. Eighteen months on, the house had been rebuilt and the grounds planted with mature olive trees, cypresses, vines, and a profusion of other trees and plants. A year after that, Paolo had added a small olive-oil factory to his domain and his estate began to grow. Whenever he had the opportunity, he bought land and property – residential and commercial. In the following years, his wealth grew exponentially and today he was considered a very rich man. As Italy was swept into the new millennium and the Eurozone, he had calmly ridden the wave, and now his shrewd business sense had built him a fortune, a reputation, and a new sanctuary.

*   *   *

It was almost dawn when Paolo finally came to a winding road through dense vineyards, and the sleek car began climbing the kilometre-long slope that led to Miraggio. He had broken his record of four hours, forty-five minutes, and had made the journey in just under four and a half hours. The tall, iron gates at the entrance to the estate were usually closed, especially at night, but he had rung Antonio, the caretaker, from the hotel before leaving Venice and so they had been left open.

As he drove up the avenue of lime trees, he could see, glimmering through the leaves, the lighted, beautifully proportioned house and he breathed a sigh of relief. He had reached his resting place, his haven, and that was all that counted for the moment. In the morning he would sort out his confused mind; now he must get some sleep – though he knew that with sleep came his demons, and they would call to him as they had done ever since he could remember.

CHAPTER 5

In the quiet luxury of her dimly lit bedroom, Venetia undressed for bed, her head and her heart in bitter conflict. Her thoughts were flitting in all directions. The evening had been a golden moment that she could neither forget nor wish undone. Had she been right to rebuff Paolo so adamantly? She kept remembering that lost and wounded look in his eyes when she had told him she couldn't give him what he wanted. Past and present collided in her mind, making it impossible, more than ever, for her to make any plans about the future, whether or not they included Paolo.

She went into the bathroom, brushed her teeth, sluiced her face with cold water and brushed her hair vigorously, a habit Nanny Horren had inculcated in her since childhood. Coming back into the bedroom, she put on a silk nightdress and slid between the freshly laundered sheets, wondering unhappily if her experience with Judd would always tarnish everything. Venetia had thought that she would forget the loss of her first love with time, but the shock and the pain of it still lingered in her heart; strangely enough, meeting Paolo had brought all those bittersweet memories to the surface.

She told herself that Paolo's Italian imagination had been at work fabricating a great romance between them to which she had been curiously sensitive; but how could she deny the way she had felt in his arms or the knowledge that all she really wanted was to be back in his embrace? It only reinforced the fact that she was emotionally vulnerable, dangerously so.

Was it just her sex-starved body that had reacted so passionately to his touch, or had Paolo moved something deeper within her, which could blossom into a new love? What gave him the power to sway her so utterly? At times he seemed stamped with an air of mastery, which couldn't fail to stir Venetia's blood; but every now and then he gave the impression of someone half dreaming of other things, making him equally fascinating. His mercurial nature surrounded him with an atmosphere of doom that appealed to her in the same way a moth is compelled towards fire. Always, wherever they met, there came a sense of crisis, as though everything was intensified and had suddenly become dramatic. Somehow the inessential faded out when they were together, and another reality, sharper, perhaps harder, yet more visceral and more poetic, rose up instead. What was behind Paolo's ambiguous half smile? What vague suggestion lay in his voice? Why did his words always seem to beckon away beyond themselves, alluding to hidden emotions in him she didn't understand? Trying to rationalise her feelings towards him was an impossible task. One thing Venetia recognised was that even though she was a different person from that innocent young girl who had hurled headlong into a passionate romance, behind the confident façade she had built up against the world she was still inexperienced and vulnerable. If she were to drop her guard and let someone in, any unscrupulous man could still make mincemeat of her; and after what she had already been through, she wouldn't survive another trauma.

Not for the first time, despite herself, Venetia found that she was comparing Judd and Paolo – the two men who had made her heart beat so wildly. They were uncannily alike in so many ways and perhaps that was partly why, subconsciously, she had been attracted to Paolo in the first place. Both were dark and charismatic, and from the back they had much the same build, with a similar shape of head. Even the way Paolo's thick, black hair curled around the back of his neck reminded Venetia of her ex-fiancé. Paolo seemed to have a caring disposition, a trait that had also drawn her to Judd, but being Italian, he was domineering and rather more chauvinistic than Judd in his approach to women. Thinking about it, she didn't always understand his reactions, but then she could hardly expect to on such short acquaintance, she supposed. Still, he intrigued her, but a warning bell rang in Venetia's head – she had the distinct impression that somewhere inside that man, something had gone wrong.

And now, as she lay in the big bed, a small, desolate figure, Venetia had a dreadful sensation of loss. Suddenly she felt horribly alone in the world. It was not that she felt lonely – she had always liked her own company, and as an only child she had often spent time in happy isolation – it was more a sentiment that, out of cowardice, she was letting go of something important in her life. She gripped the carved talisman Ping Lü had given her that lay around her neck, feeling her lack of certainty keenly. *How do I know what I feel for Paolo? Why am I reacting so strongly to him when he's almost a stranger?* The same questions kept coming back to her; it had all been so swift and sudden, like a fever.

She switched off the light, but she couldn't sleep, so she turned on the radio. U2's 'With or Without You' was playing and she gave an uncontrollable start, as this eighties favourite of hers was bound up in her mind with Judd – she had listened to it again and again for years after he left her. Still, tonight, strangely enough, it was not Judd's handsome face that swam in front of her in the dark, but Paolo's eyes. They were indeterminate in colour: sometimes a luminous cobalt, the rim of his irises darkening dramatically almost to midnight-blue every now and then, imparting a look of pathos to his tanned face; and at other times, like water with the sun shining on it. Paolo, who, with his hands, his mouth, and his tender words, had brought Venetia's body back to life again.

Her senses cried out for him to possess her, ached with the memory of that brief time in her office, and then in the gondola, when his strong arms had enfolded her and she had been thrust into an urgently pulsing hardness. She had surrendered herself with wanton abandon to the whispering touch of his palms, his lips, the demands of his muscular body. Recalling those passionate moments, Venetia's breath caught and fragmented, Paolo's name a shuddery sigh that lingered in her throat.

Thoughts whirled round and round in her tired brain. Maybe there could never be any firm security in love. The mere process of loving made one hopelessly vulnerable. Maybe it was best to be content with the 'here and now', and refrain from peering back at the past or into the future. There comes a time in most people's lives when they have to stop running. Was it her time now? If it were, she wondered, would she have the courage to stand still and face the fear and the memories that haunted her? But exhausted, the conclusion eluded her as the Sandman took over and she drifted off into a deep sleep.

*   *   *

The next day, before Venetia even had time to sit down at the office, she was out again into the early spring morning. It was an exquisite, heart-lifting day, when Venice lay like a city bewitched, with skies a tender blue, the air clear and soft, the sea serene as a table of oil, and the trees a vivid green.

'Don't even bother to take off your jacket,' Francesca told her with a grin as Venetia came into the workshop ten minutes late.

'You've been summoned.'

Venetia's heart leapt and she became aware of its heavy thumping against her ribcage. Paolo was probably at the office and had complained to her godmother.

She lifted her eyebrows. 'What do you mean?'

Francesca chuckled. 'Honestly, I don't know what you do to these men, Venetia! Yesterday it was *Signor* Barone – by the way, I'm sorry I barged in on you... you must tell me all about that later,' she said with a wry glance. 'Anyhow, today *il Conte* has been leaving messages all morning that he needs to see you urgently.'

Venetia's amber eyes were momentarily shadowed by a frown. 'To my knowledge, there's nothing outstanding in that job. We've even received payment, I'm sure.'

'Well, I don't know what it's about. He sent an email yesterday at eleven-thirty at night, and this morning he's already left three messages with different departments.'

Venetia sighed. 'I suppose a phone call wouldn't do?'

'Not really! Here are the messages.' Francesca handed Venetia the three notes. 'Besides, *Signora* Lombardi asked about you first thing. She wasn't very happy, I'm afraid, and would like to see you when you come back from your meeting with the Count.'

Venetia stared at the messages in her hand as a fearful sense of inevitability rose inside her. She gave a little groan. 'I'm almost sure I know what this is about. He's going to harass me again about his marriage proposal and, frankly, I'm really not in the mood for his tantrums this morning.'

Francesca looked at her friend sharply. 'What's up? You look as though you haven't slept for a year.'

'Don't worry about it, Francesca, I'll tell you later.' She picked up her briefcase and was on her way again.

When Venetia arrived twenty minutes later at Palermi di Orellana Torre, she was not kept waiting. She shivered, an odd little chill of something between anger and dread sliding down her spine as she was ushered into the vast room at the top of the building, which was Count Umberto's office.

Il Conte stood at the wide picture window overlooking Venice, his back to Venetia. He waited a few moments, motionless, before turning towards her.

'*Buongiorno* Venetia, did you have a nice evening last night?' he asked point blank, his slate-grey eyes narrowing almost to slits, watching her through his lashes like a cat observing its prey. His cutting tone belied an outward calm, but Venetia had worked for months with him and didn't need an explosion to guess there was a storm brewing inside.

Oh God, she thought sickly, realising what he was alluding to. Was he also having dinner at La Lanterna? But that was almost impossible: Francesca had said he had sent an email at eleven-thirty at night, and anyhow, the restaurant wasn't so big that he would have gone unnoticed.

Umberto signalled for her to take a seat, and sliding behind his desk he sat back in his chair, still looking at her, a sarcastic expression dancing on his lips.

'Yes, La Lanterna is an amazing restaurant,' Venetia answered calmly, ignoring the barbed question and forcing herself to hold his gaze.

Umberto scoffed. 'It's the hunting ground of our mutual friend. He likes to take his women friends there.'

Venetia smiled stiffly, refusing to rise to the jibe. 'Were you there? I didn't see you.'

Umberto's eyes travelled over her insolently. 'Oh, you wouldn't have, *cara*, you were so wrapped up in your... what shall we call it, passionate embrace? I was in one of the gondolas that passed yours and I saw you. I must say, that for someone who doesn't feel ready to get involved romantically and regards men as friends only, you have an extraordinary way of showing your appreciation of friendship, no?'

The gall of the man; he probably thought she was easy prey and was likely to double his propositions now, and would possibly be even more brash about it.

'First of all, Paolo Barone is not my lover. Secondly, I don't see that my private affairs have anything to do with you,' she flared. She was about to get up, but Count Umberto stopped her with a peremptory gesture of his hand.

'Please don't go. Hear me out, you might be surprised by what I have to tell you, and you must trust that I have your best interests at heart, yes?'

Venetia's lips parted and then she quickly closed them again. She was eager to learn all there was to know about Paolo, even from someone like the Count. After all, they were supposedly good friends. Maybe through Umberto she would find out a little more about him.

'Very well,' she murmured.

A humourless smile pulled at the corners of his mouth. 'Shall we talk about this calmly over a cup of coffee?' Without waiting for her answer Umberto pressed a button on his intercom. *'Angelina, la prego di portare un vassoio di caffè e biscotti.'* He turned back to her, took out a gold case and withdrew a cigarette. He reached forward and passed the case to Venetia. 'I know you don't smoke, but with what I am going to tell you, you may need one.' His tone was sardonic. When she refused, he returned it to his pocket, leaned back into his chair and puffed quietly on his cigarette for a few seconds, looking across at her through the smoke. Venetia sat there, to all outward appearance cool, proud and distant.

'What do you know about Paolo?' Umberto asked at last, slowly exhaling a cloud of smoke.

Venetia caught her breath; there was no reason for it, but she felt something ominous was in the air. 'Not a lot.'

There was a silence and then the Count smiled again, but she knew that something other than humour lay behind that smile. 'So has it always been with him and the various women he has been involved with over the years. He has not told you about his condition?'

Venetia's nerves contracted. 'What condition?' She clasped her hands in her lap so he should not see they were trembling; she was sure he was going to announce that Paolo was married.

He gave a soft, cynical laugh. 'Ugh, why am I not surprised? The man is utterly dishonest when it comes to relationships.'

Angelina brought in a tray of coffee and cakes. Umberto waited until his secretary had served them and left the room, closing the door behind her, before resuming the conversation.

'I really don't know how to put this to you, so as to dull the shock. After all, you must be emotionally involved with Paolo ... if not, how does one explain your behaviour yesterday night, no?' he asked, his voice light as he stubbed out the cigarette and took a languid sip of coffee, his hard gaze intently fixed on Venetia's face.

She was sourly aware that Umberto was perversely dragging on the suspense, trying to rattle her. Her mouth twisted in a grimace of irony. 'Don't worry about my sensitivities, Umberto. Just tell me what you have to say.'

'Well, *cara*, to put it bluntly then, Paolo is amnesic. He lost his memory in a car accident ten years ago, while on honeymoon. He and his wife were returning from a nightclub; his wife was driving, and she died on the spot. He was badly hurt and was in a coma for several months. When he woke up, he had forgotten his past – a total loss of memory.' Count Umberto paused, as if to ascertain whether or not his words had provoked some reaction on Venetia's part but she merely continued to look at him, her face empty of expression, waiting, and so he pressed on. 'He's originally from Verbania, but he moved to Tuscany to reinvent his life and lives there with his regular mistress, Allegra, who is his caretaker's niece. A most alluring young creature, I must say.'

Venetia listened to Umberto in appalled disbelief. His words were like a douche of cold water that left her chilled to the core. She wet her dry lips. 'How devastating for Paolo,' she whispered, forcing herself to sound as calm as she was trying to appear.

'He comes to Venice to have fun.' There was a silent and menacing hostility as Umberto spoke, his tone cold and accusatory, the rancour in his eyes formidable. 'It would have been interesting to have met him before the amnesia, but now... He's known here as *l'Amante delle Quattro Stagioni*, "the lover of four seasons", because he changes his girlfriends every three months, with the change of season.'

Feeling almost sick, Venetia cleared her throat. 'Is that all?' she enquired coolly, once he had finished. She lifted herself slowly out of the chair, her fingers curved rigidly. 'May I go now?'

In two strides Umberto was next to her. 'You're cross with me, *cara*, I can see that.'

'I'm not cross with you, Count Umberto. I'm just amazed that you could pour out so much bile about your best friend. Presumably, *Signor* Barone had entrusted you with his secret. All I can say is, with friends like you, the poor man doesn't need enemies.'

Il Conte's hand came down on Venetia's arm lightly, but firmly. 'You have misunderstood my motive here, *cara*. I could not bear to see you being taken advantage of.'

'There are other means you could have used to protect me if that's your only intention,' she retorted.

'I have told you again and again about my feelings towards you – besides, is it not an English proverb that says all is fair in love and war?'

She ground her teeth. 'And I have repeatedly told you that I do not love you.'

Umberto paled and drew in his breath. 'But that's not true,' he said obstinately. 'I know the ways of you English girls, you're just playing games.'

'Certainly not! That isn't my style, so please once and for all…'

A muscle twitched along Umberto's sternly clenched jaw. Catching her suddenly and pulling her against him, he held her close. Before she had time to react, he was forcing her head back angrily, crushing her mouth with savage, bruising kisses; careless of hurting her. Venetia struggled wildly, but Umberto was much stronger, towering over her, his eyes blazing.

He gave a soft, cynical laugh. 'You fight like a she-cat, my beautiful Venetia – we could have such fun together! I like my women with a bit of fire in them. It makes the conquest so much more satisfying, don't you think?' He pinned her arms even more tightly. 'You're merely whetting my appetite with your airs of a grand lady and your apparent disdain of my caresses.'

She saw the glint of possessiveness in his eyes as his fingers ran greedily across the smooth skin of her throat and paused where her pulse was beating in time with the rapid thrumming of her terrified heart. 'How madly runs your pulse, *cara*… Is my touch arousing you so, belying your cruel words, mmm?' His breathing was ragged as he devoured her with his piercing gaze. 'You are ripe like a delicious fruit, yes, trembling at the edge of its branch, ready to be picked.' He pressed her against his aroused body, subjecting her with a primitive demand to the hardness of his desire.

Venetia's face was scarlet. 'Let me go, you bastard!' she uttered through clenched teeth. With a violent effort, she pushed him off and lifted her hand to wipe away the imprint of his mouth on her lips. But Umberto caught it before she could accomplish the task.

'I wouldn't do that,' he warned, a nasty glint in his eyes as they moved hungrily over her face. 'No woman has ever wiped away my signature from her mouth, *cara*. I would only feel obliged to brand you again.'

Indignation flashed in Venetia's eyes. 'You're despicable!' she hissed, and lifted her hand again, but this time to strike at him.

Swift as the wind, Umberto's agile fingers clamped down around her wrist, tightening his grip until she thought her bones would snap. Venetia's heart leapt in fear at the gathering mask of black fury that blanketed his features. Umberto's mouth curved into a cruel smile.

'You're inflaming my senses to your own detriment, *cara*, with your unreasonable belligerence. The more you fight me, the more I want you – you are enormously appealing in this state of anger.' A distinct sneer of contempt passed over his face. 'I could have you here and now if the pleasure took me. See what you do to me…'

Venetia cried out as, taking her by surprise, Umberto unzipped himself, the animal looking out through his eyes as he tried to pull her numb fingers down inside his trousers to fondle him. She wriggled and twisted, attempting to wrench herself from him, fighting like a wild animal in the hope of disentangling her arm from his steel-like grip. Horrified, she watched as he drew her hand closer and closer. Umberto had almost covered the fully aroused bulge in his trousers with her palm, when she was aware that his pupils had glazed over. She lunged away from him unexpectedly, jerking herself back and stumbling shakily, her eyes shimmering with unshed tears of shame and disgust.

Hurriedly, she picked up her bag, and fled from the room. Aware of Umberto's voice swearing savagely behind her, she prayed that he would not follow her and her legs would not give way, at least until she got out of the building.

Venetia didn't wait for the lift, which was too slow in coming, and ran down the stairs, hardly knowing what she was doing. She stepped out of Umberto Palermi's offices with a nervous shudder of relief. Once in the road, the dazzling light and the blue sky of Venice greeted her. The cool air, full of delightful spring scents, revitalised her, easing the hammering of her heart and her shaking limbs.

Damn all men! she cursed, as she joined the bustle of strolling people out in the sunshine. She was feeling physically ill, not only because of Umberto's despicable behaviour – oddly enough, that was the least of it – but mainly because her brain was endeavouring to cope with the shattering revelations just thrown at her out of the blue. The shock of learning that Paolo was not only amnesic, but also that he had been married, widowed, and now had a regular mistress, heaped up in a mass of chaos in her mind.

Venetia was bewildered by his deceit, but also hurt. How could he have been so underhanded? She had always thought Paolo was an enigma, but she had been miles away from suspecting he was hiding so many devastating secrets. *L'Amante delle Quattro Stagioni*, the lover of four seasons... her mouth trembled piteously as tears of anger quivered on the edge of her lashes. It was humiliating to think she had been just another one of his conquests.

Though, even in her unhappiness, Venetia could not bring herself to hate Paolo. Her mind turned over the tragedy he had experienced – how frightening it must be to live without a past, how sad to have death ravish the one you love at the very dawn of a new life together, and so heart-wrenching to be deprived of the beautiful memories of that love. Venetia could just imagine the horror of it all.

He desired me though. The potency of his arousal had certainly not been deceit, she reasoned; men, unlike women, couldn't fake that sort of thing – nevertheless, it had been only desire, not love. Anyway, what did it matter now? Before these revelations, despite her overwhelming attraction towards Paolo, she had already decided that he was not for her... hadn't she?

Venetia stopped in front of Ping Lü's shop. Her legs had unwittingly led her to the old Chineseman's emporium; but it seemed that this day was fated to provide her with one disturbance after another: the blinds were drawn and there was a sign in the window saying: 'Closed until further notice'.

That's just my luck, she thought. She would have liked to unburden herself to the wise, friendly little man. There seemed to be even more paradoxes surrounding Paolo now; maybe Ping Lü would have had some logical answers to her questions and given her his sage advice. With a sigh she turned away and started back to the office. At Bianchi e Lombardi's reception she was told that her godmother had asked to see her as soon as she got back from her appointment with Count Umberto.

Giovanna was sitting behind her desk, scrutinising the company's book of accounts, when Venetia was showed into her office by Sabina, her assistant. Looking up as her goddaughter came in, her face lit up with a tender smile.

'Ah, there you are, Venetia. What did that so-and-so of a Count want from you, *carina*? I bet he's still hectoring you about marriage.' She spoke with the warmth and spontaneity that she reserved for her loved ones, but which was always held well in check behind an appraising coolness with strangers.

Venetia smiled lamely and sighed. 'Yes, you could say that… Unfortunately he won't leave me in peace.'

'Well, he'll have great difficulty in finding you when you go to Tuscany.'

Oh no! Venetia's stomach made a strange somersault as the reason became clear why she had been called to her god-mother's office with such urgency.

The alarm must have shown on her face because Giovanna burst out laughing. 'Venetia, *cara*, don't look so horrified. I had an email this morning from *Signor* Barone, saying you had turned down the restoration assignment for his chapel, alleging that you had too much work.'

'*Zia* Giovanna, I don't see how I can leave the workshop to Francesca. We have a couple of difficult restoration jobs which she would not be able to handle on her own, let alone finish by the handover dates agreed with the clients.'

'Be realistic, my dear girl. The project *Signor* Barone is offer-ing us is huge in comparison to those two small restoration jobs you've mentioned. He's not only talking about the mosaics in the chapel, but also the reconstruction and refurbishment of the entire villa, *and* the building of a resort.'

Venetia's shoulders went back and her spine stiffened. 'Well, exactly. What he's asking for is a huge job,' she exclaimed. 'I can't just relocate to Tuscany for a few months. Anyhow, he was talking about me living at his home, which quite frankly is unacceptable.'

'No, no, no. You misunderstood him. We had a long conver-sation over the phone this morning and he explained to me that he has a separate cottage in the grounds of his property that he uses to accommodate guests, and he is proposing to have you stay there. Alternatively, he would be happy to rent a cottage in the village for you, if you would prefer. The man is bending over backwards to accommodate us.'

'Really, *Zia*, I think it's most impractical and —'

'Listen to me, Venetia,' Giovanna interrupted her, raising her hand firmly, 'I don't often put my foot down, but this time I must insist. This is a sizeable commission that we simply cannot afford to turn down. I have accepted the appointment and I will not hear otherwise. I will pay for you to come back to Venice every weekend if you wish – though to be blunt,' she added, eyeing her goddaughter, 'as you don't have anyone special in your life to come back to, you might as well explore fresher pastures – so please set aside whatever misgivings you have and be ready to leave on Monday.'

If Venetia had been the sort of woman to stamp her foot, she would have stamped it right then, but instead, she planted her feet firmly on the ground and folded her arms across her chest.

Giovanna Lombardi was quick to interpret the aggressive downturn of her godchild's mouth and the two glaring flames Venetia's amber eyes had become. She raised an eyebrow. 'Don't look at me like that, Venetia. It may intimidate others, but not me,' she said curtly. 'If I didn't think that the firm needed this assignment, I wouldn't have forced it upon you.'

'Can't we just get the architecture part of the job?'

'No, *Signor* Barone insisted that it would be either all or nothing.'

'And that didn't strike you as strange.'

'Maybe, but you are no longer a child, and to be honest it's high time you grew up and got over this fear of men, which has been stifling you for so long. It will be good for you in every way. *Signor* Barone has a certain reputation, it's true, but I'm hardly asking you to marry him. A little fun wouldn't do you any harm, if he is interested in you. Anyhow, as your dear mother used to say, no man can get from a woman what she doesn't want to give. You are neither the first nor the last girl to have had an unhappy romantic experience.'

'But...'

'The matter is closed, Venetia,' her godmother told her firmly and turned her attention back to the book of accounts.

Venetia viewed Giovanna mutinously, but refrained from any untoward remark and turned on her heel to leave the room. She knew that once Giovanna had made up her mind about something, there was no leverage for discussion, especially when the decision taken had to do with the business.

'*Signor* Barone is taking care of the travel arrangements,' Giovanna said, without looking up from her papers. 'You'll be flying to Pisa, which is the closest airport to Porto Santo Stefano, where he has his villa. He promised to email the details before lunch. Ask Karina, she's probably received them already.'

Venetia scowled and made an impatient sound. 'That man's a control freak! How did he think I would get around once I'm in Tuscany? I'm not flying, I'll drive – it can't be more than three or four hours. It's obvious that I'll need a car down there.'

Her godmother glanced up. '*Signor* Barone is only trying to be courteous, Venetia, and save you the trouble of a long and tiring journey – more like five or six hours if you're a sensible driver. He said that he would of course provide a car at your disposal, but if you prefer to drive down, suit yourself,' Giovanna retorted, returning to the scrutiny of her books, 'but please let him know your plans and ask Karina to get in touch with his office to find out all the necessary details.'

Venetia left her godmother's office and made her way up to the workshop. *Six hours is a long drive*, she thought. Should she be gracious and accept his invitation to fly? Or maybe she should take the train and rent a car when she got to the other end? No, she would drive down and show this man that she could not be bossed around, and was quite capable of managing a journey of six hours on her own.

Francesca was waiting for Venetia in her office. 'It's almost time for lunch, where have you been all morning?'

'Don't ask. It's been one of those days already.'

'You look really frazzled. Let's go and have a spot of lunch and you can tell me about it.'

So over a tomato and mozzarella salad, Venetia told her friend all that had happened that morning, including her unpleasant encounter with the Count. Francesca dropped her fork, her eyes wide.

'You're not going to let that bastard Umberto get away with his outrageous behaviour, are you? You must report him!'

'The man is poison and it would be his word against mine, Francesca. I'm sure he's got half the police force of Venice eating out of his hand. And, anyhow, I'm going away, which after all may not be such a bad thing,' she admitted, a small part of her secretly relieved that the decision had been forced on her. Perhaps this was Fate pushing her in the direction she needed to go.

'I find the thought of that animal getting away with it really galling. He'll just try this sort of thing again with someone else.'

'He'll try it anyway.'

Francesca sighed. 'I suppose you're right.'

The two young women sipped their coffee in silence.

'Shouldn't you tell *Signora* Lombardi the truth about why you're reluctant to take on this job?'

'No, please, let's leave my godmother out of all this. You know that I'm a very private person and don't like talking about my affairs, even to her. She's like a mother to me and would only try and meddle. You're my friend. It's different.'

'What are you going to do about Paolo? Are you going to confront him with what you've found out about him?'

'No, I'll confine our relationship to business, and there'll be nothing intimate or personal between us. It's the only way I might be able to handle the situation.'

'I mean, face it, Venetia, less than twenty-four hours ago you were in the man's arms – you even admit to having had a magical evening. Don't you think that you'll find it difficult to work with him after what's happened between you? Attraction doesn't evaporate just like that,' Francesca snapped her fingers.

'Yes, yes, I know, I'm all confused. To be honest, I'm really appalled at the effect Paolo has on me. I thought I'd become stronger than this. When Judd left me, and even more when I lost the baby, I thought my heart would snap in two, and that nothing in the world was going to be right again.' Venetia paused and gazed off into the distance before looking back at her friend. 'As you know, for the past ten years I haven't really looked at another man. I just dated them to pass the time.' Her mouth quirked up in a wry smile: 'I don't know what it is about Paolo… what it is that makes me melt inside whenever he looks at me.'

Francesca nudged her hand and gave her a sideways glance. 'He's an expert lover, that's what it is – *l'Amante delle Quattro Stagioni,* as his friend told you.'

Venetia's pain ran deep, but pride made her dredge up enough poise to shrug. 'Yes, you're probably right. They're all the same, these men. As I told you, I had turned down Paolo's assignment anyway, even before hearing about the complicated details of his life.' She sighed. 'But Giovanna is adamant, the firm needs the work. Look, don't worry about me, Francesca. I'm quite capable of dealing with this crisis. God only knows

I've been through worse and come out the other side. I'm just furious that I haven't been given the choice.'

At Umberto's revelations, Venetia had felt as if a chill wind was blowing over her and a dark cloud had blotted out the sunlight pouring into the Count's office. However, she had the profound feeling that a piece of the puzzle surrounding Paolo was still missing. Something did not ring true about all this. It hardly seemed possible that the man who had almost declared his love for her the night before might have been feigning, and merely playing a cruel game of seduction. Yet, hadn't Judd sworn his undying love to her too, then at the first real obstacle deserted her without even a word? No, she had to face reality. Men couldn't be trusted, full stop.

Although Venetia would have preferred not to be faced with Paolo again for some time, she was aware that deep down she couldn't help but feel a strange excitement at the idea of working close to him for the next few months, and her heart beat faster in anticipation. She would try very hard to be her usual self in his company and not give the slightest inkling of what she knew about him; she only hoped to succeed in fooling everyone... but was she such a good actress? And could she conceal her feelings from him, which she reluctantly accepted now had nothing to do with either friendship or business, knowing she must stifle them, if only for her own sake? Of course she could, she told herself: she was an adult, mentally and emotionally. The young woman resolved instantly that, whatever it cost her in self-restraint, she would not make a fool of herself.

Back at the office, Venetia went straight to Karina, who was in charge of all travel arrangements at Bianchi e Lombardi, and dictated an email for Paolo, telling him of her decision to drive down to Porto Santo Stefano. After his arrogant manipulation to get her appointed to the job, she wasn't about to give him even more access to her by including her mobile phone number, that would be playing far too easily into his hands; so with a small degree of satisfaction, she told Karina that *Signor* Barone could contact the office if he had any questions. Venetia also asked the secretary to buy a couple of maps that would help her on the journey, especially given that Fabrizio told her that although the route from Venice to the west coast was pretty straightforward, as it was mostly motorway, the last hundred kilometres or so across country were more complicated to negotiate. He had also suggested driving Venetia there, with a hopeful expression on his face, but she turned down his offer as kindly as she could, saying that she would take it slowly and would enjoy the drive.

During the coming days, Venetia worked furiously in an effort to damp down the excitement that kept surfacing. Yet, she was conscious all the time that she was merely trying to escape thinking too closely about Paolo and what the future might bring. He had rung the office a few times to speak to her, but she had always either been in a meeting or out, and deliberately did not return his calls. Finally he had resorted to sending her an email, simply saying he was delighted that she had decided to take on the assignment and he would be at Miraggio to welcome her when she arrived.

As much as she tried, and no matter how busy she was, Venetia couldn't keep Paolo out of her mind. The more she fought against it, the more thoughts of him haunted her, especially at night in the most erotic dreams she never knew her imagination could conjure.

After a while, she had to admit that one part of her mind – the wounded, self-protecting, cynical part – remained aloof from all other considerations, and occupied itself in turning the new situation round and round, examining it from every angle.

There seemed to be an unreality about everything in her world now, as if her romantic 'real self' was sitting away somewhere up high, at an altitude, looking down upon the poised and controlled Venetia, restorer of mosaics, as she went about her normal routine: walking along the crowded streets of Venice, entering the equally crowded restaurants, choosing and eating lunch with Francesca as usual, and afterwards walking back to the office. Then, having waded doggedly through the great bulk of the day's work, Venetia would return to her flat to join that other remote self in silent battle, concentrating entirely upon the dreams that might come true, balancing all the delights they would offer against the embarrassments, and even the temporary unhappiness they might bring as their penalty.

Nonetheless, at the end of each deliberation, she remained appalled at how she could have surrendered her stronghold, knowing how much pain it promised. *You don't fall in love with someone you hardly know, almost a stranger, whose heart is already given elsewhere,* she repeated to herself, endlessly. How could Paolo have become so firmly entrenched in her heart that, despite what she now knew about him, not only could she hardly bear the prospect of not seeing him again, she couldn't wait to be with him once more?

*   *   *

On Monday, Venetia went to pick up her car at the garage, where she had taken it to be checked over before her journey. It wasn't ready and she was forced to wait around for almost an hour, so it wasn't until noon before she set off.

The trip down to Tuscany was not exactly a pleasure. The weather changed with dramatic abruptness; the false early spring disappeared and was replaced by rain. The first four hours on the motorway were grim, but Venetia was used to driving long distances on motorways. She had always preferred to travel by car than plane or train, and she cruised along steadily, listening to the radio, unfazed by the fog and drizzle. She hadn't had much breakfast that morning so she stopped for a snack and a cup of coffee at one of the ubiquitous Autogrill SpA restaurants on the Italian *autostrade*.

It was almost five o'clock when she got off the highway and began zigzagging her way down to Porto Santo Stefano, the small seaport town on the north-western promontory of Monte Argentario. Grey wisps of storm clouds, heavy and soft, trailed about the hills, and, as she drove along the wet, tortuous country lanes of Tuscany under the dripping, bowered trees, nothing could be seen of the countryside.

The weather forecast on the radio had threatened a storm, and now a gusty wind began to blow. The first ear-splitting crack was followed by a barrage of rumbling thunder and flashes of lightning from the west, the rain adding its fury to the storm concerto as it hit the aluminium bonnet of her Porsche sports car. There were no other vehicles on the road as she sped through the downpour; the whole region seemed empty in the darkening day.

Venetia felt strangely alone, her only company the monotonous swish of the windscreen wipers and the merry chatter of the radio. Maybe she should have accepted Paolo's offer and taken the plane instead of stubbornly insisting on driving down. She was tired and was not enjoying this part of her journey one bit. She had been to Florence, Pisa, and the more touristy cities of Tuscany, but had never explored the Tyrrhenian coast and its surroundings. She had thought that travelling this way would be fun and that she would see a little of the Tuscan countryside, but she hadn't reckoned on the storm.

Venetia sighed and changed the station to pop music. The radio show was streaming out back-to-back hits for the new millennium. The recognisable tumbling strings of Robbie Williams' 'Millennium' played out and for a while she lost herself in the lush harmonies and insistent rhythm. The next song came on, the Italian hit '*la Fine del Millennio*' by Vasco Rossi, jolting her out of her reverie, its fast, hard rhythms such a coarse contrast. She wondered why the Italians had chosen a rasping, unmelodic song to represent the millennium when they were such a deeply romantic nation. Frowning, she quickly retuned again, landing on a nostalgia radio station. Demis Roussos was singing his achingly romantic seventies hit, 'Forever and Ever', and of how his destiny followed his love eternally. At that moment, inexplicably, the words caught at her heart. Overwhelmed by that deepening of emotion which solitude bestows, Venetia's throat constricted and for a brief moment her eyes welled up with tears of self-pity. They trembled at the edge of her lids, but she was quick to restrain them, chastising herself for being so weak and spineless.

A couple of hours later, she had passed Grosseto. The land around was undulating; it now ran up from sea level and down over the main range of hills. Up and down she went for miles, between the hills that branched from the main ridge, down towards the Tyrrhenian Sea. *In better weather the view must be breathtaking*, she thought as she came to a junction and followed the signs for Orbetello, an important Natural Reserve along the coast only five miles away from Porto Santo Stefano, where the coast of Tuscany connected to the promontory by three fingers of land. As she drove across to Monte Argentario, with the distant shadow of the sea on both sides and the wind whipping up keenly, in Venetia's mind it was as if she was crossing into a kind of mysterious isolation from the life she had left behind. This was Paolo's domain now.

She was nearly there, and for a charged moment Venetia forgot her weariness and her heart beat a little faster in anticipation of seeing Paolo. She could feel swelling up inside her again that languorous weakness edged with excitement that flowed through her every time she thought of him, but she grimly clung to her self-respect, fighting off this unwelcome rush of desire that reminded her she was not yet indifferent to him. She smiled to herself as an Italian proverb Francesca often used crossed her mind: '*quando ci si priva di cioccolato, se ne ricorda sempre il sapore dolce,* when you deprive yourself of chocolate, you always remember the sweet taste'. Would she perhaps lose her craving for Paolo if she mixed with him day in, day out, not only as a friend, but also as a lover, she wondered. Was giving in to him the cure for this strange, feverish addiction?

The directions that Paolo had sent the office to reach Miraggio from Cala Piccola, a tiny village outside Porto Santo Stefano, were clear and detailed. Venetia had no difficulty finding the unlit narrow lane that led uphill to the property. The storm seemed to have stopped as abruptly as it had come on, and although the view was still nebulous in the fading twilight, the wild wind had scattered the clouds, and the sky was faintly luminous. As the Porsche wound its way upwards, she was aware that she was climbing a mighty cliff overlooking an endless expanse of sea on one side and a wide scene of undulating countryside on the other. In front of her, despite the approaching night, she could just make out a magnificent, walled building in the distance.

Finally, at the top of the cliffs she came to the towering grey-stone walls that gradually loomed out of the darkening sky. They were interrupted by tall wrought-iron gates, standing open on a plateau that half jutted out over the ocean, and which looked as if it been carved out of the hillside a long time ago.

This is it, Venetia thought, her pulse quickening. She hesitated and slowed the car for a second, before sweeping through the entrance and round the slow curve of a lime-bordered avenue leading to a gravelled courtyard. There, a large and beautifully proportioned turreted dwelling stood outlined in the obscurity: Paolo's home in the clouds.

Venetia drew the Porsche to a halt outside the imposing front door. The house was in darkness, the place looked deserted. Perplexed, the young woman sat in her car on the verge of laughter or tears; she didn't know which would win. Had she got the date wrong? Was this not Miraggio? She was sure she had followed the directions accurately and anyhow, there had been no other buildings in sight at the top of the cliffs on the narrow plateau. What was Paolo playing at? Was this his idea of a joke to punish her for driving down instead of flying as he had suggested? Or even for not being readily available to speak to him when he called? Such a tumult of feeling was rushing through her that for a moment her vision blurred, before she became aware that someone with a flashlight, and an Alsatian in tow, was coming towards the car from the far end of the courtyard.

The man approaching had a heavy limp and his right shoulder was slightly twisted. He was well over six feet in height and broad with it. A giant of a man, he had a great head of shaggy, grizzled hair which covered a very dark, bronzed face with coarse features. Venetia thought he looked much more menacing than the German Shepherd following him. He reminded her of the Roald Dahl children's character, The Big Friendly Giant, but there was nothing that seemed either friendly or gentle about this man.

'*Buonasera, signorina, posso aiutarla,* can I help you?' he asked, flashing the torch on to Venetia's face in a somewhat antisocial fashion, while the dog stood rigidly next to him, staring upwards towards the young woman and emitting a steady long growl.

Dazzled by the torchlight, Venetia lifted a hand to her eyes. '*Buonasera… è questa la casa del Signor Barone?*, is this the house of *Signor* Barone?'

'*Sì, sì, siete a casa del Signor Barone*, but the *signore* is absent.'

An unpleasant feeling gripped Venetia. Had she been brought all this way to be sent back again, the victim of some humiliating misunderstanding?

'I am *Signorina* Aston-Montagu. I was engaged for the restoration of mosaics in *Signor* Barone's villa,' Venetia explained, trying to keep the dismay out of her voice.

'*Sì, sì, lo so*, but we didn't know you were coming today,' the giant replied, gruffly. 'Bad weather, so Santo Stefano airport is closed. *Signor* Barone's flight is cancelled. We thought you would be arriving with the *signore*, after the airport opens again.'

Venetia's spirits quailed as wretched thoughts went racing through her mind. Was she going to have to look for a hotel so late in the evening? Timetables were chaotic in this part of world, flights cancelled, and airports closed at the drop of a hat, it seemed. What if the flights were not reinstated for another few days?

The giant must have noticed the worried look on Venetia's face. '*Non c'è problema, signorina*, the *signore* asked for the cottage to be made ready a couple of days ago. I'll take you to it,' he added, much to her relief before she had time to ask about hotels. '*Io sono Antonio, il custode*,' he bowed respectfully and smiled, showing off great toothless jaws.

Venetia's heart gave a lurch as Umberto's words came back to her in a flash. '*He's originally from Verbania, but he moved to Tuscany to reinvent his life and lives there with his regular mistress, Allegra, who is his caretaker's niece.'* So this was the uncle of the woman in Paolo's life? She felt a familiar surge of anger. Her instinct was to turn back and leave Miraggio immediately but it was not in her nature to give up, and so she tried to keep her voice deceptively low when she spoke.

'Thank you, Antonio. Where should I leave my car?'

'If you give me the keys, I'll park it in the garage next to the stables. It's a walk, you know. Maybe you city folk aren't used to walking. Got your cars to take you round everywhere instead of your feet.' He eyed her speculatively. 'The storm has messed up the grounds – we've lost an oak tree.' He grunted and lifted his brows. '*Il signore* will be upset, he's very fond of his trees.'

Venetia looked out of the window and down towards the dog, who was still grumbling menacingly. She frowned. Alsatians could be quite aggressive and this dog did not seem happy at all. Venetia was distinctly wary of him.

The caretaker read her mind. 'Don't worry, *signorina*, Rufus won't harm you. *É un cane bravo*, he is a good dog. He's only doing his job, protecting his owner.'

'Is he your dog?'

'*Sì, signorina.*'

'Will you ask him then to stop growling and be a little friendlier?'

Antonio gave a hoarse, croaky laugh. 'He's not growling, *signorina*, that's just groaning. There's a difference.'

Venetia sighed; she was not familiar with dog language. 'If you say so!'

Reluctantly, she opened the door and set one hesitant foot on the ground. Rufus seemed more relaxed and was not making eye contact with her any more. She stood up and, after pausing a moment, gave Antonio the keys – she didn't much like her car being driven by other people. Her father used to say that

women and cars should only be used by one person: the owner.
A rather coarse comparison, she had always thought, but
William Aston-Montagu found it a great joke, and Venetia
agreed that at least about cars, he had a point.

Venetia rounded the vehicle, making sure she did not pass
near Rufus, and opened the boot to take out her luggage.

'I'll bring your bags for you, *signorina*.' Antonio reached into
the boot and negotiated the young woman's two suitcases with
surprising ease as he moved ahead, followed by his wolf. Despite
his disability, he was athletically built and Venetia could see
now that his shoulder only looked twisted because of the way he
walked. This was a strong man, and coupled with his dog, they
made mighty guardians. It would be very courageous robbers
indeed who took on that formidable pair; Paolo's assets here
were well protected.

There was no moon, but the windswept sky was so clear now
that the stars glittered with icy clarity, and the black leaves of the
trees sparkled with rime and diamond drops. Venetia followed
the caretaker along a short narrow path with coarse grass on
either side, which had a delightful, aromatic scent and led to a
picturesque stone dwelling, facing the lawns of the main house.
Half her mind was concentrating on her surroundings and the
other half was thinking of Paolo, wondering when she would
see him again and why he had not informed Antonio that she
was arriving today.

The cottage where Venetia would be spending the next few
weeks was made of stone and stood snugly behind the big house,
alongside the cliff, nestled in its own sunken garden. Two very
tall, elegant Italian stone pine trees stood guard on each side
and bougainvillea cascaded in profusion over the low rocky
walls that surrounded it. In the semi darkness, the garden
looked old and somewhat untidy, set in the side of a terraced

slope that rose steeply away from both the main house and its small, stony companion. A little mossy flight of steps ran through the garden up to the cottage, which was covered by a great many flowering bushes, a tangle of pergola vines and climbing roses.

'La Sirena,' Antonio rasped, shuffling to a stop and waving his torch in the direction of the little house. There was an enormous magnolia in bloom on the lawn next to the cottage, and a pond with rushes and other plants that she couldn't recognise in the dusk. Like a large part of the main house, the cottage, enclosed on three sides by its low walls and thickly clustering bougainvillea, had a magnificent view over the sea on the fourth side, and the sight of it had Venetia transfixed.

Antonio looked back. 'This way, *signorina*,' he called out as he unlocked the door to La Sirena, interrupting her reverie. He led the way in and ordered Rufus to wait for him outside.

It was a single-storey dwelling. The caretaker switched on the lights at the entrance that gave into a lobby. The inner door was open and through it Venetia could see a spacious sitting room. A floor-to-ceiling picture window with a sliding door swept the length of the room, looking over the cliffs, past a belt of trees, down to the Tyrrhenian Sea. Even on this moonless night, Venetia could appreciate the dramatic view of rocks and the turbulent sea below. Immediately outside the room was a long flowery terrace with two recliners and four painted resin chairs, arranged around a stone table set with a furled umbrella.

Venetia drew in a sharp breath. 'It's utterly charming,' she whispered.

Looking around her, she spotted a great wooden bowl filled with fruit, creating a lovely splash of colour on the coffee table, and a vase of tastefully arranged bright-yellow roses and blue irises in an alcove.

Antonio followed her gaze. 'Ernestina, the housekeeper, came in this morning and made sure the cottage was ready for you.' He scratched his head. 'We didn't expect you tonight so there's no meal. But there's a loaf of bread, tea and coffee in the kitchen, and some cheese, milk *e una bottiglia di vino nel frigorifero*.'

Venetia could not help but be warmed by the attention to detail paid to ensure her comfort and she wondered if Ernestina had acted on her own initiative or Paolo's instructions.

The caretaker put down Venetia's cases on a rack in the vast bedroom. The double bed in the corner was so high that it reached the windowsill, and there was a sofa and two armchairs, a small dressing table, a bijou desk, and built-in cupboards. Leading off the bedroom was a separate cloakroom and a magnificent marble bathroom in iridescent rose-petal pink, which was divided in two with a sunken bathtub and basin on one side and an open shower area on the other.

'There's plenty of hot water and you'll find clean towels in the bathroom cupboard.'

'Thank you, Antonio, this is perfect.'

He gave her a curt nod. 'Staying long, are you?'

'As long as I'm needed by *Signor* Barone to finish the work.'

'Heh, long enough then.' He looked at her suspiciously, making her feel that she wouldn't be becoming firm friends with the giant any time soon.

She smiled as sweetly as possible. 'Yes, I suppose. Is that a problem?'

'*Nessun problema, signorina*. Antonio likes to know what goes on around here, that's all. Well, *buonanotte, signorina*. Have a good night.' With that, Antonio lurched out of the door, whistling for Rufus to follow him.

After the caretaker had left, Venetia made another quick exploration of the cottage. The main sitting area and the bedroom were tastefully decorated in tones of beige and yellow, with shaded lamps here and there. Lightweight curtains gave privacy without blotting out the light and Venetia could imagine them billowing and swaying in the breeze. The walls were hung with watercolours depicting the surrounding countryside, and over the mantelpiece in the living room there was an oil painting of a turreted house in a landscape of pale blue and powdery green, where cypresses pointed stiffly upward in the silvery air. Venetia presumed it was an illustration of Miraggio, but on looking more closely she saw printed on the frame underneath the picture, *La Torretta, 1969.*

Venetia threw one of the two windows of her bedroom wide open and leaned out. How wonderful! The sky had cleared; a damp, sweet air blew in, laden with moist scents. Over the shoulder of a nearby dark hill, the stars sparkled, large and bright; in the faint light, a small *ruscello* could dimly be discerned splashing down through the grass, and, in front, slanting across that little stream and swaying in the breeze, leaned the branch of an apple tree. She loved the purity of that air, fraught with wildness and wet. *No wonder poets were invented,* she said to herself, leaning out into that freshness, unwilling to come back into the room; but she was exhausted and finally closed the windows.

Venetia had to admit that she was disappointed not to have seen Paolo, and it made her a little sad. Her confusion about what to do, what to feel, had not abated. Still, she would have a long hot bath in the sunken tub, make herself some bread and cheese and a hot glass of milk, and go to bed. Hopefully, tomorrow would be a better day. At least she could explore this dramatic place and see if it shed any light on its enigmatic owner.

CHAPTER 6

It had been late when Venetia had finally retired to bed, but nonetheless she had not been able to sleep. Although the storm had subsided and the night was still, her brain refused to cease its chaotic tumble. Everything that had happened since she had met Paolo came back to torment her. At last she drifted off and, like most nights, was visited by a succession of erotic dreams that left her breathless and her heart pounding when she awoke in the dark.

The next morning dawned tranquil and warm after the tempest of the day before. In the bright April sunshine the earth lay damp and steamy, the sea calm. The hillside, which at night had been shrouded in darkness, was now bathed in a mellow saffron light. Among the olives and vines, standing erect, were pointed cypresses and massive ilex trees, which formed great blocks of dark foliage.

Venetia woke up to a cacophony of birdsong in the trees outside her bedroom window. Instead of pigeons perched on ancient city roofs, here there were thrushes singing in the garden, building their new nests high up in the tall Italian stone pines she had noticed the night before.

Her first thought was for Paolo, wondering whether he had arrived during the night and, if he hadn't, if she would see him today. Venetia listened for a moment to the distant, happy twittering, then stretched her limbs lazily. She lifted herself up and leaned against the pillows, her eyes still full of sleep but drawn to the scenery outside the open window. How serene, how fresh it all looked. Beyond the garden, across a narrow valley, were the terraced vines, the silvery-grey olive trees, and the hills with their flower-sprinkled slopes, so jewelled with colour they might have been the background for any legendary story.

Throwing back the covers and sliding out of bed, she padded barefoot to the other window, which had remained closed all night, and pushed the shutters open. Shafts of incandescent sunbeams spilled into the room. Dazzled by this sudden brilliance, she lifted her face to the warm rays, relishing the feel of them on her skin, and hugged herself. Below, the land fell away in a scattering of white rock and scrub to a semi-circular bay, almost landlocked by wooded promontories. Everything was clear in the crystal air, sparkling in the sunshine and filled with the fresh, tangy smell of salt, seaweed and iodine.

The Tyrrhenian coast glowed under the wide arc of a burning, cloudless blue sky, the sea a shimmering golden mirror; the sweeping coastline looked out over the distant islands of the Tuscan Archipelago, echoing their beauty with its wild and mountainous landscape, the pale rock densely interspersed with exotically green pine groves, and its almost luminescent aquamarine waters lapping the shores. In the still atmosphere, the picture was overwhelming.

Miraggio was a name that suited the place well. Hanging on its narrow bluff, it almost hovered in the void like an imaginary vision. Paolo's precarious home in the clouds seemed fitting for a man robbed of his past, a hunter of memories who, without an identity, could neither live comfortably in the present nor plan for the future. Looking at it from his point of view, Venetia almost sympathised with *l'Amante delle Quattro Stagioni*'s attitude to life.

The young woman gazed down in sheer awe at the magnificent scenery below, with the cliffs standing sentinel on each side of the cove. She felt as though, swept up by the sun and the wind above a primitive, surreal world and suspended in the air, she had left behind civilisation to embrace, for some time at least, the uncertain wildness and grandeur of Paolo's universe – a thought that excited her, even as she found it disturbing and almost frightening.

Glancing at her watch, Venetia saw it was nearly nine o'clock. If Paolo had arrived during the night he was probably still asleep, but somehow he didn't strike her as a lotus eater, so she thought she had better get herself ready for the day's work.

She showered and took a few minutes to ponder on what she was going to wear. Her choice fell on a peach-coloured, softly tailored Valentino trouser suit – smart but still comfortable if they were going for a site inspection. The long mirror reflected her: tall, slender and long-limbed. The pastel hue of the outfit brought out the warmth of her colouring and the glitter of bronze in her chestnut hair when the rays of the sun caught it. Today she had massed it in a sophisticated bun, held in place at the nape of her neck by an almost invisible net. It made her look a little severe, she thought, but it was appropriate in the circumstances. She was here to work and Venetia wanted the message to be clear, in case Paolo had other plans.

After making her bed and tidying up her room, she was just about to turn on the kettle when there was a knock at the door. Venetia caught her breath sharply. Her heart did a somersault in her breast and her pulse quickened as she went to open the door.

'*Buongiorno, signorina,*' said the smiling woman who stood on the threshold. She was holding a silver tray loaded with a plate of pastries, a large *cafetière* of steaming coffee, and a pot of thick honey. 'I thought you might like some breakfast.'

Venetia returned the woman's smile as she stepped aside to let her in. '*Grazie*, how very kind.'

'*Sono Ernestina, la governante di Miraggio,*' the housekeeper introduced herself, once again beaming and showing off a set of surprisingly milk-white teeth. 'Where would you like to have your breakfast – in the bedroom? The *salone*? Or maybe you would prefer to sit on the *terrazza*? It's a beautiful day.'

'On the terrace would be lovely, thank you.'

Ernestina was a woman in her late fifties or early sixties, with a bountiful figure and a benign face. She might have been younger, Venetia thought, as she followed the servant into the house; it was true that women from her walk of life, tasked with manual work and often outside, usually aged more quickly. Ernestina's tanned skin was coarse and lined, her features strong and clean-cut. Her beak of a nose and firm mouth might have been engraved on a coin.

Venetia watched the servant place the tray on the table in the living room before going into the kitchenette for the china and silver, and she noticed how neat she looked in her black frock, which reached almost down to her ankles, and the red woollen shawl draped about her shoulders. Her iron-grey hair was pulled back, neatly gathered up on the top of her head and held in place by a tortoise-shell comb.

'*Ha dormito bene?*'

'I slept like a log, thank you – the air is so pure up here.'

'*Sì*, and you must have been tired driving in the storm. I saw your car in the garage.'

'Yes, it was a long drive from Venice, but the directions I was given were very clear and I had no difficulty finding my way, despite the bad weather.'

Venetia moved out onto the terrace, picking up a little radio she had spotted lying on a nearby table, and Ernestina brought out the tray, now laden with everything for her breakfast.

'The *signore* is not yet back,' explainéd the housekeeper, with a frown. 'When Antonio went into town this morning, everybody was talking about the accident. Apparently one of those small planes crashed on the tarmac and the airport in Pisa is closed for now. We have not yet heard from the *signore*. He was due to arrive on the early Alitalia flight, so no doubt this will have held him up.'

Though Venetia's spirits sank at the news of Paolo's delay she was relieved that, without having to ask, she had received an answer to the question that had been at the forefront of her mind since she had arrived at Miraggio the night before. Still, she was a little put out that Paolo hadn't had the courtesy to ring the house to enquire whether she had arrived and inform his staff that the airport was closed.

She put down the radio and took a seat at the table, which was elegantly rustic with its wrought-iron frame topped by a cream slab of stone.

'Have you had a lot of damage on the estate because of the storm?'

'*Sì*, we have lost a very old oak tree. *Ma quel che è peggio*, but what is worse, the tree fell on our telephone post and our lines are down. That is why Antonio went into town this morning. He was hoping to bring back an engineer to mend the lines, but the storm has caused *tale devastazione* that it will be weeks before we can get someone to come over here.'

'Perhaps I should have given *Signor* Barone my mobile number,' murmured Venetia.

Ernestina shook her head. 'Those things don't work out here, *signorina*.' She shrugged. 'Ah, *questa nuova tecnologia…*'

So Paolo really wasn't to blame after all for the lack of communication. She realised that she had been a little unfair.

Ernestina was considering Venetia with a perplexed frown. '*Mi permetto di chiedere,* can I ask, the *signorina* is not Italian?'

'You're right, *io sono Inglese,* but I've lived in Italy for three years.'

'Your Italian is *perfetto,* if I may say so, *signorina,* but, yes, you don't look Italian. Your skin is like the skin of a peach that has been lightly touched by the sun – *molto bella.*' The housekeeper nodded and smiled approvingly.

Venetia laughed. 'Thank you very much for the compliment, Ernestina.'

'Do you have everything you need here?'

'Yes, *grazie,* the cottage is really comfortable, and so charming.'

'*Signor Barone sarà felice di sentirti* ... he supervised the refurbishment of La Sirena himself... *sì, sì,*' she nodded, 'and made sure it was *assolutamente perfetto.* The cottage had been closed for many years and needed a lot of work. The *signore* had not bothered to start it until he knew you were coming. *I lavori sono stati fatti molto rapidamente,* the work was done very quickly. It was all finished in two weeks. *Incredibile!*'

'Well, that's very kind of *Signor* Barone, and I will make sure to tell him how agreeable and comfortable it is.'

Ernestina gave Venetia an oblique look. 'You must be a good friend of *Signor* Barone. As I told you, La Sirena has been closed *per molti anni,* for many years, and the *signore* never has anyone up here. The poor man leads quite a lonely life, you know, cut off from the rest of the world – when he isn't away on business, *naturalmente.*'

'My acquaintance with *Signor* Barone is purely one of business. He has commissioned my firm with a job and I'm here to work on this assignment,' Venetia replied guardedly.

It seemed as though her reserved response spurred Ernestina's interest. 'The roses in the *salone* are from *Signor* Barone's rose garden and no one is allowed to tend to them but the *signore* himself… *sì sì, completamente proibito.* He gave specific instructions about the flower arrangement before he left and he also asked for a bowl of fruit from the orchard to be put in your room. *Non l'ha mai fatto prima*, he's never done that before.' Ernestina shook her head, a puzzled look on her face. 'Have you… has your firm known the *signore* long?'

Though Venetia could not help but feel warmed by Paolo's detailed attention to her comfort, she wasn't about to satisfy Ernestina's curiosity. 'All I know is that we value *Signor* Barone's custom and do our best to please him, as we do with all our clients.' Venetia smiled sweetly at the housekeeper. 'This coffee will soon be tepid if I don't drink it quickly,' she said, pouring out a cup of the strong brew. She helped herself to a *biscotti* and some honey, before turning her attention to the beautiful view that stretched out into infinity before them, indicating that the conversation was closed.

'*Se mi permette*, I'll do your bedroom now, *signorina*,' Ernestina said meekly, taking the hint and turning to go back into the house.

Venetia smiled. 'That's very kind of you Ernestina, *grazie mille,* but I have done my bed and tidied up my room and the bathroom. You don't need to trouble yourself.'

'It is no trouble, *signorina*, this is what I am here for. As I have told you, it's not often we get visitors at Miraggio.' She shook her head, waving her finger, '*e mai*, never sophisticated ladies like yourself.' The housekeeper's jet-black eyes settled pensively once more on Venetia's face and she sighed as she turned away. 'The *casa* has many rooms, too many of them unused.' Ernestina shook her head again, this time in disapproval. 'Some days, Miraggio is more like a tomb haunted by ghosts than a home,' she muttered as she disappeared into the house.

Left alone, Venetia's mind turned once again to Paolo. So, *l'Amante delle Quattro Stagioni* kept his conquests well away from his house in the clouds. That was most likely because of Allegra, the woman Venetia had seen with Paolo at the restaurant, *la favorita*, the one he always returned to. At that thought, she was seized by a moment of desolation so sharp that it seemed almost to take physical form. She shivered and shook the feeling off, knowing that such corrosive ideas were folly to entertain – after all, what right did she have to command Paolo's sole attention? Hadn't she declared the last time they had been together that friendship was all she had to offer him?

She was mad to have come here. She should have explained the situation to Giovanna, but she had deliberately kept quiet because deep down she was curious about the man who had touched a chord at the centre of her being, making her heart beat again. The man who had drawn her with a mysterious, addictive, primitive impulse that made her body vibrate and sing with a fire that she thought had been extinguished forever.

Venetia had assumed that her experience with Judd had beaten the romance out of her, but since she had met Paolo, all the romantic dreams that had filled her imagination way back were teasing her again with growing potency, and she was behaving like some clichéd heroine in one of the romantic novels she devoured in her teens, for some inexplicable reason finding herself drawn to a stranger. She was disturbed that her heart could behave this way, when her common sense told her that everything she now knew about Paolo meant he was wrong for her.

Recently she had been re-reading Blaise Pascal, the French theologian of the seventeenth century she much admired, and a phrase that seemed conceived solely for her predicament had leapt out at her: '*the heart has its reasons, which reason does not know*'. How painfully true. Why could she not decipher the workings of her own heart? Was she so wrong to hope that maybe she and Paolo were soulmates who had found each other after life had dealt them each a cruel blow? Venetia sighed as she turned on the radio. She tuned into the Don Giovanni show and its Italian nostalgia songs and heard 'E Salutala Per Me' by Raffaella Carrà playing. Finding herself humming along to the beautiful, haunting melody, she smiled ruefully as the voice sang mournfully of those who win and lose in love and questioned the mystery of men. She sighed. Would she win or lose? Despite all that she knew – of Paolo's reputation as a womaniser, of her own heart's mystery – Venetia was secretly beguiled by the notion that some small magic might befall her one day, and destiny would show its felicitous hand. She closed her eyes, reprimanding herself for her foolish, adolescent mooning and let the soft sea breeze soothe her face.

In spite of the riotous whirl of her thoughts, nothing could spoil Venetia's delight in the view before her. She sat there drinking it all in: the dreamy peace, the scent of flowers and burning brushwood floating in the air, and the tang of the sea. Her drooping shoulders rose philosophically. 'Quel che sarà, sarà,' went the Italian saying. It was a glorious morning, and moping around churning up black thoughts was doing her no good at all; she might as well take this opportunity to explore the grounds and maybe drive into town for a spot of lunch.

There are things that need to be put away in a little compartment at the back of the mind where they can be hidden and ignored until either the time comes to revisit them, or the day arrives when they are altogether forgotten. So it was with Venetia. She pushed aside all thoughts of Paolo and decided to enjoy her day.

As Venetia was about to get up, Ernestina came bustling on to the terrace again. 'I have attended to your room, signorina.

There was not much for me to do. You must leave everything to me in the future, as I have told you. This is my job and *Signor* Barone would be very upset if he knew that I was not attending to it properly.'

Venetia gave a crystalline laugh. 'Well, Ernestina, if you insist – I wouldn't like you to get into trouble on my account. But you must at least let me make my bed. A bed is a very personal thing, don't you think?'

Ernestina chuckled harshly, shrugging. '*Dio mio, questi Inglesi! Va bene,* as you like.'

'The weather's so lovely, I think I'll change into something more comfortable and go for a walk in the garden.'

'Of course, you must. The grounds are beautiful and you need to visit the *signore*'s rose garden. But be careful if you walk along the edge of the cliffs: the slope is slippery and the earth is all loose, especially after yesterday's storm – *molto pericoloso*,' Ernestina warned her with a wave of her hand as she left the cottage.

Venetia switched her trouser suit for a pair of tight-fitting cotton beige slacks, drawn in at the waist by a brown suede belt, and a bright-orange silk top with small round iridescent buttons. She undid the more sophisticated hairstyle she had adopted that morning and tied her hair into a loose ponytail instead. Then, armed with a pad and pencil, just in case she felt like sketching, she went out into the sunshine.

The cottage garden was a riot of colour, shimmering in the sun. Although on first sight it seemed unkempt, Venetia had guessed at its luxuriance the night before in the dark and she had been right. The enclosure, rimmed by a stone parapet, was smothered in bougainvillea that fell in purple and yellow cascades to the cliffs below. The walls of the cottage were framed in jasmine and brilliant clusters of begonia. Polyanthus and tulips looked like sparkling gems in the beds scattered on the grass, and the apple tree in front of Venetia's window was thick with white and rosy buds. Trickling splashes from the small brook running through the garden added a sort of tranquillity to the surroundings. The hovering breath and scent of spring was everywhere.

Curious to see what the main house looked like in daylight, Venetia walked out of the sunken garden and retraced her steps along the narrow path, back to the courtyard where she had left her car the evening before… and there it stood in splendour.

Constructed in an unusual pale, golden stone, Miraggio, with its Gothic turret at one end, was an imposing old building that commanded sweeping views of the surrounding countryside. Like a Goliath, solidly rooted on a rocky outcrop jutting into the Tyrrhenian Sea, it was framed on one side by stretches of well-tended vineyards, olive groves and fragrant orchards, and on the other by a great expanse of glittering deep-blue and turquoise water. The awe-inspiring residence was erected on four floors with a subterranean level built right into the rock. Its great masonry walls were smothered in climbing roses that poked at the elegant, tall windows and rambled over its beautiful, arched wooden front door, softening the building's austere appearance. A colonnaded veranda encircled three-quarters of the crenulated turret and the remaining open space included a south-facing terrace. The columns were festooned with flowering vines, and huge earthenware pots of climbing geraniums stood between them.

The architect's vision was clear to Venetia now. The great structure was dramatically positioned, and the itinerary to reach it unfolded in a sequence: it showed a procession, from the first distant view of Miraggio hovering over the ocean as visitors approached the estate, to the moment one penetrated the great walls and drove up a long avenue of lime trees to arrive in the gravelled courtyard, where the imposing house provided exquisite views and a sensual awareness of the countryside that surrounded it. Paolo's home, Venetia thought, had both beauty and grandeur, as well as a veil of melancholy laid on it from times long past. She loved it.

Venetia went over to the parapet, built along the top of the cliff. Quite near the rocky edge, leaning out into the void, grew a mimosa tree. Its fernlike silver-grey leaves with bright yellow flowers grew from its limbs in tight clusters. In the burning silence they shone like little golden globes offering adoration to the sun. Mimosa trees planted too close to an open area of land usually become a weed and spread. Strange how this one had just sprouted there, she thought, a lonely sentry slanting out from the rock in which its roots were embedded. It hung poised over the drop in perfect stillness, yellow against deep blue, with no other vegetation around it.

Not far from the tree, Venetia noticed broad steps that had been cut in the face of the rock. The craggy staircase snaked down to what looked like a private sheltered bay, lying in the dazzling morning light far beneath. *There must be more than a hundred steps,* she thought, and wondered whether Paolo ever went down there to bathe in privacy. An unexpected feeling raced down her spine and pooled deep inside her at the thought of his tanned, muscled body glistening as he waded out of the water; and for a few moments she stood there, dreamy-eyed, imagining what it would be like to swim naked with Paolo in the moonlit sea.

It was a perfect day for sketching and painting. There was so much to see and admire. Venetia settled herself on one of the steps in the shade of the mimosa tree and took out her sketch-book. She looked at the clefts in the rocks at the bottom where the tide surged in and out and at the seagulls perched in sedate companies on the ledges at the top of the cliffs. They were such a curious sight, like newly-painted wooden toys, with their glistening white feathers and heavy orange beaks, their feet close together, alert eyes very bright as they stood there motionless, an air of blank solemnity on their vacant faces.

She loved the solitude, the vastness of sea and sky, the movement of the shadows, and the way that areas previously in the shade now appeared, shining with brilliance under the sun. Timeless, and devoid of any evidence of modern life, it could be the background to a calm mediaeval picture, and the young woman wondered if perhaps Charles Lamb was not right when he wrote that, '*as men when they die are not really dead, so perhaps their habitations still persist in the unseen world*'.

Venetia took out her pencils and peered at the horizon, then began to sketch a distant white liner sailing into Porto Santo Stefano. She could understand why Paolo had settled here after his accident and the loss of his wife – it was a good place to heal.

'This is not a playground for the public or a recreation park for tourists. You're trespassing!'

Engrossed in her sketching, Venetia nearly jumped out of her skin at the sudden aggressive reprimand. Shielding her eyes from the glaring sun, she lifted her head and was met with the termagant expression of a young woman gazing down at her from the top of a bright bay mare, eyes as wild as those of her mount.

'How did you get in, anyway?' went on the unfriendly rider.

A cold anger ran along Venetia's spine when she saw that it was Allegra, the young girl who had been with Paolo at the restaurant, but she gritted her teeth and contrived an air of insouciance, allowing a smile to touch her lips.

'I came in through the front gates, of course.'

Raw little flames seemed to smoulder in the dark eyes of her interrogator as they scanned Venetia from head to toe.

'Well, you can get out the same way before I call the police.'

Venetia, unmoving, coolly looked up into the hostile pupils

of the Italian girl. 'I'm afraid that you'll have to put up with my company for a little longer.'

Her standoffish answer seemed to take the wind out of Allegra's sails, and the girl stiffened imperceptibly, before recovering her composure in a flash. 'And why is that? Who are you? Or, more appropriately, who do you *think* you are?' she taunted, keeping her impatient horse still with a tug of the reins.

'I'm Venetia Aston-Montagu. I'm the architect *Signor* Barone has appointed to carry out some work here.'

The rider arched an eyebrow. 'What works? *Signor* Barone is away, and he left no instructions about this.'

'Perhaps you should check with *Signor* Barone in that case. I can assure you that he's aware of my presence.'

A malicious smile hovered on Allegra's full, rosebud lips. 'Paolo and I speak every day. He would have told me if we were expecting anyone. During his absence we're not allowed to let anybody on the premises for security reasons. I must insist that you leave.'

Liar! Venetia was on the point of remonstrating, but kept silent, counting to ten instead. She had made herself known, and there was no point in locking horns with Paolo's mistress, who had taken great satisfaction in establishing their intimacy.

Her chin came up a fraction. 'Unfortunately, I must contradict you on this point. I was let in yesterday night by Antonio, the caretaker, and I spent a very comfortable night in one of the estate's cottages,' she replied calmly.

The Italian beauty contemplated her opponent with undisguised venom. Venetia felt as if the girl was summing her up, stripping her naked as she contemptuously dismissed her in one burning look from under silky, black lashes. Allegra flung up her head, small hands clenching and unclenching on the reins, and then gave the mare a cup on the neck that sent the creature bounding forward, and they disappeared in a cloud of dust.

Shaking uncontrollably now with fury and humiliation, Venetia watched Allegra gallop away. For the second time in less than twenty-four hours, her first impulse was to go back to the cottage, pack up her bags and leave for Venice – or even as far as England! But she had never run away from a job or a person in her life, and she wasn't about to start now, all because of some arrogant, spoilt girl's devious machinations.

Still, Venetia knew that Allegra was not just any young girl; she was as luscious and beautiful as a flower in its early bloom, with silk-smooth, jet-black hair covering her shoulders like a cape, satin warm-coloured skin, and the most expressive, dark, velvety bedroom eyes she had ever seen. The girl possessed an impertinent tilt to her small nose, which gave her a kind of haughtiness that Venetia sensed few members of the opposite sex could resist the need to break down – she was the dream *inamorata* par excellence of a million men. Venetia had no doubt how easy it must have been for Allegra to bamboozle a rich, widowed amnesic man, and she momentarily pitied Paolo.

Yet it was with a burst of frustrated anger against herself, and a rush of antagonism towards the Italian girl, that she recognised the jealousy that swept over her like lava at the thought of Paolo in the arms of the dark-eyed virago, a feeling that left her suddenly cold and implacable. Gathering her sketchbook and pencils, she walked back to the cottage, her heart a little heavier than it had been when she had started out that morning.

What was so special about this man? He was not that handsome – not in a conventional way, anyhow; quite the reverse. Certainly he didn't have the fine bone structure that had so attracted her to Judd, or the aristocratic regular features and Norse god colouring that had earned Umberto the title of Mr

Venice when he was twenty. But Paolo's whole being held something else, something much more powerful: a primitive look that made him different to other men, as the jungle animal is different from its domestic counterpart; a savage harshness, which gave his face a certain sexual appeal that she found almost irresistible. Obviously she was not the only woman on whom he had this effect. She had seen how others flocked to him, the way their heads turned and their eyes followed him, so it was not overly surprising he had been nicknamed *l'Amante delle Quattro Stagioni.*

Back at the cottage, Venetia found a tray waiting for her with a salad of baby vegetables, a plate of cold meats, a loaf of crusty bread, olives, cheese and a bottle of red wine. The large bowl of fruit was still standing untouched in the alcove where she had noticed it the night before. She had planned to go into town for lunch, but this uncomplicated meal was a far more attractive alternative – Venetia had always admired the Italian art of living simply and exceedingly pleasantly. Exploring Cala Piccola and Porto Santo Stefano in the afternoon seemed a good option, and maybe she could ask around to find out if the airport in Pisa had reopened. On reflection, it was quite astonishing that Paolo hadn't just taken a train or driven down to Miraggio. It seemed strange that neither course had apparently crossed his mind, she thought, a little miffed at this somewhat cavalier attitude, given his insistence on her coming down.

Although the sun was as brilliant as ever, it was not too hot to sit on the veranda, so Venetia opened up the umbrella and settled herself to look out over the beautiful Tuscan countryside surrounding the property, with the ground sloping down in parts to the valley and the main road from Miraggio, to the far-off town of Porto Santo Stefano. Wisteria was in full bloom now, clambering over the rough whitewashed walls of the sheds and stables on the estate.

Venetia's heart gave a little squeeze as the purple clusters brought back the memory of the magical evening she had spent with Paolo at La Lanterna, only spoilt when he had taken that phone call, an action that had raised all her defences. She had ended their date ungraciously. He had asked why she was deny-ing them simple happiness when the fire in her eyes reflected the passion that filled her soul, and she could not answer him... nor could she forget the sad, almost bewildered expression on his face when she had pushed him away with words she had not even believed herself. *My tongue – my dreadful tongue!* What had possessed her to let it run away with her like that? The answer was simple and she knew it: the deep-seated fear of relationships that had plagued her life since her devastating experience with Judd all those years ago.

Still, had she not saved herself from a more terrible heartache by rejecting Paolo? How could she regret the way she had reacted to his advances in view of the present circumstances? It was all for the best, she told herself for the umpteenth time. Yet deep down, Venetia knew that something irrevocable had happened to her when she had met him. It was as if the far-off echoes of her love for Judd, the only true love she had known, were coming back to haunt her; and fight it as she may, Venetia doubted very much she would be able to stifle the flame that seemed to burn relent-lessly day and night, hot and fierce, in her breast... although this new flash of passion, she knew, was not burning for Judd.

It's only chemistry, a voice at the back of her mind whispered. But could it really be only sexual desire that meant when Paolo kissed her, when he held her so close against him, and she could feel every hard muscle in his body, it was somehow never enough? Was it simply physical attraction that made her want to be closer, so much closer, to feel his warmth seep into her, his skin against hers, so not only their bodies, but their souls would blend forever?

She sat absorbed in thought, unconscious of the passing of time. It must have been an hour later, at least, when she heard someone come into the cottage, and a moment after, Ernestina appeared on the veranda.

'Oh, *signorina*, you didn't like Ernestina's salad?'

'On the contrary, Ernestina, I enjoyed your salad very much, thank you, but I'm not used to having a large meal at lunchtime,' Venetia said hastily, realising guiltily that she had hardly touched her food.

'Not even a glass of wine? *La cucina piccola fa la casa grande*, a small kitchen makes a house big, and anyone will tell you, Ernestina has the best kitchen around here. The bread was baked this morning. The *signore* will eat only homemade bread and ours is *delizioso, squisito!*' Pursing her lips, the housekeeper made a little sound to express the delectability of the crusty loaf for which Venetia had not shown enough appreciation.

Venetia smiled a little sheepishly; the last thing she wanted was to ruffle the kind old woman's feathers. 'If you don't mind, I'll have some tonight with my dinner. I'm really not hungry right now.'

Ernestina gave a pert nod, as if placated by this answer, then her brow furrowed slightly. 'I hope the *signore* will be back for dinner,' she said, almost apologetically. 'The telephone lines are still down and Antonio hasn't had time to go into town again to ask about the airport.'

'Not to worry, I'm going to explore Porto Santo Stefano this afternoon and I'll investigate and let you know.'

They went back inside. As Venetia was picking up her bag from the sofa, her eyes fell on the painting over the fireplace that she had been looking at the night before. Having seen Miraggio in daylight, she had no doubt now that La Torretta and Miraggio were one and the same. The only difference was the profusion of climbing roses and other vegetation that now dressed the somewhat severe walls of the house and gave Miraggio the air of a fairyland castle instead of that of a medieval fortress.

'This is how Miraggio used to look before *Signor* Barone bought the place,' said Ernestina, noticing Venetia's pause in front of the picture. 'La Torretta was derelict in those days. It belonged to *un cantante d'opera ben noto*. God save us from such evil, but this opera singer was murdered by one of his mistresses, and some say the house is haunted by *il suo fantasma*.' Ernestina looked up and crossed herself before carrying on. 'But we mustn't think about that. Bad thoughts bring *vibrazioni negative*, and the house has had many owners and a long history. Although the *signore* has had them blocked up, the dungeons are still in the original part – you know, facing the lake. And there's still that old, clunky machinery for flooding the lowest dungeon.'

'Miraggio also has a lake?'

'Yes, it's small *e molto inquietante*, and very spooky. Nothing grows well around it and *Signor* Barone never goes there. Legend has it that in medieval times, the owners of La Torretta used to tie their prisoners to iron rings in the dungeon walls and drown them slowly, inch by inch. Later, they let the water out again and put weights on the bodies before throwing them into the sea.'

Venetia let out a horrified cry. 'How morbid!'

Ernestina shrugged with Italian matter-of-factness. 'An effective way of disposing of *i tuoi nemici*, your enemies, all the same!'

Venetia shivered; it all sounded extremely macabre. She picked up her bag. 'Where is the garage, Ernestina? I gave my car keys to Antonio yesterday and he hasn't returned them.'

'They'll be in the car. This place is very safe, *molto sicuro*. No one can get to the garage without passing the stable block or outbuildings, where there's always someone working, even during the *siesta*. And at night, that wolf of a dog Rufus is on guard. Come, I'll show you.'

They went out into the sunshine and took a wide path along the back of the cottage, past a vine-covered pergola, haylofts, and other outbuildings, each overshadowed by age-old oaks, cedars, and beech trees, with here and there a tall, elegant cypress, the very signature of Tuscany. A couple of men were working outside and Venetia felt their curious eyes scrutinising her as she passed by – they were obviously unaccustomed to having strangers on the premises.

When the stable block came into view, a single glance sufficed for Venetia to assess that this was a state-of-the-art equestrian building. U-shaped, it comprised five stables, a wash room, a tack room, and a feed room, set in lines on either side of a dramatic stone archway with wisteria and Virginia creeper hugging its walls. Built in hardwood with oak posts, beams and stays, it had high eves with a tiled overhanging roof in brown asphalt shingles. A fleeting peep inside showed the stalls to be spacious, with fresh straw on the ground, and four beautiful, well-groomed and contented-looking animals housed there.

Venetia had ridden all her life. Sir William owned extensive stables in Berkshire where he used to hunt. She herself had never participated in that sport, but had been given her first pony when she was seven and had been through pony club, dressage lessons and competitions, and had even won a trophy when she was sixteen. Judd was an accomplished rider and she had wonderful memories of their horseback hikes around Hyde Park in the early mornings during summer. A pang of sadness gripped her once more, as she took in these familiar surroundings.

'*Signor* Barone is an expert rider,' Ernestina told her, jolting her out of her reflection. 'He oversees the work on the property *a cavallo*, on horseback, instead of going round with a car or one of the estate trailers.'

And he's obviously always accompanied by his mistress, Venetia thought hollowly. For two pins, though, as pride gave her a poke, she would have asked the friendly housekeeper about the young girl she had seen that morning on horseback, but she kept silent. *Everything comes to him who waits,* she told herself philosophically.

'And that is where Antonio lives,' muttered Ernestina she hurried past the large stable cottage. It was larger than La Sirena but somehow not as charming. Venetia suddenly realised that Allegra must also live there and it took all her willpower to bite her tongue.

The garage was near the stable block. The Porsche was there and Venetia noticed it was cleaned of all the mud that had been splashed over it on the journey through the storm. The key was in the ignition.

'*State attenta*, drive slowly, *le strade sono molto insidiose*, the roads are very treacherous.' Ernestina said, as Venetia climbed into the front seat.

'Don't worry, I'm a good driver.' She waved at the house-keeper as she pulled away down the gravel track towards the great entrance gates.

The scenery going down the hill towards Cala Picola was quite different from the craggy splendour of Miraggio, but just as dramatic. The little hamlet with its cottages, beaches, vineyards and its little church looked like a miniature village under the blazing sun. It was a brilliant day, a day as different from the bleak greyness of yesterday as could be imagined. Venetia could hardly believe this was the same route she had driven only twenty-four hours ago. The coastline as she approached Porto Santo Stefano afforded a most breathtaking view, though less dramatic than the one coming up to Miraggio. Here, wrought-iron gates led down to private coves and large millionaires' villas; and beyond them, the coastal road led on to stuccoed houses covered with flowering creepers that perched precariously on the bank, and to quaintly painted cottages whose stone steps were lapped by the blue waters of the Tyrrhenian Sea.

When she reached the port, Venetia left her car in the main car park. The town was modern with bright, clean shops and charming *caffetterias*, and with luxury hotels, their terraced walls festooned with climbing roses. There was not much to do in this pretty port but shop, laze in the sun, swim or take a boat on the azure-blue ocean. Venetia stopped to buy some postcards, and glancing at the headlines on a local newspaper read that the airport at Pisa had reopened and scheduled flights were running on time. Though Giovanna would doubtless be expecting an update from her immediately, Venetia felt oddly reluctant to call her godmother – already she'd sent a text message saying that she'd arrived safely and, besides, there was nothing else to report since the client had yet to make an appearance.

The market, its stalls piled high with gaily coloured fruit, sausages and cheeses, and souvenirs appealed to her artist's eye. She found an outdoor *caffetteria* with a cheerfully striped awning, and sat under a red umbrella sipping a *caffè shakerato* that had been poured into a wide-mouth, martini-type glass. It was Fabrizio who had introduced her to this frothy and creamy fresh-brewed espresso drink, shaken with ice and sugar. Venetia found that there was nothing more refreshing on a hot summer's Italian afternoon. She smiled inwardly at the thought of her colleague. Why couldn't she have just given Fabrizio a chance? Handsome, with so many excellent qualities, he would make some woman a wonderful partner. Some woman... but not her, oh no! She needed tortured, complicated souls to spark her interest, she thought derisively... a glutton for punishment, her father always said.

Women in the market, mostly wearing sombre black shawls over their shoulders, were clearly the housewives of Porto Santo Stefano. As they shopped, they prodded and poked, chaffered and bargained, in the manner of housewives all over the world, and their dark clothes only served to enhance the effect of bright sunlight and deep shadow, the colour in the fruit, vegetables and flowers. Venetia was so enjoying the scene before her that she wished she had brought her sketchbook. Undeterred, she asked the waiter for a pen and paper and was soon at work.

On the pavement in front of her people of every age and nationality passed by, and Venetia's ears picked up snatches of at least a dozen languages. But what struck her most was the laughter that rang in the clear atmosphere, the expression of happiness on old faces as well as young. Evidently, tourists from all over the world came to Porto Santo Stefano to enjoy themselves, and did so in a way that was simple, healthy, and joyous; so very different from the hectic holiday schedules in Venice and the world's other great cities she had visited.

The afternoon flew by. The church clock chimed five o'clock; the sun would be setting soon. The market stalls had long put away their goods. Boats were discharging their last passengers, and the beach was all at once peaceful. The last of the strollers were heading back to their hotels.

It was time to go. Venetia paid the bill and reluctantly started on her way home. After such an enjoyable afternoon, she felt rested and calm, and prepared to confront anything the days ahead might hold. She knew that, whatever happened, when Paolo returned, nothing would be easy.

*   *   *

The evening was still. Venetia sat on the veranda of the little cottage, La Sirena, sipping a glass of chilled white wine, while trying to concentrate on a book on Buddhist philosophy that she had bought after her session with Ping Lü. She had changed into a sleeveless white shift dress made of thin cotton and had undone her pony tail, leaving her lush, chestnut hair falling casually over her shoulders. She looked up to her left, gazing at the crimson sun that was declining drowsily on the horizon, its burning light making golden patches on the sea, smooth as a lake at this sunset hour. To her right, the distant countryside lying beyond the trees seemed bluer with those powdery white branches of apple blossom, and as the shadows lengthened, it deepened to a celestial Italian blue. The old brick of the outbuildings was empurpled, shining with an intense, yet soft glow. The luminous light was magnificent; the fiery orange, bright pink and patches of serene blue giving way to the swift advance of dusk.

Miraggio spread before her eyes, hugging the coast and folded in safely by hills, utterly remote from civilisation. There was something about this place that made it too beautiful for anyone but lovers; for them alone its wanton loveliness was the right setting. Yes, Venetia could understand why Paolo didn't bring anyone to his Paradise where he was king and Allegra his queen. Pain jabbed at her lungs, almost making it hard to breathe at the thought – she didn't belong here.

Venetia took up her book again: *'and attain a state where craving and feeling cease,'* she read, and laid it down. She smiled ruefully: detachment was a distant thing indeed, if merely the thought of Paolo with another woman could create in her breast and mind such incomprehensible jealousy. Why had he manoeuvred things to get her here? Was he trying to hurt her because she had refused to become another of his conquests? Venetia sighed, her eyes on the garden and the darkening sea. How strange the scenery looked in the empty light. The evening air breathed of cooling earth, the dusk full of little sounds. She felt restless; where was Paolo and why wasn't he already here? The flight from Pisa to Porto Santo Stefano was only two and half hours. She wanted to see him, even though she knew that if she did, all her confusion would no doubt be intensified rather than resolved. Venetia finished her glass of wine and went down into the garden for a walk. How she hated waiting!

It was the hour of the Evening Star, before the moon repeated the circuit of the sun and flooded the valleys with silver radiance and sharp shadows. A necklace of lights was strung all along the far-off coast. The gardens of Miraggio lay in silent splendour, and Venetia walked to the wooded area she had noticed that afternoon, which sloped down to a balustrade, overlooking the sea. By now, all the birdsong had ended. There was only the croak of a bullfrog from the reeds of a lily pond she passed on her way down, and the odd cricket chip-chipping here and there.

She hadn't been there long, absorbed in her thoughts, her gaze lost in the scenery, when she was aware of a slight movement in the shadows. Startled, Venetia spun around, rocketed out of her daydreaming. Her heart gave a jerking throb, and yet she stood motionless, feeling her limbs heavy, although pulsing with life. Perhaps it was the effect of having waited for what seemed like ages, even though barely twenty-four hours had passed since she had arrived at Miraggio, but she was acutely aware of Paolo's presence, more strongly than ever before.

He stepped out of the shadows and stood very still. They looked at each other dumbly in the penumbra, almost as if they had been strangers. For an instant, they were alone in the world, isolated in this little wood under a starlit sky, their souls exchanging a message that their lips could not utter. Paolo's eyes found hers and stared into them, his gaze raking questioningly over her face. A strange duel of tension battled between them. Venetia's heart seemed to have snapped its moorings, and felt as if it was careering about inside her. He was so close that she could hear his breathing and see the almost imperceptible trembling of his mouth.

And then, just as she was thinking that she could not stand another second of this searing tension, Paolo held out his hand to her. He was only a few feet away; all she had to do was accept it. Yet she couldn't find it in herself to do so: her morning altercation with the beautiful Amazon had left her hurt and humiliated, and she stood in silent mutiny, her amber eyes burning with all the indignation that had been building up since Umberto's revelations. How dare Paolo bring her to his love nest!

'*La persona che è assente ha la sua scusa con lui.*' Paolo's eyes held hers, and he dropped his hand. 'I apologise for not being here to welcome you, *cara*, but I was in a very difficult position. All the plans and documents of the project we'll be discussing in the next few weeks were in my luggage on the plane, and in addition to that, I was accompanying an important client whom I couldn't just drop.'

Venetia assumed a casual air. 'There is nothing to apologise for. As you say, the person who is absent has his excuse with him, and yours is quite acceptable.'

A smile moved about his dark eyes. '*Eccellente,* so we are still friends?' He extended his hand again.

Venetia looked at it for a second, but ignored it. 'If you say so,' she replied.

'I thought you'd decided you didn't want the job. But you are here after all, *cara*, isn't that the only thing that counts?'

Venetia looked up at Paolo, anger momentarily banishing her pain. 'May I remind you that I am just an employee at Bianchi e Lombardi. I'm afraid *la Signora* Lombardi does not believe in nepotism – I did not have much say in the matter.'

Paolo gave a small regretful sigh. 'That saddens me, *cara*. I was under the impression we enjoyed each other's company, and that you were here because you realised that too. People always think they can ignore their feelings but it's like ripping out a part of yourself when you try not to care for someone.'

'*Care?*' Venetia gave a slight, derisive laugh. 'We hardly know each other.'

Paolo moved a little closer and glanced at her, an enigmatic expression crossing his face. 'Do you have a wooden heart?'

The question startled her. 'No.'

His blue eyes were still and dark as they met Venetia's amber stare. They slid slowly over her slim figure clad in the shift dress and it was as if he was running a hand very lightly over every part of her. 'If I remember rightly, neither do you have an insensitive body, *sì?*' His voice was low and husky.

Venetia's cheeks flamed and she turned away abruptly from him, her gaze desperately searching about her for some avenue of escape, even as her heart palpitated at the overpowering memory of that not so far-off evening they had last shared.

'Don't go, *carissima mia*,' he murmured.

'Stop calling me *carissima*. I'm not your darling,' she flared.

'Supposing I really did fall in love with you, what would you do?'

His words disturbed Venetia more than she wanted him to know, and she could not take the intensity of his eyes on her, so she lashed out with the first thing that came into her head.

'Is that why you brought me to your love nest? Is not one woman enough to warm your bed, *signore*? Or have you decided to break the usual pattern of *l'Amante delle Quattro Stagioni*?'

She thought for a moment that she saw a certain look of pain etched into Paolo's features. 'So that is the opinion you have of me, Venetia? I see you have been listening to vitriolic tongues. No one gossips about another person's virtues. People who spread rumours usually have an ulterior motive.'

'One of my father's favourite quotes is by Winston Churchill: *"There are a terrible lot of lies going around the world, and the worst of it is that half of them are true."* The rumours I've heard about you, Paolo, come from more than one source. Can you deny that you're a notorious womaniser? As far as I can tell, love for you is a game of musical chairs that you play whenever you're in Venice... a fickle and cruel game of which I want no part.'

Paolo's mouth tightened into a grim line. 'That's not fair, Venetia. You've condemned me without knowing all the facts.'

'I haven't condemned you. Why should I bother, since I don't care? I'm here on business and our relationship is, and will remain, strictly a business one.'

Venetia saw Paolo's jaw muscles clench and something leapt into his eyes, a tiny gleam of challenge that made his irises look like glistening sapphires in the dark. She felt her heart strangely gripped by their intensity, her treacherous senses responding to the flame of desire reflected in his face; and still, somewhere deep inside, she knew there was a kind of tenderness for this man that melted her to the core.

She swayed a little, and he caught at her wrist. She wondered if he could feel her pulse pounding under his touch, as the yearning for him flooded her loins. In a few heartbeats, the passion of anger had turned into something very different, and they could both feel it.

Paolo gently drew her to him, still holding her by the wrist, and Venetia made no attempt to stop him. In the intimate shelter under the trees it was as if he were a god possessing his chosen mortal. Now, she dared not even raise her eyes to his ruggedly masculine face. Everything seemed to be happening in some sort of slow motion, with an inevitability that made her acutely conscious of each detail. He cupped her chin in his strong, wide palm and lifted it towards him, but he didn't kiss her immediately; instead, his gaze bored into her as though he were searching her soul.

Venetia could feel the strange trembling of her thighs, the ache low down in her body, the desire to part her lips for his mouth, but still he did not move. Though only inches apart, she found herself wanting to be closer still, and arched a fraction towards him. He let go of her wrist and placing that hand in the small of her back, pressed her against the length of his hard, aroused body, making her feel how much he wanted her, and her head instinctively tilted back. Their eyes locked; their breath almost melded and yet still he did not kiss her.

Venetia's heartbeat was quickening and she knew she could, and should, stop now, but the knowledge of his desire for her acted like a primitive spur, urging her on. The heat coming through the thin material of his shirt was palpable, and her nipples hardened to stiff peaks beneath her dress. Everything other than Paolo ceased to matter now. She edged a little more towards him, lifting her face to him, her eyes pleading for release, every part of her body crying out her need for him and her surrender to his mastery of it. She parted her dry lips, her breath fluttering in and out of them, like the wings of a small caged bird beating to be freed, and yet imprisoned by a longing far stronger than any bars. Very gently, Paolo ran a long index finger along their yielding outline, making her feel faint with the longing to be kissed. Only then did he bend his head and his mouth closed over hers, muffling her weak moan.

Oh, the sweetness of that kiss! Venetia's heart trembled with emotion. There was something so infinitely tender in his possession of her mouth that any remaining thoughts she might have had of resisting him were drowned beneath a wave of pure sensation. Her hands went up and tightened around his muscled upper arms. The shadowed garden swirled around her and her lips cleaved to his as if she depended on him for her every breath.

And then his tongue was playing a game of tormenting her, tracing little circles around the edge of her lips, one hand pinning her against him while the other slipped into her hair, weaving his fingers through its silk-like mass, and stroking it gently back, flooding her with the warmth of his touch, flames spreading through her lower limbs arousing her to fever pitch. The back of her head had always been sensitive and so Venetia's thoughts flew to the only other man she had been with, the only one who had explored her body inch by inch, and who knew each receptive part almost better than herself. It was a memory of pain and dreams that had died in the face of reality – Judd, a distant voice echoed inside her head; Judd, the love of her life, the one man she had lain with and with whom she had discovered the wonderful secrets of her body. Judd, the father of her unborn child.

'Oh, Judd!' it was almost a stifled sob that escaped Venetia's lips.

Paolo thrust her from him. He looked as if she had slapped him. She saw his face strain, drawn of all colour, and his heavy dark brows contract in the uncertain light. He watched her in silence, bitterness etched on his rigid features, his nostrils quivering. The anger that flashed in his eyes drained all the heated urgency out of Venetia's body in an instant.

'I am not your Judd, *signorina,* for whom you tremble with such passion. In case you've forgotten, my name is Paolo,' he growled savagely, his words like the lash of a whip and, pushing past her without another word or a backward glance, he lunged into the dark and strode off, disappearing into the night.

Venetia stood beneath the stars shivering, hugging her trembling body, desire still beating deep inside her like a feverish pulse, her flesh crying out for a satisfaction it had not received, and a longing in her bones that was solidifying into actual pain.

Slowly the world returned, but her mind remained confused and uncertain. Judd... It was always Judd... she had to face the fact that she wasn't over him, and might never get over him. The echoes of the past would forever be there to haunt her. She walked back to the cottage. Once in her room, she flung herself on the bed and buried her head in her arms.

When Ernestina came over to call her for dinner half an hour later, the housekeeper found the young woman still lying there in the dark, staring at the star-studded sky through the open windows, the night air blowing in on her as she listened to the sound of whispering waves that mixed with her mournful thoughts.

'*Signor* Barone is waiting for you to come to dinner, *signorina.*'

Oh no! Facing Paolo tonight was too much to ask, Venetia thought. She would brave the situation in the morning, once she had put some order in her bewildered brain. She had behaved appallingly, and confronting him tonight after what had just happened was more than she could bear.

'Would you please send my apologies to *Signor* Barone. I have a bad headache. I'll feel better after a good night's sleep, I'm sure. I must have caught a touch of the sun, but I'll report for work tomorrow morning without fail.'

Ernestina gave her a quizzical frown and Venetia's cheeks flamed under the servant's keen eyes.

'Shall I bring you a tray, or maybe just a cup of *brodo di pollo*?'

'No, thank you. Really, it's been a long day and all I need is sleep. I'll be fine in the morning.'

'As you wish, *signorina*. I'll let the *signore* know. I think he will be very disappointed. *Buonanotte, signorina, spero che vi sentirete meglio la mattina,* goodnight, *signorina,* I hope you feel better in the morning.'

'*Grazie,* Ernestina. *Buonanotte,* and please convey my sincere apologies to *Signor* Barone.'

'I shall do so, *signorina*. Sleep well.'

With Ernestina gone, the cottage sank back into silence. Venetia sighed. She got up and went over to the window looking out on to the stable yard. Paolo might be disappointed for a few moments, but he would soon forget his troubles in the arms of Antonio's beautiful niece, she reflected bitterly.

A deep-seated ache began somewhere inside her at the thought and she bit her bottom lip. What on earth was wrong with her? A few hours ago she had almost told Paolo to go to the Devil, then she had clung wantonly to him, dizzy with desire – was it only her sex-deprived body that was reacting to the novelty of a man's touch? No! She rejected that thought even as it crossed her mind. Paolo reminded her of Judd in so many ways that she was clearly transposing her love for her former fiancé on to the Italian tycoon. She closed her eyes against this frightening admission, which seemed the only answer to her erratic behaviour. Anyhow, it was irrelevant now, she concluded. She knew very well what Paolo must be thinking, and was scorched with shame from head to toe. She had made such a mess of things this evening; it would be he, now, who would draw back from her. And, even if she hadn't ruined everything, wasn't it now more dangerous than ever before to get involved with *l'Amante delle Quattro Stagioni*?

CHAPTER 7

Paolo poured a large measure of scotch into a heavy crystal tumbler, raised it to his lips and took a fiery gulp. Standing by his bedroom window, looking out to sea, the book he had been trying to read, unsuccessfully, was held against his chest and his blue eyes clouded over in sombre reflection.

The large room was unmistakably masculine, with its oak four-poster double bed and a magnificent Renaissance wardrobe, two comfortable armchairs covered in navy blue leather, and a big round table set in the middle. The walls were painted light blue and were hung with oils by local painters whom Paolo sponsored. A beautiful Murano glass vase with a tasteful flower arrangement had pride of place on a Renaissance chest of drawers, which matched the wardrobe and stood in between two tall windows. The gilded chandelier that hung from the white ceiling could be described as a piece of old-world charm with a dash of contemporary sophistication.

Paolo was brooding on the enigma of Venetia. To him she spelt intensity and contradiction. There was something about her that was both girlish and mature; she seemed innocent and at the same time experienced. Her eyes had a look of candour, but they held a certain secretiveness when she was thinking or judging. And he felt that judging was something she often did when it came to him. She appeared to Paolo much older in mind than her peers – he had the impression she had already seen a great deal of the world.

Venetia's looks were also a contradiction. Although energy and feminine force showed in her long limbs, he had seldom seen a woman as graceful, except in the world of ballet – the allure of a temptress and sometimes the still grace of a summer flower. Who was Judd – the man whom Paolo was now sure was the reason why Venetia blew hot and cold, one moment resisting his advances and the next trembling with wanton desire under his touch? Had he been foolish to pursue her, to allow himself to dream of love with a woman so headstrong, maddening, complicated, and so utterly beautiful that he believed he could lose himself completely in the intensity of her golden eyes? He had let himself believe that she could love him too, even with the dark burden he carried...

A surge of cold, hard anger rose inside him as he thought of the way Venetia had treated him since they had first met. And now she had even called him another man's name in the heat of passion. Then again, she was not a woman to give herself lightly; no doubt Judd had been an ex-boyfriend, but a boyfriend who had meant much more than just that. Maybe he had been a lover... a fiancé... or even a husband? The one thing he was sure of: this man had hurt her and the wound was still tender. He had to shake off his biting jealousy and move on. Already he had lost enough of his life to dwell on obstacles; he didn't want to lose Venetia too. Something more powerful than he recognised drew him to her, overshadowing everything else.

There was a knock at the door.

'*Avanti.*' Paolo put down the book on the table next to him but continued staring out of the window.

A beautiful young woman with lustrous dark eyes and a mass of raven-black hair covering her shoulders came into the room.

She was clad in a revealing scarlet nightdress of shimmering soft silk, which clung to the fullness of her hips and to the sharp nipples outlined under the thin fabric.

'I couldn't sleep,' she whispered, encircling her arms about his waist, pressing her curvaceous body against him and laying her cheek on his back.

Paolo pulled away, disentangling from the young woman's embrace. 'What are you doing here, Allegra?'

Reproach clouded the fiery black eyes momentarily. 'You never have time for me any more, Paolo.'

'I have a lot on my mind at the moment.'

'That's no reason to have dinner in your bedroom,' she huffed.

'It's been a difficult twenty-four hours. I didn't get much sleep yesterday because I didn't bother booking into the airport hotel. The wreckage of the plane was supposed to be cleared last night, so I was hoping the airport would open, if not yesterday, then at least in the first hours of this morning.'

'That's no excuse,' she went on relentlessly. 'You could've had dinner with me and then gone to your room, as you usually do when you come back from your journeys.'

A quick glance at Allegra showed Paolo that she was in a reckless state of mind. He ran his fingers through his thick black hair. 'I'll make it up to you, *cara*,' he promised, trying to look contrite, 'but tonight I'm in no fit mood for company.'

Planting her hands on her hips, Allegra probed Paolo's face with her dark eyes. 'Who is this woman living at La Sirena? She says she's an architect working on some project of yours.'

'Yes, that's right.'

'What project? You never told me that you were involved in a new project.' Allegra's tone was almost aggressive.

Paolo gave her a dry smile. '*Cara*, I don't tell you everything about my work.'

'You never let me in on anything,' she seethed.

'Must we have this conversation tonight, *cara*?'

'Why are you pushing me away from you, Paolo?'

'You've always known the score, Allegra. I haven't changed my mind. You're trying to alter the nature of our relationship. I've told you before, it's not an option.'

Allegra lifted her burning eyes to Paolo's austere face, and her arms dropped to her sides. 'But I love you, *amore mio*.'

'And I care for you very deeply.' He gave a reassuring smile.

'But obviously not enough.'

'*Dio mio*, Allegra...'

'I know you well, Paolo, too well. It's not like you to bring your work to Miraggio, and it's certainly not like you to bring a woman to your home. This woman means much more to you than you're admitting.'

He turned from her and picked up a pack of cigarettes that lay on the night table next to his bed. 'What's between *la Signorina* Aston-Montagu and myself is purely business.' He did not want the young woman to read the lie in his eyes.

'She could have stayed at a hotel in Porto Santo Stefano, like the businessmen that you usually deal with.'

Paolo ripped the pack open and put the Zippo flame to his cigarette, then blew it out and replaced the lighter on the table. Smoke wreathed about his dark head.

'La Sirena was there,' he gestured. 'Sooner or later, I had to renovate that cottage. Besides, this is a long and difficult construction project which I'll be working on for months and I need an architect on hand.'

'Does this mean that the *signorina* will be staying at Miraggio for months?' Allegra demanded, her eyes wide with indignation.

'Not at Miraggio but at La Sirena, which neither impinges on your privacy nor on mine. *Dio mio*, the estate is large enough for us not to fall over each other, don't you think?'

'I saw how much of your own time you've put into renovating La Sirena, and how much money too. More than one would expect for a small cottage.'

Paolo swung round to face her, a ribbon of smoke twisting from his lips. 'Have I ever stinted on a project, or on anything else for that matter?'

'No maybe not, but you usually leave these sort of things to your employees.' Allegra trailed a finger round the edge of the table next to her, pouting and glancing up at him. 'Even Ernestina and Antonio were surprised at how pernickety you were about the planning of every detail before her arrival. Apparently, you insisted on picking the roses for the living room yourself.'

Paolo caught the rasp of jealousy in Allegra's voice. Silence fell on the vast room for a few seconds; he tossed off the remainder of the whisky in his glass.

'Allegra, this jealous scene is totally out of place. You're acting like a spoilt child.'

'She's beautiful,' the young woman remarked tonelessly.

Paolo gave her half a grin. 'Next time I'll make sure to hire an ugly person.'

She glared at him. 'Don't be flippant.'

'And you stop being unreasonable and childish.'

'You didn't breathe a word about this to me – you were underhand, which proves what I have said before, this woman means much more to you than you're admitting.'

'You can read what you wish into this, *cara*, it's your prerogative, but I'm afraid I don't owe you any explanation,' Paolo stated firmly.

Allegra came to him. With an air of possessiveness, and cat-like movements, she let her nightdress fall off her shoulders and slip to the floor, and brought her arms up around Paolo's neck, plastering her flawless frame to his length. 'I wasn't aware you went for the stiff, cold Nordic type,' she purred. 'I was under the impression...'

'Come now, this conversation is ridiculous and you know it,' Paolo disengaged himself firmly from her, picked up the nightgown and gave it to her. 'Allegra, this is embarrassing for both of us. You need to have some pride; think of your self-respect.'

There was a void of silence between them, with only the sound of the sighing sea coming in from the open window. Allegra's face was flushed and Paolo could see that she was fighting back tears as she put her nightdress back on with trembling fingers.

His face softened. 'I didn't intend to hurt you, *cara*. Contrary to what you may think, you mean a lot to me.' Slowly but firmly he led her towards the door.

Allegra pushed away from him. Her perfect breasts lifted with a deep inhalation as her chin came up proudly and she looked him straight in the face, singeing him with the little flames that shone deep in her eyes.

'You'll regret this, Paolo,' she muttered, her lower lip still trembling with the effort of controlling herself. 'You might be used to treating other women with contempt, but I'm made of sterner stuff! This Englishwoman doesn't know you the way I do. I promise you that I will make sure you eat the words you've said to me tonight,' she flared.

Wariness flickered in Paolo's eyes. 'Too bad, *cara*, if you insist on taking it that way. I have nothing to reproach myself about. You can threaten all you like, but the last thing I need tonight is a melodramatic scene from a hysterical girl.'

Allegra gave him a last vitriolic look before swanning out of the room, her head high.

Paolo sighed and returned to the window. What was he going to do with Allegra? He was used to her antics. It happened every time he came back from a business trip; but tonight she had gone too far. She was beginning to get out of hand, and he was concerned at the manipulativeness she had shown of late.

'Women!' he muttered.

His thoughts turned back to Venetia. His earlier anger towards her had evaporated and now his eyes reflected love, the love that he had finally allowed to flood his heart; and yet their cobalt depths were troubled – *the first love of my short life, since I've no memory of any other,* he thought with a self-mocking smile. But was it an impossible love? He was filled with panic for a few seconds at this prospect. For so long he had thought no woman could love someone like him, a man with no life, a shadow man; but he had snapped out of it. He had to resist such pessimism; after all he was lucky to be given a chance at love at the age of thirty-eight, he reasoned.

He wondered whether Venetia was asleep. Ernestina had said that she was in bed with a headache when she had called her for dinner. It wasn't surprising she wanted to avoid him after he had stormed off earlier, the rage of jealousy and rejection searing inside him. Paolo wanted Venetia more than he had wanted any other woman before – and he'd had women: plenty of women, of every creed and race, to furnish the void the amnesia had created in his life.

His fantasy took him to the bedroom appointed with Venetia in mind. He imagined her outstretched on the bed, and it was as if his gaze roamed over her near-naked, exquisite length, while he ran his fingers through the silken mass of her hair, something he now knew would make her tremble with delight. He imagined her mouth, parted, tempting him to sin, letting him bend her to his will and at the same time making him surrender to the erotic power she wielded. His lips wanted to trace the curve of Venetia's cheek, the line of her neck and the sensuous hollow below that beautiful throat that was made for a man's mouth. And he wanted to go beyond, to explore every secret part of her body, his tongue sliding into the depths of her aching desire.

He yearned to linger on the curves of her breasts that he had imagined beneath the flimsy dress she had worn tonight. He had wanted to peel off that dress as soon as he laid eyes on her. That dress, through which he had felt her nipples harden wantonly against his chest, almost driving him insane with an aching urge to rip it off her and take her there and then, burying himself in her softness, releasing the torrent of what they both wanted, what they both needed.

The fantasy was almost enough to let loose the primitive lust quivering beneath his skin. Now there was passion and hunger in his midnight-blue eyes. The fire in them spoke of unrealised dreams and the hopes he still nurtured. Images and thoughts skidded through his mind, reckless and wild; but they were only thoughts, and tonight he would be sleeping all alone in his bed.

*   *   *

When Ernestina brought breakfast to the cottage next morning, Venetia was already dressed and ready, wearing a lightweight, stretch twill, straw-coloured trouser suit. The few hours she had spent sketching in the sun the day before had given her skin a warm, apricot glow that was enhanced by the pale yellow shade of the ensemble.

'*Buongiorno, signorina.* I hope you're feeling better this morning. Did you sleep well?'

'Yes, I'm feeling fine, thank you. The air here clearly has an effect on me, and the sound of the sea lulls you to sleep. I had a very restful night.' *Liar*, a voice at the back of Venetia's mind whispered – she was ruefully aware that she had hardly slept. It had been a hot night, and a restless one; she had spent most of it sitting on the veranda, contemplating dark thoughts.

'Where would you like to have your breakfast this morning?'

'On the *terrazza* is fine, *grazie*.'

'*Signor* Barone will be waiting for you at ten o'clock in his office. I will take you to him when you're ready.'

Left alone, Venetia sat there, sipping her coffee and staring out at the placid Tuscan countryside, which was in such contrast to the storm carrying on inside her. She hoped that the cloud above her head would be lifted once the ordeal of her meeting with Paolo was over. Then, perhaps, they could resume their relationship civilly without either of them bringing up the awkward occurrence of the previous evening. Paolo had been a gentleman in his dealings with Venetia, but he was an Italian man with a capital M and she feared that the culture of Latin machismo to which he belonged would gain the upper hand and he would not be so forgiving. Twice before, both on Torcello and at the La Lanterna restaurant, she had given him cause for annoyance when she had swung between warm surrender and frosty rebuttals, but each time he had said nothing more and had continued on the same easy footing with her. She hoped that he might do so again this time, although her offence yesterday was in a very different category.

Still, the prospect of a meeting with Paolo was not the only reason a ripple had crossed Venetia's brow this morning. Why had she spoken Judd's name in a moment of passion, when everything in her mind and body in that instant was about Paolo and no one else? She poured herself a second cup of coffee, her thoughts chaotic, trying to make common sense conquer emotion, but failing dismally.

Venetia had spent plenty of time in the sleepless hours of the night chasing this question around in her head. Although aware that thoughts of Judd haunted her as never before, she was forced to admit that it hadn't been the memory of his caresses that had robbed her of sleep. Yes, in many ways Paolo reminded Venetia of Judd: his height, the breadth of his shoulders, the way he moved and held himself, even some of his mannerisms, like the habit he had of always blowing out the flame from his Zippo instead of just snapping it shut, and of running his fingers through his hair when restless.

But there was another thing: Venetia was aware of a poignant tenderness about Paolo, a surprising vulnerability in such a big man. She had never noticed it in Judd who, unlike Paolo, had possessed a hard edge. Judd was the soldier par excellence, trained to attack and defend, and though he had never talked about it, Venetia was sure he had killed. Both men exuded strength, but manifested it in different ways. Try as she might, Venetia couldn't understand why the memory of Judd was refusing to loosen its grip on her.

Then, on top of all this, something else had given a searing edge to the torment of her feelings. Last night, while musing on the veranda, Venetia had caught sight of Allegra in a clinging red satin nightdress making her way towards the big house from the stables. She wondered painfully how much the Italian Amazon meant to Paolo. It was impossible that any man would not be moved and flattered by the attentions of such a beautiful and assured young woman – a woman who could fire his passion as she never could. Paolo was a passionate man too. They would take each other by storm.

If Venetia had been questioning Paolo's feelings before, fearing that he did not care enough, this had removed all doubt: he didn't care at all. The realisation was a bitter blow and she felt an atrocious sense of loss resonating in the depths of her once more; but how could she feel that when Paolo had never been hers to lose? She had rejected him again and again, so she only had herself to blame if he looked for comfort in another woman's arms. *Besides, the other woman was there before you came along,* a nagging little voice reminded her bitterly, worming itself into her thoughts. All night, the misery had lain like a weight in her heart and she had sat for hours looking into the night shadows, staring at the starry sky, the cypress trees, the shimmering sea, and waiting for the first glimmers of dawn.

So it was with mingled excitement and nervousness that Venetia followed Ernestina when the housekeeper came to fetch her at ten o'clock.

That morning, Miraggio was swimming in a haze of sunshine, making its muted yellow stonework glow warmly. As the solid oak front door towered above her, Venetia was acutely reminded of its owner, as if the power of the man was reflected in the leviathan proportions of the house itself.

She went inside with Ernestina. The inside of the house sprawled round a central gallery, which stretched from one end of the building to the other. Though it had been made comfortable for present-day use, somehow Miraggio remained tinged with melancholy and steeped in romance. The scent of flowers and wax polish mingled in the wide hall, and Venetia was vaguely conscious of the beauty of the blackened oak beams, the twisting staircase with broad, shallow steps, a gleaming copper bowl of blue flowers, and the soft Persian rugs strewn about the polished floor.

'I will go and fetch *Signor* Barone,' Ernestina told Venetia as she led her into Paolo's spacious study.

The room was curved, in a U-shape, affording a 180-degree view from the eight glass picture windows that punctuated its walls, leaving the place completely exposed to the exterior and making the most of the wide-ranging, stunning vistas. It was surrounded by sea, rocks and trees, allowing the landscape to penetrate the space and become another decorative feature, and capturing as much daylight as possible, especially the last rays of the setting sun.

It was painted a luminous white, complemented by the dark wood of the antique furniture, especially the enormous Italian Renaissance desk standing in the recess curve of the room. The burgundy and golden yellow in the rugs covering the floor and the accessories on the sofa, as well as in the two armchairs placed in a corner next to the door, added splashes of colour, providing the study with a sophisticated air. This part of the house looked as if it had been given a complete facelift, compared with the darker, more gothic appearance of the rest of Miraggio. Here, with its light and airy feel and its mixture of antiques and modern design, Paolo had created for himself a contemporary space within a historical setting. It was fabulous.

Venetia was standing with her back to the door, contemplating the only painting in the room. Set on the wall behind the desk, the huge portrait was of a beautiful young blonde woman with deep-set, laughing blue eyes that looked down at her mischievously. The artist had captured the obvious *joie de vivre* that shone through her smile. *Paolo's dead wife,* Venetia thought, and her heart ached for him as she wondered how someone would get to grips with the tragedy of losing not just a loved one, but also one's own identity.

She crossed over to the opposite wall, between two of the huge windows, where floor-to-ceiling bookcases stood. Glancing round, she could see that more vast bookcases stretched up between three other windows. Clearly Paolo was a voracious reader. Running her fingers over the beautiful leather-bound tomes, she walked alongside the shelves and suddenly stopped as something caught her eye, lying sideways on the top of the books.

She picked out the small volume, a copy of *Canti* by the Italian poet and philosopher Giacomo Leopardi that she had always admired. This was an antique version of the same book Judd had bought her when they were one day browsing through the antiquarian bookshops of Charing Cross. Her heart lurched in surprise at the sight of it, and a painful reverberation coursed through her. Was Fate yet again sending her a message of some sort, pushing her towards this man who seemed to steal inside her soul at every turn?

She heard the door slam shut and her head jerked round nervously to confront the smiling face of Paolo standing behind her. Hastily she returned the book to its shelf and, caught by the gleaming eyes that stared boldly at her, Venetia's previous emotion gave way to an alarming, all too familiar reaction. She felt a disturbing tumult of her pulse and a nerve tightened at her throat. His presence seemed to shrink the room. This morning he was dressed in black: slim-fitting jeans and an open-necked shirt, sleeves rolled back, dark glasses perched on top of his forehead. It was unfair that one man should possess so much masculine appeal.

'*Buongiorno*, Venetia. I've just been out to refill the car, that's why I'm a few minutes late.' His eyes rested on her with a rakish twinkle. 'I've made you wait again, I apologise. *La puntualità è la cortesia dei re*, punctuality is the courtesy of kings,' we say in Italy. I obviously don't have blue blood running through my veins.'

Paolo's sudden appearance when she'd been so engrossed in her thoughts had caught Venetia completely off guard, startling her into the present. Hearing that deep tenor set her heart pounding; it was infuriating the way her nervous system insisted on responding to his presence. Still, with relief and some surprise, she recognised Paolo's light-hearted mood. She had feared there would be an uncomfortable uneasiness between them, given the last time they had met had been so highly charged.

Picking up the thread of humorous banter he was throwing her, she managed to smile coolly. 'I think I can forgive you, Paolo. Actually, I don't know who said that punctuality is the virtue of the bored. I can only believe that you have so much on, there are not enough hours in the day.'

'*Perfetto*, I would hate for you to wait for me impatiently,' he mocked.

'No fear of that! As we say in England, "Punctuality is the art of guessing how late the other person is going to be." I will bear that in mind next time we have a rendezvous.'

Paolo growled a half laugh, his piercing blue eyes alight with amusement.

'*Touché, mia cara*. I stand chastised.'

There was a faint pause as they both looked at each other.

'This is such a fabulous room,' she ventured, changing the subject.

Paolo grinned. He was obviously pleased by the compliment. 'When I bought Miraggio, the place was derelict. This part especially had been partly destroyed by fire and was almost falling into ruin. I tried to rebuild the house without making any modification to the original structure on the exterior, but when it came to this room I let my fantasy play.' His voice was low now, and he looked at Venetia with the hint of a challenge curling his sensuous lips.

She cleared her throat a little too loudly, trying not to look at his mouth. 'And what did your vivid imagination come up with?' she asked, a suggestion of irony in her voice. She could still only manage a glance at him.

'It was too much of a temptation to create a link between the architecture and the surroundings, and the only way was to use these big expanses of glass that would make the most of the stunning views.' His gaze was unwavering. 'Let's make ourselves more comfortable, shall we?'

They moved to the far end of the room and, slipping behind his desk, Paolo gestured towards one of the leather chairs facing it. He placed his sunglasses on the desk and for a few moments he seemed content to relax, elbows on the arms of his chair, fingers steepled in front of his mouth. He regarded Venetia through his thick black lashes with a disturbing intensity that made her feel uneasy.

Venetia fidgeted in her seat. Despite herself, her eyes kept returning to the beautiful woman in the portrait, whose smile seemed to be challenging her. *Not only must I contend with a sexy mistress, but with the memory of a beautiful dead wife.*

'You paint, don't you?'

Paolo's question interrupted her train of thought. Venetia started guiltily, and her face flushed, wondering if he had known what she was thinking and had deliberately broken the thread.

'Ye-yes,' she stammered, 'just a little. I mainly sketch – nothing very impressive, I'm afraid.'

'You must paint Miraggio for me one day, *cara*.' His voice was soft again, like warm honey, and he was scrutinising her. Venetia's blush deepened. It was maddening – why did he have this effect on her?

'I noticed a painting of the house in the cottage.'

'Yes, *La Torretta*. That was its name before I bought it, but I changed it to Miraggio.' A shadow passed over Paolo's face. His eyes sought the far horizons beyond the sunny room to the scintillating sea outside, and Venetia felt that his mind had also wandered off for a few seconds before he turned to her again, his mouth curving into a sardonic twist. 'The name seemed more appropriate.'

'It's a lovely name for a most beautiful house,' Venetia whispered, and her smile was tender for the man who didn't know that she was aware of his tragedy.

Paolo gave her a strange look, as though probing the sincerity in her eyes, before giving a slight perplexed shake of his head. 'You're a very sensitive and compassionate woman, *cara*. You fascinate me...' He stroked his bottom lip with his long index finger and it seemed as if he was about to add something, but he changed his mind.

Venetia stared back at him, mesmerised by the finger on that beguiling mouth, trying to sort out her thoughts. Her body, her heart and her senses were clamouring hungrily for him, as they had from the moment she had set eyes on him, but she still remained confused, uncertain as to what she wanted.

With an abrupt change of mood, Paolo leapt up from his chair. '*Andiamo*,' he said cheerfully. 'I was going to show you the photographs and plans of the site before taking you there but I think it would make more sense for us to visit the location first so you can get an idea of the place, and then we'll discuss it on paper at leisure. If we leave now, we'll get there before the afternoon heat and can have lunch on the way back.'

Following suit, Venetia stood up. 'That sounds very sensible,' she replied, giving him her most charming smile.

'I'll show you around the house some other time. In some parts, the architecture is very old and I think it will interest you.'

'Thank you, Paolo, I'd like that very much.'

Paolo's dashing blue Ferrari Maranello was parked at the front door, shining and ready for their escapade. Venetia was not surprised that it was one of the more expensive models around – Paolo was rich and successful after all – but she wondered at his recklessness. As far as she knew, the car was the fastest on the market. Not so long ago, she had seen a documentary on Italian television about international sport cars and the Ferrari Maranello had been at the top of the list for speed. Had the accident not left any trace of fear in him, even if he had no memory of it? He held the door open for her and she took her place in the passenger seat.

'The site is on the other side of Monte Argentario. We should be there in about half an hour,' Paolo told her, as he slid in beside her and released the latch to the roof, which slipped back noiselessly. He turned on the ignition and made the car roar twice, grinning as he did so, and they were off, leaving a cloud of red dust behind them. Seeing the unimpressed look Venetia gave him, he feigned a sheepish expression, with an almost boyish smile that made her stomach flutter. His eyes twinkled wickedly. '*Scusa*, it's all part of the fun of having this sort of toy.'

And Venetia couldn't do anything but smile too. 'Thank God for small joys!'

The smile he gave back to her was wry. 'Most people seem continually to be making arrangements to live, and never actually living. Life is too unexpected, too short, *non credi?*'

For the second time that morning Venetia's heart went out to him. *He's thinking of the accident, the loss of his wife and his memory.*

The Ferrari climbed and twisted alarmingly along the rugged coastline, and through perched villages, on roads fringed with pink, yellow, and red wildflowers. Cars and buses roared past, racing and swerving round hairpin corners. The sun was as brilliant as ever, the air clear and stimulating, and everything aflutter in the sunny breeze. The shimmering hillside, planted with olives and vines, sloped steeply down; beyond the motionless spires of cypresses stretched the blue and green hills of

Tuscany. The hollows and little valleys were brimming with whitish haze and the flat elder blossoms spread unmoving in the heat of this glorious day.

On the seaward side, they overlooked a necklace of small, sun-drenched, white sand beaches, separated by coves and craggy coral rock outcroppings. Viewed from far above, the shoreline was spectacular, with the great Tyrrhenian Sea stretching out beyond, sprinkled with islets and dotted with boats on its turquoise surface. The Ferrari tore past clusters of pastel-hued cottages framed by flowering trees, nestling in the hills that rose to windswept bluffs, where every turning had a picture-postcard view of sprawling green land, coloured villas and blue waters. Golden sunshine poured down, and Venetia's face was bright with pleasure, chestnut curls flying across her face. She loved the feel of the wind in her hair and the smell of the sea.

With a contented sigh, she leaned back in her seat. Aware that Paolo was looking at her, she blushed.

'I'm just happy being with you,' he told her, echoing her own thoughts, and she wondered if this was also his way of telling her that he knew what she was thinking, and there was no need for her to feel self-conscious. 'I hope you'll like the site. The location and the views are quite magical but to create my dream will need a lot of work. The villa is derelict and the various historic buildings surrounding it are also in very poor condition.'

'You seem to have a compulsion to restore derelict buildings.'

'I would say it's more of an irresistible urge to build, to turn waste into something worthwhile and useful. The landscape of Tuscany for the past three thousand years has been as much the result of man's work as nature's gift. If I'm able to put something back into the pot, make my contribution, why shouldn't I?'

Venetia could see it now: how this man was driven to transform things out of destruction into something new – a metaphor
for his own life, perhaps. She shook her head. 'Don't get me
wrong. I wasn't criticising you, I was just making a statement.'

'So you're not telling me off, then?' His gleaming teeth
showed a moment in his smile, as his eyes followed the
coastal route.

Venetia loved to see Paolo smile; she couldn't say why, but
somehow it was important to her that he should be happy. She
turned to face him, her lashes hiding her thoughts.

'Now would I?' she said playfully.

He turned to face her, momentarily taking his attention off
the road, and she stared into his eyes, a piercing blue, mottled
with deep flecks, and their darker midnight rim.

He flashed her a wicked grin. 'I'm not sure, *cara*. You're so
unpredictable, very much like your English weather: one minute
sunny and the next incredibly stormy.'

'I'm sorry about last night,' she stammered suddenly. 'What
I said to you – I want to apologise. I'm really so very sorry – I,
I really don't know what came over me. Judd was part of my
life once, but I haven't seen him for ten years. I would quite
understand if you didn't want to have anything to do with me
after that.'

She was aware that this breathless, apologetic rush of words
was not at all the cool and dignified speech which she had
intended if the subject had been brought up; but he had hit her
with his teasing half-reproach when she had least expected it
and it was all she could manage.

'*Non c'è bisogno di scusarsi*, no need to apologise.' His eyes had
returned to the road, his expression impenetrable, but there was
an almost imperceptible clench of his jaw. 'If this Judd left such a
lasting impression on you, maybe I should look at the issue from

a different angle and be flattered that I remind you of him,' he said gravely. 'Most of the time, people only see what they want to see. I've learnt that the power of visualising is very important in life, that is, if you want to survive. Carl Jung said: *"It all depends on how we look at things, and not on how they are themselves."* I think he had a point.'

He had stated his thoughts so simply and dolefully that Venetia felt her defences crumbling – already they had begun to fall away, even before he had appeared in his study that morning. Her certainty that Paolo was an unprincipled philanderer was slowly beginning to dissolve – only an uneasy suspicion remained, which in that moment she would have given anything to have had proved wrong.

Now they could not see the sea, as it was more or less screened by trees, but Venetia lost herself in the beauty of the hills. Around every bend in the road was a new vista: a slash of cobalt-coloured ocean through tall hedges, an old water mill, a disused olive oil factory of crumbling brick, a severe fortress church that could have been designed by Giorgio de Chirico, and houses painted in pastels as if a stage designer had created them for a seaside opera, some with laundry outside, spread to dry on bushes like huge flowers.

Venetia watched Paolo stealthily. There was that daunting air of power about him of which she had been conscious since the first day. She felt like a teenager again – a strange feeling – he couldn't be that much older than her, but something about him told her that he was a man who would welcome dependency and would never let anyone down. Despite her aversion to overpowering men like her father, it was strange that part of her craved someone to lean on.

Paolo's eyes flickered to her and Venetia hastily looked away again.

'We'll soon be there,' he remarked, as they started the descent towards a small spectacular bay of clear blue water, sparkling like a jewel at the bottom of the cliffs. 'I'm afraid we'll have to leave the car down here,' he told her as they rounded the cape and came out on to a large plateau. On it stood a little church with a cemetery surrounded by pine trees. He drew up on to a shelf of rock next to it, an area where people parked to admire the view.

Paolo stopped the car and turned off the ignition. 'We'll walk up to the site. For the time being, there's no road that leads to it,' he grinned. 'It's all part of the challenge.'

'I'm game for it,' Venetia replied, getting out of the car. What she didn't tell him was that she had done quite a lot of mountain climbing in Scotland with Judd, and climbing a steep hill wouldn't be an issue, even though she wasn't as fit as she used to be.

They went up the rough and stony lane, which hadn't been used for decades. The hillside was bathed in warm, calm sunshine. Butterflies zigzagged in and out of the beating sunlight, across the path. Yellow Banksia roses and purple wild wisteria fell in tresses and clusters over crumbling walls and broken stone columns; Venetia caught whiffs of their fugitive scent in the air as she went by. The clumps of elder and bramble were thick and caught at the twill of her slacks. She was thankful she had worn trousers; the claw-curved thorns seemed to reach out and catch their unsuspecting legs as they passed.

The silence was as tense as if a spell had been laid upon the place, and Paolo and Venetia's steps sounded loudly as they picked their way over shifting, clinking stones. At one point, Venetia almost stumbled and their fingers brushed slightly. There it was again, that jolt of electricity through her, as if she had touched a live wire, sending heated darts of excitement deep down to the apex of her thighs.

Paolo stopped still and his eyes held hers as if he had felt it too. Venetia looked for a distraction and pointed to some bits of broken wall and rubble that lay on one side of the path, almost covered by grass.

'Any idea what this is, over here?' she asked, her voice breathy.

'That's reputed to be the remains of an Etruscan shrine,' Paolo answered, his voice husky, mirroring hers. 'There was an Etruscan city at the top of this hill, as well as a Roman theatre and a Franciscan monastery.' He gestured for her to go ahead, and Venetia passed in front of him on the rocky path, aware of his eyes following her.

As they walked up the hill, pausing occasionally to cool down, they talked about the three civilisations – Etruscan, Roman and Christian – gathered there. Venetia was surprised at the extent of Paolo's knowledge about the art and the history of his country. It was as if she was peeling away new layers and discovering different sides to him. She found him more than interesting, with an eager mind. In some ways, it was as if he belonged to another period; she could quite imagine him at the time of the Renaissance, joining in with the circle of scholars that gathered round Lorenzo de' Medici, the erudite patron of poets and artists. He seemed to have an affinity with people of that era, discussing mythology and legends, dreams and fate, and such things as Michelangelo believed in.

'Where did you get all this knowledge? Surely they didn't teach you history of art at business school?' she asked.

'I spend a lot of time reading about beautiful things and like to surround myself with them. Albert Einstein said: "*The pursuit of truth and beauty is a sphere of activity in which we are permitted to remain children all our lives.*"'

'Are you saying you're some sort of Peter Pan? You don't strike me as such.' A child was the last thing she thought of when looking at him.

Paolo smiled sadly. 'Sometimes, one doesn't have the choice – it's the only way to keep sane,' he whispered.

Venetia barely caught his words; they were indistinct, as though spoken to himself.

She drew a trembling breath, realising how unintentionally insensitive she had been. Of course, Paolo had created his own Neverland, Miraggio, where he could hide in his universe of fantasy, like J.M. Barrie's character. She slanted a glance at the firm, austere profile… and again something stirred within her, an emotion akin to tenderness, but so much more. There were a hundred things Venetia wanted to ask him. She hated the thought of him being trapped inside such loneliness, but she could not admit to knowing his secret. She wished she could put her arms around him and comfort him – was this only compassion and pity she felt for Paolo, or was the strange sentiment that softened her heart towards him part of something deeper and more meaningful? Her resistance was so fragile now that she wanted more than ever to cross the narrowing divide between them, but she was too afraid to take the final step.

At last, hot and tired, they reached the crest of the hill. There, lay a vast expanse of ground that held an old Roman temple surrounded by venerable trees and, to the right of it, a huge arena. The temple was derelict; some trees had fallen across it, smashing the columns. The circles and steps of the Roman theatre lay almost intact in the sunshine. The air around it was full of the heady perfume of olives and the myriad tiny flowers almost hidden in the grass. And then much further to the right stood a crumbling villa and a chapel in beautiful pink stone, which, originally, would probably have been reached by a courtyard attached to the main structure. As far as Venetia could assess, the two buildings dated from the late nineteenth century.

The Florentine-looking villa was surrounded by its own derelict garden, with a wrecked gazebo covered in clambering ivy and brambles standing under two ancient Judas trees in flower.

Outside the garden, a viewing terrace had been built on top of a small knoll. Impressive stone steps led up to a colonnaded and paved long rectangular platform, with far-reaching views towards the Chianti countryside.

'This is incredible!' breathed Venetia, gazing around her. They had stopped among some large stones and Paolo rested his foot on top of one, folding his arms and looking straight ahead. Standing next to him, Venetia was acutely aware of the closeness of his black jeans stretched over his thigh, and deliberately looked away.

'The plans show that the palace was built over the ruins of the Franciscan monastery and that most of the mosaic murals of the chapel date from that time.' He scanned the site, squinting against the sun into the distance. 'I won this place at auction. It was destroyed during the war. No one has ever reclaimed it. My lawyer couldn't find any documents concerning the ownership of the plot, only the old plans remain. After World War Two, the Italian government seized it and put it up for auction. It was brought to my attention by my good friend Umberto, who knows that I'm always on the lookout for this sort of project.'

Venetia coloured. *His good friend Umberto…* She wondered if Paolo would still feel the same if he knew what a snake in the grass the Count had been. She wished she could warn him against Umberto, but how could she, without letting him know that she was aware of his predicament?

They walked around the site. On the ground between age-old vines, banks of wild iris were just beginning to flower, there were also some tiny daisies and forget-me-nots, bluebells, buttercups and the frailest of scarlet poppies – the very carpet of *primavera* to walk on. Despite its untidy look, the area had a kind of enchantment that was captivating.

'It's such a beautiful place,' Venetia murmured, taking in the wonder of it all. 'Botticelli must have set eyes on exactly this sort of vivid tapestry of spring. I can understand what attracted you to it. It needs a lot of work and a lot of money spent on it, but I agree, this place could make the most magical resort.'

'I'm pleased you like it, *cara*. Your opinion is important to me.' He glanced at her, his eyes burning with an emotion that made her mouth go dry. 'I told you it had been neglected for years and I know it will need much spent on it but after all, what's the use of money if it isn't for creating beautiful things? Unfortunately, I neither paint, nor do I write poetry.' He turned to look out at the scene before them. 'The only way I know to give back to art is by restoring and reinstating what has been abandoned.'

Venetia thought again of Paolo's compulsion to transform, mesmerised by the rugged outline of his face that stirred so many dark and complicated emotions within her. He then shot her a dazzling smile, making her legs turn to liquid, and nodded questioningly in the direction of the small hill.

'Shall we?'

'Yes, I think we should.'

They went up the steps to the terrace that lay in the sunshine. Here, tawny bees hovered and settled on the wild roses and honeysuckle that smothered the balustrades and columns in a tangle, the tranquil air pervaded by their fragrant scent, made stronger by the heat.

A panoramic view met them. Venetia looked around and then over the parapet. Down among the broken rocks were several fragile-looking reptilian skins that could not have been shed earlier than this spring. Venetia thought of the lovely lines from Shakespeare's *A Midsummer Night's Dream*:

And there the snake throws her enamell'd skin,
Weed wide enough to wrap a fairy in.

The idea of fairies seemed very apt in such a place at such a time. Not a stir, not a sound; she and Paolo might have been alone in the world. She could hear nothing except for the humming of bees resounding loudly in the silence. The whole place left the impression of peace and they stood there for a while, neither of them speaking, absorbing the atmosphere of another epoch.

A deep melodious bell chimed once in the church below. The sound echoed up to them, and suddenly a cloud of pigeons swept out of one of the old stone pines with a whirr of wings, circled in midstream and returned to the tree, vanishing in its dense green foliage. For a moment, Venetia turned, half startled to see that Paolo was staring down at her with unusual intentness; but he looked away and glanced at his wristwatch.

'That's the toll, "*Il tocco*" in old Tuscan dialect,' he told her. 'It's one o'clock. Bells chime only once during the day, at this time… a custom in Tuscany to remind people that it's lunchtime. Before we go for lunch, I would like you to have a look at the mosaics in the chapel attached to the villa.'

'Yes, of course – after all, that's why I'm here.'

'Is that the only reason?' he said softly, taking her hand to help her down the steps, his concentration on her face.

The sun was warm on Venetia's back; Paolo's hand was warm around hers. The place was one of the most romantic she had come across, and suddenly all she wanted was to be in his arms. She didn't answer his murmured question, instead giving her whole attention to the steps, fearful lest her legs should give way, so conscious was she of his proximity and of the thumb now sensuously caressing her wrist. It was such a light touch and yet it sent her hormones rioting as her heart skipped a beat.

Venetia knew he was watching her, felt him trying to read her mind, compelling her to look at him. Her pulse was racing, and panic quickened in her throat as she desperately tried to bring herself under control. She untangled herself from his hold and in doing so tripped, letting out a small cry.

Paolo sprang forward to stop her from falling, shielding her with his body; but as he caught hold of her waist he tumbled with her, holding on to her as they hit the ground so that Venetia landed on top of him, his strong arms tightly clamping her to him. Her mouth was inches from his, so close, too close, his sparkling blue eyes boring into hers with piercing intensity. For moments they lay still, his head and chest slightly raised from the ground, cradling her against his body. Venetia could smell the faint trace of aftershave lotion that lingered on his skin, and could hear his thick breathing; she could feel the potency of his virility pressing against her. The intimacy of that burning contact was feeding her desire like fuel poured on to a smouldering fire, which would soon erupt into flame.

Heat flooded her loins and her head span. Her heart, her senses were letting her down; she was not proof against this, against those lighted eyes, that look which she knew, the significance of his clasp, the strong beat of his heart. He had to be aware of it because she was trembling. She wanted him to reach down with that mouth and kiss her now, more than she had ever wanted anything. Paolo closed his eyes and took a deep breath. He opened them and there was a look of hesitation, and then steely resolve.

'You've had a shock, *cara*, you're trembling,' he said in a choked voice as he loosened his embrace before placing his large hands on the side of her shoulders and gently sliding her off him. 'Have you hurt yourself?' He jumped up and held a hand out to her.

Venetia ignored it, chilled by his rejection of her willing surrender, and leapt to her feet, brushing the dust from her clothes and smoothing her trousers over her hips. 'No, no, I'm fine, thank you. Are *you* all right?' she asked breezily, trying not to sound too disappointed. 'You're the one who took the brunt of it.'

A glimmer of a smile lit up his eyes, blue as the Tyrrhenian Sea. 'On the contrary, Venetia, I can put my hand on my heart and say that for me it was a pleasure.'

A pleasure? Then why hadn't he taken advantage of the moment? She'd been in his arms, ready and willing. Paolo was an experienced womaniser, and even if he hadn't been, he couldn't have failed to notice the symptoms of her need. Venetia knew that her eyes, her mouth, her whole body had been crying out for him, and he had just ignored it and pushed her away. Was this his revenge for her slip of the tongue the previous night, or was Paolo playing hard to get? Whatever the reason, Venetia felt a little humiliated. The ease with which he had been able to cut himself off hit her with a shock, and her amber eyes darkened with a mixture of desire and confusion.

Paolo stared down at her, something very serious in his gaze. Had he sensed her change of mood? But all he said was, 'Maybe we should call it a day, and I'll take you to lunch. We can come back some other time.'

'No, no, really I'm fine. I'd like to get on with visiting the rest of the site, please.' Now awash with humiliation, she wanted to move away from him as quickly as possible.

'Well then, I'd better hold on to you. Next time we may not be so lucky, *cara*. What would I tell *Signora* Lombardi if you returned with a broken leg?'

And before Venetia had time to protest, he had taken her hand again and was holding it as though he had no intention of letting it escape from his grasp. Compelled against her will, she looked up at him and met the steady gaze that held a dozen different expressions: dominant, possessive, challenging and... tender.

The old villa inside was nothing less than she had expected, with generous proportions and elaborate ornamentation. Within the ruined, beetling walls, the place was faintly lit by the diffused glow of daylight, which came through the shuttered windows with their half-open or broken slats, and shafts of sunlight that penetrated here and there through holes in the main structure and ceiling. There was a particular fragrance in the air, for the whole villa and its treasures were redolent with the glories of a past age. The faded curtains and tapestries, though magnificent and irreplaceable, were not only worn and shabby but torn. The place represented the splendour and lavishness, the decadence of earlier years.

Paolo and Venetia walked slowly over the disused floor, alive with vegetation in some places, picking their way through rubble, large portions of broken stone, some of which were still coloured with gold and pastel hues, chunks of solid wood with beautiful carvings, and fractured rods of wrought iron. She was glad of Paolo's grip now. The colour scheme in the main reception room had once been reminiscent of a spring garden on a sunny day, with wooden columns depicting exotic trees climbing from the baseboards up onto the coved ceiling. Today, the walls were stained and peeling and the superstructures rickety, with ivy, maidenhair and acanthus creeping down them, forming fantastic bowers at the entrances to the rooms.

There was a Gothic Room, a Renaissance Room and most extraordinary of all, a Moorish Room, which seemed to have been added at a later date and had a meretricious air, a shoddiness beneath its carved arabesques, a hint of dirt and gloom behind the grilled arches. Hanging on the walls were rusty, curved swords and spears. The atmosphere was secret and mysterious. The utter stillness of the place, broken by the occasional cry of a bird outside, imparted a sinister expectancy to such luxuriant silence, as though some witchery lurked behind it all. Venetia shivered.

'This is no Elysium,' she murmured, peering through the gloom, 'but more like a sinister, enchanted dwelling. I wonder who it belonged to.'

'It looks as if it's had many owners,' Paolo mused as he handled one of the unsheathed weapons, fingering the sharpness of the old worn steel.

Venetia slipped free of his clasp and preceded him through an arched door and into a charming small courtyard, where the sweet, strong, sensual scent of jasmine prevailed. The flowers were strewn on the ground like a white carpet. The arcade, its pillars with climbing wild clusters entwined over the pink marble, gave shade all around the little green space. Two dry fountains, in the form of lion heads, stood at each end. Venetia could just imagine them spouting water out of their gaping mouths. In the middle, pomegranate bushes lifted their creamy and scarlet blossoms to the full torridity of midday. A weight of heat, a brooding stillness, filled the place with a heavy peace.

'I have a great vision for this part,' Paolo told her as he moved towards one of the white marble columns in the shade of a horseshoe arch. He leaned against it, gazing dreamily out at the peaceful scene. Flicking his lighter, he lit a cigarette and then blew out the flame before inhaling deeply. 'For me, this is the home of djinns and wizards: the enchanted pavilion of Scheherazade. Have you visited the Alhambra in Granada?'

'Yes, many times – Granada is one of my favourite holiday destinations. I must have a bunch of this,' she said as she went to pick some of the jasmine. 'Jasmine and orange blossom were the two scents I loved best in Spain.'

'Jasmine is an emblem of sorrow, *cara*. You had better choose orange blossom,' he answered, smiling ruefully. 'I have plenty growing in the garden at Miraggio. I'll pick you some when we get back to the house.'

'I never knew that jasmine was associated with grief.'

'Yes, according to an Oriental legend.'

Venetia burst out laughing. 'Another one of your legends, Paolo! You're incorrigible. How do you remember them all?'

He shrugged and laughed as well, though a tinge of bitterness had crept into his eyes. 'I read a lot – I guess I'm a storybook person.'

'Tell me the legend.'

He raked long fingers through his hair. 'You really want me to tell you the legend? It's rather sad.'

'Of course! I love the way you always pull these tales out of a hat. Besides, I've always liked stories. I had a Scottish nanny who used to tell me the most incredible fairytales. She would call me her little princess and for a long time I really fancied myself as a fairytale princess – I suppose some of Nanny Horren's romantic notions rubbed off on me.'

He nodded his head. 'Very well then. Once upon a time, there was a princess who was in love with the Sun, but failed to win his heart, so she committed suicide. From her ashes rose the Jasmine Tree – the type that you see here. And because her love had been unrequited and she could no longer stand the sight of the Sun, she only bloomed at night and shed all her flowers before the Sun rose. That's why this special strain of jasmine is called Night Jasmine.'

'Indeed, it's a very sad story, but nevertheless very touching.'

Paolo regarded Venetia steadily, his eyes narrowed and

thoughtful. A muscle jerked in his jaw. 'That's why I think the rarest, most vital moments are those lived at the highest pitch of being and are of greater worth than a drawn-out fulfillment of another kind.' He paused briefly and then asked, 'Do you think someone could commit suicide out of love?'

His question took her by surprise. 'How should I know?' she tossed out on the spur of the moment, 'I've never been there.' She felt the little vein beat in her throat, which was always a tell-tale sign when she was uncomfortable.

Paolo came towards Venetia and, seizing her chin gently in between his thumb and forefinger, tilted it up to meet his steady gaze. 'Why do you lie to me, *cara*?'

She swallowed a retort, and tried to keep calm. 'I'm not lying.'

'Yes, you are. I can tell by this tiny blue vein that is beating much too quickly at the base of your throat, just there,' he said, reaching down and stroking the pulsing nerve with the same finger, then slowly removing his hand.

Venetia coloured and put her hand to her throat, trying to ignore the dangerous heat shooting down between her legs at his touch. She let out her breath, realising she had been holding it in. 'You noticed it?'

'I notice everything about you, *cara*.'

His face was still so close and she looked at him, wide-eyed.

'Men are not usually aware of little details.'

'I'm an unusual man – you must have realised that.' Paolo's face was serious, his eyes impenetrable, although perhaps there was a questioning in their depths.

Words deserted Venetia for a few seconds as her gaze locked with his, finding it increasingly difficult to sustain their penetration. He seemed to be stripping away her shallow defences. The warmth of his touch was invading her, making her feel weak and vulnerable, her limbs turning to water. She felt a sudden fear – he was so adept at reading her – what if, looking into her eyes, he was able to see more than she was prepared to divulge? Already she had given him proof of her wantonness once today.

'Why should I give you details about my life? You have hardly told me anything about yours,' she retorted, pulling away from his grasp.

Paolo's mouth quirked up as if he was trying to suppress a smile. 'Maybe that's because I think that you already disapprove of me enough.'

'It's not my business to disapprove of important clients.'

His amusement seemed to deepen. He looked mischievous. '*Dio mio, che disastro, cara. Vedo che dovrò lavorare sodo per redimermi.* My God, that sounds bad. I see that I'll have to work harder to redeem myself.'

Paolo's lighthearted tone exasperated her. Surely he was mocking her? She lifted her shoulders in an eloquent little gesture. 'We'd better have a look at the chapel,' she said coolly, hoping to sound dignified and remote.

He grinned and saluted her. 'At your orders, Captain!' His hand reached out in an attempt to take her arm, but Venetia avoided it. 'No?' he asked, raising an eyebrow.

She was tempted to respond to the compelling sparkle of fun in his eyes, but instead she shrugged again without answering.

'What's wrong, Venetia? What have I done this time? Is there no way I can please you?' His tone was still light, but there was a hint of annoyance there.

Suddenly he looked tired and drawn, sadness clouding his deep-blue eyes, and Venetia fought the twinge of compassion that twisted her heart. She didn't want to feel any sympathy for this man, whom she was finding increasingly irresistible. The emotional havoc he was creating was making her act like a spoilt and unbalanced teenager. She didn't like how she sounded and she liked even less the way she felt. Still, she gave him a wan smile.

'Sorry, I know I sound horribly ungracious,' she said, a little unsteadily. 'It must be the heat that's making me fractious.'

'You're tired, *cara*, but you still want to go on?'

'Yes, please, if we're going to discuss the project on plans later, I need to at least have an idea of the work I'm going to be involved in.'

Paolo winked at her. 'It's your English upbringing that speaks here – never give in to weakness, eh? What do they call it... *Stiff*?'

'Stiff upper lip,' she laughed, and the coldness she had been at pains to show him abruptly vanished.

'So let's go and discover this deteriorating jewel which you will turn into a fabulous treasure. I have not been to see it since the auction.'

Through a somewhat ruined gate at the side of the villa, they entered a walled courtyard. It was a great neglected space, over-grown with lanky weeds, its irregular ground covered with stones and bushes. In front of them was the chapel, which, from close up now, looked much bigger than Venetia had thought. The entrance, locked by a tall and handsome carved door, needed extensive restoration; it had lost its original lustre and there were deep cracks in the wood. Venetia didn't think it was restorable. Pity it had to be replaced – the workmanship was of a class that was difficult to find in this modern age, where machines had taken over man's skilled work.

Paolo produced a large wrought-iron key that was also very fine, and unlocked the door. 'You'll see that the chapel is still in quite good order in comparison with the rest of the place, prob-ably because it has been kept locked all these years.'

Indeed, the chapel was a jewel. It was almost intact except for the impressive mosaic murals that adorned its walls and the statues of saints placed on pedestals high above Paolo's and Venetia's heads, with painted and lavishly decorated robes that had faded with time.

The sun that shone with broad, warm midday beams through the richly coloured windows tinged the marble colonnades with an effective glow, half illuminating them, drawing lines over the marble floor, and giving grotesque effects of light and shade, and mystery to corners full of soft tones and shifting colours.

'It's a rare treasure you've found here, Paolo. I'm surprised the Government put it to auction and didn't turn it into some sort of monument open to the public.'

'In my opinion, it's too bitty and too untidy for it to be of interest as a historic site. Still, it's the exact project I needed. My friend Umberto is the one who heard about it and tipped me off. He, of course, moves in the right circles and is very influential. He's a great networker – I think he pulled a good many strings. I owe him.'

Venetia felt the blood rise to her face. She was so angry she almost blurted out, *he's not your friend but a deceitful and treacherous bastard*, but it was not her place to interfere in Paolo's life. She was here on a job, she reminded herself, and that was all.

'You look angry, *cara*.' Paolo interrupted her thoughts. 'Have I said something wrong?'

Venetia placed her hand on his arm, and stared up at him in earnest. She had to say something; she couldn't just leave it at that. '"*A man is his own easiest dupe, for what he wishes to be true he generally believes to be true.*" Not my words – Demosthenes.'

'Why do you say that – you don't like the Count?'

'No.'

Paolo glanced sideways at her. 'Yet I know that he's very taken with *you!*'

'That really doesn't make a difference,' she retorted a little too quickly.

'He's been discourteous towards you?'

Venetia flushed self-consciously. 'I'd prefer not to talk about it.'

Paolo laughed. 'He can be very enterprising with women sometimes, and I have yet to meet a woman who complained about Umberto's boldness.'

'Well, to take your lead, let's say that I'm an unusual woman.'

'I've noticed.' The blue eyes held mild amusement. 'Still, I'm very pleased to hear that you haven't succumbed to Umberto's famous charm. On the whole, people – men and women – find him irresistible.'

Bully for them, Venetia thought, but refrained from speaking her mind further.

'One day you will open your heart to me, *cara*?' he asked softly.

'*Chi lo sa*, who knows!' she said lightly, suddenly feeling frivolous. 'And now that I've seen the chapel, you can take me to lunch – I'm starving.'

'Excellent idea, *carrissima. Andiamo!*' Paolo gave a cheerful smile, tucking his arm through hers. Deciding to go along with his mood, Venetia allowed him to do so.

CHAPTER 8

Paolo took Venetia to lunch at a small restaurant in a picturesque resort village called Baia Delle Onde Mormoranti, along the coast outside Porto Santo Stefano. Notched into the rocks, its curiously shaped houses leaning together stood at the head of a little creek filled with sailing and fishing boats, all of which blended perfectly together with the low rocks, the vineyards, olive groves and the pine trees on the headlands.

La Mezza Luna was a tiny restaurant of whitewashed stone and red tiles set on the pale gold sandy beach, surrounded by palm trees and overlooking water that glittered in the sunshine like wet cobalt paint. A lean-to loggia adjoined the building, with a bamboo matting roof providing shade from the hot afternoon sun. Grape vines were trained from large earthenware pots up each corner post, their green tendrils reaching through the bamboo, and eight tables with green checked tablecloths and bamboo armchairs with round green cushions stood underneath.

The friendly owner, who to Venetia looked as if he had stepped out of a Sergio Leone spaghetti western, greeted Paolo effusively. It was almost three o'clock and most of the customers had gone, but he assured them that there would be no problem conjuring up one of his specialities for the pretty *signorina* and for his friend, Paolo.

'Just settle yourselves at a table and *pronto*, I will bring you some *antipasti* and a bottle of *vino Ernestinato*, our very special house wine, while you wait for your lunch.'

They sat down at one of the little tables overlooking the bay, its deeply etched coves rimmed by sheer cliffs. Far off, lay the harbour of Porto Santo Stefano bathed in syrupy golden light with hundreds of sailboats dozing in their slips under the luminous blue Tuscan sky.

Venetia wrinkled her nose slightly and smiled. 'How do you dig out these quaint places?' she asked Paolo once the restaurateur had disappeared into the kitchen at the back of the restaurant.

Paolo grinned. 'Simple – I like to eat well. Do you cook, Venetia?' He made the question sound somehow intimate in a way she found confusing. Sitting to the side of her, rather than opposite, his nearness was disarming.

'Yes, but I don't have the opportunity to do much cooking nowadays. I live alone and I usually grab something to eat in town before going home in the evenings, or I go out for dinner with friends.' She always filled her life with work and nearly said so, but now it felt uncomfortable to admit it.

He gave her a quizzical look, as though he was going to ask a question, but the owner of La Mezza Luna was already coming back with a bottle of wine, a bottle of sparkling water, a loaf of *ciabatta* bread and a delicious-looking plate of what he announced to Venetia as *Caponata a la Siciliana*.

'*É completamente diversa da qualsiasi altra caponata servita in Italia*, it is completely different from any other *caponata* served in Italy. It is the king of *caponata*, the original Sicilian recipe which was handed down from my great-grandmother.'

'Mario is from Sicily – most of the dishes he serves here are Sicilian dishes that you won't find in Northern Italy,' Paolo explained.

Venetia's interest was piqued. 'I've had *caponata* in Venice and in Florence. How does this one differ from the others?'

'In addition to the aubergine, the capers, the olives, raisins, tomatoes, onions and pine nuts, my great-grandmother's recipe includes octopus, shrimp and grated tuna roe,' Mario answered, smiling proudly. 'It is a more, *come si dice...* aristocratic version of the dish.'

Venetia had great difficulty in keeping a straight face. 'It really sounds very original.'

Mario poured Venetia a glass of wine with a quick flourish. 'And for you, Paolo, a glass of sparkling water, as usual?'

Paolo flicked a glance at him. 'Yes, yes, I'm driving.'

As usual. Venetia noted the two words, and she had the sudden impression that Paolo seemed a little uneasy now. This must be one of his special rendezvous haunts. Who did he bring here – his Venetian girlfriends, Allegra? In her mind's eye she saw the young woman as she had espied her the night before, clad in a bright-red satin nightdress. Painfully aware that she had no right to be jealous, she hadn't the shadow of a doubt that the Italian beauty had been on her way to meet Paolo at the house. However unreasonable it seemed, the thought of him with another woman suddenly made her feel ill. Still, she mustn't dwell on that now, she told herself. She should make the most of this beautiful afternoon.

'I will go and prepare you the *arancini*. You will not get it in any other restaurant in the North.' Mario placed the bottles neatly in the centre of the table. 'The Italians consider *arancini* a street food, but it's a national Sicilian emblem, *veramente deliziosi!* I promise that you will not be disappointed.' And with that he swivelled on his heel and hurried back to the kitchen.

'Mario comes from an old family of Sicilian fishermen.' Paolo broke off a piece of ciabatta. 'He spends eight months of the year down here, but goes back to Sicily for the winter. His daughter and her husband run a *trattoria* there, which is just as successful as La Mezza Luna and has the same name. You would never think that his daughter is Sicilian – she's as blonde as he is dark, with pale blue eyes. She must have taken the colouring of her Norman ancestors.'

Was Mario's daughter another of Paolo's conquests? Venetia's heart squeezed unreasonably again. *Don't be ridiculous,* she chastised herself: just because Paolo had remarked that the woman was blonde and blue-eyed didn't mean that he had carried on an affair with her. *And even if he has… since when do you stoop to such lowly emotions? Are you so insecure?* She had no right to any personal interest in Paolo, she reminded herself.

Paolo spread some *caponata* on a slice of *ciabatta* and offered it to Venetia. 'Taste this and take a sip of Mario's very special *vino Ernestinato*. According to Mario, his *rosé* would warm the heart of a statue.'

'What am I supposed to glean from that remark?' Venetia blurted out the question without thinking and was suddenly aware that she was being too touchy and that Paolo's statement contained nothing personal. She wished she could eat her words but it was too late; she had just invited intimate comments, and Paolo didn't disappoint.

He gazed lingeringly at her. 'How can I compare you to a statue, *cara* – a fierce enchantress, maybe, but never a statue.' His voice was low, the look in his eyes dark and deep where anything might lurk for the woman drawn into them. 'I've felt your body tremble in my arms like a storm coming. Whatever you show to me on the outside, I know is not how it is on the inside.'

Paolo took Venetia's hands in his, and held her fingers tightly until she could have cried out. His eyes had kindled and were searching hers intently. 'You've bewitched me completely.

Be mine, Venetia. I want you with all my heart, with every fibre in my body… with every breath. *Dio mio,* I need you! Be my root, my anchor.'

He sounded hoarse with emotion and she was profoundly moved by the wistful note of longing in his almost desperate words. The expression on his face, as he struggled with something inside him, pleading for her understanding, tugged at her heart as she confessed in silence that she really cared for this man. A tremor surged through her body; she came alive at the mere contact of his hands, and remembering the sensations of how his touch had indeed made her tremble, she wanted to break apart. Whatever the sentiments that possessed him now, they were genuine, strong and profound. Yet she needed more. She sat there, tense and still, as if mesmerised.

'But how can I be yours when I know nothing about you?'

'What do you want to know?'

'You tell me. Isn't there anything I should know? Up until now you've always been a blank page.' She was willing him to confide in her, to confess what she already knew about him.

Paolo's eyes settled on Venetia's face steadily. 'You're right, *cara,* there's plenty you don't know about me, but trust me when I tell you that it's of no importance – I want to start my life with you.'

His gaze slid from her eyes to her lips with a fire that made her burn with uncontrollable longing. 'I've had this strange feeling ever since I met you that we're meant for each other, that we've been together in another life. When I hold you in my arms, it's as though you've always been mine.'

Venetia's lashes flickered; she caught her bottom lip in small white teeth. Paolo's words echoed her own feelings. Surely this meant something? Somewhere deep inside her she had instinctively recognised him as the man of her life… the only man who could replace Judd in her heart. Her mind and body locked horns; she would be swept away if her body won. She craved his arms about her, craved his kiss, the feel of his heart beating hard against her, his mouth on her breasts and the feel of him shuddering strongly inside her, even just once – but it would never be *just once*! Still, despite the temptation to give in to this desperate yearning for him, if only once, she stifled the impulse with a supreme effort of will; her pride wouldn't allow her to surrender to a man who, just now, hadn't even pronounced the word 'love'.

Venetia laughed shakily. 'How many women have you said these beautiful phrases to, Paolo?'

'I have teased, I've flattered and I've had sex with many women, that's true, *carina mia*... but I've never wanted to – and never have – made love to anybody as far as I can remember.'

This was the opportunity Venetia had been waiting for. Was he going to tell her about his amnesia?

'As far as you can remember...? Do you have such a short memory, Paolo, or have you had so many women that you have lost count?'

She saw him start, saw the quick colour rise under his tanned skin; he winced, as though her question turned a knife in an agonising wound. He had always known how to read her, knew what she was saying. Jerking his head back, he ran fingers through his hair in a nervous characteristic gesture. There was a long silence while Venetia waited for his answer.

Finally, he looked full at her and spoke in a barely audible voice.

'How long have you known, *cara*?'

'Not that long.'

'Who told you? Not many people know about it.'

'Your good friend, the Count.'

Paolo's face whitened, though his eyes were dark. '*Umberto?*'

'Himself.'

Paolo's hands clenched. '*Che stronzo!*' He gritted his teeth. 'Just let me get my hands on that bastard!'

Mario came back at that moment with a large plate of golden brown rice balls surrounded by finely ground meat, egg and cheese.

'*Eccola,*' he said as he placed the plate in the middle of the table. '*Arancini* are as typical of Sicily as hot dogs and apple pie are of America.' He seemed not to notice Paolo trying to regain control of himself but instead looked at Venetia with appreciative eyes. 'I have made these freshly for you, *signorina.*'

Venetia helped herself to an *arancini* and was just about to bite into it when Paolo's now calmer voice cautioned, '*Sono molto caldi, fai attenzione a non scottarti,* be careful not to burn yourself. When they're piping hot, as these are, it is better if you split them like this,' he said taking one, breaking it in half and giving it to her.

Venetia nibbled at it gingerly. 'This is amazing!' she exclaimed. 'What is it made of?'

'The *arancini* are usually made with creamy risotto, or any other day-old rice mixed with leftovers,' Mario explained, clearly pleased at her curiosity. 'In these I have put some olives, tomatoes, ground veal, onions of course and a pinch of saffron, which makes all the difference. But don't fill up on them, they are only *antipasti!* The next dish is *finochio con sarde,* fennel with sardines served with homemade *pappardelle* pasta.'

As soon as Mario had disappeared back into the kitchen, Paolo's eyes narrowed.

'What else did that *mascalzone* tell you?'

Venetia did not speak; she flushed, feeling both uncomfortable and vulnerable, not wanting to remember any more of the unsavoury episode than necessary, and certainly not wishing to relay any of it.

Paolo regarded her anxiously. 'Ah, it's he who told you that I'm nicknamed *l'Amante delle Quattro Stagioni* in some circles.' His lips curled into a bitter smile, and he leaned back in his chair on one elbow, tapping his lighter distractedly on the table. 'Society is cruel, Venetia, one must not believe everything one hears.'

'Can you deny that you pursue women only to get them into your bed and that you drop them as soon as you tire of them?'

'No, Venetia, I cannot deny that, but I can defend myself. These women you talk about, they always know the score from the very beginning – sex without ties. Like any normal man, I have needs. I have no attachments, and since my accident I've lived for the moment. There's been no reason not to... until now.' He turned his lighter over and over between his fingers and regarded her watchfully.

No attachments? Liar! her heart screamed out as she stared at him silently. *And how about the luscious Italian woman in a red satin nightdress who warmed your bed last night, and probably every night when you're at home?*

'You must believe me, *cara*, when I tell you that I was a different man before I met you. To live without a dream is a frightening prospect,' he went on huskily, tracing his lip with his finger and drawing her attention to his mouth again. She wished she could look away. 'Meeting you has given me a lust for life again. You're the sunshine that has brightened my sad, dreary days. Thanks to you, I dream, I hope and believe in love, and in all the wonderful things that the world has to offer. We are made by our past, and mine is gone... but when I'm with you I'm not anxious about not having a history any more. All that was yesterday is unimportant, because today and tomorrow belongs to me... to us.'

Still Venetia did not speak. She tried to summon the energy to tell him that it would never be *us* for them, but all she could manage was a small sigh that contained her stifled longing and frustration. Paolo's manner of talking to her was making her weak and she could not afford to be so.

He was staring at her, the pupils of his eyes dilating until they filled the blue irises. Venetia could read an emotion in them that she couldn't fathom. He sounded genuine enough... but no, he was an expert at handling women, his desire for her was a fleeting thing... he would soon tire of her and cast her aside as he had other women. She must not let passion cloud her judgement; if she listened to him any longer she would be lost.

Venetia half turned away from him and looked down at her hands. They were kneading one against the other as though they had a life of their own.

Paolo's eyes narrowed. 'Why are you running away from me, *cara*? There's something about me that worries you; that puts you on the defensive. I'm not a wolf, and you are definitely not a lamb.'

He had such a picturesque way of putting things and his words were remarkably apt: she might not be a lamb, but yes, she felt on the defensive because when he spoke like this, it was more of herself that she was afraid than of Paolo. Logic told her that the sensible way forward would be to talk this whole situation out; to admit to the attraction between them and untangle this mess. After all, she still had to work with Paolo; if she couldn't find some reasonable and workable solution to the confusing way things stood with them, how could she carry on being so close to him, day in day out? It should be so simple to confront him about Allegra, yet something deep inside her feared his answer, and she knew that emotionally she simply wasn't strong enough to do so.

Mario was back with a steaming plate of pasta. He frowned as he noticed that the plate of *arancini* had gone almost untouched. 'You've hardly eaten any of my *arancini! Non sono di vostro gusto?* You didn't like it?'

Paolo grinned at the restaurateur. 'You must forgive us, Mario. We're just beginning to get to know each other and we've been lost in conversation.'

'*Ah, l'amore, l'amore,*' Mario sighed and shook his head. '*Persino quando sei innamorato non puoi vivere solo di amore e acqua fresca,* even when you're in love, you cannot live on love and fresh water.'

Venetia felt her face flame. How dare Paolo make such an implication?

'I hope you will honour this dish.' Mario winked at Paolo. 'Sardines, like most oily fish, are well known to be a powerful aphrodisiac – *buon appetito!*'

'How could you let Mario believe that there's any romance going on between us?' Venetia whispered urgently as soon as the restaurant owner had turned his back.

Paolo gave her a half smile as he sipped his water. 'Is that not what's going on between us, *carissima?*'

'Certainly not,' she retorted haughtily – she had to defend herself against the mad feelings that were invading her.

'*Sì*, we're flirting, finding out what makes the other person tick.' His eyes narrowed almost to slits – Venetia was beginning to know that cat-like look, playful and yet edged with danger – and just to prove to her how wrong she was, he leaned over, lowered his head and took her lips with his in a couple of biting kisses that sent a tremor through her limbs, and her pulse racing.

'We kiss and arouse all kind of vibrations, light all sorts of fires and we burn, *sì?*' he murmured, looking at her mouth, his face still close to her. 'There is no shame in it. A man and a woman should feel this way when with each other, as though they need nothing else but to be together, alone in a world made up of their dreams.' He dug his fork into his pasta and began to eat slowly, watching her, his smile subtle, with a mixture of challenging amusement and something far darker.

Venetia had to look away from him, her teeth clenched hard as she fought for control. His words were kindling the glowing embers trembling inside her that threatened to erupt into flames, despite all her attempts to stifle them. She despised herself for what she felt towards Paolo. She didn't even know what it was, only that he exerted a hypnotic power over her and she had lost all of hers to him. He only needed to look at her for her mind to cloud and her body to wish to surrender completely.

They ate their pasta with *finochio con sarde* in silence, listening to the sounds of the waves as they carried on their own flirtation with the shore and the breeze gliding across the water and through the palms, causing them to sway back and forth and rustle like smothered footfalls.

They ended their meal with a Sicilian *gelato*, ice-cream flavoured with *grappa*. Mario told them that ice-cream probably originated from Sicily, because during the Roman times, relays of runners used to bring snow down from Mount Etna to be flavoured and served to rich patricians. His little anecdotes between each new course lightened the atmosphere and by the time they were having their coffee the tension between them had calmed down.

It was almost sunset when they pulled into the drive at Miraggio. Paolo went round to Venetia's side and opened the car door for her. 'Would you like to have a tour of the house, or would you prefer to wait until dinner?'

Venetia climbed out of the car. 'Now would be perfect. I'm not used to eating so much at lunch. I would prefer to skip dinner if you don't mind.'

'Would you like Ernestina to bring you a tray at La Sirena?'

'No, really, you're very kind and I have still to finish the wonderful bowl of fruit that was set out for me in the cottage. Thank you.'

Antonio, with Rufus in tow, came over to take the keys and park the car. The dog contented himself to sniff at Venetia, but this time didn't growl as he had on her arrival.

'Please tell Ernestina that there will be no dinner tonight, and I will have a *panino al prosciutto* and a cup of coffee in my study.' Paolo stood back from the car.

'But *signore*, Allegra has…' the caretaker protested.

Paolo was quick to interrupt him before the man was able to finish his phrase.

'I have urgent work that needs to be attended to.' His tone was cutting and allowed for no argument.

Something akin to anger sparked in Antonio's eyes as he turned to look at Venetia, but it was gone in a flash, and he climbed into the car and drove off in the direction of the garage. The man resented her; she had felt his reticence when she had first arrived and by the looks of it nothing had changed. Like his niece, he probably regarded her as a threat to what must be a very comfortable situation.

Allegra, the dusky beauty that furnished Paolo's nights, was no doubt waiting impatiently for him, Venetia told herself. *Well, at least it seems as though he doesn't need the young Amazon's services tonight.* And though her scalp had prickled at the sound of Allegra's name, suddenly her heart felt light and warm.

The imposing arched wooden front door was wide open to let the late afternoon sunshine in, as Paolo led her through the hallway. The house itself, Venetia assessed, was half manor, half fortress and was fascinating. In the morning she'd had a glimpse of the hall; now she saw the spacious interior in all its splendour with its vaulted and cupola ceilings, archways and beautifully etched cornices, and the various levels and areas connected by passages and corridors. The rooms were simple and comfortable with polished old mahogany and glowing bits of silver, glass and china; the subtle nuances of the pale-hued walls made them look unusual in their shape, arresting, and the elegant, tall narrow windows ensured they were full of light. Large vases and bowls of flowers added daubs of bright colour to the more sedate furnishings.

It was a romantic house, far larger than it appeared at first glance, and yet built for a patriarchal life and a self-contained one. It was not unfriendly, but it guarded its secrets; very much like its present owner, Venetia thought, who himself was open and friendly yet gave an impression of reserve, a man whose smile was frank but also grave and serious. Everything glittered with squeaky cleanliness; for someone who never entertained, Paolo's home was surely well looked after and that fact in itself was as much an enigma to Venetia as the master of the house. Was he so damaged by the loss of his past and the people in it that he now had no desire to build a future, and no impulse for the company of others?

Listening to Paolo recount the background to every piece of furniture and the story behind each ornament, Venetia was amazed at the difference in him. As at the site that morning, he had thrown aside his armour of coolness and became passionately alive, vibrating with the force of his emotion almost as if he was talking to her about love. The furniture was real to him, the ornaments and paintings were full of colour and the fabrics that he touched were alive. It didn't surprise her – Paolo had substituted art and its history for his own history; as well as collecting stories to populate his imagination, he had furnished his life with beautiful things to compensate for the lack of beautiful memories. It was understandable and she was full of sympathy for him.

At the door to his study, as they came to the end of their tour, Paolo smiled.

'It's six-thirty. Will you join me in a glass of wine? I always have one at this time.'

He opened the door to the room Venetia had sat in that morning. It was now bathed in the incandescent colours of the most dramatic sunset as the great red ball sank below the horizon and an array of magnificent tints painted the sea and flushed the sky. It took her breath away and she was drawn into the room, spellbound by the enchanting glow, dazzled for a brief moment by its luminosity.

Unintentionally, Venetia's eyes moved up to the painting that dominated the room. It was crowned with a light that was almost unreal. She met the enigmatic gaze and shivered – the beautiful blonde looking down at her seemed very much alive.

'My wife,' Paolo announced to her in a matter-of-fact way that took Venetia a little aback. 'She died in the accident which robbed me of my past. I don't remember her – for me it's as if she never existed.'

He took out a couple of glasses from a drawer in his desk and poured Venetia a glass of white wine from a bottle that stood in a bucket of ice on a small table next to it. 'I don't grieve for her as much as I grieve for my lost life. We were on our honeymoon. She was driving, so I don't even have the privilege of feeling guilty – I might as well be dead.' His voice hardened as he spoke.

Venetia's heart gave a sharp twist as if she had been stabbed. An overwhelming and unexpected emotion surged within her, frightening in its implication. Not for the first time that day she felt a passionate desire to put her arms around Paolo and comfort this lonely, unhappy man. She looked at him, her eyes wide and tender, the golden lights in them quenched, their colour deepened. Still, she fought it down, refused to recognise it for what it was.

'You mustn't talk that way, Paolo. Look around you – you've created so much beauty. You're talented and creative – a visionary who has plenty to offer.'

'You mean a mirage. A ghost,' he said, without looking at her. His eyes had taken on a wintry expression as he gazed, unseeing, at the view of the indigo sea that stretched to infinity beyond the window, while he turned the stem of his wine glass round and round in abstracted fingers. Venetia saw the lines around his mouth deepening, and the tragic weariness steal back into his face, which earlier had been relaxed and amused, almost youthful.

'Not at all! How old are you? Thirty-five? Thirty-six?'

'Thirty-eight, going on ninety.'

'Nonsense! You're a passionate man with plenty to live for. What will all those women who pine after you do if you desert them?' Venetia spoke with more lightness than she felt.

Paolo turned his gaze upon her.

'You've not been through what I have, and God forbid that you ever will, Venetia. You can still play with words and play with feelings, but I've been broken. Life has maimed me inside and out. The truth is that all the experience and substance that was once me is now dead, and I can't remember how anything feels, or *should* feel. I can't go hunting with the hounds of imagination any more… I don't want the fine flowers of life. Something has gone with my memory – the carefree big-heartedness of youth. But when I met you, I glimpsed a way out of this abyss, a glimmer of hope. All I know now is that you have lit up the darkness with a dazzling light and the whole current of my being flows to you. It's you, and you alone, who can make me whole again.'

He paused. Dusk darkened the room and the silence was heavy.

Venetia shook her head. Paolo's hard voice made her realise the pain that drenched him, and at his slightest movement a strained trembling came over her. The pain etched into his features was too raw to be feigned – this man was not playing games.

'Of course, if you persist in being blind and pushing me away,' he said, 'I will not pursue you any more. I'll be your friend as you asked from me once, and I'll try to quench my thirst at more accessible streams.' He laughed a rough, deep, humourless sound that shimmied its way to the far end of Venetia's soul. 'I've been doing it for so long now – bitter water they might be after you, *cara*, but I will have no other solution, and I will "*dream the rest, and burn*" for you, "*the secret food of my fires unseen.*"'

Venetia sighed, her eyes on the darkening sea. 'Oh, please, don't talk like that,' she cried out, looking at his face set in such rigid lines. She knew the poem well, 'When Passion's Trance is Overpast', of which Paolo had just cited a couple of lines. It was one of Shelley's miscellaneous works that she loved so well.

'You're right, *cara*,' he said, suddenly springing to his feet. 'The sun has gone down and it will soon be dark. Besides, I'm boring you with my maudlin talk. I get into this mood from time to time – you must ignore it when it happens. It never lasts long anyhow.' He smiled at her. 'Come, it's been a long day and you must be tired. I'll walk you back to the cottage.'

Venetia didn't answer – there seemed nothing more that could be said, or at least, nothing else she felt able to say. As they came out of the house there was a charcoal line on the horizon where the sun had struck on to the sea, and along the dark grey strip a fishing-boat sailed westward, its pointed sails black against the still pale blue water. Mysteriously chilling to the spirit, it filled her with unreasoning melancholy, as though all the beautiful things of life were being borne away upon the waste of the ocean in that little craft. A breeze got up and made a steady rustling noise, driving along the path that led behind the house to La Sirena, and tint upon tint of grey enveloped everything as they walked slowly back.

*   *   *

Venetia woke up with a hoarse cry. She was sitting up in bed, panting, her eyes wide open, disorientated for a few moments. Her hair clung to the back of her neck and her head was pounding as if a hammer had been taken to it. Although the windows were wide open, the room seemed hot and airless; her lips were parched, her skin was warm and tight and her chest felt heavy as if her heart was made of lead. She couldn't remember the details of her nightmare, but she knew that it was about death, and that it concerned Paolo.

Sliding out of bed, she went to the bathroom. She splashed her face under the cold tap and poured a glass of water to calm herself. The day she had spent with Paolo had been emotional, to say the least, and it had deeply affected her. He had bared his soul to her with touching fervour and she had found his words disturbing. Could she not lay herself open to him too, and trust in his response? Why could she not bring herself to be his salvation?

Listening to Paolo, Venetia had feared for him. She had always considered him a handsome man – not good-looking in the traditional sense, but distinguished, charismatic and hard. Yes, he could look extremely hard at times. But there was also a suggestion of melancholy, even of tragedy, which quickened her interest. Ignore it as she may, Venetia couldn't fool herself any longer: she was falling in love. The fact that Paolo reminded her of Judd was neither here nor there. Something of the one was present in the other, of that she was sure, and that certain something seemed disturbing, although she was not clear why; but deep and tender feelings had been resurrected that were as much part of her as her own mind and body. In the past, after Judd had gone, when she had found the painful remembrance of such thoughts and feelings coming, she had done her best to put them away. But now she knew that although this might have been the reason for her initial attraction to the owner of Miraggio, there was a sea of difference between the two men.

There had never been anything tragic about Judd, nor the slightest hint of vulnerability; he was a soldier in every sense of the word. His vigour and courage had been part of what she'd admired about him. Paolo was strong too – you had to be strong to have suffered such terrible misfortune and still manage to adjust, to be successful, to have a life. But he was also fragile, and it was this that made him touching, human.

Venetia glanced at her watch. It was five-thirty, almost dawn. She was still feeling restless and hot; maybe a cold shower would cool her down and make it possible for her to sleep for a couple more hours. The water felt lovely and refreshing on her skin, as it slowly washed away the tension of the previous day.

Stepping out, she put on her bathrobe and padded to the veranda to watch the dawn come up over Miraggio. She stood leaning against the stone balustrade, her back to the countryside, looking towards the sea. There was no horizon, nothing yet but the soft dusk everywhere so that she couldn't tell for a while where the sky began. Then, oddly, the sea became darker before the first streaks of colour lit the sky. Venetia wondered what created the unearthly greens and blues and mauves in the sky before the first bars of gold heralded the sun.

Gradually, moment by moment, as she watched entranced, the pale translucent green grew more lovely till at last it seemed as though all tender colours – shiny rose, wisteria, pale blue, the transparent purity of emerald – played on the shimmering fields of the sea, and touched the liquid curves which stretched away and away. Those softly changing colours altered dreamily, as if a divine artist were entertaining kindred spirits with a magnificent show before allowing the sun to bathe the world in molten gold. The array reached up to the horizon and overflowed, spreading over the sea, blotting out the entire colour with sheer light. Colour and light and space... never could one drink enough of such beauty, Venetia thought, as she bathed in that golden glow with her hair rippling gently across her shoulders in the early morning breeze.

As she prepared to go back into the house, her attention was suddenly riveted by a figure standing nearby, across from the cottage. Dressed in a navy-blue silk robe, Paolo was leaning against the trunk of a tree smoking, bathed in auroral light, looking positively unearthly, like a powerful Roman god in an ancient, timeless myth. What was he doing there at this hour? Was he restlessly finding a moment of beauty, as she was? How long had he been there? She hadn't noticed him when she had first come on to the veranda. He seemed to be in a world of his own. Had he seen her?

And then he turned and looked up to where Venetia was standing and she caught her breath. His presence was so potent that it was as if a current passed directly from him to her. Sometimes one moment can cut off a whole period from another and so it was now; that breathtaking instant held an almost mad exhilaration as though the colours, the scent, the entirety of nature, were intensified for her. And finally, as their eyes met, she realised that a veil had been abruptly dropped: there was no mask, no barriers, nothing more between them but their fire, and their hunger for each other.

Nothing stirred at this early hour: it was as if some spell had been laid on this unworldly scene that no one had the power to break. Paolo's eyes were still fixed on hers. The silence deepened; the blush of daybreak seemed more brilliant. What beautiful danger was this, rolling in with the dawn? Some wave of strange life seemed to carry them far from anywhere they had ever been and almost drowned them in its gold, glowing splendour before it lifted them on to an unknown shore. Scarcely breathing, they gazed at each other. The leaves in the garden fluttered in a sudden sigh of the breeze, whispering their mysterious message. Venetia turned and went back in, knowing that *he* would come to her.

And then Paolo was standing there, inches away from her in the sanctuary of the open door, staring hesitantly at her, mutely asking, *are you sure?* Venetia swayed a fraction towards him, her whole body tensing almost to the point where it was impossible to move, forgetting all she had planned: her determination to be cool, composed and a little haughty towards him. *You can still change your mind,* she told herself. *It's not too late, not if you react now, tell him to leave.*

Paolo pushed his hand through his hair and slowly crossed the short distance between them, his eyes gentle with concern, the features that had seemed so hard to her in the library last night now softened into a questioning frown as he looked searchingly into her face. She watched him, eyes locked on his, still paralysed. The heat of his body was producing a scent, subtle yet wildly male, prompting a pulse of startled recognition along Venetia's senses. His hand reached up and touched her hair as though he was touching something beautiful and rare. She couldn't help but close her eyes momentarily and lean in to his hand as her nerves awakened and sang.

'*Dio mio, si cosi bella,*' he whispered, his face transformed with awe, making Venetia's heart flutter helplessly.

Lifting wide amber eyes again to the search of his piercing blue gaze she reached up for him now, her hand sliding over his shoulder and around the back of his neck. As he urged closer, her body curved towards his in a gesture that told him what her lips could not yet say. Paolo let his fingers tangle into Venetia's long silken chestnut hair. The faint caress of his cool fingertips against her skin sent almost painfully sensual tremors through her, drowning whatever good intentions her mind may have had, in the fiery, uncontrollable response of her body.

She saw his eyes smouldering darkly above that sculptured mouth she wanted on her parched lips, and then he plucked her to him. Only the touch of his warmth on her skin and his hardness against her gave away that her bathrobe had been discarded, baring her naked body to his feverish gaze. Her slenderness, her smoothness were lost in his embrace and his strength, his power incited fierce needs in her flesh. She felt the sweet ache between her thighs and wanted to feel him hot and damp, sliding against her.

'Venetia!' He breathed her name before his lips touched her temple, her cheek, her ear, and then traced the shape of her mouth with his own, stroking the surface of her pink full lips, murmuring words that thrilled against her skin.

Her hands needed to touch him, discover the strength of his naked flesh and muscle, to feel the driving urgency that was igniting her. Venetia lifted her arms to push away the silken dressing gown from Paolo's back, but at once he gathered her up, swinging her effortlessly into his arms. His hands were like steel bands where he held her tight, cradling her against his chest, his mouth hot at her ear, pouring out passionate words of desire, and before she knew what was happening he had carried her into the bedroom and laid her gently on the bed, stretching out beside her.

'I want to feel you,' she murmured, her fingers running over his muscled shoulder and attempting once more to free him from his robe.

With a movement that was lightning fast he caught her hand and whipped it aside, pressing closer to her so that their bodies were almost touching.

Venetia searched his face questioningly. 'Why?' she breathed. 'I want to feel you... touch you.'

'Venetia...' He tensed and stared at her for a moment, but there was a new intimacy in the way he spoke her name, sensually low and seductive with barely controlled restraint. His face was in shadow but she saw the sadness that clouded the intense blue of his eyes; they seemed so light now, gazing down at her with an almost tactile caress, while he drew his hand delicately, almost hesitantly over her body, raising a wave of gooseflesh, making her shudder as she felt the excited response of every sinew under his touch.

'Let me,' she whispered again. This time he didn't protest but kept his eyes on hers as she pulled the garment away. Venetia sucked in her breath. Deep scars criss-crossed his shoulders, sliced across his lower torso, and the side of his thighs. The marks showed up more sharply because their strained pallor contrasted so dramatically with the tanned colour of the rest of his skin. It struck her that with scars like this, the car accident must have left him in agony for weeks. All she could do was look at him, containing her emotion.

'You are so beautiful and I'm…' his voice trailed away.

But Venetia laid her fingers against his lips to silence him, and lifting herself up she pressed her burning lips against his trembling mouth. She wanted to kiss away the pain of all those terrible injuries.

He smiled ruefully. 'The beauty and the beast,' he murmured against her mouth, pushing her gently back into the pillows. '*Amore mio*, let the beast make love to his beauty. Will you let me, Venetia?' His voice held a hoarse, driven sound which seared the blood in her veins.

'Yes,' she whispered.

Paolo lifted his head back and his erotic gaze held her totally at his mercy, moving over her sensitised flesh, caressing every part of her. The passion and desire she read in his eyes was fuelling her own need, exciting every nerve, making her pulsate with aching anticipation.

'I want to feel you. Do you have any idea how much I want you?' And then he rolled her back so that her hands were pinned above her head in one of his, in an iron-like grip that was almost painful but not quite. He was stiff against her thigh and she arched slightly, feeling the ache in her nipples and the moisture between her legs.

'Paolo,' she murmured, pleading for him to touch her, with no thought in her mind other than that she loved him and would do anything for this man. Nothing else seemed to matter in this electric moment of expectancy and desire.

And so he bent to brush her lips, and it was as if fuel had been poured over flames; for good, for ill, forever; the world ceased to exist.

At the silken stroke of the down on his chest against her swollen, naked breasts, a great shuddering sigh shook her. Paolo's mouth was firm and demanding, and Venetia closed her eyes as a furnace deep inside her body made her lips part hungrily beneath his and match his ardour. And as his tongue met hers, she gave herself up to his urgent plundering, gripping his muscled back and upper arms as she floated in the euphoria of pure feeling. His hand slid down her spine, circling the soft curve of her behind, caressing and squeezing, pushing her against his hips, moving her against his hardness. She moaned into his mouth and answered his movements wantonly, her fingers clenching his solid shoulders.

Then their tempo slowed. They found a beautiful sensual delight in kissing, caressing and tasting each other, setting out on an erotic journey of intimate discovery, and wanting to savour every second without haste. Their hands, their mouths, their tongues stirred, stimulated, soothed, heightening every fragment of awareness that would lead to the final merge of their bodies and their souls into one.

Now, Paolo's hand was cupping her breast, the pad of his thumb moving rhythmically across the hardening tip as he captured her mouth with infinite tenderness and let his tongue coax hers slowly and erotically. His hands on her skin were skilled, sensuous and feathery, almost worshipful. They trembled as he traced the feminine contours of her body. Every stroke, every kiss, every lick revealed his devastating need for her, as he murmured his adoration against her quivering flesh, always returning to her mouth. She existed only where he touched her, making her limbs fill with a melting heat that spread quickly to her whole body.

His warm, sensuous lips left hers now to travel the length of her throat, down over her silk-like skin to the swollen curve of her other breast, taking his time, playing her, taunting her, flicking his tongue to wet the fiery nipple, each stroke an explosion of fire, intensifying the burning ache she felt between her thighs.

Her fingers curled deep into his hair as she cried out against the sensations sweeping through her.

Attuned to her need, Paolo laid his other hand on the soft triangle between her legs and began a languid caress. Her wet readiness slicked against the skin of her thighs as his fingers glided further and deeper with each pass, parting the swollen lips that concealed the heart of her desire, finding the moist, tumescent bud and rubbing over it delicately, persuasively with the tip of his finger.

She moved frantically, responding to the powerful urgency of her desire with every fibre of her being, whimpering, giving way to pleasure, revelling in this delicious torture he so expertly afflicted... it had been so long! Paolo knew just how much pressure to use, sometimes stroking and at others applying the firm touch she ached for.

Venetia gasped when his fingers moved away, but before she had time to miss him, his lips had found her core and he was tasting her, drinking her, loving her as she pulsated under his teasing strokes, each gentle drag of his tongue on her hot centre making her tremble harder. He made her peak again and again as he decreased and increased the rhythm in time with her need, each climax greater than the last.

And now she was pleading with him to give her more. 'I want you inside me, Paolo. Love me, now... please, now,' she panted, her entire body a wriggling mass of febrile nerve endings.

Paolo pulled away and gave her a questioning look. 'But *cara*...' he whispered, and she could read the pent-up tension and overwhelming desire that burned in his feverish eyes, which had deepened to the most midnight of blues. '... Are you sure this is what you want?'

She smiled at him, comprehending his generous sacrifice. 'Don't hold back,' she breathed, her hands moving to find the pulsating maleness between his thighs, her love for him mirrored in the tenderness of her features. 'It's been a very long time, but I'm not a virgin. You know how hungry I am for you, Paolo. I want you so much, I want all your love. Now.'

Her words were inflaming, meant to break down the last barriers of inhibition between them; and as Venetia's fingers encircled his hard need, she saw the wonder in Paolo's eyes and he groaned savagely. '*Amore mio, Venetia, il mio tesoro*, my treasure,' he said in a choked voice, burying his face in her neck and nuzzling at her skin, 'you're driving me crazy, I want you...'

Venetia could feel the silky virility of his manhood in her palms swell, harden and pulsate even more beneath her erotic ministrations, turning her bones to liquid, and she delighted in pleasuring him as he was pleasuring her.

But Paolo had not finished with her. As he moved on top of her now, his hands were part of her hair, massaging her scalp, tilting her head back as he claimed her mouth again, this time in a savage, bruising kiss, branding her his – the gently flowing river of feeling turning into a raging torrent of passion. The finely curling mat of hair across his chest was rubbing against her over-sensitive skin, exciting her, making her reel, and her body called to his with all the craving for fulfilment of which she had been deprived for so long, and which she knew only he could satisfy.

Paolo responded. Explicit, demanding hands roamed eagerly over the same curves he had worshiped so tenderly earlier, crushing Venetia to him, probing, sucking and nipping at her responsive skin, overwhelming her with his need; and she revelled shamelessly in this manly possessiveness with only one thought in mind, to surrender to it.

Flames licked up inside her; she wanted Paolo within her. He'd taken the edge off her hunger, but she needed more, the real thing: to be his. Her body arched in invitation. She saw his eyes flare as she parted her thighs to receive him, stroking the swollen life force of his flesh, guiding the silken head into her. She was tight, and she sensed his momentary hesitation, his hands gripping at her shoulders, fighting for self-control. His breathing was harsh and his mouth opened slightly as he gazed down at her.

'Are you all right, *cara*?'

She nodded, her eyes wide, her hands on his back. 'It's been ten years,' she breathed, trembling with unbearable anticipation… and then he was there, where she most ached for him to be. Paolo thrust into her with one swift movement, piercing her with a sweet pleasure that brought tears of emotion to her eyes. It was like a match to kindling, triggering a blaze, and she cried out in relief as hot pokers consumed her senses, her body and her mind.

She heard Paolo stifle a harsh sound of pleasure in his throat as her body softened, expanded to welcome the powerful strength of him. He stilled for a moment, letting her get used to the feeling of him inside her.

'There are so many things I cannot put into words that I can only express with my body… *Amore mio*, are you ready for me…?' Paolo muttered huskily, in a raw, halting voice.

'Yes,' Venetia breathed.

He thrust into her again and stilled as she cried out.

'… How much I want you…'

She groaned as he did it again, her body wanting more.

'… How much I love you…'

He then took her with agonisingly slow, deep thrusts, holding her pinned to him with one arm, while caressing her moist, super-sensitive core with his free hand.

As he sunk into her, inch by gentle inch, liquid heat coursed through her, beginning somewhere deep in the pit of her stomach and spreading gradually throughout her body. With every invasive shift of his strong, hard body Paolo was driving her to a greater height, teaching her that there was no end to pleasure, no boundaries either. Her hips writhed and squirmed while his deliberately languid movements inside her electrified her with all-consuming delight. She could hear herself crying out his name again and again, her soul and her body totally receptive to his possession.

Venetia's hands raked up Paolo's back, burying themselves in his thick black hair, and then shifting from his hair to his powerful thighs; she arched towards him, wrapping her legs around him, inviting him deeper, wanting to feel all of him. Her eyes were shut in wanton abandonment. Space and time disappeared as he moved inside her faster and faster, building up the tension. Matching his rhythm, she was swept away as they danced together to a melody of a love that echoed inside her like the returning memory of a dream long forgotten.

And now he was hauling her closer still, tipping her back slightly. Venetia felt him shudder against her as he plunged so deep into her that her breath came in short staccato gasps while she revelled in the sovereignty of his powerful body over and inside hers. The pleasure centres of her brain overloaded with sensation, the crescendo and excitement of it multiplied and peaked, her muscles began to spasm just as she heard Paolo's rumbling, agonising groan. She felt the strain of his body still wildly pulsing within her, and then the hot streams of his climax flooded her, blending with her warmth as they reached the ultimate fusion of their passion. And as the volcano exploded and an all-consuming furnace engulfed her, Venetia soared and swooped, crying out her ecstasy, sobbing and convulsing under the shattering power of the most intense orgasm she'd ever experienced.

They lay entwined and motionless for a long while in the silent room, bathed in the rising sun. 'A new dawn to our love,' Paolo whispered as he looked into Venetia's eyes. 'Are you still hesitant, *amore mio?*'

She shook her head, smiling up at him, mind and body deliciously languid and fulfilled.

It had been a curious experience for Venetia, having a man make love to her for the first time after so many years of abstinence. Somehow she was aware that there had been, for both of them, a familiarity in the meeting, as if they had always known each other and been parted for a long time. When Paolo had moved inside her, he'd felt exactly as she'd known he would feel. The echoes of a previous time when she had loved and been loved reverberated through her. *We were meant to come together,* she thought as she closed her eyes and drifted off to sleep with a sweet sense of blissful security, safe in the knowledge that after stumbling and falling in the wilderness, they had finally found one another.

CHAPTER 9

Venetia moaned and twisted her head to still the tickling sensation on her cheek. The first thing she saw as her heavy lids lifted was Paolo's face inches from hers, smiling down at her tenderly.

'*Buongiorno, tesoro,*' he whispered, his eyes caressing her features intently. 'I'm sorry to wake you, but I would prefer if Ernestina didn't see us in this… how to say… um… compromising position. She's a very kind person and an excellent housekeeper, but she's also a big gossip.'

Venetia stretched languorously. 'It can't be that late already,' she groaned softly, looking up at Paolo through sleepy eyes, her skin gently prickling under his burning gaze. She remembered worrying about the latent morning-after embarrassment as she had drifted off to sleep, wondering if in daylight she would regret the intimacy they had shared, and this honeyed feeling which flooded her now was a surprise.

The shadow of dark stubble over Paolo's jaw enhanced the masculinity of his bronzed face and she stared up at him, drinking in its hard planes and angles and the glitter of desire in his eyes. With his broad shoulders, strong arms, the silky down that furnished his bronze, muscled ribcage, and the taut hardness of his virility that she could see outlined beneath the sheet, he seemed once again like a primitive god seducing her mortal body and soul. Her need for him hit her like a bludgeon and she felt herself turning into a hot pool of longing.

She raised herself on one elbow and let her fingers run over his disfigured chest, lingering lovingly on the deep, discoloured scars. Paolo's body tensed and she felt him shake slightly under the feathery contact of her fingertips. He lifted her hand and brushed the inside of her wrist with his lips, and then sat up, leaning against the pillows.

'Don't go yet,' she murmured as she inched over, questing after the wonderful effect his touch had on her senses.

Venetia didn't need to ask twice. Paolo breathed in sharply and pulled her towards him, sweeping her up so she was straddling his legs, her nakedness on display for him. She liked the smouldering way he was looking at her, desire and passion etched on every one of his features, and the way his hands ran over her curves with a possessive firmness that made her long for him to dominate her and take her on the spot.

Paolo sensed her urgent arousal and his eyes blazed.

'What are you doing to me, Venetia?' he murmured against her lips, before hauling her sharply to him, so her head went back almost in supplication and her breasts were touching his chest, the nipples swelling to form taut peaks rubbing against him. He groaned deep in his throat as she pushed her hips further against him, feeling him grow harder in response.

Paolo pressed his lips against her tortured throat, punctuating its length with fierce kisses and bites, cupping the hardened curves of her breasts in his warm hands, kneading and stroking them with his fingers, faster and faster.

Venetia's breathing became sharp and shallow; her head began to whirl, her pupils dilating with her own dark desire, every muscle and nerve-ending tightening in anticipation of his penetration. But Paolo was a master at love making, as he had proved to her all night. His mouth was hot fire on her lips, crushing them, urgent and commanding, submitting her to his own avid need, which only served to increase her excitement.

His hands spread over her body, followed by his tongue, exploring, tasting, encouraged by the high sounds in her throat as each erotic sensation moved tantalisingly, irresistibly, up and down her body. Her senses reeled, demanding more and more, needing to satiate the gnawing hunger for relief that was torturing her, and yet not wanting it to end.

'Oh, please, don't stop, Paolo, don't stop!' Her speech was almost slurred, her mouth becoming drier, and the need for him to bury himself in her strengthening by the second.

Still, he seemed to have more to give, her ardent response kindling his own arousal, stimulating his own pleasure.

'Do you know what I'm going to do to you now?' he rasped, his eyes blazing with passion, which made her suppress a moan.

They were mutually driving each other on. His hands still caressed with a feather-light touch her breasts, her stomach and the sensitive skin between her thighs, while his head dipped and gently glided down her body, to the secret core of her femininity, which longed for him so much. Pushing her legs apart so Venetia's arousal was in full view of him, and parting the moist, silken pink petals with his forefinger, he stroked the edges sensuously, making her wait a few seconds before flicking his tongue against the swollen burgeon, licking it, while rubbing it with the tip of his fingers in an unbearably rapid rhythm, urging her pleasure to burst and send rippling shocks through her already strained nerves. The waves were coming, Venetia could feel her loins trembling; soon she would be flooded.

'Now, Paolo, now my love, now,' she pleaded for release, tears rolling down her cheeks. Paolo's aroused body required no more preliminaries; his velvet hardness found her moist, satin softness with a kind of primitive possession, and together they fused in an all-consuming blaze of fire, total and rapturous that left them completely spent and satiated.

It was almost nine o'clock when Paolo, showered and clad in his navy-blue silk robe, emerged from La Sirena. Venetia, her own white silk dressing gown wrapped around her, accompanied him to the gate. There was still no one to be seen; only Rufus lay stretched asleep on the grass behind the house. A breathless quiet hung about the place, and the scent of flowers and of newly mown grass drifted on the wandering air, sweetening the atmosphere.

Mushrooms gleamed fresh and pearly in the soft, close lawn and the sun, already very warm but with its light misted, shone down upon Miraggio and its surrounding grounds. The trees that dotted this part of the property stood along the bottom of a slope, bunchy and motionless in the still air, thick with leaves. Like trees from an ancient tapestry, they seemed as if nothing would ever change them, as if they would always wear this plumage of full blue-green.

The garden seemed spellbound: not a leaf quivered in the warm air, not a sound came through the veiled sunshine that suffused it all, and no word came from Paolo, who stood by Venetia's side as if he couldn't bear to part with her. He bent his head and took her lips to his. They stood for a few more moments in their caressing warmth until, almost with the effort of someone rousing from a trance, Paolo dragged himself away from her at last, just as the sound of cantering hooves made them both turn abruptly.

A few paces away, a fierce-looking Allegra atop her handsome bay was regarding them steadily, animosity sparkling in her coal-black eyes.

'*Buongiorno, Allegra,*' Paolo called out to the young woman with an engaging smile, though Venetia noticed that his body had tensed slightly. '*Vieni qui che ti presento la signorina,* come here so I can introduce you to the *signorina.*'

Ignoring him, Antonio's niece shifted her dark gaze slowly and disdainfully over Paolo's visage, then raising her chin slightly she huffed, turning her mount on itself, and without so much as a glance in Venetia's direction, she cantered off towards the stables.

Venetia's stomach contracted in a sickening knot. Her heart was beating so urgently she was sure that Paolo could hear it thumping against her breast. She met his impassable eyes for just a moment before he gratified her with another smile.

'Allegra is Antonio's niece. She's a very intelligent and talented young woman, but also extremely wild. She's only twenty-one and Antonio is very severe, so the poor girl does not have much opportunity to get out of Miraggio, apart from the few times when I take her with me to Venice for a couple of days.' Venetia was sure she could sense a slight strain in his voice, despite his open gaze.

Ernestina appeared around the corner carrying Venetia's breakfast, just as the young woman was about to retort that his great friend Umberto had already enlightened her about the relationship that existed between himself and the fiery Amazon, and that he should spare himself the effort of lying to her, and the humiliation of having to listen to his fabrications.

'*Buongiorno, signorina… signore,*' said the cheerful house-keeper as she came level with the couple.

Paolo scowled and shook his head, his expression one of great frustration, as if this was the final straw. He swore under his breath, '*Maledizione!*' and then '*Buongiorno, Ernestina.*'

'Should I set up a place for you for breakfast, *signore?*' she enquired with deceptive quietness, but Venetia could see in the way she looked at them that the servant was excited and could hardly contain her curiosity.

Paolo's face took on a closed look. 'No, no thank you, Ernestina, I will have my breakfast in my bedroom as usual.' Turning to Venetia his eyes locked with hers. 'I'll be in my study in about an hour if you would like to join me, umm…' he paused deliberately and grinned down at her in a way that put her teeth on edge, 'to continue our conversation and maybe look over the plans.'

He had the gall to grin! Venetia stared at him. The fact that he mentioned Venice showed that he remembered she had seen them there together and, guiltily, he was trying to justify the reason why he was taking the caretaker's niece out for lunch in such a prestigious restaurant. If the young woman hadn't appeared suddenly, would he have even bothered to admit that she lived with him at Miraggio? She could pack her bags and leave in a huff, or take what he was subtly offering her, just an affair. Venetia's mind and heart waged war once more, struggling to find a balance between her pride and the burgeoning love she felt growing inside her for this man.

'I'll be there,' she returned, trying to keep her voice even and strode away, following Ernestina into the house and not looking back at Paolo.

'I'll have a shower and dress before breakfast,' she told the housekeeper, hoping that she could tidy up the bedroom and bathroom, eradicating the tell-tale evidence of a night of love before the servant went about her daily cleaning.

'*Va bene, signorina.*'

Soaping herself under the shower, Venetia was vividly aware of her body in a way she hadn't been before, even ten years ago. Her breasts were tender to the touch, her nipples still sore from Paolo's love bites, while she could already detect faint bruises on her shoulders, evidence of his passionate hold on them as he had reached his climax that morning. She trembled at the memory of their lovemaking, and wondered at her own wanton abandonment.

But she could not delude herself about her feelings for Paolo that were blossoming fiercely in her with the overnight glory of a tropical flower. Those flashes, intuitive, swift, and primitive, that were transmitted between them disturbed her oddly; it was almost as if, in spite of the tangible world that divided them, her mind could speak directly to his and receive an answer. There was a palpable harmony between them; it was exquisitely sweet and she was sure that Paolo had been aware of it too, since the first time they met.

Still, a grey cloud marred the euphoria she would have felt if Allegra hadn't appeared, and if Paolo hadn't lied to her... but had he lied to her? Venetia tried to argue in his favour. He had only shielded the truth from her at that moment. Did she really expect him to admit there and then that Allegra was his mistress, even though the Italian girl was probably history after their passionate interlude at dawn? That wouldn't be very gentlemanly of him, and Paolo, she had the deep conviction, was a gentleman. How foolish she was to be feeling this way.

When Venetia went back into the living room to have her breakfast, she was surprised to see Ernestina still there. She noticed that the servant was holding on to the discarded bathrobe that Paolo had slipped off her shoulders before carrying her into the bedroom, and which she had not picked up from the floor.

'I wasn't sure if you wanted me to set up your breakfast on the *terrazza* as usual or if you would prefer to have it indoors. It's going to be a hot day and the sun is already very strong.'

The servant's eyes darted quickly from Venetia's lush mane of chestnut hair left loose this morning around her shoulders to her long shapely legs under the summery floral dress.

An unwitting flush of pink rose to Venetia's cheekbones when she realised what Ernestina must be thinking, confirming the housekeeper's surmise of a night spent in the arms of her employer.

'*Grazie*. I will just have some hot coffee on the *terrazza*.'

'*Ve lo porto subito*, I'll bring it to you in just a minute.'

There wasn't a ripple on the pale blue sea and not a cloud in the sky. It was a warm morning, no air stirring, and the heat had the heavy dampness of windless days upon a sea coast. Ernestina was right: the temperature was climbing, the golden orb beating down on the countryside. The horizon was faintly hazy, and the line of hills rising far away behind the estate, almost veiled and dazzling white in the hot sunlight, looked as if they had been cut out of cardboard; the flowers in the garden below stood bravely lifting their cups to the sun. Nature looked as if it was holding its breath.

Ernestina also looked as though she was holding her breath when she came onto the terrace with the cup of coffee. Her dark eyes met Venetia's, containing all sorts of insinuated questions, and finally she decided to speak.

'If the *signorina* will permit, I would like to say something.'

Venetia lifted her eyebrows, feigning a surprise she did not really feel.

'The *signorina* must be careful.'

'I don't understand.'

'*Bisogna stare attenti a quella piccola strega*, you have to be careful of that little witch.'

'I still don't understand what you're telling me, Ernestina. *What* witch?'

'Antonio's niece, Allegra, the young woman riding a horse this morning who passed by you when you were...' the servant gave an embarrassed little cough, 'umm... with the *signore*.'

Venetia felt her cheeks burn. 'I don't see what this has to do with the young lady in question, or with you for that matter,' she replied calmly.

'Please don't get me wrong. I'm not trying to intrude, *signorina*. God forbid that I should meddle in either yours or *Signor* Barone's business, but this girl is dangerous. She has the *Malocchio,* the evil eye.'

'It's very kind of you to worry about me, Ernestina. But you see, I don't give credence to all these superstitions, if some kind of hocus-pocus black magic is what you're meaning to suggest. Anyhow, things like the evil eye don't affect people who don't believe in them.'

'*Signorina*, with all due respect, you may think that I'm an ignorant, superstitious Italian peasant, but Antonio and his niece come from Elba, like me, and we are from the same small village of San Stefano di Camastra. I knew the family, and Allegra was born bad to bad parents. She was treated cruelly, it is true, but it was like pouring petrol on a fire already out of control. Whether it was bad genes or the evil that surrounded her, *chi lo sa*, who knows, but from a young age, she was *cattiva*, manipulative. Already as a child, she started dabbling in witchcraft. She fell in with *un cerchio del male,* an evil circle, which was poisoning her mind even more with their wicked rites of sorcery and black magic. That's why in the end Antonio had to move to the North when Allegra was seven. He spent some time in Porto Ercole and when a few years later *Signor* Barone was looking for builders to help with the restoration of Miraggio, he found *buon lavoro,* steady work here for him and his niece.'

'Where are Allegra's parents?'

'They died when the child was only five. The father, Antonio's brother, was a drunkard. Her mother was a well known *matta*, madwoman, and the town strumpet to boot. She and the father completely neglected the small child. Antonio and his wife, Angelina, were kindly folk and they took in the little girl. When Angelina suddenly fell ill and died, Antonio continued caring for Allegra, but she was still wild. Then the father ended up dead in a ditch not long after – no one knows how, but no doubt to do with his drinking. Ah, *madre di dio!*' Ernestina lifted her arms to the sky. 'That's when things became even worse. The child's interest in the dark arts grew, and Antonio took her away to the North. By the time they came to Miraggio, Allegra was eleven. She was as fully developed as a girl of sixteen, and she knew all there was to know of good and evil – mainly evil. She had been taught by a preacher to read and write and add up sums, but the girl had no affection for anyone. She was moody, headstrong, and beautiful *come un angelo*, but she brooded in that cottage the *signore* provided for her and her uncle, and roamed the hills. Occasionally, she came out with furies and rages that frightened anyone who happened to witness them. It was me who spoke to *Signor* Barone about her in the end. She was causing trouble among the workers and I wanted him to dismiss Antonio because of the girl.

'Anyway, that got the *signore*'s curiosity going, and he asked to meet with the child. I brought her to him. *Madre di dio*, I will never forget how she looked up at him with her black, lovely eyes and stretched out her arms to him with a cry: "*Portami via, Portami via*, take me away." The rest followed quickly.' Ernestina sighed. 'The *signore è buono come il pane*, he's as good as bread, *è molto sensibile*, very sensitive, and he took her under his wing. This exquisite child could not be left to rot, he said. He would save her.'

Yes, Venetia thought, it would be so like Paolo to want to save another thing, a person this time, from destruction.

'So he put her in a convent, where she rebelled at first, but her cleverness and ambition soon won over her wildness. She was shamed by her own ignorance and set herself to study to become a lady. The girl quickly realised that sullenness and furies got her nowhere... *era più saggio accattivarsi le persone,* it was wiser to win people, make them worship her. And she succeeded, but she herself never knew affection for anyone. *Cambiano i suonatori ma la musica é sempre quella,* the singer changes but the song stays the same. She will never be a good girl.' Ernestina shook her head. 'All this is to tell you, *signorina,* that Allegra is very possessive of *Signor* Barone. I know for sure, she does not only regard him as her protector, but both she and Antonio are hoping that he will marry her one day... *Come Dio mi é testimone,* as God is my witness, I have heard them plotting this with my own ears that will be eaten by the worms one day.'

'And what does *Signor* Barone think of that great plan?' Even though Venetia thought the old woman's words were some-what melodramatic, she couldn't resist asking the question, quietly eager for a clue to Paolo's feelings for this dangerously alluring girl.

'The *signore* is a lonely man, *signorina,* and the girl is a *scaltra tentatrice,* beautiful and wily temptress. When she speaks to him she knows how to make her voice soft and caressing... *una puttana in incognito.*'

'I really don't see what it has to do with me, and why you're telling me all this.'

'*Signorina,* may the sky fall upon me if I speak out of turn, but... the *signore* is blinded by his affection and pity for this young woman, who he has seen grow up. And, as far as I can see, he has invested *un sacco di soldi,* a stack of money, into the bargain. He is a very melancholy man, the *signore*. He still grieves for his dead wife who he has never forgotten. Allegra brings colour to his life *sicuramente* and if I thought that she would make him happy, I would not have talked to you in this way, *signorina*. But she has a biting tongue, and a cruel heart – hurting people is her way, and most of all she doesn't love him. *Lei è come una sanguisuga*, she's like a leech, always asking for this and that.'

Venetia raised her eyebrows. Clearly Paolo had forgotten his wife but she was not about to bring up his amnesia with Ernestina, knowing next to nothing about the housekeeper or how much she knew about her employer. She wondered what else was unreliable about Ernestina's information.

'My dear Ernestina, you seem to think that I have influence over *Signor* Barone. I'm here to restore mosaics in an old church, not to meddle with my client's problems of the heart.' Venetia inwardly winced at the irony of her own words.

'*Signorina, mi permetta di dire*... I saw you and the *signore* this morning... *come dire*... you know... I was going to go back to the kitchen from the garden when I saw Allegra go past you, so I stood behind the tree as I knew she was up to no good, and then when I saw that *Signor* Barone was leaving, I came over.'

'Well, since you saw us this morning, I don't know what you're worried about. Doesn't that show that maybe your fear of Allegra's power over the *signore* is a little unfounded?'

'I also saw the hatred in her eyes. She was born under a Black Moon, which some say is a bad omen. I tell you, she has a dark power that, whether from this earth or from another world, is dangerous. She will harm you if she can, *signorina*, even if it means hurting the *signore*, and you must guard against it.'

Venetia stood up. 'You're very sweet, Ernestina, to worry about me. I can't speak for *Signor* Barone, of course, but really, I don't believe in all this mumbo jumbo and so I assure you, it can't touch me.' She smiled and kissed the old servant on the cheek. 'And now I must go and join my client in his study. Whatever you saw this morning, that doesn't mean that we don't have work to do.'

The woman seemed touched by Venetia's affectionate gesture. 'I knew as soon as I saw you, *signorina*, that you would be good for our *signore*... *un balsamo che se messo su una ferita la curerebbe,* a balm which if put on a wound would cure it. He carries a lot of sadness in his heart and there's a kindness that radiates from you. You're good for him and him for you, because I can see in your eyes that you have also known unhappiness in your life. We say in Italy, *"siete entrambi della stessa stella,* you're both of the same star," which means that you two are born for each other.'

As Venetia made her way to Miraggio she wondered again at Ernestina's words. She hadn't mentioned anything about Paolo's amnesia, and probably knew nothing of it, judging by her comments about his dead wife, so probably her reference to his sadness must concern his widowhood and the tragic way it had come about.

Again, it was not clear from Ernestina whether or not the young woman was in fact Paolo's mistress, though the housekeeper would see Allegra and Paolo together all the time and would know if Antonio's niece was scheming to marry him. And if that was the case, surely the young Amazon had already weaselled herself into his bed, and surely Paolo being the hot-blooded man he was, he wouldn't have pushed away her advances? Venetia's heart became heavier with every step, as she made her way through the big house towards Paolo's office. Why should she expect more from him than other men? *He's human and Allegra is so beautiful, so utterly seductive. What man could hold out against her?*

*   *   *

Paolo sat at his desk in the study, staring unseeingly out of the window, questions reflecting in his eyes. Why did he feel so restless... so lost... so utterly confused and in turmoil? The emotional charge he had felt in Venetia's arms that morning was like nothing he had experienced in this new life, and yet it had not been completely alien... He had read numerous books about amnesia and it was believed that some people only remember through touch, taste or smell... and for a split second, when he had reached his shattering climax inside her, he had felt that he was going back in time. There was something there, the return of something specific, and he momentarily surfaced on the shore of familiarity; but then immediately, like each time he had seemed to put his finger on a memory, the mirage lost itself again in the tragedy of his life.

One thing he was sure of: he was irremediably in love with Venetia. There had been no preparation for this, no leading up in soft degrees. It had been this way since that damp, misty evening he had rescued her in Venice, when looking into her eyes in the first few seconds it was as if he had pulled back a curtain. The intensity of the emotional flash memory that had come into his mind was so strong, so beautiful, he almost felt relief, but again it had vanished nearly as quickly as it had occurred, to join the dead wreckage of his past.

And now Paolo knew he could not live without Venetia. Was that because, somehow, she was jogging his amnesic memory? The psychologist who had followed his progress for two years, until he was quite sure Paolo could stand on his own two feet, had told him that the return of memory could not be prompted by somebody else, it had to come back from within.

Still, when he was with Venetia, Paolo felt secure; even without regaining his forgotten identity, she represented the promise of a life where he could find happiness. Together they would make their own past, live in the present and plan for the future. Venetia had also been aware of that connection; he could feel it.

Paolo allowed his mind turn to their lovemaking that morning, playing back the moment when Venetia let the robe slide from her shoulders to the floor. A new fantasy took over, where he was kneeling in front of her and drawing her towards him, gently probing the delicate, secret corolla of her most intimate part with his lips and his tongue to taste the soft ripe fruit that trembled inside her, sending a series of erotic images dancing across his mind's eye. He could almost hear the helpless little moans in the back of her throat, see the mixture of yearning and rapture in her eyes, which turned flame-coloured when she was aroused, making the insistent, throbbing ache in his groin intensify to an unbearable pitch.

It would soon be Easter; he would take her away to Capri, or perhaps to one of the islands for a few days, and after that ask her to marry him. There was no time to waste; he had lost enough years. Was he being unrealistic, building castles in the clouds, pretending that nothing more divided them now? Was he living for this singular moment in a golden haze, outside time? Would she want to take on a man of whom she knew almost nothing? And even if he told her what had been related to him about himself and his past, would she believe him? It was all so extraordinary.

Paolo knew a moment of panic. When Giovanna Lombardi had rung him to say that Venetia would be taking on his assignment after all, he had amassed a whole store of words to say to her when she arrived – the truth about himself, everything he'd wanted to tell her right from the start. Now that store was distressingly empty. He didn't want to frighten her off. There was an anxious side to Venetia, and until he'd found out the hurt that was eating away at her, he believed it best to tread with muffled steps.

She had rebuffed him so many times, even though everything in her eyes and the expression of her face spelt out that she was drawn to him as passionately as he was to her. He always sensed a resistance in her when they talked, a kind of pent-up belliger-ence, and only in his arms did she become tender, docile, submissive and infinitely generous. She had given herself to him that morning without restraint; her body had revealed itself to him like the petals of a flower opening up to expose itself to the sunshine; she had taken him with avidity, but she had loved him back with equal fervour.

A sudden thought crossed his mind: Allegra. Venetia might have wondered why she looked so angry on seeing them together that morning. She had been at that new restaurant in Piazza San Marco where he had taken Antonio's niece some time ago. Paolo frowned as he wondered what conclusions Venetia had reached regarding his relationship with the girl. He had so many regrets when it came to Allegra, and he had been too weak.

That Allegra was infatuated with him and wanted to marry him was indeed unfortunate. He also realised that she had developed more dissipated inclinations and he was well aware of her esca-pades into Porto Santo Stefano whenever his back was turned. He had never confronted her with the rumours, too fond of her to hurt her feelings; however, his protective instinct, and his guilt, had led him to speak to Antonio. The caretaker had assured him that it was all malevolent gossip, but Paolo was not duped.

Of late, even though he had stopped asking Allegra over to the big house for an occasional meal, she had become clingier, and the scene that had occurred the other night in his bedroom left him uneasy. Ernestina had always warned him against Allegra, insinuating the girl was evil. Now, he wouldn't go that far, but he sensed that she had some rather unsavoury instincts and a scheming nature from which he should guard himself perhaps, and certainly protect Venetia.

Paolo glanced at his watch. Venetia would soon be there. He lit a cigarette and started to make a series of phone calls to agents in various parts of Italy to secure a hotel over Easter. He would give Venetia the choice of place, and take her wherever she wanted to go.

*   *   *

When Venetia walked into the room, Paolo was just putting down the phone. His eyes flicked over her slender figure outlined in a delicate sleeveless white dress. He was wearing an open-necked indigo shirt that gave his irises a cerulean tint, making them even more striking. His raven-black hair was swept back, but slightly ruffled, and his features had lost the tautness she had been used to – he seemed relaxed.

Paolo got up and came towards her, his smile sweet and tender. 'I've missed you, Venetia,' he whispered, his voice husky as he drew her gently into his arms.

She wanted to resist, but how could she? The way he spoke her name alone made her feel desirable – all woman. Her mind clouding, Venetia gave herself up to his kisses, her body on fire with sudden heat. She closed her eyes, the hard strength of Paolo's body along the full length of hers, drowning in his embrace, engulfed in the possessive demand of his lips and surrendering to them without the slightest hesitation.

When at last he released her, she kept her eyes closed a few seconds more, her senses immersed in a sea of deep, aching need.

'Come, sit down.' Paolo moved over to his desk.

Venetia followed and took a seat opposite him, her eyes lifting a little sheepishly towards the huge portrait looking down, watching her enigmatically.

Paolo smiled ruefully. 'She wouldn't mind, *cara*,' he murmured, as if interpreting the anxiety on Venetia's face. 'I think she'd like to see me happy.'

'It's very difficult to have someone you cared for so much as a rival, especially since she disappeared from your life in such dramatic circumstances.'

'Please, *amore mio*, don't give it another thought. I have no past – only the present and the future hold importance for me now.'

Venetia hesitated before formulating her concern, her ultimate fear. She glanced down at her fingers, knotted together in her lap. 'Paolo, can I be very candid with you?'

'Of course, *tesoro mio*, you can say and ask whatever you want. I will always try to answer you truthfully.'

'What if your memory came back one day and you discovered that you were still in love with your wife?'

There was a short pause before he answered, his tone grave, his eyes denuded of all expression. 'Please believe me when I tell you that there's no chance of that – the past is dead for me. The woman you see up there is and will always remain for me a figment of the imagination of the artist who painted her.'

Since they were on the subject of 'the other woman', Venetia was burning to ask Paolo about Allegra. She had to stop that nagging little voice tugging at her heart, telling her that she was running headlong into another disaster, just as she had with

Judd, and the only way to stop the war inside her was to hear the truth straight from Paolo himself.

She was about to take the plunge when once again he spared her the embarrassment of asking the question. 'I can see the watchful look in your eyes and read the troubled thoughts that are going round and round in your mind, *cara*. You're puzzled about the... um... *come dire...* relationship between Allegra, the young woman you saw this morning, and me. You're saying to yourself, why should he take the caretaker's niece around with him in Venice, and in such a well-known restaurant? *Deve essera la sua amante*, she must be his mistress. Not so?' Paolo asked calmly.

Venetia stared at him, dumbfounded. He was so attuned to her that he was always one step ahead of her thoughts, interpreting them with finesse and answering her fears with tact. How was he able to perceive her inner thoughts with such perspicacity? Was she so transparent? She had always prided herself on having a 'poker face' when necessary, but it was almost impossible for her to hide anything from Paolo – as it was in bed, where he seemed to anticipate every one of her reactions and thoughts, leaving her totally vulnerable to his uncanny clairvoyance. With Paolo, she was unable to sustain the persona she so successfully projected to the outside world. He could see right through to her soul; her emotions, her feelings, and the intimate way her brain worked appeared no secret to him, as she lay there naked, exposed to his mystifying perception. And although it unnerved her to be so transparent to the man she had come to care for so deeply, she knew that it was no use pretending, she just wasn't strong enough emotionally to try and protect herself any more; besides, she realised, she trusted him.

'Yes,' she murmured, 'I did wonder, especially as Umberto told me that she's your mistress... and then the hatred I read in her eyes this morning when she saw us together only seemed to prove his words. Added to that, I caught sight of her the other night looking very fetching in her red satin nightdress, obviously going to meet you at the house.' Venetia felt the colour rise in her cheeks at the thought.

'And you believe this?' Paolo's eyes widened as they searched her face.

'There is a great deal to be said for the power of positive thinking, but I'm not going to hide my head in the sand like an ostrich, Paolo.' Venetia tried to rein in her temper. 'What would you think in my position? After all, she is really very beautiful.'

'*Dio mio,* Venetia, I am thirty-eight and she's not yet twenty! I'm almost double her age – I could be her father. Do you really think I'm the sort of man to go after a *bambina*?'

'Are you telling me that there's nothing going on between you? That you, *l'Amante delle Quattro Stagioni,* has kept his hands off this beautiful girl?' She found it difficult to keep the jealous anger from flaring in her voice.

Paolo shook his head. 'How little you know me, *carissima.*' He made an effort to smile but, exasperated, ran a hand through his hair. 'When I took on Antonio to help with the renovation of Miraggio, Allegra was just a child. Unhappy and wild, left to her own devices without discipline or supervision. I had just come out of a deep depression, having left my home to start a new life, with no hope really of marrying again and ever having children. Allegra was a beautiful *bambina*, intelligent and lively, and I decided to take her under my wing – in some ways very much like a guardian. I put her through a good private school, a convent where she excelled, and gave her singing and violin lessons because she had a lovely voice and showed an aptitude for music. In my eyes, she always remained a little girl and I didn't realise that the *bambina* had turned into a young woman.

Soon, I'm sad to say, she developed a sort of infatuation with me and began to send me anonymous gifts, which became more intimate, with attached love notes, which she eventually signed, making her feelings known.'

Venetia coloured again, not wanting to hear this sort of detail, even though she had pushed Paolo to be honest with her. He glanced at her and frowned, seeing her reaction, but continued, his voice sounding strained and cautious.

'I explained to her, as well as to Antonio, that this had to stop. But then I was told she was spending nights in Porto Santo Stefano, selling herself to the sailors from the liners and boats which passed through the port.'

Venetia blinked, wide-eyed. 'Did you talk to her about this – at least tell her off? She was obviously seeking your attention.'

Paolo sighed. 'No, I was weak. At the beginning I thought it was just malicious gossip, and then I exercised, as you say, the politic of the ostrich… I'm not proud of the way I've handled things with Allegra.' He pushed his hand through his hair again, his mouth pressed into a thin line. 'It's true, I should have spent more time providing her with the guidance she sorely lacked from Antonio, and perhaps been firmer in laying down boundaries between us. But eventually I decided to take her to a psychologist who was recommended to me in Venice, in the hope that he would cure her of this ridiculous adolescent crush on me.'

'And?'

'Well, even though I'm very fond of Allegra and admittedly that strange relationship of guardian and ward has created a strong bond between us…' Paolo broke off when he saw the look in Venetia's eye. '*Dio mio*, how couldn't it? I've seen her grow up, what do you take me for, *cara*…? Let's just say that she will grow out of this puppy love, as you say in England.'

'You have a rather notorious reputation as a womaniser,' Venetia said quietly. 'You can't blame people for thinking the worst if you exhibit yourself with a young beauty in a city where you are well known and where everybody gossips.'

Paolo shifted in his chair and again raked his hair with his hand. 'People, people... I don't care what people think, *cara*. It's *your* opinion that counts for me. And yes, I will not lie to you and say that I've lived like a monk. I know that I have gained a reputation, but I'm a man of thirty-eight,' he gave a self-deprecating smile, 'and even though I have a defected mind, that doesn't make me half a man. I am normal and there is still a lot of fire in me. Perhaps... perhaps it's partly a drive to escape myself or look for something that's missing, I don't know.' His eyes had darkened momentarily with a flicker of frustration. 'As I've told you before, I'm no saint, but I like beautiful women and I have – to my knowledge – only pursued those women who didn't want a commitment any more than I did.'

'I'm neither criticising you nor am I reproaching you, Paolo – I have no right to, anyhow. But I was just... um... a little concerned.' Venetia flushed and looked down at her feet. She was jealous, that was the real reason for her angst, and she was sure that he was aware of it.

Still, even if he had read her censuring thoughts, he went on as though he hadn't guessed at Venetia's actual feelings. 'I would never, never try to seduce a *bambina* whom I almost think of as my daughter, were she the last woman on earth.' Leaning back, he rested his elbows on the arms of his chair. He looked pensive and his frown deepened. 'But to return to Allegra, I'm now aware that there's an ugly streak in her. Her mother was a well-known madwoman and whore, and she died from some nasty disease, though it might have been worse for Allegra had she lived. Ernestina, who apparently knew the child from their days in Elba, and the mother too, has always insisted she's evil. I must admit I don't believe Allegra is a bad girl, she's just had a difficult life and now is a little spoilt – and that's probably my fault. One day she'll find *un buon marito* who will know how to calm her down – at least that's my hope.'

A small frown of worry creased Venetia's forehead. Even after Paolo's long explanation, doubts still clouded her mind, although she tried to push them away. Was she being manipulated? He sounded so sincere. She could just hear Francesca's voice, telling her not to be so naive: *'He's probably got a string of women he's beguiled with charm and the right words into believing him, trusting him, and then dropped them as soon as he's had his fun.'*

Paolo's warm gaze caught and held hers in a sudden charged silence. He then stood up and came round his desk. 'I love you, Venetia. *Ti amo piu' di qualsiasi cosa al mondo*, I love you more than anything else in the world. You are the ray of sunshine that I've been waiting for all these years.'

This was useless; how could she think straight when he was standing so close, pulling her up into his arms, murmuring such beautiful words while smoothing out the anxiety lines that furrowed her brow with a caressing touch?

'You don't believe me, *cara?*'

Her sigh whispered between them as he searched for her lips, his kiss melting her inside and then spreading through her whole body. They broke apart and Venetia met his sapphire eyes shining intensely as she searched them with her own. 'Though I feel as if I've known you forever, I realise I have a lot to learn about you, don't I?'

'You're doing fine, *amore mio!* These last hours I've spent with you have given me more happiness than I can ever remember.'

He smiled a mischievous smile. 'That is, even if my memory only goes back ten years.'

Venetia's eyes then filled with a soft light. She couldn't bear to think of the ordeal he had suffered, and continued to suffer. 'Oh Paolo, I promise I'll furnish your memory with so many golden times that it'll be a treasure book to replace the old ones, and all you ever need.'

'Let me take you away for a few days, *cara*, so we can begin to fill this wonderful album then. Where would you like to go?' He nipped her chin with his thumb and forefinger.

'Are you really asking me to choose?'

'*Naturalmente*. The world is vast and I'll take you wherever you fancy.'

Venetia's crystal laugh filled the room. 'You're so extreme, Paolo – I don't need the world, though it's very sweet of you to offer. There are so many places in Italy that I haven't explored. I've always wanted to visit Sardinia, I suppose, and never had the opportunity, and apparently it's quite unspoilt compared with the other islands. I usually go back to England for Easter, but my father is spending the holiday in Scotland with friends this year, so I was thinking of going back to Venice next week, on Good Friday, to spend it with my godmother.'

'Sardinia is a wonderful idea. I myself would also have chosen one of the islands of Italy.' He had his hands locked behind her waist, arching an eyebrow as his secret smile returned, 'And Sardinia is my favourite – it has a unique way of celebrating Easter. Events take place all through the holy week. The Monday before Easter, the *Lunissanti*, is a very emotional ceremony in Castelsardo that starts at dawn and ends at nightfall. If we leave by plane from Pisa to Alghero tomorrow, we could be in Castelsardo in time for the evening procession, which is the most moving part of the event. *Bene*. I'll rent a car for the week from the airport. *Me ne occupo immediatamente*, I'll make arrangements at once.'

But Venetia was wrestling with doubts. Everything was going a little too quickly. She remembered Nanny Horren's favourite saying: '*The devil takes a hand in what's done in haste.*' If she were sensible, she wouldn't be going anywhere with him, at least not yet.

'Are you sure? You don't want to think about it?'

'What is there to think about, *cara*?'

'You're so impulsive, Paolo! And then, it's a whole week you're talking about here, not just the Easter weekend. We haven't yet gone through the documentation of your project. Is it very wise?'

Venetia knew she was making excuses, playing for time... all she needed really was a little push to get her to cross the slim line between *Maybe not* and *Why not?*

Paolo gazed down at her. 'Venetia, you must take the opportunity when it arises. *Life's too short* is my motto, and so I make sure that important things come first. Spending a few days together in a beautiful place to get to know each other better is what counts for me, *carina*. All the rest is *senza importanza*.' He gestured dismissively.

'You definitely don't waste any time.'

A spasm of pain crossed his face. 'Having lost one life, I've been very fortunate to be allowed a second chance at living, and I intend to do that to the full and not waste a single moment in procrastination. I accept what is given to me today and I intend to enjoy it all.'

And as Venetia met his deep-blue brooding eyes she realised her decision was made.

She went back to La Sirena to start packing. There was a dress she was particularly fond of that she wanted to take with her, but it was missing a button. She went looking for Ernestina to ask for a needle and thread and found her sitting at the door of the stables with Antonio and Rufus. The dog sprang forward, barking ferociously as Venetia walked towards the housekeeper, and she leapt back, her heart pounding. She was not usually afraid of dogs, but she found Rufus intimidating.

It took Antonio a few seconds before he ordered the beast to sit down quietly. He smiled at Venetia slyly. 'You mustn't show that you're scared of him, *signorina*. Rufus is usually a friendly dog, but animals, they can smell fear. Intelligent creatures, dogs. See, Rufus, here, knows he's frightening you. He feels threatened, and that makes him act up.'

Ernestina shook her head. 'How many times has the *signore* told you to keep that animal in check, eh? One day he's going zto injure somebody,' she told the caretaker reprovingly. 'You were looking for me, *signorina*?'

'Yes, I was wondering if you could lend me a needle and some purple thread. I need to sew back a button on one of my dresses.'

Ernestina beamed, showing off her brilliant white teeth. 'I have a box full of threads of all tints and colours, *signorina*. Give me the dress and I will match the thread and sew the button on for you.'

'Are you sure? I wouldn't want to trouble you.'

'There's no trouble, *signorina*.'

'That's very kind of you.'

'*E'un piacere servire la signorina*. It's a pleasure to serve the *signorina*.'

At that point, Antonio whistled at Rufus to follow him and lumbered off. The two women walked back together to the cottage. Venetia took the dress out of the cupboard. A beautiful Parigi purple chiffon dress with a puffball full, short skirt and low-backed ruched bodice, it fastened at the side with twelve tiny buttons made of the same material.

'Oh, *signorina*, you will steal the spotlight wherever you go in this!' The housekeeper passed her hand lovingly over the flounces of material. 'The colour is *squisito*.' Then, noticing Venetia's suitcase open on the table, she frowned. 'But you are leaving us already?'

'No, no, no, just for Easter,' Venetia answered quickly, hoping that she wouldn't pursue her interrogation.

At that moment there was a knock at the door. It was Paolo coming to take her out for lunch.

'Are you ready, *amore mio*?' He almost entered the room and then stopped in the doorway as he noticed the housekeeper holding the dress. This time he merely looked at Venetia, completely unembarrassed by Ernestina's presence.

'*Oh, com'è bella!* What a beautiful dress, *cara*. In it you will look like a purple butterfly, so dainty, *così eterea*, so ethereal.'

Ernestina was eyeing them with her bird-like glance and Venetia felt herself flushing.

'Give me the button that's missing, *signorina*. I'll sew it back on and return it to your room. You'll find it done when you come home after lunch.'

'Thank you, Ernestina.'

The housekeeper left, carrying the dress. Paolo turned to Venetia. '*Andiamo*?'

'Yes, I'm ready.'

'Have you finished packing?'

'Almost, there's only that dress and my wash bag.'

'Splendid then, let's go for lunch.'

That afternoon, after lunch, they worked solidly, going over the plans, assessing, arguing. Venetia made suggestions, many of them in direct contradiction with the original designs, and though Paolo listened, discussed, and gave his ideas, she noticed that if the plans didn't comply with her propositions, he usually altered the project here and there as they went along in accordance with her advice, almost encouraging her to make it her own. They functioned well together, taking pleasure in each other's company, entering into each other's enthusiasms. She was amazed at the way they got on, their brains clicking with the same perfection and compatibility as their bodies had shown that morning. They sparked off each other and when they disagreed on a point, it was only because their contrasting ideas complemented one another.

Paolo laid his hand on hers as they were studying the plans spread out on the table in front of them. 'I'm happy that you've taken on this assignment, Venetia,' he said, grinning and curling his arm around her waist, pulling her gently towards him, 'not only because it will keep you near me, but also because you're a brilliant architect and restorer, with a flair and taste that I've seldom seen. For any other firm, it would just be another contract; they would look at the project from a purely business point of view but I know that you will look at it with the eyes of your heart. You'll weigh all the elements: aesthetics, history, conservation, and business too, and you'll give each aspect its fair due without compromising on any one of them.' He cocked his head and his eyes shone with admiration and love.

Venetia blushed and smiled playfully, holding on to his forearms. 'Well, that's certainly a vote of confidence, *Signor* Barone, which I hope I'll live up to. I must admit that, to start off with, I didn't want to get involved with the project for reasons that you might have guessed.' She looked up at him shyly through her long lashes. 'But although it's a challenge, now that I've visited the site and seen the plans I'm really very excited about it.'

In the late afternoon they went for a stroll in the garden. Paolo had a firm arm about Venetia's shoulders. The clear golden sunshine crowned the hills. They couldn't see the sea, it was behind them, but the hills were beauty enough to gaze at and lose oneself in for hours at a time; and besides, they didn't need the scenery, they had each other.

'I've been starved of the warm, sweet touch of a woman and I'm hungry for more of you. I had read about this wonderful feeling... I'd heard other men talk about it and still I hadn't found it, until today, in your arms.' Paolo's eyes were intense, wandering over the scenery and then back to Venetia as he spoke.

Venetia gazed up at him, seeing above her his wide shoulders rampant with masculine force and his strong protectiveness. She wondered how such a hulk of a man could be so vulnerable, and she leaned further into him as they walked, immersing herself happily in that thought. They sat on the edge of a fountain that played in a round stone lily pond and watched the goldfish swim out their circular lives.

At this hour, the garden was teaming with birdsong. A blackbird, perched on the branch of a small pine tree, was sending forth his notes, which tumbled out on to the air like a little fairy trill cascading over invisible stones. Here and there, he seemed so thrilled with the loveliness of his own song that he got the notes all jumbled up and they came out like a veritable splotch of music. From a distance away somewhere, a mistle thrush sent out his ringing like a question: *Did-he-do-it? Did-he-do-it?* And from farther away still came the cawing conversation of rooks. Venetia could see their black shapes flapping about the sky, the outlines ragged. They might have been pieces of black paper caught up and blown about in the wind. She revelled in the calm beauty of it all. The air, only just moving in a light breeze, felt clean, and it was so soft, passing like folds of invisible velvet over her skin. She hadn't felt as happy and serene since those far-off days when she used to go for walks with Judd in Kew Gardens.

Later, Paolo and Venetia had dinner on the *terrazzo* among the dwarf potted lemon and orange trees and the large Etruscan urns overflowing with flowers. All around them was the scent of freesias, whose sweet fragrance rose like incense from the sunken garden to the terrace. They watched as the sun slipped steadily lower and lower, chasing the long shadows from the valleys, and with remarkable swiftness changed its golden flame for coral-red, as bright as a branding iron. The sea turned purple, and above, the sky darkened and began to glow with the phosphorescence of night. Then, overpowering everything else, the Tuscan islands of the Tyrrhenian Sea started to shine and blaze with hot ochre light. It seemed as if the sea itself was steaming from the immersion of these burnt-sugar creatures, covered with ice-green lichens that here and there occurred and vanished in the broad consuming glow.

After dinner, Paolo walked Venetia back to La Sirena. The moon was shining, the stars winking at them happily in the navy velvet canopy above. The sea was like a table of amethyst liquid, glistening with moonlight. In the distance, the Port of Santo Stefano wore her lights as a woman wears her diamonds, sparkling and glowing against the darker bulk of the hills behind. There was something infinitely peaceful and refreshing now that the sun had gone down; the air was as wine – cool and reviving, intoxicating the lovers.

Paolo stopped at the doorway. Their eyes met for a brief moment as Venetia hesitated, and in that instant she was conscious of every detail about him, which was enough to send wild yearning surging through her. She shivered.

'Let's go in,' he murmured.

'Oh, Paolo,' she breathed as he tried to pick her up, while fire shot to life inside her. 'We have a long way to go tomorrow. You need to have a good rest. You'll be driving, and you mustn't be tired.' Her voice was gentle to match the quiet of the night.

He gazed down at her. 'I'm never tired when I'm with you.'

'Well, perhaps just a small nightcap.' A little smile flickered around her mouth. 'But you must promise me that you'll go back to the house after. I don't want to be worrying tomorrow.' She looked at him shyly.

'Looking at you now, *cara*, hard as it will be, I promise I'll go.'

He wandered into the sitting room to pour them both a shot of *grappa*, while Venetia headed for the bedroom to fetch a cardigan. The temperature had dropped somewhat and she was beginning to feel slightly chilly.

Then with a little cry she stopped in the doorway, rooted to the spot. Appalled, she came into the room, unable to believe her eyes. There, lying pitifully on the ground in an unrecognisable pile was the beautiful purple dress that she had entrusted to Ernestina. It was ripped from the oval neckline through to the hem and, as if that had not been enough, the ethereal purple chiffon had been slashed in the most savage way, the shredded lengths of it scattered around the room. A cold, sick feeling gripped Venetia's heart, crushing it with a mixture of fear and anger. It was a deliberate expression of violence and malice. She could think of only one person who could have wrought such a wanton, passionate act of hatred... Allegra.

'Venetia, what's wrong?' Paolo came bursting into the room.

'I've just found this.'

Paolo looked horrified as she held up the garment. 'But how... who could have done that? I can't believe that anybody could do something so utterly evil.' Something indefinable flickered for a moment in his eyes but his expression was ferocious.

'Jealousy is very corrosive.' Venetia stared back at him, trying to control her emotion.

'You mean Allegra?'

'I haven't the faintest idea, but there are not so many people at Miraggio who would have a bone to pick with me.'

'Though I know Allegra can be swayed by her passions, I think it very unlikely that she would attack you in this under-handed way. She would be more likely to start a fight with you, I think. This is the work of someone with a tortuous mind – it is more likely to be Antonio than his niece.'

Perhaps this was true. To Venetia's knowledge, the girl hadn't had a chance to see the dress. Could it have been Antonio? She had difficulty imagining the caretaker doing such a thing, but maybe... As she picked up one of the pieces of ruined fabric, her eyes brimmed with unshed tears of outrage and resentment.

'Here, *cara*, let me see.'

She handed it to him, but didn't look at his face. Somehow, she couldn't let him see how much it had affected her. Bringing it up to the lamp, he examined the thin purple cloth closely.

'As I thought... it's the work of an animal. Rufus... See?' He gave her back the dress and paced the room, looking pensive. The holes made by the sharp incisors were showing clearly in some parts of the material, still damp with the dog's saliva.

'Yes, you're right. Antonio must have set Rufus on it,' she said quietly.

'I don't like this one bit.' Paolo suddenly looked up and saw the look on Venetia's face. '*Cara*, are you all right?' He gath-ered her firmly into his arms, pressing his mouth against her hair. '*Comportamento scandaloso*, outrageous behaviour! I will ring my lawyer tomorrow to terminate Antonio's contract – I want them both off Miraggio.'

'Don't be so quick, Paolo,' Venetia said. She turned her face up to his, watching the scowl darken his features ominously in a way she hadn't seen before. 'Wait until we get back and then maybe you can have a talk with him and sort this out. I don't want to be the cause of a rift between you and Allegra. After all, you do love her as a daughter and maybe you'll be able to talk her into being sensible about...' she hesitated, '... about us.'

It wasn't exactly her first impulse, she thought uncharitably, but despite her bitter feelings towards the Italian girl now, she knew she would regret it later if she didn't try to give Allegra a second chance.

There was a warm light in Paolo's eyes. 'Oh, *amore mio*, you have such a kind heart. It's one of the things I love most about you. I'm so sorry about this nasty mess – it's very disturbing and, yes, I'll put it right as soon as we get back to Miraggio after Easter.'

Venetia felt herself relax a little and pulled away from him. 'I think I could do with that drink now.'

They walked back into the sitting room and Paolo handed her one of the shots of *grappa* he had poured. She sipped at the fiery amber liquid and welcomed the warmth in her stomach that seeped through her limbs. She watched as he downed his own drink in one gulp. Seeing her raise her eyebrows, he glanced at her.

'I needed that too,' he explained. His features had grown tense and distracted again, and she knew his mind was playing on what he was going to do.

'Paolo, please don't worry.'

He set his glass down and started pacing again, the fingers of one hand loosely on his hip, the other combing through his hair. 'Of course I'm worried, *cara*. I think I should stay with you tonight.' He stood in front of her, his piercing blue gaze anxious.

She hesitated for a moment, putting her own glass on the small coffee table, next to the bowl of fruit. 'No, Paolo – you don't need to do that, I'll be fine.'

'Venetia, how do you think I can leave you tonight, after this?' He reached out and traced his thumb along her bottom lip. 'If something ever happened to you because of me, I could never forgive myself,' he murmured.

She sighed, blinking up at him. 'Paolo, please, we'll sort this out. If it was Antonio, he wouldn't actually harm me. He wouldn't dare. It's obvious this was just meant as scare tactics. Nothing's going to happen. I've been on my own since I was nineteen and managed fine.'

'But, *cara*, you're not on your own. You have me, now.' He took her chin in his hand.

'Yes, I know, and it's wonderful, believe me, Paolo. But I'm a big girl and I can look after myself. I can't explain… it's just important that I still can. Besides, if you stay, they will have won, whoever they are. I refuse to be intimated. My English backbone will see me through, you know that.' In an attempt at teasing she touched his raised forearm and gave him her most plucky smile. She would not give Antonio or his niece the satisfaction of knowing they had got to her.

Paolo's eyes were still wary but he nodded his agreement. His hands pulled her close, and she held up her flushed face. For a minute or two, he held Venetia tightly, and the hard pressure of his lips on her mouth as he bent down and kissed her was so thrilling that she almost weakened and asked him to stay the night. The temptation to lie in his comforting arms until dawn was almost overwhelming. The only measure of time was the pounding of Venetia's heart and, unconsciously, her hands moved towards his face as the kiss slowly ended.

'*Ti adoro,*' he whispered huskily, now placing a chaste kiss on her forehead. 'You mean everything to me. I will never let anything happen to you, Venetia.' His eyes were shining with passion but there was also a trace of sadness as he stroked her cheek softly with his finger. Taking her hand as they both went to the door, Paolo kissed her once more. Then he walked away towards the house.

Venetia stood in the doorway until he had disappeared and she could no longer hear his steps on the gravel. Finally she went in.

She walked back to the bedroom, undoing her blouse, her mind and body still full of Paolo. Sitting on the bed, she was jolted back to reality by the sight of the pieces of ripped fabric still littering the floor. Who on earth would go to these lengths to separate her and Paolo? If Ernestina had left the door of the cottage open after having hung up the dress in the bedroom, perhaps the dog could have come in and mangled it. It was a rather far-fetched idea but, without a witness, who knew what was possible? No, surely it was the caretaker: Antonio. Ferociously in favour of his niece, obviously aware of the relationship developing between Venetia and Paolo, he had declared his own war on her to make her leave. Or Allegra herself had perhaps put him up to it. A beautiful Amazon, a nasty giant and a dangerous dog… Venetia shivered, feeling frozen to the bone in a world of hostility from which she could see no chance of escape, at least for the moment.

She glanced at her watch. It was late; she should get some sleep. She picked up the tatters of her lovely dress and stored them away in the cupboard and then, on a second thought, shoved them into her suitcase.

That night, she went through a dreary hell while she lay for hours in her bed, staring out of the open window, gazing at the moon and the stars, trying not to think of the frightening possibilities. Her imagination worked at a hundred miles an hour, conjuring all sorts of dreadful scenarios. What ogres the mind calls forth in the darkest depths of night can be dwarfed in the warm light of morning, carried away on the wings of dawn. And so Venetia told herself that she would look at things differently tomorrow. She got up, made herself a cup of hot milk, and went back to bed, finally dropping off into a restless sleep.

*   *   *

The next morning, Paolo dressed quickly and made his way to his study. Perhaps Venetia was right, he thought, as he strode through the dark gothic corridors of the house; he ought to wait to deal with Antonio until after they returned from Sardinia, when he had calmed down.

But he'd made up his mind: the man had to go. That the caretaker could have let his dog into the cottage with the deliberate intention of scaring Venetia, even if she wasn't there, was unthinkable. And if she had been there, what then? Would he have hurt her, even accidentally? Antonio had always been protective of Allegra, and would probably do anything for her if he thought she was threatened in some way. He had never been any trouble before, but Paolo wouldn't be able to trust the man again. He had been thinking about the problem of the caretaker and his niece even before Venetia had come on to the scene. And if he and Venetia were to be together... No, Antonio was finished at Miraggio.

He frowned deeply. As for Allegra... He hadn't promised Venetia that he would defer dealing with *her*. At first light, when

Ernestina had brought him coffee in his room, he had asked the housekeeper to tell Allegra to meet him in his study in an hour. He was going to have it out with the girl before he set foot on a plane to Sardinia. This was a conversation he couldn't put off. His fury at her behaviour was unlike any he could remember since taking her in all those years ago. Had he misjudged how damaged she was?

Her constantly dissolute ways were one thing – he had shown weakness there out of indulgence, and a mistaken faith that she would grow up, change. This new outrage wasn't just designed to get his attention, like her other unsavoury antics; this time, she had involved Venetia. Well, she had his attention now, she could be sure of that. He had loved and trusted her like a daughter but she had repaid him with bitterness and betrayal.

As he strode up the steps to his study, Paolo tried to calm himself, wrestling with disappointment and anger. When he opened the door, she was already there, draped in one of the armchairs near the door. She was wearing a low-cut green dress, fitted at the bodice with a flowing skirt that was hitched up around her thighs as she hung her shapely legs over the side of the chair. Paolo regarded her coldly. It was now even more distasteful to him that she persisted in flaunting herself with such unsubtle and adolescent clumsiness.

'You wanted to see me, Paolo?' Allegra stared at him, her voice sweetly purring and her smile innocent, though it did not reach her eyes.

'Yes. Was it you or Antonio?' He cut straight to the point.

'I've no idea what you're talking about, Paolo.'

If he was unsure before, Paolo now knew the truth. Just by looking at her he could tell that she knew exactly what had happened, and a fierce mixture of all the anger, disappointment and guilt that he'd been feeling towards her surged through him. He stood in front of her, his hands behind his back, struggling to keep his composure.

'What you did was unforgivable, Allegra. An act of pure malice that I would never have thought you capable of! Now I know better, and I cannot forgive you for that.'

The young woman watched him through her thick, black lashes for a moment, seemingly unfazed by his outburst, but didn't answer.

Paolo glowered at her and gritted his teeth. 'The dress, Allegra – Venetia's dress! You got Antonio to set his hound on it, didn't you? Thought you'd try and scare off your "rival", no?'

'Fine, the dress, Paolo! Yes, I might have asked *Zio* Antonio to help me make you see sense. It just isn't fair that you spend so much time with that woman. What can she give you that I can't?' She pouted and shifted sulkily in her chair.

Paolo blinked, incredulous. 'So you thought breaking into the cottage and getting Rufus to savage her clothes was the solution? What if she had been there? She would have been terrified!'

'So what? Perhaps being a little scared would have made her reconsider her stay here and she would have run off back to Venice, where she belongs.'

He paused, trying to rein in his temper and his voice was dangerously low. 'She belongs here with me, Allegra, and I cannot give you what you want from me. You'll just have to accept this is the way things are.'

The raven-haired girl suddenly jumped out of her chair and rounded on him, her eyes now wild.

'I will never accept that Englishwoman as long as I breathe!'

His brow furrowed. '*Dio mio*! Stop acting like a child, Allegra.'

'I'm not a child. I'm a woman and the sooner you see that, the better,' she hissed acidly. 'This Englishwoman cannot give you the kind of love you need. She doesn't know you – *I* do!'

Paolo's eyes frosted and his stare was unwavering. 'This is the first time I have found real love with a woman and I mean to marry Venetia.'

Stunned, the young woman took a step back from him. He could see in her eyes the realisation that she was finally defeated.

'Yes, Allegra, it's true. I have never met a woman that I cared about enough to replace my wife. Now I have. And I will not have you jeopardise that through your misguided, adolescent feelings for me. I care about you, but not in the way you want. I've never given you any cause to think that I have.' His voice softened a little. 'I'm sorry, *cara*.'

She gazed blankly back at him and seemed to gather her wits before her features contorted with frustrated rage. 'Then she will know what it is like to yearn for a man and never have him! I have learned things that will teach her the meaning of despair,' she spat, her hands clenched at her sides while her breathing came thick and fast.

Paolo blanched, but ice-blue anger flashed in his eyes. 'Leave her alone. I mean it, Allegra. If anything happens to Venetia, I'll hold you personally responsible and you will never see me again.' His voice was low and restrained but with an undercurrent of something more menacing.

Allegra stared at him, fear and longing sparking in her dark eyes. Paolo knew at that moment that he still held a power over her. She took a step forward, desperation now in her gaze, but for him she had passed the point of no return.

Paolo turned and faced the tall picture window, flicking his Zippo lighter open. He dragged on his cigarette then blew out the flame, his eyes empty, scanning the vista of cliffs, forests and the rolling Tyrrhenian Sea stretching away from the house.

'As it is, I want you gone from Miraggio. You leave me no choice. I am buying a small house for you in Porto Ercole, where you should be comfortable. If you agree to take up your studies again and make something of yourself, you will also receive a regular allowance from me, enough to see you through to a career of your choice.'

Allegra scoffed. 'Studies? I know all I need to know! I have plans of my own,' she whispered, the proud emotion trembling in her voice. Paolo turned and saw the dark rebellion in her face. Resigned, he waved a hand vaguely in the air.

'As you like, Allegra – the offer will always be there.'

Allegra turned on her heels and stalked towards the door. Throwing a glance over her shoulder, she muttered, 'You can keep your Englishwoman, I don't need you any more, Paolo.'

He looked at her, a mixture of sadness and relief washing through him, but he said nothing. They exchanged one last look and she was gone.

Paolo sighed. Perhaps Allegra would cool down, change her ways, and they could re-establish some kind of relationship. He was still fond of her and wanted to see her rise above the wretched misery of her childhood and learn how to be happy. The house he had spotted in Porto Ercole would provide a good life for her and for her uncle. She would still be close enough for him to visit from time to time, but also far enough to be out of Venetia's way and not cause any trouble.

He looked out into the sky as it clouded over and narrowed his eyes, turning his lighter over in his fingers.

'So many complications,' he murmured.

CHAPTER 10

Venetia and Paolo left early the next morning for Pisa to catch a plane to Alghero in Northern Sardinia. The sun was brass-bright and high when they got off the plane at Alghero's Fertilia Airport, and Venetia was glad that she could peel down to her loose cotton sleeveless blouse and mini-skirt. The island, with its distant serrated mountain peaks, seemed to shine with borrowed gold in the sharp glare, like stairs leading into a huge blue-domed basilica of sky overhead. Venetia was dazzled by the vibrating landscape. She inhaled deeply the intoxicating rich, dry odours of summer herbs, and was suddenly overcome by one of those wild surges of happiness that had eluded her since those far-off years when she had basked in Judd's love. She shivered a little despite the heat and slipped her hand into Paolo's as they crossed the tarmac.

On arrival at the car hire company in the airport, Paolo picked up a Ferrari 550, the same model as the one he had left behind at Galileo Galilei, Pisa.

Venetia arched an enquiring eyebrow as he held the door open for her. 'Same car, why is that?'

'I'm a man of habit,' he replied, his eyes gleaming as she slid past him closely and into the front seat. 'If you know something works, why go looking elsewhere?'

How very logical and disciplined, she thought, as he closed the door and came round to the driver's side. He started the engine and let a Ford Mustang pull out slowly in front of them on its way to the exit. How odd to see an American car, she thought absentmindedly. As he turned on to the main road towards Sassari, Paolo glanced at her with a questioning look.

'Happy, *cara*?'

'Oh yes, Paolo,' she whispered, and beamed at him. She *was* happy, she realised. She hadn't felt like this for so long. He grinned back at her, squeezing her knee, and Venetia watched him so relaxed behind the wheel, the sleeves of his crisp, white shirt rolled up to reveal his muscular, tanned forearms.

At first she had only seen in Paolo a human being weighed down with problems, and her heart had gone out to him; true, along with the sympathy, she had felt a certain amount of curiosity, and then of course there had always been the undeniable chemistry between them and the uncanny, singular impression that she had known him all her life.

Still, on top of all these visceral attractions, the more she got to know Paolo, the more Venetia respected him, although from time to time he gave the impression of being overwhelmed by melancholy in a way that made her wonder if there were still unanswered questions about this man beside her. He seemed to have so many intriguing layers to him, not least his courageous acceptance of the amnesia and his philosophical matter-of-fact approach in dealing with it. She admired him for that. She was also surprised at the simple way he had clarified the ambiguous situation between him and Allegra, the manner in which he'd spoken about his dead wife, and how he had justified his notorious reputation.

But, as ever, her mind was invaded by creeping doubts. Had he manipulated her into thinking his explanations were all acceptable and natural? Could she trust him? Was it possible he could deliberately blind himself to Allegra's seductive behaviour just because of the difference in their ages? Perhaps Venetia was being naive in believing him just because she knew her emotional involvement with Paolo was already too far gone.

One thing was for sure, Paolo had now been more forthcoming than she herself had been about her own past. Venetia had told him nothing of her involvement with Judd or the tragic loss of her baby. He knew before they had made love that she was not a virgin; still, he had tactfully made sure she really wanted to give herself to him before taking entire possession of her body, and then had asked no questions. And now, as Venetia sat quietly next to him, her hands in her lap, looking at his strong profile etched in sharp outline against the open window, she felt a pang of guilt. It wasn't right that she should know so much about him, and yet Paolo be kept in the dark concerning a part of her life that had left her so deeply scarred, and had shaped a substantial portion of her psyche.

They rolled along in silence, almost overpowered by the weight of nature around them – for now, to either side, the majesty of this mountainous island began to impress itself: on one side towering black humps racing far into the sea, while on the other the near slopes of the *macchia* rose up, small hills so thickly covered with aromatic scrub that the high-ridged hilltops looked smooth and furry like convulsed green baize against the blue sky.

'The air smells delicious,' Venetia noted as wafts of sweet fragrance floated through the window from the many odorous plants that carpeted the countryside.

'Apparently, more than two thousand, five hundred species of wild flowering shrubs grow on the Isle of Sardinia. In ancient times, oarsmen of boats knew this island from a distance because of the perfume that drifted far out over the sea.'

Venetia smiled fondly at Paolo's love of encyclopaedic pronouncements. Thinking about the stunning gardens at Miraggio, she wondered at his obvious love of horticulture and how at odds this was with the tough physicality of the man himself.

'I've never asked you about your rose garden.' Something that Ernestina had said came back to her. 'Why do you never let anyone else tend it?'

'Ever since I woke up in that hospital bed, battered, with no memory, I've regarded myself as an abomination, an abhorrent creature.'

'Oh no, but Paolo…'

He lifted his hand and smiled ruefully. 'Let me explain, *cara*… I value my peace and my privacy now, to be left alone with my thoughts. The rose garden is my sanctuary. And there I can indulge the fanciful side of my mind perhaps. You know that fairytale, "Beauty and the Beast"? Well, like the Beast I guarded my roses jealously, maybe in the hope that one day a beautiful and kind-hearted lady would enter my garden, close her eyes to my defects and release me from my pain.' He glanced at her, reaching across with one hand and stroking Venetia's cheek with the back of his fingers, a tender gesture that she was beginning to recognise. 'You are my rose now, my beautiful and compassionate Venetia. The Beast feels a man again – I just hope I'll be worthy of your love.'

'Paolo, you're the most worthy man I've ever met,' she whispered and they needed no words in the silence that fell between them for a moment. Venetia gazed out of the window at the epic landscape with its evergreen hills and dwindling trees that seemed so timeless in its beauty.

'It's amazing countryside, so wild and yet so vibrant in colour and in texture… and so varied,' she breathed.

'Legend has it that after God created all the dry land and

seas, he created rocks, which he then casually cast into the sea and trod upon. From his footprint sprung an island, a little continent unto itself containing every conceivable type of landscape. Then, to make it perfect, he took all the best of what he had already created elsewhere and dispersed it across the surface of what is today called Sardinia.'

She laughed out loud, delighted at the picture. 'Have I ever told you that you're a tremendous raconteur, Paolo? How do you remember all these legends?'

Paolo grinned and shrugged. 'My memory is not clogged up with useless material, and I make sure I store in it only things that interest me, that are pleasant and that I like.'

'That's remarkably philosophical.' She studied his profile. 'I was only thinking a moment ago how I admire the way you deal with your loss of memory.'

'What else am I to do, *cara*? Of course, every breath I draw can be a reminder of the loss I've suffered, but time has a way of robbing the grim satisfaction from making one's life miserable. It has a way of obliterating pain, and you get used to what life has dealt you and learn to accept and make the most of it... Not so?' Paolo slanted her a look.

That was his overture, his gentle invitation for Venetia to open up to him. She tried to avert her eyes, hoping to avoid answering him and get off the subject he had skilfully manoeuvred them on to.

'You still don't trust me, *cara*?'

'It has nothing to do with trust.' Venetia's tone was clipped, her expression harried.

Paolo said nothing for a while and then his eyes darkened.

'This man Judd, you still love him?'

'Of course not,' she was quick to answer. Paolo was silent again and Venetia glanced at him. She let out a long breath.

The time had clearly come; she could no longer avoid telling him everything.

'I was very young,' she began in a low voice. 'He was my first love and my parents didn't approve of our relationship. Even though I was forbidden to see him, we continued to meet and I got pregnant. He was away when I found out. I wrote to him and told him I was going to have his child, but he never answered and I never heard from him again. Such an ordinary story,' she ended ruefully.

Paolo raised his eyebrows, but made no comment, his gaze fastened intently on the road in front of him. Venetia couldn't tell what he was thinking and her eyes clouded with uncertainty.

'I don't love him any more, if that's what you're wondering,' she said, her voice breaking with anguish.

He seemed not to have heard her. A muscle pulled in the side of his jaw and his mouth was set in such a grim line that for one quivering moment she thought he might change his mind about her. 'So you have a child, Venetia?'

'No… no! I had a bad fall at the beginning of my pregnancy, which resulted in my losing the baby.'

Numerous emotions seemed to cross his face and he blinked slowly.

'You've had your share of loss, *cara*. Perhaps that's why you seem to be so attuned to mine. I have always felt we are kindred spirits and now I know why: we've both been touched by tragedy, but we're survivors. And happily we have found each other.'

'I thought I'd never love again, that I'd never trust a man enough to…'

'To give yourself with the passion you showed me yesterday?' Though he was still watching the road, Paolo's voice was low and husky.

Venetia nodded, her body flooding suddenly with yearning, a longing for the feel of him at the centre of her being, for possessing and being possessed by this man whom she had known only a couple of months. Desire bloomed wildly inside her.

She could feel Paolo sense her change of mood, and could almost taste the same need in him to seize this moment, as the atmosphere charged instantly between them. Without even glancing in the mirror, he quickly pulled over to the side of the road and turned off the engine.

'I want you, *amore mio* – now,' he murmured, leaning across, his eyes devouring her. He drew in a sharp breath and lifted her hand to his lips, pressing fervent little kisses across her palm, making Venetia shiver, robbing her of every thought. Then before she could catch her breath, Paolo was out of the car and holding her door open.

'We'll stop here for a while.'

It sounded more like a command than a suggestion, but she didn't care which it was.

'Yes,' she murmured. Oh yes, she couldn't wait! Her mouth went dry. She wanted him now, to kiss him, caress him, love him… to make him feel as precious to her as he had shown she was to him.

His eyes were scorching as, holding her hand, he gently but firmly pulled her along next to him, up the rocky path from the roadside.

How quiet everything was. No forest murmur here, no longer any trees to move in those slight breezes that fanned the two shores; only sometimes the silent glint of a bird skimming the low branches, or curving up suddenly like a feather kicked on the hot air. Hand in hand, they climbed one of the low hills, and though steep and tiring, the climb was a joy: a sense of great freedom among such wind-washed luxuriance in the warm spring sun, and one of anticipation as the ache low in Venetia's abdomen increased by the second.

Finally they reached the hilltop where the moss-green ground was soft and even, with nothing around them but emptiness and the great sky, blue and wide. At last Paolo, more alive than ever, drew her into his arms and with expert deftness released himself of his clothes as Venetia stood before him, mesmerised.

She ran her tongue over her dry bottom lip and Paolo's gaze flicked over her scantily clad figure. His eyes gleamed, filled with desire.

'*Dio mio*, I want you now… right here.'

Paolo's hands went to her hair and he tugged at it so that her head tilted back, exposing her smooth neck to his mouth. Breathing fast against her skin, he lifted her mini-skirt and hooking his thumbs in her panties, peeled them off and swept her up to him. He ran his palms over the quivering curves of her hips and parted her thighs to let his long, deft fingers trace the infinitely more sensitive and intimate place below the soft chestnut triangle of curls. Venetia let herself drift into the sensuality of his closeness and his touch. She could hear herself moaning and then whimpering his name as she wrapped her legs tightly around his waist and her arms about his neck, clinging to him, desperately wanting to feel him inside her; but he did not enter her, instead brushing the velvet tip of his male hardness lightly against the moist soft-ness of her femininity.

'Now, Paolo, now,' she pleaded, but his touch controlled her, taking her to the edge and just as she thought she was going to tip over, bringing her back, making her cry out for more.

And then he laid her down on the soft, mossy grass. They were both naked now and Venetia had no idea how that had happened; the only thing that mattered was that she could feel herself dissolving under his warm skin, and her fingers tangled with his hair.

Paolo started off by making love to Venetia's mouth, letting his tongue trace the contour of her parted lips, his minted breath fanning her cheeks. Then moving down to her throat he lingered there for a few seconds before burying his face in her sweet scented hair and the warmth of her neck. He showered butterfly kisses down her throat, running a hand over her with a whispering touch as he went along his sensual journey, gripping her in a desperate hunger that escalated with each caress.

His thumbs grazed over her taut nipples as his mouth explored the valley between the ripe mounds of her cream-fleshed breasts, before fastening on the pink swollen peaks. Venetia's hand ran down the length of his spine to press him still closer, every cell of her skin impatient, begging for the scorching contact of his desire.

And now his lips scrolled down over her flat stomach, running his tongue so slowly over her flushed skin, sending impatient messages to the core of her need. A torment of sweet sensation sent rippling, drugging waves through her trembling limbs.

'Please, Paolo, love me,' she pleaded again, her eyes closed, abandoned in a haze of heated anticipation, but he was deliberately making her wait, she knew, so the release would be so much sweeter and more powerful.

Instinctively her hand moved down, tracing the long muscles of his thighs and the contour of his buttocks until she felt the extraordinary contraction of his muscled arousal beneath her fingertips. Paolo sucked in his breath and groaned as she fondled him, teasing and tantalising, stroking and caressing. Venetia watched as his eyes became pools of muted sapphire, swimming with surges of emotion that made them look darker from moment to moment, as his body pulsated under each stroke; he was almost beautiful. She sensed that Paolo had abandoned himself to her, enraptured by her caresses, revelling in her touch. In turn she was giving back some of the pleasure he had lavished on her, making him realise how much she loved and cherished every part of him; and the knowledge that she was pleasing him and stirring in him all the exquisite and sensual trembles of approaching climax fuelled her own excitement.

'*Rallenta, amore mio,*' Paolo said thickly, his breathing quickening and she felt a shudder run through his length and saw his eyes glazing over. 'You excite me more than any woman I have known,' he groaned again. 'I need you, Venetia, take me inside you, *amore mio!*'

She could sense the straining tension of his body poised on the brink, the urgency of his desire that could not endure any more delaying, and so she gently guided him to where they both wanted him to be. She let him slide into the damp warmth of her, receiving him with all the love she had, allowing him to stretch her, enthralling her as he pushed deeper and deeper, faster and more urgent, an aching sweetness accompanying his invasion. And then suddenly Venetia felt his convulsions as if they were her own – they *were* her own – they were panting and groaning together as body owned body in an act of possession that was totally overpowering. Waves of release pulsed through them again and again, the echoes of their cries of ecstasy breaking from their throats, filling the air around them.

Paolo lay on top of Venetia, heaving, his face buried in her lush chestnut mane.

'Your touch is so sensual, *amore mio*, so erotic…' he breathed softly, still trembling with the emotions she had provoked, 'that I will never stop begging you for more. How do you do this to me? You have bewitched me, Venetia, body and soul.'

His words, more than all the voluptuous sensations she had suffered at his hands, flooded her with pride and pleasure.

She had never thought any man could make her feel fulfilled as a woman ever again, but he had.

'I love you, Paolo,' she murmured, cradling him and stroking his head with infinite tenderness. 'You've given me back my soul, my ability to feel real emotion again.'

She kept her arms wrapped around him until finally he moved off her, releasing her of his weight. She let out a tiny startled sound as for a flash she felt cold and lost without the warmth and security of his body.

'We must go, *tesoro mio*,' he told her as he helped her up and once again stroked her face with the back of his hand. 'It'll soon be dusk and we still have some driving to do if we don't want to miss the procession.'

The spicy scent of stocks, of pinks, and of lean spikes of lavender came to them, deepened by the moisture of the afternoon haze. A wood pigeon began cooing in a nearby tree with that liquid note as though it came up through water. On one clump of scarlet wildflowers four butterflies were spread, the black of their wings like velvet on the sunny petals; they seemed to be quivering with joy and drawing up the stored sweetness from the heart of the blossom. Venetia gazed at them as if they were mirroring the overflowing joy inside her; at last she too was tasting the sweetness stored up for so long.

They lingered there a little, looking about them as they dressed, and then turned to walk back along the path by which they had ascended over an hour ago. Finally, they reached the side of the road where the car was parked and Paolo opened the door for Venetia, leaning forward to kiss her gently on the mouth. As she climbed into her seat, she noticed a bright red silk scarf caught on a thorny bush being whipped about in the breeze. It hadn't been there before when they had parked, she thought, as the car's engine revved up and they started off towards Castelsardo. Had someone been there? So close to where she and Paolo…? Not wanting to spoil the idyllic afternoon with such uneasy thoughts, she dismissed the idea.

Paolo threw her a glance and rested his hand on her knee. '*Cara*, you look a million miles away.'

'Yes, I was. But now I'm back again.' Smiling up at him, she closed her hand around his and watched the road speed past.

*   *   *

The road to Castelsardo in the late afternoon was glowing with colour and light. The natural beauty of the scenery was breathtaking. For most of the way, vineyards and orchards covered the slopes from a height of about two hundred feet to a deep-blue sea that frothed on dark-red rocks, or lapped gently on the sands of small beaches. The hillsides were dotted with villa after villa, each one escorted by guardian pine trees and gardens brilliant with roses and semi-tropical creepers – a landscape unchanged in appearance since the nineteenth century. On the landward side, the dense *macchia* rose up, steeply broken here and there by masses of different copper-coloured rock.

The Ferrari snaked its way around the curving rocky slopes, heading across the top of the island to where the town of Castelsardo awaited them on the north coast. A green valley fell away from the road to their left and they passed only a few other cars and trucks. Glancing in the side-view mirror, Venetia caught sight of the American car she'd spotted at the airport a distance behind them. She was sure it had turned the opposite way out of the hire-car parking lot. Probably a lost American tourist, she thought.

Suddenly, as they turned a corner, her attention was instantly distracted. 'Gosh, what's that?' she gasped. There, in the distance, on the edge of the road loomed the enormous jagged shape of a prehistoric elephant, its head and trunk turned towards the highway.

Paolo chuckled, slowed down and then stopped the car in a layby so Venetia could get a better view.

'The legend has it that when Hannibal was crossing the Roman Empire with his army, he brought over one of his elephants but actually, it's a natural sculpture made out of the rock by the wind and rain. If you walk through Sardinia's woodlands, you'll find many granite boulders that the strange atmospheric phenomenon of this island has chiselled into a multitude of fantastic shapes, rusty natural relics that take you back to the prehistoric age.'

Venetia peered at the bizarre formation. 'Have you come here before?'

'Yes, over the years, I've travelled to all the Italian islands,' Paolo told her as he started the car again. 'My favourite is Sardinia, not only because it was the first one I visited, but also because the sun here shines all year round. During this week, I'm looking forward to rediscovering it with you, *cara*.' He glanced at her, his eyes shining, as he pulled out on to the road again. 'It's an earthly paradise, with a wealth of secluded places and open spaces to take your breath away, really. In between myth and history, there's the theory that Sardinia could be the lost Atlantis.'

Venetia laughed. 'Any more legends that you haven't told me about?'

He raised his brows. 'Plenty, *carina!* You must remind me to tell you about the *Janas*.'

'The *Janas* – what are they?'

'They're the fairies and witches of Sardinian popular folklore. *Domus de Janas* means "House of the Fairies" in Sardinian. They're types of prehistoric chamber tombs resembling houses in their layout and were cut into the rocks by the Ozieri and

Beaker cultures, dating back to the Copper and Bronze Age. The walls of the tombs and their corpses were painted a sort of ochre red and, like the pharaohs of Egypt, they were buried together with daily-life objects, like tools, food and jewels.'

'Yes, I've been to Egypt – such a fascinating civilisation. But to bring us back to your *Janas* and your fairy stories, I want to know more about *them*.'

Paolo laughed. 'You sound like a little girl pestering her parent.'

'As I'm sure I've mentioned before, my nanny used to tell the most wonderful fairy stories. I could stay for hours listening to her, spellbound. She used to bribe me into doing my chores by beginning a tale and interrupting it just at the crucial moment with a promise to tell me the rest once I'd finished my work.'

'Ah, you've revealed one of your weaknesses, *cara*.' He shot her a mischievous smile. 'I can now bribe you with a story so you make love to me as you did earlier.'

Her cheeks heated at his boldness, shyness and desire pooling in her eyes. She was becoming more comfortable with his flirting, and her pulse fluttered, watching his sensual mouth twitch as she knew his own pulse was firing into overdrive.

'You don't need to bribe me, Paolo. I would gladly make love to you at any time, as I did earlier, and more.'

Paolo gazed down at her, pleasure quirking his lips. 'More?' The husky monosyllabic response held a flagrant indication that he was fully aroused again.

'A great deal more,' she whispered as she felt a surge of desire so powerful throughout her body that it almost brought tears to her eyes.

'If it wasn't that we are already late for the *Lunissanti* procession, *amore mio*, I would… I *will* take you to horizons of heaven that you've never imagined, even in your wildest erotic dreams – tonight.' Paolo fixed Venetia with a fiery stare for a few seconds and then, turning his eyes to the road, he took her hand and slid it very gently down to his lap. 'This I shall be feeling all evening, waiting to touch you, wanting to do things to you, inventing ways of pleasing you.'

'Paolo…' was all she could whisper as she felt his need expand under her fingers, powerfully loquacious, and her own soared to meet him. She shuddered, her arousal shockingly intense at the feel of him, so strong and so virile under her hands, the thought that he wanted her so much sending her blood singing. Without thinking, she began to stroke him and fumbled with the zip of his jeans.

'Not now, *amore mio*, not now,' he said, lifting her hand to his lips and kissing it. 'I'm sorry, I shouldn't have done that, but I couldn't stop myself. As I'm driving, your touch would make me lose control. The waiting will make tonight even sweeter.'

'I shall look forward to it in that case,' Venetia said quietly and the two of them exchanged a look, the air between them dancing with charged anticipation. She told herself that she must control her hormones and quickly changed the subject.

Raising an eyebrow playfully, she said, 'Anyhow, you still haven't told me about the *Janas*.'

'Oh, you're an obstinate woman, *cara*,' he chuckled. 'Let me see…' He slowed down to go around a shepherd and his unruly flock of bleating animals, waving courteously, and then speeded up again. 'The legends of Sardinia say that the *Janas* are tiny, white-skinned fairies who live in underground caves, in the *Domus de Janas*, or literally "fairy houses".

'Wrapped in purple-red cloaks, they only go out after midnight so that the sun doesn't burn their snow-white skin, which becomes luminous when they scurry about on moonless nights. Inside their tiny caves, on golden looms, the *Janas* weave the finest, most beautiful fabrics, embroidered with magic.

While they work, it is said their sweet, melodic singing can sometimes be heard from far away if you're lucky.'

'How delightful. And I suppose no one has ever seen these little people?'

Paolo shot her a mock-serious look. 'Of course not! They're fairies, *cara*. They only make themselves known to children during the night, approaching their cradles to bestow good luck. And like all good fairies, they possess mountains of treasure.'

'Of course, I'd be disappointed if they didn't.' Venetia smiled, looking out of the window at the slopes of the scrubby *macchia*.

Paolo grinned. 'Some say their treasures of gold, silver, pearls and diamonds are guarded by fearsome, insect-like creatures. According to some tales, if the treasure of the *Janas* is stolen, it instantly transforms into coals and ashes in the hands of the thief. Other parts of the legend say similarly that if you hear someone call you three times during the night while you're sleeping, it is the *Janas,* and they will take you to look at their huge stash of treasure but if you try to touch it even once, everything will turn to dust.'

'Mmm, I see. A sober little lesson against greed.'

'Indeed, *cara*. The material world can be merely a trap and an obstacle to true happiness.' He smiled as he spoke but Venetia noticed something else flicker across his face.

She watched the sweeping green meadows give way to the rocks and sea in the distance, shimmering in the softening light of the afternoon. Venetia wondered about the story of the *Janas* and how they transported dreamers to their glittering treasure that could never be touched. She thought of those dreams about Judd that still haunted her, and her feelings for Paolo, both somehow strangely out of her reach. Perhaps if she ever succeeded in putting her finger on them… perhaps then everything would turn to dust for her too, and the dream of her happiness would disappear? At that moment, she felt Paolo's hand on her knee again and looked up into the sparkling cobalt of his eyes, and her unsettled thoughts evaporated.

They rode without speaking for several minutes, enjoying the scenery and each other's proximity.

'There it is,' Paolo said, pointing to a small town set on a rock overlooking the sea, illuminated by the last half-hour of sunlight. The sky, already streaked with long strokes of petal pink, announcing that the sun would shine tomorrow, looked almost lilac in the strange light. Sea, sky, *macchia mediterranea,* and grey and ochre rock lay calm and innocent on the edge of dusk, wrapped in bluish tint.

'It's such a moving sight,' Venetia marvelled. 'Quite extraordinary... so blue! At twilight the scenery is usually veiled in bright pinks and yellows.'

'The distance and the reflection of the granite rocks give it this blue colour. It varies in intensity according to the time of day.' He paused then glanced at her. 'I've booked us into a hotel for the night, but tomorrow we'll drive to Cagliari, where I've reserved a villa on the beach.'

Venetia smiled, excitement warming her. 'It sounds great.' She tried to focus on the drive, and not on thoughts of Paolo's wet and glistening body wading out of the sea. They were still driving, after all. She gave him a teasing look. 'So tell me something about Castelsardo – I'm sure you're not short of a fact or two.'

He grinned. 'I know a little.' As the car climbed up towards the small town, he gave her an overview of its history.

'Castelsardo is a true example of a medieval town, built around its castle and fortifications. It was founded in the twelfth century by the Genovese family of Doria, who built it in a strategically high position, as a defence from possible attacks from the sea, and it passed under the Aragonian domination during the second half of the fifteenth century. The ceremony of *Lunis-santi*, which started at dawn this morning, and the end of which we are going to attend tonight, is a tradition that probably dates from the eleventh century and was introduced by the Benedictine monks from the neighbouring basilica of Tergu.'

'You never fail to disappoint, *Signor* Barone.'

He nodded and raised an amused eyebrow. '*Prego, Signorina* Aston-Montagu.'

Something made her look in the side-view mirror once more, but there were no cars behind them as they made their way up the hill. Relaxing, she smiled at Paolo.

The road curved around the hillside and began to slope down to the promontory where the town nestled. The Ferrari started to pick up speed, hurtling round the bends.

'Paolo, *rallenta*. You're going too fast!' Venetia glanced at him, worried.

'I'm trying.' Paolo slammed his foot down on the brakes but the car kept flying round the twists in the road. In an attempt to keep control of the vehicle, he swung the steering wheel wildly. 'There's something wrong with the brakes. Hold on tight, Venetia!'

There was nothing Paolo could do but try and stay with the unruly movements of the car, turning the wheel sharply this way and that. A truck loomed towards them round another corner, sounding its warning horn as it swerved to miss them. Paolo shifted down a gear and kept pumping the brakes as the car's engine made a rebellious rasping noise. They raced through a short tunnel and out the other side to where the road was straightening. Venetia gasped. Far ahead she saw another herder, this time with a flock of goats, crossing the road.

'Paolo, we're going to hit them!'

'No we're not.' He gritted his teeth and pushed the car down through another gear. The engine screamed as the Ferrari careened over to the opposite side of the road. Although they had slowed down slightly because the gradient was levelling off now, Paolo hit his horn repeatedly as they sped towards the goat herder, still at an alarming rate.

Venetia could hear her own cry of terror. *Oh my God, we're going to die,* she thought, her knuckles white on the dashboard, her neck glowing with perspiration.

Suddenly the goatherd looked up, and seeing them hurtling towards him and his herd, cried out something; he began beating the last of his flock with his stick, pushing them away on to the dusty verge on the other side, just before the swerving car screeched past them. Venetia didn't bother to look behind her as the vehicle roared on, now edging scrubby fields.

'Brace yourself, I'm going to try and stop the car now,' Paolo shouted at Venetia, who closed her eyes for a moment, panic crushing her chest.

He began to pull the handbrake up slowly, straining his forearm for control and moving the steering wheel round with the other hand. The Ferrari span round one hundred and eighty degrees, carried on travelling in reverse and then span again to come to a halt sideways across the road.

There was silence in the car as both occupants breathed heavily. Venetia's heart was hammering as Paolo pulled off his seatbelt and leaned over to her.

'Venetia, are you alright?'

'I need to get out.'

She stumbled out of the car on to solid ground, her head and stomach churning.

'*Cara*, are you all right? Are you hurt?' Paolo was beside her in an instant, his hands touching her head, her face, scrutinising her all over. His eyes were blazing with an almost primal, feral instinct, then he pulled her tightly towards him as if he never wanted to let her go.

'Yes, yes, I'm fine.' She pressed her face against his chest and breathed him in. 'Oh my God, Paolo! I can't believe that just happened.' She looked up into his face that was strained with tension, but only with the concern that she was unharmed. Paolo seemed almost unaffected by the brilliant manoeuvring that had saved their lives, though. 'Are *you* okay?' she asked, gripping his arms tightly.

He nodded briskly, stroking her cheek. 'Yes, *carissima*. I'm fine.'

Paolo's eyes had grown calm again, the concern for her now mixed with a steely expression of concentration as he gently broke away. He walked around the car and crouched down by the front wheels, touching something under the chassis. After rubbing his wet fingertips, he sniffed at them.

'Brake fluid's gone.' He straightened, looking grave.

'How?'

'I don't know. It's pretty unusual for a car like this. Almost impossible, I'd say.'

'So how on earth could it have happened?' The dragging sense of unease Venetia had been feeling all the way from the airport now began to take on a more alarming aspect.

Paolo saw the look on her face and stepped towards her, sweeping her into his arms.

'I'm sorry, *cara*. You must have been terrified.'

'Well, yes.' She pulled away and looked into his face. 'But it seemed like you knew exactly what to do. How on earth did you manage it?'

He paused, his gaze oblique, then said: 'I took a specialist driving course after my car accident. You never know...' He trailed off and drew her back, resting his chin on her forehead. 'We're fine, *amore mio*, and that's the main thing. Come on. Luckily, there's a petrol station just a kilometre up ahead on the outskirts of town, where I can find out who to call to have the car towed. We'll take a taxi into town and come back for our luggage on the way. We can still make it into Castelsardo before dinner.'

Venetia gave a weak laugh. 'Yes, at least we've made good time now!'

He grinned and turned her round in his arm. 'You're right, *cara*. And soon I'll have you alone all evening in the comfort of our hotel room, and I'll make all this disappear. You'll forget it ever happened.' He drew her against him, kissing her brow and they started walking.

The town seemed to have been completely overtaken by crowds when they reached Castelsardo in the taxi that had picked them up from the petrol station. This event was obviously a popular one, Venetia noted, as the taxi driver endeavoured to manoeuvre the car through the clusters of people flooding the place.

They finally arrived at Rocce Sarde, a small, secluded hotel at the top of the hill with a view dominating the Tyrrhenian Sea. The vast suite Paolo had booked for the night overlooked the harbour. It had far-reaching views of the coast, with miles of sandy beach stretching in front of pinewoods, and the hills of the *macchia* rose up in successive tiers of violet that became deeper as the light of the day declined. Sailing ships floated across the sea, which had a soft opaque light, bringing out to the full the colours of the little crafts, and the rocks and buildings on the mainland.

Venetia stood on the veranda looking down at the still yet smiling water, mesmerised by the romance of the view in the evening's blue dusk. It was nearly enough to dispel the trauma of the near-accident with the car, which still lingered in her thoughts, but she gazed over the sea and leaned on the balcony, letting the evening fragrance of the sea calm her.

After he had taken delivery of their luggage, Paolo joined her there.

'We'll walk down to the entrance of the town to meet the procession,' he suggested, putting his arm around her shoulders and squeezing her to him. 'We'll join it and come back to the church of Santa Maria, which is not far from here, just below the medieval Doria Castle. Come, we don't want to miss it.'

It was night by the time Paolo and Venetia left the hotel and finally joined the masses on the pavements. All lights had been extinguished and the town of Castelsardo with its narrow streets, alleys and squares lay shrouded in inky darkness except for the silvery light of a brilliant full moon.

They took their position outside a bar at the corner of a twisting narrow street, in the dense crush of people herded in the roads waiting for the procession. Between houses, the crowd completely filled the canyon; every window, every balcony that promised a view was taken, and even the rooftops offering a point of vantage were turned into grandstands. Sardinians were clad in all their finery, the women somewhat austerely dressed for the most part in black, and coiffed with black or white lace *mantillas*, a tradition left behind by the Spanish, who had occupied Sardinia for four hundred years.

Groups of men and women were wandering in and out of *caffetterias*. Some were chatting and fanning themselves, pausing for gossip between their prayers, or mouthing them as they fingered their rosaries; others sat astride the wooden barriers separating the pavement from the road, their arms crossed, engaging in banter with the other spectators. Blending in with the crowd, Venetia was aware of the happy reverence and the good humour of these people and she felt in touch with it.

As they waited for the pilgrims, she turned to Paolo.

'Being here makes me realise how Venetian I've become. Everything is so different in Sardinia. I've seen all kinds of religious ceremonies and cultural processions in Italy and other countries before, but tell me more about the *Lunissanti*.'

Paolo stood close to her, leaning against one of the barriers. 'It all begins before dawn with a mass in the church of Santa Maria, where the wooden cross of the black Jesus is kept, and where members of the *Confraternita di Santa Croce* – the Oratory of the Confraternity of the Holy Cross – meet. From there, a long procession unfolds. Two brotherhoods have the main roles. The *Apostoli*, who follow each other carrying the offerings, which are different objects relating to Jesus's crucifixion: the chalice, the glove, the pillar, the chain, the scale, the crown of thorns, the cross, the ladder, the hammer and tongs, the spear and the sponge. The second group, the *Cantori*, is made up of three choirs of twelve members each, who sing the *Miserere* and other pre-Gregorian songs.'

'Have you ever taken part in this procession?'

'Yes, the first year I settled in Tuscany I came here for Easter. I had only just bought Miraggio, which was in the early stages of the restoration work. I wanted to get away from everything and go somewhere isolated to take stock of my life. Taking part in the procession of *Lunissanti* did me a lot of good.'

'In what way?' Venetia didn't wish to pry too much but she was curious for more insight into Paolo's accident and his amnesia.

He ran his hand through his hair. 'It is a profoundly spiritual ritual. I found it cleansing somehow; I needed that. I also stayed for a couple of weeks after Easter with some monks in a monastery not far from here – I needed to find my new self.'

'If you don't mind me asking, where did you get married and where did the accident take place?'

Venetia felt Paolo stiffen. She kicked herself for raising the matter. *The thought of the accident, even though he can't remember it, must still be painful for him.*

Paolo didn't answer immediately. His eyes skimmed over the crowds. 'Oh, we married in Verbania, and the accident happened on the way to Pallanza, where we were going for our honeymoon,' he said evasively, his mouth set in a line. 'But I have no memory of all that. For me, today, that episode of my life never existed.'

'Yes, yes, of course, how tactless of me. I'm sorry, Paolo.'

'After the Holy Mass, the pilgrimage continues during the morning to the Basilica of the Pink Madonna of Gerico of Tergu,' Paolo went on, still watching the passers-by and ignoring her apology. 'There, the religious mysteries carried by the *Apostoli* pilgrims are offered to the Virgin Mary during a Pontifical Mass, accompanied by the crying song of the death of Christ. After the mystery plays and the mass, a long parade goes to the old town bastion wall, and returns to the church, where everybody enjoys lunch.'

Suddenly from afar burst the swelling melody of the *Miserere*, throbbing through the night, sung by a perfect choir and perfect soloists. An impressive silence blanketed the town while they listened to the exquisitely mournful sound. Soon the procession came marching up the narrow medieval street on its slow way home to the Church of Santa Maria, where it had all started at dawn.

Men that were part of the *Confraternita di Santa Croce* were dressed in white tunics and cloaks with thin, high-tapering hoods – a costume that could be nothing other than medieval in inspiration, reminding Venetia of the processions of the *Semana Santa* in Spain, where she had attended a more elaborate ritual in Seville when she had been working on a restoration job there a few years back. The cowled men and the pilgrims all held torches or candles, the golden glow of which threw a warm tone over the attendant multitude, swarming like bees to get a nearer view. As the procession passed by, the crowds lining the streets fell devoutly upon their knees.

Paolo and Venetia joined the worshippers on their way to the Church of Santa Maria, following the wooden cross and the human skull set on a tray, both carried by the apostles and accompanied by prayers and religious chanting of the three choruses.

There was an intensity about the worship which Venetia had not observed before, even in Spain. It was as if a great mystical shadow was being cast by the twenty-four hooded men and it stirred Venetia's emotions profoundly. She could well understand how this sort of rite recalling the Passion of Jesus and involving legions of devotees would awaken a lagging faith and leave an indelible and unforgettable impression for all time – for who could ever erase the memory of one of these processions wending its glimmering way at night through the narrow medieval Sardinian streets into the immensity of the dark, waiting church?

From time to time, Venetia had glanced up towards Paolo and was surprised to discover that he was totally immersed in the ceremony, praying and chanting with the devotees as if he had lived all his life in Sardinia. It touched her. She could see that a man who had such a heavy cross to bear as the one Paolo was carrying could certainly find solace in the spiritual experience of the *Lunissanti*. She had sometimes wondered if Paolo had a faith, and now she found a potential new facet to his personality that intrigued her. Her heart flooded with compassion and love for him. At that moment, she wanted nothing more than to make him happy, to compensate for all the countless years and memories he no longer had.

The procession moved on through the streets, the crowd humming and swaying in one sweeping wave of bodies, in time with the ritual. Candlelight flickered on faces engrossed in their chanting and cowled heads bent in quiet supplication as they walked. The lines of people standing at the side of the road knelt in a slow ripple of motion as they passed by. Out of the corner of her eye, Venetia saw a sudden movement in the crowd and looked up. Only one person had not knelt. The back of a young woman's head was fleetingly visible, her long raven tresses spilling over her shoulders as she pushed into the throng away from the road, and disappeared. She looked so like Allegra at that moment that Venetia sucked in a breath. *Impossible, there's no way that girl could be in Sardinia.* There was any number of black-haired young women in the crowd who looked just like Allegra. Venetia shuddered. *Get a grip*, she chided herself. She was becoming far too jumpy. Looking back at Paolo, who was still standing with his eyes closed, lost to the ritual, she took a deep breath.

After the procession returned to the church and Mass was celebrated, Paolo and Venetia left the local populace heading off to the main square of the town to celebrate the rite of thanksgiving for the *Lunissanti*. They made their way back through the dark cobbled streets to their hotel, after deciding to have dinner at La Grotta E Il Tempio.

'It's an amazing nightclub that opened last year with two different dance floors, one inside and the other outside,' explained Paolo. 'I haven't been to it, but I've read about it and many of my friends have told me that it is an experience not to be missed: *molto originale*, different, fun.'

Venetia hooked her arm through Paolo's. 'I'd better dress accordingly in that case.'

Back at the hotel Venetia sifted through the clothes she had brought that were now neatly hanging in the cupboard. She had intended to wear her purple butterfly dress in Sardinia and the unwelcome image of the torn fabric flashed sharply in her mind. She swallowed slightly, not wanting these dark thoughts that kept following her to triumph when she was feeling so happy being with Paolo.

Paolo leaned against the edge of the small desk, watching Venetia, his dark brows gathering into a slight frown, as if he had read her thoughts.

'I can just imagine how beautiful you would have looked in your purple dress.'

Venetia stood there with her back to him, not answering. She didn't want to spoil the evening by discussing the incident again.

Paolo came towards her. 'You seem upset, *amore mio*. I shouldn't have mentioned it, I'm sorry. You'll look beautiful in any outfit – and I prefer you anyway when you're not wearing anything.' He turned her around and drew Venetia to him, letting his hands roam over her curves. His eyes sparkled mischievously. 'Ah, but that is only for me, and as we're not dining alone, I wouldn't like to share you with the rest of Sardinia,' he told her, kissing the tip of her nose.

She shot him a gently scolding look. 'I should hope not! Yes, let's not think about disagreeable things tonight. We're together, that's all that matters, isn't that so?' Her eyes shone as she smiled up at Paolo. She turned back to the cupboard. 'I've brought other dresses with me, and the good thing is that you've hardly seen any of them.'

Venetia looked at him and saw his mouth twitching as if he were trying to stop himself from laughing. As she watched, the effort at control became too much for him and Paolo's lips parted in an indulgent grin.

'Yes, *amore*. I wondered what you had brought with you in that large suitcase the porter nearly dropped on his foot. Now I know!'

Venetia giggled. 'Oh, don't tease! So, what shall I wear? Mmm… what about this?' She took out a sunglow-yellow strapless lace mini-dress, which she had bought on one of her trips to Paris. The warmth of the colour had struck her and, as it was on sale at half price, she had bought it on the spot, but had never worn it.

'*Meravigliosa!*' Paolo folded his arms and looked appreciative.

Venetia showered and applied some mascara to her lashes and a tinge of gloss to her cheekbones and lips before stepping into her dress and zipping it up.

With its subtly structured boned bodice and waist-clinching grosgrain belt, the yellow dress moulded itself to Venetia's curves like a glove. For this occasion she wore her hair up in a sophisticated topknot. Every now and again she glanced at Paolo, who watched her silently, his eyes alight with fascination, longing and intensity. She clipped to her ears a pair of twenty-four-carat gold, wood-effect pendant earrings.

'Venetia, you are utterly beguiling,' he murmured. 'You look like a ray of sunshine – the ray you brought into my life.'

'I love nature-inspired jewellery.' She smiled shyly at him and slipped into cut-out golden leather high-heeled slingbacks. 'I'm ready,' she said, grabbing her glamorous box clutch sprayed with glitter that she had won at a tombola raffle at one of her godmother's charity parties a year ago in Venice.

Paolo stared down at her, a blazing look in his eyes she now knew so well. 'It's already past midnight. Let's go, *cara*, before I change my mind about going out tonight and carry you on to the bed that's looking at us so invitingly.'

On the way out, catching sight of her reflection in the mirror by the door, Venetia hardly recognised herself. Gone was the defensive, guarded young woman of not so long ago: her eyes were shining, she positively glowed.

La Grotta E Il Tempio nightclub was a stone's throw away from the hotel, at the top of the hill, looking down on the main town and the wide stretch of beach. The night was cool and balmy. Under the moonlight, the sea was fashioned of opal and pearl. The waters lay resignedly beneath an almost mauve sky; there was no wind.

The club had a most unusual setting. Set back from the road, its high rectangular entrance was cut into the dark cliffs that reared up almost sheer, like a rocky palace hugging the coast. From the street-level entrance, Paolo and Venetia descended almost fifty feet, along a narrow rock path that was interspersed with stairs leading deep into the cave. Halfway down, they could hear the soft strains of dance music. The path then widened out into a series of large grottoes, partly natural but in many places cut out to enlarge the cave into a stunning space. The first dance floor was set around the natural crevices. The rock was mostly the clean bluish-grey of limestone, but it was veined with red clay and sparkling white seams of spar. The acoustics were good and the lighting subdued, giving the place a real enchanted grotto atmosphere.

The place was not overcrowded and Paolo and Venetia sat down for dinner in a corner far away from the dance floor. They were given the house appetiser with the compliments of the chef, which consisted of thin slices of *Buttariga* and *Pane Carasau.*

'I've never had this before. What is it, Paolo?' Venetia broke off a mouthful and tasted it.

'*Buttariga* is smoked mullet caviar marinated in olive oil. *Pane carasau* is also known as *Carta di Musica*, music bread, because it's so dry and thin that it resembles pages of a score. The shepherds combine it with tomato sauce and eggs, so it makes a hearty dish that they call *pane frattau.*'

'I really love this. I'll buy some *Buttariga* to take back with me. I'm sure my friend Francesca will be amused – she's a great one for trying new things.'

'It keeps for months, so does the music bread.'

The waiter, when he came to take their order, recommended the homemade *carraxiu*, which he explained was achieved by laying a suckling pig, a calf, or a lamb in a hole dug in the ground and covering it with aromatic myrtle leaves. 'The pile is then covered with firewood which gradually cures the meat, *e ne fa una prelibatezza davvero succulenta,* and makes it a really succulent delicacy. Tonight, *signore e signorina,* it is suckling pig.'

Paolo looked at Venetia. 'So let's try this truly "succulent delicacy", yes, *cara?*'

'Why not? I'm all for having a totally Sardinian night.'

Paolo glanced up at the waiter. 'And what do you suggest for the main course?'

The man nodded courteously. '*Costata di Vitello alla griglia con Funghi Spadellati, Crème brûlée di Mais.* In Sardinia we have a great variety of mushrooms. This dish is made with the *dittula* mushroom, which is rare and has a most delicate flavour.'

They both ordered the grilled veal with mushrooms and Paolo requested a bottle of the local red wine, *Torbato,* which came from the region of Alghero where they had arrived by plane that morning.

The service was quick and the food delicious. Soon Venetia had forgotten about Allegra with her fiery black eyes, Antonio, Rufus and the incident of the torn dress, their near car crash – everything but the present, with its music and fun and laughter. She was enjoying every moment with a new gusto – that of a healthy young woman who felt good about herself and about the man who was sitting at her side, gazing at her with adoring eyes.

Soaking up the romantic atmosphere, Venetia smiled back at Paolo. 'So, aren't you going to tell me any more legends?'

'If that's what you'd like, *cara*, I will oblige,' he said, grinning and lighting a cigarette as they waited for their coffee. 'There's a very famous legend about the Gulf of Cagliari, which is called "Bay of Angels". As the visitor comes into the Port of Cagliari from the sea, the first image that appears is the promontory of St Elias. Its most distinctive aspect is a limestone ridge at the top of the hill – it's called *"Sella del Diavolo"*. Legend has it that after the seven days of Creation, God decided to give the angels a land where they could live in peace, with the condition that it had to be a place where there were no wars or evil. The angels searched long, until they came down on our earth and discovered the Gulf of Cagliari with its emerald sea, its green vegetation, and the pure white of its cliffs.

'"Here is our uncontaminated place," the Archangel Gabriel said, "we will make it our city of love and peace."

'The angels settled in what is known today as the Bay of Angels but this prompted the envy and anger of Lucifer who, before he was cast out of Heaven, rode his horse and, with his army of demons, declared war on the angels. The angels then brought about a storm, creating big waves in the Gulf and they made Lucifer fall from his horse. Archangel Gabriel rose into the air with his shining sword and the defeated Lucifer in fury threw off the saddle of his black steed. The saddle immediately petrified, forming the promontory known today as "The Devil's Saddle". '

Venetia gazed at him. 'I could listen to you for hours.'

'And I can't wait to take you into my arms. Let's dance.'

'Shall we go outside? I'd like to see the other dance floor.'

They made their way down some more stony steps that suddenly emerged out into the starry night at the base of the cliff. At the archway, there were two big lime-kilns, their massive stonework still intact. It crossed Venetia's mind that they might have been the infinitely old watchtowers of some primitive tribe that had once lived there. A smooth slab of broad stone sloped down into the sandy beach and was joined by a cluster of flat stepping stones that led across the sand, whether natural or man-made it was difficult to say, so seamlessly did they blend with the surroundings.

The enormous second dance floor was set on the beach surrounded by widely spaced columns and conifer trees, giving the impression of an open-air Roman temple. Here the mood, the lighting, was ultra-romantic. The wild design of the nightclub was open and sparse, with no discernible railings or walls to inhibit the view or set boundaries for where the dance floor ended and the beach and sea began – a chimerical temple set in idyllic surroundings, a place made for lovers.

Paolo and Venetia were swept into the ocean of rhythm and glorious melody as Peppino di Capri's smooth vocals seduced them with his classic rendition of 'Luna Caprese'. The lilt and romantic ecstasy of the soaring strings and piano lent wings to their feet, transporting them a thousand miles from Sardinia. There was no desire in either of them for speech, the moment was too emotional for coherent thought; they simply let themselves drown in the passionate sensuality that surrounded them. Venetia looked up. The stars that blazed in the night sky above them matched those in her eyes. They seemed to be watching over them, full of promise, she thought. Her heart was tumbling with joy, fire flaming over her and through her. Paolo held her lightly but firmly, as if his hands were accustomed to her form. They were so perfectly attuned, not only in their steps but also in their cadence and flow of movement. Brushing their bodies against each other in measure with the music, it was clear to Venetia that, like her, Paolo was enacting in his imagination erotic gestures, warming her up for a night of rapturous lovemaking.

When the music swept to its finale she was a little breathless with the intoxication of it, and it was hard to open her eyes to the crowded stage, to come back to earth. All she craved was to melt into Paolo and rest there forever.

'Let's go for a walk on the beach before going back to the hotel,' Paolo suggested, his mouth still against her hair. 'I don't know where the time goes when I'm with you. It's almost dawn and I'd like us to watch the sun come up together. Suddenly he paused and moved his head back, studying her anxiously. 'Unless, of course, you're tired, *carissima*.'

But Venetia was wide awake, her head and heart awhirl, her pulse beating a little faster. She was elated, her whole body flooded with the adrenaline that Paolo's nearness and the romantic atmosphere on the dance floor had brought about.

Her uplifted, radiant face answered his question. Paolo paid the bill and they headed for the beach.

Venetia took off her sandals and Paolo his socks and shoes. The ash-coloured sand was cold and damp under their feet as they made their way closer to the shore. A wind blew in soft and cool from the wide dusk-blue Tyrrhenian; such a light breath, a zephyr, which floated over the rocks to where Paolo was heading.

'Have you come to this beach before? You appear to know your way quite well.'

'Yes. When I first visited the island, I stayed at a small hotel not far from here. But it's all changed now – you know, built up. It was almost deserted in those days.'

Walking now on the wet sand by the sea's edge, Venetia felt the night-cooled water fresh over her toes, a delicious sensation. The wind touched her cheek and she looked up quickly at the greyish light. The moon was fading but was still flooding the dark glassy surface of the water with metallic light, creating a silvery staircase leading from their feet all the way to the moon. She took out the clips that held her hair up, her eyes lingering on the reflected image on the sea. 'It's so beautiful,' she sighed.

Paolo slipped his arm from under hers, stopped, and drew her to him. 'You're the one who's beautiful, *la mia bella sirena*,' he whispered.

How she loved the feel of those firm strong arms round her. His eyes as he looked directly into her face were bright, but they and his whole expression were infinitely serious. Somehow, she felt closer to him than she had ever done before, almost as if a door had suddenly been opened, admitting her to the part of his life hitherto hidden from her. It was altogether a wonderful, but also a very frightening feeling – as though this burgeoning love of theirs was so fragile, it could be shattered by the outside world any time, and her happiness snatched away from her in a flash. Her mind returned to that night in Venice when they had taken a gondola ride, when she had first allowed herself to surrender to the intoxication of romance and passion that Paolo knew how to stir up in her blood.

'Will you take me to your palace in the moon, where the stars shine always bright, and the angels sing all night a beautiful lover's hymn?' She gazed up at the deep-blue eyes that watched her intently.

Paolo smiled wistfully. 'You still remember, *amore mio*?'

'How can I forget? I was already in love with you then, but didn't want to admit it.'

He took her hand and they began to stroll slowly along the sand again.

The beach was deserted, apart from two or three solitary dark shapes of fishermen wading to and from their boats, carrying tackle and jars by lamp-flare, the residue of a night's fishing.

They found a solitary rock and sat on it by the fringe of the clear and laughing water breaking softly on the sand at their feet. Behind them there rose a semicircle of mountains. The sun was not yet up, the air redolent with the fragrance of the sea breathing all around. It was lighter now, the sky not yet coloured by the sun, but brilliant, as the blue expanse caught whatever glare there was in its imperceptible movements. And then suddenly above the surface came the full flush of a red dawn. Glowing rose, fuchsia and bright red, with flaming oranges and golden yellows, it reached out to the rest of the island: to the towering cliffs and near mountain tops; over the small craggy town; on the aerial lines of straight cloud all the way to the north; and on the Tyrrhenian Sea. Over its wild blue, there stretched this blazing rainbow of vibrant hues, burning its colours across the vanishing greys of paleness.

Paolo turned towards Venetia and took her in his arms. When he spoke, his voice had that quiet but intense earnestness that could come to it at times, and his gaze burned fiercely with emotion.

'I love you, Venetia, with a passion I would not have thought myself capable of. Every beat of my heart, every breath I take, and every thought in my head is overflowing with my love for you. You are all that a man can desire.' For a long charged moment he gazed at her, searching the amber eyes that were melting as they looked into his. He cupped her face in his hand. 'I desperately want you to marry me, *tesoro mio*. Will you do me the honour of sharing my life and becoming my wife?'

Venetia could not answer at once, but that wasn't because she was in any doubt as to her feelings, or what her answer might be. She had been attracted to Paolo from the minute she had set eyes on him, and their chemistry seemed to be effortless but up to forty-eight hours ago, she had not been sure as to the depth of her love for him. Yet suddenly she was possessed of richness and warmth of feeling such as she had never felt before… unless it was on that one single occasion, so long ago, when Judd had asked her to marry him. The road to truth can be winding and treacherous, and though we can ignore the signposts along the way and hurry through our lives either fearful or unnoticing, just like the sun and the moon can never be hidden, soon enough it cannot be denied. When it is spied, the heart knows in a moment of revolution that it has arrived.

So it was with Venetia as she looked into the face of Paolo.

Now she was only conscious of his closeness and the clasp of his arms round her. Now she knew the truth of her feelings.

'Yes, yes, my love! All I want is to be in your arms – to be kissed by you, to belong to you, to become your wife.'

His eyes widened, burning blue. 'The only thing I'm afraid of is that your kindness and generosity to me have been out of some sort of compassion. So I must ask you again, *amore mio,* can you love me enough to put up with my… handicap? Will you marry me despite the amnesia, and the nightmares that come with it?'

A lump rose in Venetia's throat. She gave him her heart in her answering look, gave him without pretence, what in truth had long been his.

'How can you doubt it? You've given me a new life,' she whispered as she put her arms around his neck and drew his head down towards her, pressing her feverish lips against his in a long, passionate kiss.

Paolo's mouth moved downwards and he nipped gently at the soft silk-like skin of her neck, his hands working their magic on her bare shoulders, her arms and over her breasts, which by now were hard mounds, the taut peaks pushing rebelliously against her corsage, demanding his attention.

The sun was now fully up and already it was growing hot. They broke apart slowly, and their eyes skimmed the azure levels of the sea and the turquoise ripples, which in the new morning had the transparency and depth of jewels.

Paolo looked down at Venetia amorously, his thumb moving a slow, sensual trace across the contours of her face. He smiled, moving his mouth close to hers. 'Shall we go back to the hotel? Our bodies are calling each other, and we mustn't leave them waiting, *amore.*' He gave her soft, biting kisses in between the words.

Venetia felt her blood singing and caressed his cheek tenderly. 'Yes.'

They walked back to the nightclub, where a handful of guests still lingered aimlessly. The music had stopped and the waiters were busy tidying the place.

Suddenly Venetia had the uncomfortable impression she was being stared at. She turned and met the steel-grey gaze of Umberto. She gasped and would have stumbled had Paolo not held her up.

'What's the matter, *cara*?'

'Paolo,' she said in a choked voice, 'Umberto is behind us.'

Surprised, Paolo stopped and turned. He recovered himself immediately and smiled sardonically. '*Buongiorno*, Umberto, what good wind brings you to Sardinia?'

The Count ignored him and shouted at Venetia, who had marched on. '*Vedo che vai ancora in giro con quel bastardo mutilato*, I see you're still hanging around with that mutilated bastard!'

Venetia winced at the harsh name Umberto had just called Paolo, obviously alluding to his amnesia. The man was surely off his head on something; the best thing was to ignore him.

'Did you think I'd forgotten about you, Venetia? Did you think I'd let you get away that easily after you humiliated me? I have friends in all sorts of places, you know. I had you followed when you went off to see our friend here.' He shot Paolo a contemptuous glance.

'You're drunk!' Paolo told him and turned away. Striding alongside Venetia and taking her arm, he accelerated his step towards the club's beachside exit.

As Paolo and Venetia reached the road and began the walk back to the hotel, Umberto had gained on them, and he called out to Paolo: '*Se sei un uomo mi combattere!* May the best man keep the pretty lady as a trophy!' Coming behind Paolo, he tried to catch him by the neck.

Quick as a flash, Paolo shifted sideways and turned his upper body straight, his shoulders square, as if waiting for Umberto's blow. Then, as the Count came towards him, Paolo quickly stepped forward with one leg, bending his knee, and thrust his fist sideways in a sharp movement, striking the Count in the face.

Umberto stumbled backwards, recovering his balance in seconds. Scanning around quickly, he picked up a steel pipe from the side of the road and hurled himself at Paolo, who jumped back to dodge the blow, simultaneously turning his body slightly and executing a front kick to Umberto's face, completing the counter-attack with another punch to the face, which sent him almost flying against the wall.

Venetia stood horrified, but also bemused at Paolo's agility and the precision of his blows. 'Stop it, please, stop it!' But they weren't listening, too engrossed in the fight.

Suddenly, a gorilla of a man appeared from the car park outside the nightclub. Venetia recognised him as Umberto's burly bodyguard. He was rushing straight at Paolo, carrying a huge crowbar.

'Paolo, careful! Behind you!' Venetia shouted, totally beside herself with fear. *I must call the police,* she thought, panicking, wondering if she should run back into the nightclub to ask for help.

At Venetia's cry Paolo turned, still fully on the alert, dodging quickly towards his attacker and, grasping the crowbar with both hands in a straddle-leg stance, he delivered a hard front kick to the heavy man's stomach, winding him.

By this time Umberto had recovered from the jolt and was swinging a punch at Paolo, who rocked backwards. Then, leaning forward, he put out one foot and with his arm forced the unbalanced Count to trip over his leg and sprawl face down in the gravel.

The gorilla looked stunned and then launched himself at Paolo again, coming in with a quick, springing lunge, bunched fists at the ready. Again, Paolo was already in position, and seemed to barely move. Harnessing the bodyguard's momentum, his instinct took over and he grasped a flailing fist and turned with one of the man's arms over his shoulder. It looked as if he intended to throw the gorilla. Sure enough, Venetia heard the crack of bone as the heavy weight fell to the ground, where the man curled up, nursing his broken arm in agony.

Venetia blinked at the move, which was almost graceful and clearly instinctive for Paolo. He had defended himself with an agility and speed that was surprising in such a big man. His two attackers were sprawled on the ground whereas he had barely a scratch. She rushed towards him amid the distant sirens of police cars.

Paolo gazed at Venetia, his eyes empty, without emotion. 'Go back to the hotel,' he said calmly, gesturing her quickly away. 'I'll deal with this mess.'

CHAPTER 11

It was almost eight o'clock in the morning when Paolo headed back to the hotel, having given his statement at the police station. Some tourist onlookers had witnessed the fight and had been able to confirm that it was Umberto and his henchman who had assaulted him and landed the first blow. The Count and his gorilla bodyguard had been taken to hospital, Umberto with a bloody nose and a couple of loose teeth, and the muscleman with a broken arm.

Still, Paolo had been kept in a stuffy room without windows for over an hour, waiting. He'd smoked almost half a packet of cigarettes. He shuddered. For some reason, that small room had made him very uncomfortable, almost afraid – a sort of claustrophobia bordering on panic. Something new in the dark abyss of his mind stirred. Memories seemed to hover at the edge of it; they were almost palpable, as it is when one is groping for a word and it's almost there, quivering on the tip of the tongue. But there was a block, as if his brain refused to move on, and he met with a void, the usual black hole that infested his universe. What had the Count called him: *mutilato*? Yes, his mind was mutilated… he was a man with most of his life missing, living in shadows that tormented him – now more than ever.

The *policia* had interrogated him as if he'd been a criminal. Nothing better to do, he thought bitterly. They said it was because the gorilla had pressed charges against him. 'Routine check-up' was their excuse, just to find out if he had a record. He was thankful that he'd sent Venetia back to the hotel. He didn't want her mixed up in all this, although Umberto had done his best to implicate her – giving her name and her address in Venice as he didn't know where she was staying. The police tried to extract her whereabouts from Paolo, but he insisted she had nothing to do with the incident.

He'd still be there, he supposed, if it hadn't been for the middle-aged Italian couple and another man, an Englishman apparently, who had given their versions of the events which corresponded to his statement. It was a good thing he'd had his identity card with him, which clearly hadn't been the case with Umberto. Paolo always carried around his identity papers; it was a habit he'd acquired since his amnesia. Just in case.

Umberto… Paolo had thought *il Conte* had been more than just a 'partner in crime' on nights out in Venice. He assumed he'd been a friend. *Just another mirage*, he thought bitterly, though he couldn't blame the Count for being driven to such lengths for Venetia. She was a woman who could drive any man insane for love.

The glare of the morning was mellow, a sort of rich, golden light. Overhead, a flock of white doves wheeled and dipped in the magical radiance. Paolo walked along the narrow twisting street with the swift stride of nervous fatigue, lost in thought, still a little dazed. It was strange how the brain and the body functioned. His amnesia had obviously not affected his reflexes – the years of martial arts training hadn't been lost after all. Paolo smiled ruefully. There was a moment during the fight with *il Conte* and his henchman when memories again began to push themselves forward. What was happening to him? He was aware of a new pain gathering and trembling at the surface, but it had no sharpness. It was more like a heavy ache, dragging not so much at his body as his inner self.

Paolo could not describe, even to himself, the tension he felt. There was a throbbing between his eyes. It was as if something were pushing upwards underneath his skull, a grumbling volcano about to erupt. He would never be right again... this was worse than he had ever felt. His anxiety increased to sudden gigantic proportions, pressing down on him like an overwhelming burden he would never be able to discard. And then, abruptly, tears were running down his cheeks, silent floods which he tried to swallow back but they wouldn't stop, blinding him as he half staggered up the hill.

Shocked and ashamed at his loss of control, he dragged an arm across his face. Why was he crying? He hadn't shed a single tear since he had woken up all those years ago with an unpleasant taste in his mouth, the suggestion of a headache, and a dreamy sense of having been asleep for a long, long time. Gradually, his eyes had taken stock of the hospital room with its antiseptic white walls and then he'd discovered with a scrambling horror that they reflected the white, blank sheet that was his past life, and that even his name eluded him. Paolo's thoughts raced to and fro in confusion. Was this sudden incontrollable flood of emotion caused by frustration or merely a reaction to something that ran much deeper; something he'd forgotten, that had been buried in the dark well of memories?

His forehead was pulsing. Too much had happened in the past few weeks and he hadn't slept for more than twenty-four hours... perhaps that was now taking its toll. He rubbed his eyes with the heel of his hand, which he then drew through his hair; he couldn't go back to the hotel, to Venetia, while he was in this state. Whatever the reason for this sudden outpour, he had to pull himself together. The thought of Venetia soothed him.

He paused by a low stony wall to calm himself, turning his attention to the sea.

Paolo lit a cigarette and stood with one foot on the stones, gazing up at the scintillating reach of the Tyrrhenian. It was a brisk and stimulating scene under the wide sky: the ocean surrounded by a tumble of rocks which rose to a height of two hundred feet or so, with huge gulls circling above it and perched in the high outcrop. Those fat ugly birds looked to him like the genii of the island and their loud cries sounded like ironic laughter. Paolo smiled to himself as he wondered what Venetia would say if he told her of his fanciful musings. No doubt, she would ask for a story. There ought to be a legend about those wretched feathered creatures that plagued the area. Well, his wild imagination, he supposed, always seeking out the stories behind things, compensated for a lack of memories.

A dozen or more small white steamers were tied up on the flat shore, their various destinations scrawled on blackboards attached to high posts dug into the sand. Fishing boats were also there and huge baskets of fish were being carried ashore. Out at sea, sailing craft tacked to and fro; everything sparkled, and was whipped about in the bracing sea breeze. Paolo took one last look, deeply breathed in the briny air and set off up the hill again to the hotel.

He discarded his cigarette, stubbing it out it under his shoe and pulled out his phone to call Venetia. As he lifted his head, he saw the dark-haired figure of a young woman flit across the road ahead of him. She glanced back and caught sight of him, then bolted down a side street. There was no mistaking her. Paolo shoved his phone back into his pocket and broke into a run. She darted into a blind alley and when she realised that she was trapped, spun around to face her pursuer, her back pressed against a large wooden door.

'What the hell are you doing here, Allegra?' Paolo shouted as he strode towards her. The young woman gripped her shawl tightly against her breast and stared up at him, panic flaring in her eyes.

'She's not right for you, Paolo,' she muttered under her breath.

'What are you talking about? How did you get here?' he snapped.

Allegra pulled herself up straighter and her expression became more defiant.

'Who do you think told *il Conte* where to find you?' she sneered. 'I went through your desk and found your airline tickets. Umberto Palermi was very grateful for the information. *Very* grateful indeed.' Her eyes flashed mockingly.

'What do you mean?

'Do you think that just because you don't want me, other men don't either?'

'What have you done, Allegra?' His voice was a low growl.

She threw her head back and laughed bitterly. 'What I have I done? I've done nothing except take what I needed from that preening *cafone. Uno sciocco ed il suo denaro son presto separati*, a fool and his money are soon parted. His eyes were falling out of his head when he first saw me with you in Venice. All men are the same – weak and stupid! I knew what he wanted and it was easy to give it to him. In return, he reimbursed me very handsomely for my "services". And he bought me nice things, of course. It was also convenient that he could keep an eye on you for me with your little jaunts to Venice.'

'You would sell yourself to Umberto Palermi for money?' Paolo ran his hand through his hair. 'So it wasn't just idle gossip – the men you've been seen with.' He shook his head. 'Allegra…'

'Don't look at me like that, Paolo. I don't want your pity,' she spat. 'You never gave me what I needed, so I found it elsewhere.'

'I gave you the love of a father.'

'I don't need a father! You betrayed me... with that English *puttana.*' Allegra flung out her hand in contempt. 'I decided I wasn't going to leave it to *il Conte* to confront you, so I took the car he gave me and came here alone. I followed you from the airport. I saw you and her...' Her face contorted with rage. 'It was disgusting, how could you?'

'You followed us? You spied on Venetia and me?' A terrible realisation was dawning.

'It should have been me you were making love to, not that whore,' she hissed.

Paolo's face was ashen. 'It was you who sabotaged the brakes, wasn't it?' But Allegra wasn't listening.

'I'd never seen you like that. So... happy,' she looked at him with a mixture of despair and fury in her eyes. 'Why couldn't you have just left things the way they were? I would have cared for you, Paolo, for the rest of our lives.' Her hand went up to his face, trembling, but he jerked his head away.

'I've told you before, I'm in love with Venetia. There is nothing between you and me – never has been!'

'Don't you see? I couldn't let it happen. I couldn't let you be with her,' she said, her voice rising hysterically.

'And so you wanted to kill us both?' His eyes were incredulous.

'I love you, Paolo. We were meant to be together. If I can't have you then no one will. And certainly not that *puttana!*' She had a wild look about her now that made Paolo step back from her, gaping in angry disbelief.

'This isn't love.' Pity had given way to cold animosity now, which flashed across his face. 'You don't know the meaning of the word. You're deranged... I cared about you, Allegra. I trusted you. But I must have failed you somehow to make you this damaged. I should have you placed behind bars, if not a prison, then a madhouse!'

'You have no proof.' She smiled menacingly.

'No, I have no proof.' He turned on her. 'You can keep the house in Porto Ercole but I never want to set eyes on you again. If I do, or if your path ever crosses Venetia's, if you even set foot in the same city, then it's all gone, and I won't be responsible for my actions. Do you understand?' His voice was a cold snarl.

Allegra started to say something but paused. She narrowed her eyes, which were now empty and blacker than he'd ever seen them. The girl knew she was beaten. Edging past him, she stumbled and ran. He watched her disappear round the corner and only then did he realise that his fists had been clenched.

Suddenly he felt a crushing weariness and for a moment he leant back against the wall. He knew that Venetia would be concerned as she hadn't heard from him since he'd told her to leave the beach and his phone had been turned off in the police station. What was he going to say to her? His voice would probably give away that something was wrong. He paused, then decided a brief text message to tell her he was all right and would be with her soon would be best; it gave him the chance to gather himself again. Tucking his phone back into his pocket, he lit a cigarette and left the alley, making his way up the road towards the hotel.

Venetia was waiting for him on the veranda, still fully dressed, when he came into the suite. In the limpid early morning light, her face was pinched and bleak – a pixie's face, with purple shadows under her tired eyes. As he stepped into the room, she rushed towards him, her hands outstretched.

'I've been worried sick,' she breathed as he gathered her close and kissed her.

It was hardly the kiss of a lover; at this moment he felt no stir of passion, only flooding tenderness, and a strange, sweet, unendurable pain that needed at all costs to be assuaged.

Nor was her response any more passionate; she gave herself to his arms as if within them laid her refuge and her home. It was what Paolo liked about Venetia: she seemed always to be attuned to his moods and to act accordingly.

'What happened? Did you have to go to the police station?'

He couldn't tell her about Allegra, not now. That could wait for another time. Now he just wanted to hold her. He sighed. 'Yes – it was a little frustrating because of the endless paperwork those bureaucrats love to shuffle around, but there was no doubt that Umberto had started the quarrel. Luckily, there had been some witnesses to the fight and they confirmed my side of the story.'

'I can't believe the venom of that dreadful man you call your friend!'

'He is a man passionately in love, *cara*.' He paused a moment, and frowned as if his mind was crowding with dark thoughts. But then his features softened, and he leaned forward and brushed her softly parted lips with his own. 'Men kill for love sometimes, you know?'

Venetia calmed at his touch, but shook her head. 'Umberto is a brute, despite his angelic good looks. You're different – you don't have that killer instinct. *You* wouldn't hurt anyone,' she said forcefully.

So much faith in him... it caught at his heartstrings. Paolo gave her a rueful smile. 'Wouldn't I?' He couldn't bear to lose her now. He pressed her a little closer.

'Of course you wouldn't,' Venetia looked up at him and chuckled, 'although I was very impressed by your fighting techniques – I didn't know you were a Jujitsu expert.'

Paolo half smiled. He laid one hand on Venetia's shoulder, and placing the other beneath her chin, tilted up her face. 'Ah, but I'm an expert at many things, *signorina* – didn't you know that?'

He kept the tone light, but his heart was heavy. For one endless moment he gazed down into the depths of her golden eyes with their quizzical intensity. There was still so much she didn't know about him, so much he didn't know about himself... Would their love survive in the looming shadow of such uncertainties? Still, a life without Venetia meant a hunger unappeased, a thirst unquenched. Anything was better than that.

'You were agile as a panther out there – it was quite something. Where did you learn to fight like that?'

Her question came to him through the haze of his thoughts.

'Lessons, *cara*,' he was quick to answer. 'Martial arts are a very useful way to stay fit. Besides, with the amount of crime on the streets nowadays, it's essential to know how to defend oneself.' He raised a dark brow. 'You yourself had a bad experience, Venetia, not so long ago.'

'I know. And there again, you defended me with quite masterly expertise.' She beamed at him and then thought for a moment. 'You're right – I should learn Jujitsu, Karate or maybe Tae Kwan-do. Will you give me lessons?'

Paolo felt the stir in his body as his imagination instantly conjured up an image of Venetia belted in a white robe, the two of them entangled on the floor... and all the other wonderful things that he could teach her which had nothing to do with martial arts, though he didn't think she had much to learn. He gazed at her with a wicked glint in his eyes.

'I'll give you lessons in anything you like, *cara*. But first we must vacate the room, it is already nine o'clock and we must get ready to leave after breakfast for Cagliari and our villa,' he said as he nipped her chin with his thumb and forefinger and gently uncoiled her arms, which had wound themselves about his neck.

She shot Paolo a pretend sulky look and playfully pushed him back.

'You can use the bathroom first. In the meantime, I'll call *Zia* Giovanna to tell her that you've asked me to marry you – she'll be delighted.'

*   *   *

As Paolo disappeared into the bathroom, Venetia went to the sitting room to ring Giovanna. There was no answer at the house, or from her mobile which, unusually, went straight to voicemail. Venetia looked at her watch: it was a quarter past nine. Giovanna didn't usually go to the office on Tuesdays. She kept that day for her personal work because at weekends she was busy, either with entertaining or going out with her husband, Ugo. She was always served breakfast in bed, where she read the papers, and seldom came down before late afternoon. And in any case, Celestina the housekeeper should have been there as it was not market day.

Venetia tried again ten minutes later, and when she received no answer from either numbers, she rang the office.

'I'm so sorry, *signorina*, but *Signor* Ugo was taken ill this morning as he was getting out of his car at the office,' Sabina, Giovanna's assistant, told her. 'They called an ambulance and he was rushed to hospital – I think he may have had a heart attack. I informed *la Signora* Lombardi as soon as I heard about it, and she went immediately to the *ospedale*.'

Venetia tried to stem the rising panic in her throat, but she had to be practical and so she kept her voice calm. 'Do you know which hospital? Do you have the number? And the room number too, please?'

Having obtained the information she needed, she set about getting in touch with her godmother. The switchboard at the *Ospedale dell'Angelo* tried their best to be helpful, but it was no straightforward matter. It was likely he would have been rushed into intensive care, she was told, but they could not be sure, and it was unlikely they'd be able to track the patient down quickly. There was no way of knowing if she could get in touch with Giovanna before the afternoon, or even the night, and so much could happen between now and then. Ugo was Giovanna's whole life; already she had gone through the trauma of losing her first husband while still in her early forties. Venetia could just imagine how harrowing this experience was for her darling *Zia*, while she was living it up in Sardinia and would be for the next week.

Venetia heard Paolo come out of the bathroom. He called to her from the bedroom, 'The bathroom's clear, *cara*. All yours.'

But she didn't answer, the line of her jaw tense. She felt wretched, torn between a sense of duty towards her godmother and her reluctance to spoil Paolo's holiday, which he had gone to such pains to organise.

Paolo found her in the sitting room. He was almost naked, with a narrow brief covering him, his virility only the more appealing with that edge of mystery; and despite having her mind on other things, Venetia couldn't help the instinctive arousal that stirred her body at this view. Built like an athlete, he was so tall and broad that he almost dwarfed the furniture in the room, not only with his bulk but with his personality. No wonder he had made short work of Umberto and his bodyguard.

Seeing her expression, he frowned. '*Sembri preoccupata, cara,* you seem worried. Was *Signora* Lombardi not happy with your announcement of our engagement?'

'No, no, not at all,' Venetia reassured him. 'I haven't been able to reach *Zia*. Ugo, her husband, was taken ill outside the office this morning and was rushed to hospital. They think he's had a heart attack.'

'*Dio mio.*' In two strides he was beside her, his hands on her shoulders. '*Cara*, you mustn't worry. We'll leave immediately for Venice. I'll take care of the arrangements and we'll be there before tonight, I promise.'

'But Paolo, this will spoil the whole week... all the trouble you've taken to organise this wonderful holiday, and...'

'There'll be time enough for that,' he said, ignoring her protests. 'I think there's a plane from Alghero that leaves for Pisa at midday. We can then drive to Venice. My car is already at Galileo Galilei.'

'I'm not going to have you drive all the way to Venice. I'll fly.'

He cocked his head to one side. 'You think that I will let you go alone to Venice to face *una tragedia indescrivibile*? What sort of a man do you think I am, eh?'

He made her feel so soothed and protected, and so much stronger just by his presence. Venetia smiled, trailing her fingers over the scarred skin of his powerful chest. 'I think you're the most wonderful man in the world, and I love you.'

Paolo closed his eyes, unmoving, and she felt him shudder under her touch.

'Don't do that, *cara*,' he breathed, clasping her hand and gently pushing it away. 'There's a limit to a man's willpower. If you continue down that road, I doubt we'll be in Venice even in a month's time.'

Venetia moved away a little. He stood there watching her. Looking at him standing, half-naked, his gaze so intense, it was as much as she could do not to test his willpower. His deep blue irises were stroking each of her features, tracing them as graphically as if it were his lips that were making that journey. She smiled impishly. 'And I promise, Paolo, that I'll make it up to you.'

*   *   *

They arrived in Venice late afternoon and went straight to *Ospedale dell'Angelo*. Throughout the whole journey from Sardinia, Venetia had tried to call her godmother but, without a room number for Ugo, the switchboard employee could not be of any help, and she still hadn't been able to get through to Giovanna on her mobile. Feeling deeply embarrassed and guilty for having ruined Paolo's plans, nevertheless she strived to appear calm, almost phlegmatic, even though she was intensely worried. She tried to persuade him to leave after he had dropped her off at the hospital, but Paolo flatly refused to go before she had met up with Giovanna.

'*Non posso andarmene prima di aver trovato la Signora Lombardi*, I can't leave before we've found *la Signora* Lombardi.'

'Oh, Paolo, you've put yourself out enough for me today… You've had no sleep, you drove all day yesterday. You must be so tired.'

'Don't argue, *cara*, I've told you before I'm never tired when I'm with you – I'd feel far more anxious if I left now and didn't know how things were. I promise that when we find *Signora* Lombardi I'll not intrude, and if I'm not needed I'll go, all right?'

They were lucky to find a parking place in the very restricted car park of the hospital. Having been given hardly any information for an hour, they finally learnt from one of the doctors that *Signor* Ugo Lombardi was in intensive care. He'd had a heart attack, but the situation was now under control and he was out of danger. However, they wanted to keep him in intensive care for twenty-four hours to be on the safe side. *La Signora* had been asked to go home, as there was nothing she could do at this stage and *Signor* Lombardi would hopefully be out in a couple of days. Having seen the test results, the doctors realised that his condition seemed to be less serious than they had originally thought.

Venetia was relieved. She hated the smell and the feel of hospitals and, besides, she had the impression that Paolo shared her aversion. Although he didn't say anything, he was subdued while she spoke to the doctors and, noting the shades of pain that clouded his eyes, she sensed that a sort of malaise had overcome him. He was probably reliving the time he'd spent in hospital after the accident, she told herself. And yet the degree of his restlessness the longer they stayed surprised her.

They spoke little on the way out of the hospital, or on the drive through the centre of town, heading for Giovanna's penthouse.

Paolo parked the car at the municipal car park at Piazza le Roma in Santa Croce and they picked up his launch at the Venice Marittima Port, a stone's throw away.

'I'll wait for you at Fritelli. Meet me there when you've finished with your godmother and we can have dinner,' he told Venetia when they finally arrived at the pier of Piazza San Marco.

'You might as well come with me, Paolo, and we can announce our engagement to *Zia*. It'll help cheer her up.'

'Are you sure I won't be intruding?' He looked at her warily.

She nodded. 'Quite sure – *Zia* will be delighted about the news. If she hasn't had dinner, we can take her to Fritelli together.'

When they arrived at Bella Vista and enquired at the security desk if *Signora* Lombardi was at home, the friendly porter told them that she had arrived an hour ago and that as far as he knew, she had not come down again. They were taken up in the lift by a smart bellboy dressed in a black and green uniform – Venetia had always liked this little touch of ceremony, of the kind you would find at a hotel or a smart department store. It was so like charming, old-fashioned Ugo to give his building this element of luxury; a little pompous perhaps but it had a lot of panache.

Giovanna Lombardi was surprised but relieved to see her goddaughter. 'I'm so glad you've come,' she said, ushering her and Paolo into the apartment and sitting them down on one of her sumptuous sofas. 'Just as I was about to call you from the hospital, my stupid mobile gave up on me and I had no way of contacting you. It's been horrible – I really thought Ugo was at death's door. *Grazie a Dio*, the doctors have said he's now out of danger. It was only a mild attack and he'll be back to normal in a couple of weeks.'

She was delighted when Venetia told her of the engagement. 'Isn't it rather sudden?' she enquired in a low voice, once Paolo had gone out into the hall to ring the restaurant. Giovanna looked at her goddaughter with a twinkle in her eye. 'After all, I thought you didn't particularly like the man. If I remember rightly, I had to twist your arm to take the assignment and that was only a few days ago.'

Venetia smiled ruefully, recalling how difficult she had made things at the beginning. 'I think we fell in love almost from the first minute we met, but I was still haunted by my experience with Judd.'

'Have you told him about all that?'

'Yes.'

'And the loss of your baby?'

'Yes.'

'And?'

'And nothing – he listened and we moved on.'

Giovanna looked surprised. 'He's rather broadminded for an Italian.'

'He's a widower himself.'

'Oh... I see... Actually, it could be a marriage made in heaven – you've both suffered a great loss.' Giovanna patted her goddaughter's hand gently.

'Yes, I honestly think we're made for each other.'

'If that's the case, then it's a wonderful thing. You look well, and happier than I've seen you for years. Oh, the radiance of love!' Giovanna smiled and kissed her affectionately. The words were light but Venetia caught some undercurrent beneath them and her godmother's eyes looked faintly anxious as she added, 'Perhaps you'll be the one to tame him. Anyhow, there's no rush for the wedding – that's what the engagement period is for.'

Venetia was wondering what reply to make to this when the door opened.

'I've reserved us a table at Rigoletto,' Paolo announced, coming back into the room.

'Oh, Paolo, isn't that a little over the top?' Venetia's sleek eyebrows shot up. Rigoletto was reputed to have the best dining room in Venice and it was very expensive. It had been around for more than six decades and unlike many fad restaurants that appeared and disappeared within a short period, Rigoletto had kept its impeccable high standards over the years, renovating its menus to reflect modern times while the décor was kept unchanged to reflect the nostalgic atmosphere of yesteryear.

'We're celebrating two events, Venetia. First, the reassuring news that *Signor* Lombardi's condition is not serious, and secondly, that you have granted me the honour of agreeing to be my wife.' Paolo lifted Venetia's hand to his lips, giving a secret smile against her fingers and gazing adoringly into her eyes.

*   *   *

They walked to the restaurant. The evening was mild, but Venice was crowded; tourists had started to pour in for Easter. Gondolas with lanterns passed to and fro along the Canal. The dome of the Church of Santa Maria della Salute was in sharp silhouette against the evening sky, a deep blue vault above them where countless stars were shining brilliantly. Lights gleamed from the waterside and shone on the colourfully striped, gilt-topped poles that marked the landing stages outside large buildings and hotels. Their reflections bobbed up and down on the water, a poem of black and silver in the moonlight. Happy voices sounded lightly in the air. Someone was singing to the accompaniment of a guitar and behind some pinnacled historic monument the big moon rose in glorious splendour in the navy heavens.

They had almost reached the restaurant when Venetia, who was walking while gazing upwards trying to recognise some of the stars in the sky, collided with a man who was coming up the pavement in the opposite direction.

'*Scusa*, I'm so sorry,' she said, without looking at the person she had just banged into.

'Venetia… Venetia Aston-Montagu?'

Venetia looked up at the man addressing her. In the light of the street lamp, the face looked familiar. In his late fifties, he was tall and barrel-chested, and though wearing faded jeans and a discoloured T-shirt, he was a distinguished-looking man, with receding blond hair that was greying at the temples. She hesitated, and then remembered: Mr Riley. Robert Riley, a friend of her father's.

'Mr Riley, am I right?' she asked with a smile.

'Yes, that's me. How are you, Venetia?' The man shook her hand, peering at her intently. 'It's been a long time. I see your father quite often at the club, and at our bridge nights. He told me you were living now in romantic Venice.'

'Yes, I love it here. How is Daddy? He's not very talkative when I ring.' She felt suddenly embarrassed by her father's apparent lack of interest and added: 'He's always had an aversion to the phone.'

'He's very well, actually. Getting on a little, of course, like the rest of us.' Robert Riley laughed. 'He's had to stop the wine and the good living – a few attacks of gout.'

Venetia's brows lifted. 'I didn't know – he never told me. He always says he's fine and never talks about his health. I only get to visit him once a year, at Easter, and I always assume he's well… But how rude of me, I haven't introduced you to my godmother, Giovanna Lombardi.'

'Yes, your godmother – we met years ago. *Signora* Lombardi, a pleasure once again,' the man said, taking the hand Giovanna had just extended to him.

'And this is *Signor* Barone. Paolo and I have become engaged literally this morning and we're out to celebrate. I haven't yet told Daddy, but I will first thing tomorrow.'

Robert Riley turned to Paolo, but did not offer his hand. 'Congratulations.' He nodded politely.

'*Grazie*,' Paolo murmured, hardly looking up.

Venetia glanced at her fiancé. The light fell on his face and she noted how tired he looked, haggard and drawn and showing lines she had never discerned before. 'I haven't seen Mr Riley since I left England,' she explained.

Paolo's smile was slightly wistful as his gaze travelled from his fiancée to Venetia's father's friend. 'It's a small world, *cara*.'

'Indeed, you never know who you'll bump into,' Robert Riley said. 'Well, it was lovely to see you again, Venetia, after so long.' His large hand warmly engulfed hers. 'I'll leave you to celebrate this happy event.'

'I remember him,' Venetia said, turning to her godmother as the man disappeared round the corner. 'One of Daddy's stuffy government friends! I didn't recognise him immediately. It's been more than ten years and he's certainly aged. Besides, I'd only ever seen him in a suit – he looked rather underdressed in those shabby jeans. I'd never have thought of meeting him in a romantic city like Venice.'

Giovanna watched Paolo take the lead and move ahead of them, as she leaned towards her goddaughter, lowering her voice.

'Oh, don't be fooled, my dear. These undercover MI5 and MI6 types pop up unexpectedly all over the globe. I remember him well. Your mother didn't like him much – she said he was a bad influence on your father. They'd been friends at Eton and then at Oxford. He read Political Science, like your father, who only briefly worked in intelligence. William abandoned all that to look after the family business when your uncle John died but your father kept in touch with all his friends from his secret agent days, I'm sure of that. Your mother suspected that he actually donated large chunks of money to the organisation. He's very nationalistic and I think always resented having to leave his career in intelligence.'

Venetia gave a sigh and shook her head sadly. This was one of the few times she had discussed her father with Giovanna, not wishing to remind herself of her unhappy family life before she'd come to live in Venice.

'I never knew that, but then again, I always avoided thinking about what he did, and he never talked about his work. I doubt Mother was aware of what he was up to half the time. Besides, as you know, Daddy and I didn't get on. He took no interest in what I wanted to do with my life, always dictating, always making me feel that I didn't live up to his expectations, so I gradually moved away from him. I think that secretly he wished he'd had a son.'

Giovanna nodded, signalling towards Paolo who was still walking ahead of the two women. 'Well, let's not rehash all that now,' she told Venetia in a hushed tone. 'Tonight we're celebrating a happy event and you mustn't let any dark thoughts mar the occasion.'

Arriving at the grand Baroque entrance of Rigoletto, the *maître d'hôtel* gave them a choice of two tables. They could either sit inside in the formal Italian marble dining room, dimly lit with its raspberry raw-silk curtains, leather dining chairs and walls decorated with paintings by Amedeo Modigliani, who had been a close friend of the owners; or more informally, outside in the garden where the tables were set among flowers. The riotous blooms were everywhere; not only in the ground, but growing in baskets hanging from the branches of trees, or arranged in large Etruscan vases in odd corners of the lawn, which though small and compact, like the few green spaces within the city, would have seemed bare without those colourful floral arrangements.

They chose the second option and sat in candlelight beneath a silver birch tree next to a warbling fountain. Venetia was drunk with her own intoxicating emotions, which were amplified by the beauty of the surroundings. Music vibrated in the scented atmosphere, and the rhythmic beat of its drums found an answering throb in the young woman's heart.

Still, she was aware that Paolo was not his usual voluble self. From time to time when he turned to look at her, she saw that his dark face was taut and strained – and at once she was filled with guilt. Now and again he paused to sip his whisky and leaned back in his chair, looking out at the gardens, and the happiness that had been shining out since Venetia had agreed to be his wife left his face. His expression became momentarily preoccupied, even troubled.

Venetia noticed that he'd ordered another whisky. It was so unlike him to take a second strong drink in one evening. She wondered what was perplexing him. The visit to the hospital must have affected him more deeply than she had realised. *He must be exhausted. I shouldn't have let him take us out tonight.* She and *Zia* could have stayed at home and Celestina would have made them something simple like *crema di pomodoro*, a plate of gnocchi and some salad, she told herself. At this stage in her reflections Paolo, as if impelled by her gaze, looked straight across at her and smiled. Her insides fluttered as they always did when he looked at her that way and she relaxed.

A simple meal was literally not on the menu. Venetia had a copious dinner made up of *risotto Milanese* and crispy veal sweetbreads filled with *Tartufi Neri*, which the *maître d'hôtel* insisted was an early harvest that had just arrived that morning from Umbria. She ended her meal with a dessert made of golden, fresh *nespoli* with honeycomb ice-cream and a cup of black coffee.

After dinner they accompanied Giovanna back to her apartment.

'I'll join you at the hospital tomorrow morning, *Zia*. Have a good night.'

At the door to Bella Vista, Giovanna kissed her goddaughter and then Paolo. 'Goodnight, *cara*, and thank you for the lovely evening, Paolo.'

He gave a courteous nod. 'It's my pleasure, *signora*, and I hope the first of many.'

As Venetia and Paolo were walking back to the launch, Venetia shivered for no apparent reason. 'Someone walked over my grave,' she said laughingly.

'Don't say things like that,' Paolo snapped. 'It's morbid.' He took off his jacket and wrapped it around her shoulders as though she were a rare piece of china. Then his voice softened. 'Here, wear this. You must be tired, *carissima,* you need a good night's sleep.' Venetia pulled his jacket around her and glanced at him, realising that she had never seen him so tired-looking, but she smiled and said nothing.

The tranquil night was not without its effect on Paolo and Venetia. They stood side by side a while in silence on the deserted quay, gazing over the Grand Canal's mirror of water with its quivering reflections of many-coloured lights – red, green, yellow and blue. Gondolas full of sightseers, each with their lanterns fore and aft, glided past them like blossoms moving to and fro, backed by great façades of medieval architecture lit up in grand and gracious beauty by clever lighting. The moon shed a beam as soft as mother-of-pearl across the water. Lovers, honeymoon couples in boats, and would-be honeymooners moved in dreamy wanderings on the liquid table.

'Will you come over to my place instead of going to the hotel?'

Paolo looked down at Venetia. In the moonlight, she saw the quick curve of a smile move across his face. 'If I stay with you tonight we will not sleep, *amore mio,* believe me.'

'We could try.' She smiled shyly, still staring out at the water.

'Although I admit that I'm tired, I wouldn't be able to resist you. Either a fool or a saint would turn their back on a night in your arms, *cara,* and I am neither.'

At his words, a slow wave of heat curled through Venetia's body.

Suddenly Paolo's hand went out and caught hers, squeezing her fingers convulsively. Slowly, Venetia turned her head towards him to find that he was looking at her. There was an urgency in his gaze, a pleading that caused her heart to leap in her breast. His blue eyes were glittering, and his face, lean and dark, almost terrifyingly stern with a new intensity. Then, suddenly, he removed his hand from hers, though it was only to clasp Venetia in his arms and gather her close to him. He tried to speak, but the words did not seem to come.

'What's wrong, Paolo? You look so pale and agitated suddenly.'

'Just remember this, *amore mio*: I love you, Venetia. I've known this all along, ever since the day I met you. I want to take care of you for the rest of our lives. I simply cannot live without you…'

'I know all that, my love, and I feel the same about you.'

'Are you quite sure? What if…'

'Shush, you're exhausted and it's all my fault, dragging you back down here and spoiling your holiday – there's nothing to worry about.'

Paolo shook his head in a way Venetia didn't understand and searched her eyes. Then his mouth was on her forehead and he whispered her name again and again, *'la mia piccola strega*, my little enchantress,' he breathed. He leant his cheek against hers and appeared to find comfort in doing so, but there was a kind of sadness about him, Venetia thought; she had the impression that his shoulders were suddenly bending under the weight of some predicament. Maybe he was realising now that asking her to marry him would be an added complication to his life and he was having second thoughts. Maybe it was all her imagination… Silence stretched between them, broken only by the soft lap of the water against the quay.

'Come, let's go, Paolo. Take me home and get yourself a goodnight's sleep – you'll feel better tomorrow.'

They stepped down into Paolo's launch and motored away towards the Dorsoduro district.

*   *   *

An aura of wispy dream clouds surrounded Venetia. She seemed to be a prisoner in a bubble, floating between sky and earth. Through a hazy veil, the indistinct features of her lover appeared to her like an inaccessible mirage she knew would vanish at any moment if she didn't capture it immediately.

She sighed softly, lifting herself a little, her arms stretched, reaching out for him. 'My love,' she breathed. 'My dearest love, my only love, don't go. I love you. I've never stopped loving you. I'll always love you… you… only you.'

She kept seeing the man at a distance, but the nebulous image went on fading, then coming back… she could almost see him clearly now, but then again his face melted away in the swirling brume of the unreal.

She called after him, running now, overwhelmed by a frantic need to catch up with him. And then suddenly his arms were around her. Paolo… holding her… Paolo… stroking her… kissing her. She tried to press against him… feel him, throbbing with emotion, hungry for his touch… his warmth, but she met with nothingness… emptiness… air… cold air. Why couldn't she feel him?

He was whispering in her ear. The words were indistinct, though she knew they were tender… words of love… a melody surging and echoing… *Paolo… Paolo, answer me. Is that you?* Of course it was him, who else could it be? Even though she couldn't hear the reply clearly, there was something about the voice that was familiar, like the low note of a cello, deep and barely distinguishable, but you know it's there.

Paolo, she breathed, lifting her eyes to look at him… *Paolo*… but it was not Paolo's face that she met with, but Judd's… and as tremors of fear raked her body, a shattering cry escaped her lips… *Judd's ghost!*

Venetia's mind was still echoing with those two words as she wrenched herself out of her dream to escape him. She was sitting up on her bed, panting – disorientated for a moment, eyes wide open. Her hair was plastered to her skull; her mouth, her throat dry. Afraid to move, she clutched at her chest, terrified to close her eyes, fearing she would see him again if she did… *Judd's ghost!*

The shafts of silvery moonlight that played on the eiderdown and across the walls provided the only light in the dark room. Venetia looked around her, getting her bearings. Yes, that was it… she was back in Venice. She hugged her knees and rested her forehead on them, trying to quieten her breathing and allow her heartbeat to slow down.

After a while, she felt calmer and her pulse had recovered its normal beat, enough to begin thinking rather than just feeling. 'Judd again,' she sighed aloud. 'It's always Judd.'

As soon as she believed she was rid of his memory, it came back to haunt her somehow. Venetia had run from the shadow of his abandonment for too long. Should she try and seek him out again and bring all those years of torment to a conclusion, once and for all? Maybe it would bring closure, and the echoes of this love would cease pursuing her; she would be able to get on with her life. Of course, Paolo would have to know about it, if that was her intention. But despite his philosophical nature, Paolo was a passionate and possessive man, she knew that – his condition had no doubt intensified the need for security and control. Perhaps this approach would only complicate matters. She'd have to give it more thought.

Venetia turned on the bedside lamp and turned it off again: the light was too bright. She slid out of bed and padded to the bathroom. Pulling off her nightdress, she stepped under the shower. A little shudder of pleasure ran through her as her hot skin felt the coolness trickle over it and she closed her eyes, imagining Paolo's feathery touch stroking her. She loved the way his hands moved over her, strong and firm, but tender too. Despite the passion and fire that ran through him, he'd never been rough with her, handling her body as if it were a precious jewel. Such gentleness in such a big man she had found deeply arousing, and it had intrigued her. Paolo had taught Venetia not to be afraid of her body and its demands.

Ripples of emotion stirred her as the water curled intimately between her thighs, joining the moisture she could feel pooling in her core. All too aware of what she needed right now, Venetia wished that she had insisted he spend the night with her after all – she knew he would eventually have given in. It was too early to call him. He was exhausted... he must be fast asleep. She was exhausted too; the dream had unnerved her, but it was only a dream, she thought philosophically, maybe she should try to get another few hours of sleep. Yes, that was the best thing to do: go back to bed, close her eyes and sleep. Time would pass quicker that way and then, once the sun was up, she would ring Paolo.

*   *   *

When Venetia woke up again it was broad daylight, but it was still too early to call Paolo. *Let him have a lie in*, she thought. Before dressing, she made herself a pot of hot, strong coffee. She wasn't hungry, but she needed a boost to get her going today. Taking it on to the narrow veranda, she sat in her thin dressing gown, lazily watching the traffic on the canal through the pattern of the wrought-iron screen guarding her balcony.

She could hear the cooing of pigeons and she smiled, mentally comparing this view to the one that had become so familiar at Miraggio.

It was a perfect blue and gold morning. The sky was flawless and the water seemed to dance with fluent brilliance in the warmth of the sun.

Her mobile rang and Venetia rushed to seize it from her bag with a knowing smile. *Paolo*, she thought. *He's up early, maybe he couldn't sleep either.*

It wasn't Paolo, but Giovanna, asking her not to go to the hospital but to the office. There was a large slab of damaged mosaic that had just been delivered to her department and the Spanish client was in a hurry to get it back. It was quite a substantial piece that had fragmented off a mural in Granada. Giovanna thought that if Venetia tackled it with Francesca this morning, it would speed up the work and they'd easily have it ready for *Señor* Herrera within a couple of days.

Somewhat relieved that she didn't have the ordeal of the hospital to contend with again, Venetia dressed, and before going down tried Paolo on his mobile to arrange to meet him for lunch. The phone was turned off so she rang his hotel.

'There's no answer from his room, I'm afraid, *signorina*,' the switchboard at the Hotel Cipriani informed her. They tried the dining room, as he was probably having breakfast, but he wasn't there either.

'Could you please put me through to the concierge in that case.' Venetia held on for a few minutes before the concierge came to the phone.

'*Signor* Barone took a taxi from the hotel very early this morning and hasn't yet returned. His key is still on the keyboard.'

Annoyed, Venetia put down the phone. Why hadn't he called her? Most likely he hadn't wanted to wake her – a sweet thought but nevertheless irritating. Besides, why would his phone be switched off? *You're being unfair,* she castigated herself. *He didn't want to intrude since you were supposed to spend the day with Giovanna at the hospital, so he decided to do his own thing. And there could be any number of valid reasons why his phone is off.*

Hurrying out of her apartment, Venetia joined the huddle of people at the boat stop. She had to wait a little longer for the *vaporetto* that morning. There seemed to be many more tourists this year, probably due to the favourable exchange rate with the *lire*, she mused. Once she had finally got off at San Marco, she had to walk briskly to reach the offices of Bianchi e Lombardi on time.

Francesca jumped up to greet her friend as Venetia entered the room.

'Venetia! It's wonderful and so unexpected to see you back here. I thought it would be months,' she exclaimed, embracing her friend warmly, and then added with a mischievous smile, 'We have poor Ugo to thank for that, I suppose.'

Venetia sighed. 'Yes, poor Ugo, and poor *Zia,* but the good news is that it was only a mild attack and he should soon be out of hospital.'

'What about you? You look a little tired – I hope that animal isn't giving you a hard time.'

Venetia frowned. 'What animal? I hope you don't mean Paolo?'

'Ooooooh, he's *Paolo* now,' Francesca laughed, mimicking the tender way she had pronounced his name.

Venetia felt the telltale reddening of her cheeks giving her way. 'Don't tease, Francesca… I know it's all very unexpected... As you know, I went out there really not looking for romance, but…'

'But *l'Amante delle Quattro Stagioni* charmed you, eh?'

'It wasn't like that. I did try to fight my feelings at first, but you know that I was attracted to him from the very beginning. You witnessed our kiss.'

'*Sì*, but this man is a *mascalzone*, who's had hundreds of mistresses. There are *so* many rumours about him.'

Venetia smiled sheepishly. 'I promise you that he's the most caring, attentive and affectionate man I have ever come across.'

'*Dio mio*, you're hooked, *cara*! Love is blind and I can see that this man has become your knight in shining armour now.' Francesca arched an eyebrow, distinctly unconvinced.

'He's not what you think. Let's sit down to work and I'll explain – I have a lot to tell you.'

'I'm sure you have. *Chi può fare da testimone alla sposa, se non sua madre*, who will bear witness to the bride but her mother?'

'Don't be so cynical, Francesca. I know how to be impartial when needs be.'

'I'll fetch us two cups of coffee and then you can confess all, while we tackle this *unreasonably* intricate job which they want finished in an *unreasonably* short time.'

While Francesca was bringing the coffee, Venetia rang Paolo again, but still he had not returned to the hotel. He might have gone to Torcello, she thought. *But if Paolo had been called away for work, he would have told me.* She tried to brush away the small murmurings of unease.

Venetia and her friend spent the morning working and chatting. Francesca almost dropped her cup of coffee all over herself when she told her that Paolo had proposed and she had accepted. By lunchtime, Venetia had been able to change Francesca's views about Paolo. Just about. Still, the young Italian urged her to keep an open mind and not to wear blinkers. After all, she was not married yet. '*Non c'è peggior cieco di chi non vede*, there is none so blind as he who will not see.'

At lunchtime Venetia rang the hotel again, but Paolo was still out. She rang Miraggio and fell on Ernestina for any news of Paolo when she answered. The housekeeper told her that she hadn't heard from the *signore* since they had both left for Sardinia a couple of days ago, but that if he turned up unexpectedly she would let him know that the *signorina* was looking for him. As Venetia hung up, she knew of only one thing she wanted to do that might help alleviate her rapidly growing anxiety.

'I'll take you out for lunch,' Francesca suggested, looking at her watch. 'It'll be my treat in celebration of your engagement.'

Venetia jumped up quickly and grabbed her coat. 'Thanks, Francesca, but let's leave it for another time – I have an important errand to run. I'll be back here this afternoon to continue the job.'

The two bronze giants on the top of the San Marco clocktower beat out one o'clock on a sounding bell. Venetia hurried towards her destination, in the midst of the great streams of people who came flooding from all directions in the sunlight, bringing with them the myriad buzzing and humming of the international world. For once, as she walked along, she was not admiring the Doge's Palace, which shut out the sky with its great façade supported on a double tier of arches, or the Renaissance front of the Library of Saint Mark, where she spent many winter afternoons reading and researching. She crossed the great square with its Campanile towering above, the graceful shaft flecked with the shadows of passing clouds; the severity of the sober red brick of the bell tower made the main edifice of the Church of San Marco look almost fairy-like with its wealth of white marble lace-work and golden mosaic. Hundreds of pigeons crooned and strutted round her, glorious in their opal plumage, as she walked quickly through the broad square.

Venetia was lost in thought; she needed to speak to Ping Lü. The last time she'd called on the Chineseman, the emporium had been closed but today an odd certainty came over her that she would find him and he would clear the doubts that had been creeping into her heart all morning. It was as if her strange dream sparked some unseen current that had touched and registered itself on a part of her brain. Something that matter-of-fact people would laugh at… but this was a quiet conviction she felt in spite of herself. Just as certain delicate instruments can feel an earthquake shock, although the earthquake may be five thousand miles away, the quiet murmur of knowledge inside us all can sometimes be heard above a roar. Jumping to conclusions, common sense said to Venetia. *Intuition*, an internal voice whispered.

Calle del Paradiso was teaming with people. As with each time she had visited this enchanting corner of the town, she was aware of its medieval feeling, so uncommon in the rest of Venice.

Venetia made her way, pushing and shoving, trying to forge a passage between the sea of people moving to and fro on the narrow street. She had almost reached her destination when she came upon a crowd blocking her way as they gathered en masse, peering through the grills into two dark basement rooms in one building entirely inhabited by caged birds. There was an awful stench of feathers in the air around the shop and she could hear the little creatures twittering, chirruping and squeaking. She had been told about the caged birds of Venice – imported love-birds, canaries, doves and blackbirds that were sold in ornate, gilded show cages. In fact, Fabrizio had a blackbird that lived in a cage on his sunny balcony, among the potted flowers and climbing plants. Passers-by would halt and whistle a short tune to it, which the happy little bird answered faithfully with extraordinary sweetness. Fabrizio. He was such an easy-going, happy-go-lucky fellow. Such a straightforward young man would make a fine match for any girl. Still, she could never have fallen in love with him... he lacked that elusive something that made men like Paolo go straight to a woman's heart.

Having finally disentangled herself from the scrum, Venetia reached Ping Lü's emporium. Her heart leapt with joy – the shop was open and the little man was sitting outside, sunning himself. As Venetia approached, he got up to greet her.

'I'm so glad I've found you,' she told him. 'I came once before, a few weeks ago, but your shop was shut.'

'Yes, my wife and I have just come back from a holiday in the mountains. But what brings you here, my child? I see that the shadows have not yet lifted from your face.'

'I've found love, but...'

Ping Lü stepped into the shop. He smiled his placid smile. 'Come, I will take you to my meditation garden. It is darker there, cool and silent, an atmosphere much more conducive to reflection.'

They went through the shop and passed through large double doors, which Venetia hadn't noticed previously, into a shaded exotic garden with twisted fairy trees, and curious plants and shrubs. In a corner, an ancient shrine, which seemed to have been built long ago in worship of a strange wild god, was surrounded by incense candles and stone lanterns, which threw a golden subdued light on the place. The entrance was guarded by bronze Fü dogs – the Chinese Imperial guardian lions, Ping Lü explained to her, with the male resting his paw upon the world and the female restraining her cub on his back.

'The female protects the dwelling inside, while the male guards the structure. The cub represents the cycle of life, which is important for all of us.' He nodded as he said this, giving Venetia a knowing smile. 'Come, my child, let's sit under the trees.'

The old trees, their outlines sharp against the light, resembled some that Venetia had once seen in a Japanese print; their flowers wan and elfin. The air was sweet and very still; the only sound came from a fountain, around the base of which blossoms sent out a cloying, heady scent.

Ping Lü sat on a wooden bench and he signalled to Venetia to sit on the stool opposite him. The very presence of the diminutive man gave the young woman a sense of calm. Once they were seated, his enigmatic, slanted black eyes scrutinised Venetia's face.

'So, you say you have found love?'

'Yes, his name is Paolo.' She hesitated, not knowing where to begin. 'He's a wonderful man who's had a very tragic life.'

'But?'

'Well, the problem isn't with him, you see... it's actually with me.'

'You have doubts? You are not sure of your feelings for... Paolo?'

'On the contrary, I love him more than life itself but I am haunted by dreams and thoughts of my first love.'

'Are you saying that your heart is divided between your first love and your new love?'

'No... it isn't like that. Paolo's gone, he's...'

'Have you read Heraclitus?'

Venetia frowned. Where was he going with this? 'I studied some of his philosophy at school, but I never read him as such.'

'He believes that all becoming is circular.'

'I don't understand.'

Ping Lü's eyes were on Venetia's face. They had the trick of emptying themselves of all expression, and now looked flat and dull as he spoke. 'Fire dies and is changed into air, air dies and becomes water, water dies to become earth, and so on. There is a constant interchanging of life and death between different elements, which goes both ways. All becoming is circular. The way Heraclitus put it was: *"The way up and the way down are one and the same."* Do not worry, my child, you are on the right track.'

Ping Lü's immense repose, his extreme gentleness in his manner of talking to her, gave Venetia reassurance, even though she was puzzled and didn't understand a word the old man was telling her.

'I can see that you are still confused, though if you trained in meditation the answer would have been plain to you. I will bring my tarot cards. We don't use them in China, preferring the I Ching, but my Italian wife introduced me to them, and for you I will make an exception.'

The scholarly man disappeared into his shop leaving Venetia to ponder his words. She glanced at her watch; she should be getting back to the office, but she didn't want to leave before she understood whether she was on the right track. She wanted to ask more questions, but to stay longer would be selfish. It wasn't fair on Giovanna, who had entrusted her with this work, or Francesca, who was left holding the baby.

When Ping Lü came back, Venetia got up. 'I'm so sorry, but I've run out of time already. I really need to go back to the office and I don't know when I'll be able to return.'

The Chineseman's dark eyes dwelled on the young woman's face and he smiled. 'Don't think so much, let your heart guide you. You are almost at the end of the road and the gods are smiling on you. There is still a storm you will have to weather with generosity. Confucius says: *"To be wronged is nothing unless you continue to remember it."* Crush the rose of anger, my child, so it may only leave its delicate fragrance on your hands. Learn to forgive an evil deed so you do not remain the victim of its consequences forever.'

'Thank you, Ping Lü. I will definitely think about what you've told me today. Although I don't really understand the meaning of your words, I'm sure I'll eventually find in them the answers to my questions.'

'I see you are still wearing the talisman I gave you.'

'Yes, always.'

'Then you must not fear. Remember to follow your heart and the gods will always smile upon you.'

Ping Lü accompanied Venetia to the front door. She extended her hand and he held it in his for a moment, staring into her eyes. 'I am full of wise sayings today,' he said with a half-smile. Confucius says: *"Never does the human soul appear so strong as when it foregoes revenge and dares to forgive an injury."'*

'But I forgave Judd a long time ago, Ping Lü. I have no hatred for him, just a little sadness at the bottom of my soul. But I deeply wish that the memory of him would stop haunting me, so that I can get on with my life. I love Paolo, I'm sure of that, and I want to spend the rest of my life with him.'

She had spoken passionately and the watchful old man's eyes twinkled mischievously. 'All becoming is circular, it is as simple as that. Goodbye, my child, and may the gods go with you.'

Although Ping Lü had helped to reassure her, Venetia was still anxious. Most of all she needed to speak to Paolo. *Where was he?* Realising that she'd left her phone at the office, Venetia stopped at one of the silver telephone boxes and called the hotel. 'No, *Signor* Barone is not here, he checked out this afternoon,' the operator told her. Perhaps he had left a message with Ernestina. She rang Miraggio again, but this time got no reply.

When Venetia arrived at the office she asked if there were any messages for her, but again drew a blank. She was miserable; memories of the times she had been left waiting for Judd to call or write came flooding back. A dark panic began to rise inside her. This couldn't be happening. *She couldn't go back there again.*

Francesca tried to reason with her friend, but Venetia refused to listen. There was no plausible reason for Paolo to leave Venice without telling her or suddenly being uncontactable. She'd been there before; she knew the score. Could she have been so deluded by Paolo? Had he run from her the moment she had finally given her heart to him? She felt sick to the stomach. *L'Amante delle Quattro Stagioni* was up to his old tricks. All her bright, shining dreams of everlasting love were splintered into the most devastating nightmare.

'You're jumping to conclusions, Venetia. Just wait – he might have been called out urgently on work, or there could be a problem with his phone. You can't condemn the man so quickly.'

Venetia gave a short, mirthless laugh and clenched her fists. Her deepest fear was unfurling inside her. 'And he couldn't find another phone to call me, even for two minutes? I was warned by you, and even by that dreadful Umberto – like in the past, I only have myself to blame. It's history repeating itself. I suppose at least this time I'm not pregnant.' *At any rate I don't think I am!* she mused bitterly.

She tried to concentrate on her work and was silent for the rest of the afternoon, thankful when it was time to go home. Starting to clear things away, she turned to Francesca. 'I think I'll pass by *Zia* quickly on my way out.' Maybe her godmother would have an idea of where Paolo might be.

Francesca saw the drawn look on her friend's face and patted her arm. 'Go,' she told her, shooing her out like a mother hen. 'I'll tidy up the workshop. If you'd like to have dinner later on, after you've visited your godmother, or if you'd prefer to talk on the phone, I'm not doing anything tonight.'

'Thanks, Francesca.' Venetia tried her best to smile. 'I'm in too much of a muddle at the moment to think straight. There's probably a plausible answer to all this and I'm just dramatising matters because of my experience with Judd and a strange dream I had last night. I'll go home first and then I'll ring *Zia* and find out what her plans for tonight are.'

As she was leaving the building, one of the security guards hastened down the steps. '*Signorina, Signorina...*'

She turned round. 'Are you calling me?'

'*Sì,*' the man said, coming towards her, holding out a white envelope. 'A gentleman dropped off this letter for you about an hour ago.'

Her heart gave a jolt. Paolo... Paolo had left her a message. Why hadn't he come up? But she didn't care about all that now. She breathed a sigh of relief. Silly man, he obviously didn't want to disturb her. Just like him to be thoughtful to a fault.

Venetia beamed. '*Grazie mille.*'

She tore open the envelope, almost ripping the letter inside. And then, as she looked down at the signature at the bottom of the page, her face fell. The message which she read again and again was brief and to the point:

Dear Venetia,

As a matter of urgency please meet me for dinner at eight o'clock at Buon Appetito on Campo dei Santi Giovanni e Paolo Square. I have some significant information, which might be of interest to you.

Yours truly,
Robert Riley

CHAPTER 12

The rhythm of the train as it chugged across the cold countryside seemed to measure the impatient beating of Venetia's own heart. It was a sunny April day with spring just reaching its full surge in all growing things; at last spreading its cool fresh colours to cover the greys and browns of winter. The sky was blue, with puffs of cotton-wool cloudlets, and the whole world feathered in green, the chestnut trees holding aloft their candles of pink and white blossom, the earth teaming with new life. In the fields, the first lambs were bleating, and young calves and foals experimented on groggy, spindling legs. Thick banks of daffodils and forget-me-nots bordered the rail tracks, and the trees in the copses looked rounded and buoyant; while in the orchards, fruit trees were dotted with buds. It was an English spring scene so different to that of Italy that Venetia watched slipping by, mile after mile, as the train laboured on its way.

The slowness of the country locomotive, stopping at every station, infuriated her. Even the noises she found aggravating: the gritty sound of people walking on gravel, the clatter of luggage, the voices, or the grinding noise from the carcasses of the old compartments as they started off or came to a halt.

Venetia had the carriage to herself, and even though she had brought a book for the journey, her thoughts kept rolling back to the evening before and to her meeting with Robert Riley. A hundred questions tumbled through her brain as she stared out of the window, her mind seesawing with alternate hope and despair. Her world was in turmoil; she no longer knew what was true or false. She went over and over the conversation she'd had with her father's friend: the questions and answers, the disjointed facts and bits of information, and it all still seemed too confused and fantastic to make sense.

After she had read Robert Riley's letter with a thumping heart, Venetia had almost not gone to the meeting. She had never particularly liked her father's 'cronies from the Organisation' as her mother used to call them. Always there seemed to be a cryptic feel in the air whenever they came to visit; they were the type of men she had learnt early to fear and to avoid.

She had read enough spy stories by John Le Carré and Len Deighton to recognise the equivocal language they used when they spoke, which always seemed to be focused on undesirable activities and enemies of the realm, both at home and abroad. It was the Troubles that occupied a great deal of their hushed murmurings behind the closed door of Sir William's study. Even though they hardly talked openly about the problems in Northern Ireland, Venetia knew that it was at the centre of their minds and their conversation. She had always presumed that, although her father had left the group, he was still implicated in all sorts of secret work – after all, surely once in, you never really got away? Still, she had never suspected to what extent his involvement would affect her life.

Enemies. The word formulated bitterly in Venetia's mind. *Rich, well-bred, well-groomed enemies, with claws that could be concealed so well that one never guessed at the evil going on behind the scenes. The crème de la crème of English society.* The thought sent a little shiver of distaste through her, even more so now that she knew that her father had been at the centre of it. How could a man behave with such unutterable cruelty towards his own daughter?

To think of her father, now more than ever, was like prodding an unhealed wound. All her life, William Aston-Montagu had dictated what his daughter could and couldn't do. He did it through love of course, so he told Venetia, and her mother blindly supported him. Maybe the fact that it was all for her own good should have made a difference, but it hadn't – she had felt trapped, and as soon as she'd been able to go, Venetia had fled the nest. She still flinched when she remembered the awful rows there had been between herself and her father over anything that didn't go the way Sir William wanted. *Mother could have protected me*, Venetia continued the acrid conversation with herself. *But of course her views were distorted by her love for Father, so much so that in the end she had no forbearance, not even when it came to hurting her own daughter.*

In her mind, Venetia replayed her meeting with her father's friend. Robert Riley had not told her much. He had been waiting for her at Buon Appetito, seated at a corner table at the far end of the restaurant...

*   *   *

To Venetia's surprise, he immediately stood up when she arrived and signalled to the waiter to bring over the bill.

'Good evening, Venetia, I'm glad you've come,' he said with a congenial smile. 'I hope you don't mind us delaying dinner a little. I've reserved the table for ten o'clock, actually. As Italians don't dine before then, and it's such a beautiful evening, I thought we could go for a little walk before eating.'

Venetia tried not to show her irritation at his suggestion; she was not in the mood for chit-chat. All day she'd been on tenter-hooks trying to get in touch with Paolo and wondering what this sudden summons to a meeting was all about, which, by the tone of his letter, seemed to allude to something unsavoury.

'What's it all about, Mr Riley?' she said stiffly. 'I don't really care about dinner – that's not why I'm here.'

'Suit yourself, my dear, but I think we need to talk privately.'

They left the restaurant and walked in silence for a few moments, soon finding a small public garden that skirted the canal, which at this hour was almost deserted except for a few loved-up couples kissing on the benches.

'We won't be disturbed here,' Riley told her as he led them to a bench not far from the water's edge. 'Let's sit down, it'll be more comfortable – besides what I have to tell you might come as a shock and I think you'd be better off seated.'

Venetia was distinctly uneasy but sat down without looking at him, staring ahead at the dim reflections of the buildings opposite on the canal. 'Please come to the point, Mr Riley. It's been a long day and I really don't enjoy, nor do I have the time for the cloak-and-dagger games you and your friends get up to.'

Robert Riley smiled without amusement. 'No need to be like that, my dear – I could just as easily have left you in the dark for the moment, but at some point you would have had to learn the truth. I think it's only fair that you should know sooner rather than later, particularly as, after all, it now concerns you intimately.'

She gave an exasperated sigh. 'I'm all ears, sir.'

The agent didn't answer immediately. He took out a pack of cigarettes and offered one to Venetia, which she declined. The evening had not yet surrendered to night and was almost luminous, iridescent with fireflies; the atmosphere was warm, filled with the scent of roses, and the sound of water lapping softly against the jetty was borne to them on the night air.

'How well do you know Paolo Barone?'

'Well enough, why?'

'Venetia, you must believe me when I tell you that I'm not here to hurt you, quite the reverse. Some things are meant to be and life has a strange way of teaching us lessons. Perhaps Napoleon was right: "*There is no such thing as accident; it is fate misnamed.*"' He gave a little dry laugh. 'I don't particularly relish being the one to talk to you about this, and I really don't know how to say it without being blunt.'

'Well then, go ahead and be blunt – don't mind me.' There was impatience and frustration in Venetia's voice, and contempt in her dark amber irises as she finally met his eyes.

He peered through the cigarette smoke as he exhaled. 'A long time ago, when you were about eighteen, you were very much in love with a young man.'

Venetia cringed inwardly. Why was this man bringing all that up now? It was none of his business anyhow. 'Yes, Judd Carter. That's an old story which I put to bed, as you say, a long time ago, and I fail to see what my private life has to do with anything you might have to say to me,' she snapped.

'Gareth Jordan Carter. Well, life has a curious sense of humour and sometimes things have a funny way of cropping up.'

The memories were back, and her pulse started to act erratically. Her mouth went dry. 'Are you telling me… are you saying that you're in touch with Judd and that?'

He lifted a peremptory hand. 'One step at a time, my dear, you're jumping the gun.'

At that moment, Venetia felt a momentary and irrational feeling of panic. *What was all this about?* 'You asked me how well I know Paolo, and then suddenly you're talking to me about Judd!'

Her father's friend shifted uncomfortably on the bench. 'There's actually no ten ways of telling you this…' He hesitated and threw his cigarette stub into the canal. 'Venetia, my dear child, Paolo Barone and Gareth Jordan Carter are one and the same man.'

She stared blankly at him, then the world swayed around her. A cold sweat raced through her spine. Her heart was hammering, the palms of her hands damp; the leaves on the trees were a whirling kaleidoscope of dark patches. *I'm going to faint,* she thought, and prayed for the strength not to collapse there and then. What Robert Riley had just said was insane; it made no sense at all. A hundred questions flooded into her mind but she felt too confused and faint to ask one.

'I don't understand,' she murmured, trembling with shock and disbelief. 'What on earth are you talking about? It's impossible! Judd is English, Paolo's Italian – they don't even look remotely alike. They come from totally different worlds… What are you telling me?'

'I'm afraid that I'm not in a position to give you much more information. Your father has all the answers.'

Venetia felt herself freeze. 'What has my father got to do with this?'

'Unfortunately, William played a great part in this mess and I'm sorry to say that I was also part of it.' He leaned forward, his elbows on his knees, clasping his hands together.

'What about Judd… Paolo…?'

'He is now Paolo Barone. For all intents and purposes Gareth Jordan Carter is dead and must remain that way – it's a long story.'

Venetia's eyes flashed. 'So all this affair about Paolo being widowed and having lost his memory is a pack of lies?'

'No, Paolo is totally amnesic. Gareth was very badly injured during an undercover mission in Northern Ireland ten years ago. He almost lost his life.'

'But Judd was never an agent. He was an officer in the Parachute Regiment.'

Robert Riley sighed and looked somewhat sheepishly back at the young woman. 'Yes, I know, and that is where your father and I played a not very honourable role. Gareth was very patriotic and had a bit of a chip on his shoulder about not being part of the club – no public school background, and all that. It didn't take much to convince him to play hero.'

The fog of Venetia's puzzlement started to dispel as she began to understand what he was telling her. The ruthlessness of her father was so sickening that she could hardly bear to think of it. A slow and terrible anger, quite unlike her usual volatile temper, began to rise in her. For a split second, her hatred was like a searing flame, stronger than any emotion she had ever experienced before. If what she suspected was true, her father had destroyed her happiness as surely as if he had murdered his daughter in her sleep.

'You're despicable!' Her words were choked as she fought back the tears of rage and bitterness welling up inside her. For a while, she couldn't speak. She swallowed and tried to keep her voice from trembling. 'Does Paolo know all this?'

The agent sat back on the bench, looking straight ahead. When he answered, his voice was low. 'No, Paolo Barone only knows what we told him after he woke up from the deep coma into which he was plunged for several months. There was no need for him to know more than we thought he should know. He had been totally disfigured and needed extensive surgery. Believe me, your father was assailed by guilt and had him undergo these operations at his expense with a world-renowned

American surgeon. He also donated a large sum of money to provide Paolo with a very comfortable life.

'Gareth was a great soldier, a stoic and courageous man. The dangerous mission he was assigned almost cost him his life. To everyone he knows, he is dead and must remain so, as there's a price on his head. Paolo is very precious to our enemies, who think that he perished with the warehouse of ammunition he blew up. We had to invent for him a new identity, a whole new life. For two years he was trained until he became this new person. It wasn't that difficult for Gareth to embrace Paolo's personality, because of his amnesia. We set him up in Italy because we have close relations with the Italian Secret Service. He has been and will remain always, for obvious reasons, under surveillance.'

Venetia, who had listened silently, scarcely able to believe what she was hearing, looked at him aghast. 'You mean to say that Paolo is followed everywhere? That his phones are tapped and he has no privacy?'

Robert Riley smiled grimly. 'Not in the dramatic way you put it, my dear, but we have our methods. That's how I knew how to get in touch with you in the first place. The altercation Paolo had with Count Palermi di Orellana put your name on the map. One of our agents was there and it's thanks to him that Paolo was released so quickly. The Count's body-guard had put in a complaint, saying that it was Paolo who assaulted them first. The Italian police, because of Umberto Palermi's status, would otherwise have kept him there for twenty-four hours.'

'Does Paolo know that he's being followed?'

'Yes, to a certain extent, but he's been trained to ignore it and forget about it. After all, we're there to protect him, not to intrude in his life.'

Venetia huffed. 'No, you're not intruding… Perish the thought that you should stick your noses into other people's affairs!'

'It's for his own protection, and Paolo is quite aware of that.'

'How did you know we were coming back to Venice? We had intended to spend a week in Sardinia. It's only because my godmother's husband was taken ill that we returned.' She shuddered at the thought of how much she and Paolo must have been watched over the last few days, when she had been so lost in her happiness and thoughts of their future together.

'We knew you were both coming back to Pisa because your names were on the passenger list. Whenever his name comes up at any port or airport in Italy, and a few other countries, we're alerted. And then from there it was easy – our agent followed you to Venice.'

'So, meeting you yesterday was not a coincidence.'

'Well, yes and no. We were alerted when you and Paolo first met by accident and I can assure you, that set the cat among the pigeons. But we watched and waited, not knowing for sure what would happen between you. Then it became clear that we would have to intervene soon. I flew into Venice that afternoon when I knew that was where you were headed. I was going to contact you at your home to speak to you, but then we bumped into each other on your way to the restaurant – that was a coincidence. When you introduced Paolo Barone as your fiancé, I knew that I had to act quickly. I rang your father and we decided to tell you the truth immediately, hence my note to you and this meeting.'

'Still meddling… Does Paolo know you?'

'Yes, of course – I was involved with him from the very beginning and we meet twice a year to touch base.'

Venetia thought about Paolo's behaviour since they had met, all the ways in which her own sixth sense had tried to tell her something about him, and how finally, it all made sense. She swallowed again, the enormity of the truth dawning on her afresh.

'Have you told him the facts now about this whole mess?'

'Yes, we spoke yesterday evening.'

'So you've interfered again and ruined my life for the second time,' she threw out vehemently. She got up from the bench and walked away a few steps, hugging herself. If he'd told her all this before speaking to Paolo, despite her own shock she could at least have broken it to him gently in her own way, with all the love she felt for him, now more than ever. She stared across the canal. 'No wonder Paolo disappeared and couldn't face me – I can't believe it!'

'I don't think I've ruined your life, Venetia,' the agent told her in a calm voice. 'It's clear that Paolo loves you very deeply.'

She remained silent, not wanting to discuss her feelings for Paolo with this man who, along with her father, was responsible for so much loss, so many years of misery and confusion. She looked back at him coldly.

'I was unable to get in touch with him today. He's checked out of his hotel and he's not at home. Nor is he answering his mobile. He's obviously disgusted with this whole business and I don't blame him if he never wants to set eyes on me again.'

'He's at a monastery in Sardinia. He went there once before, after he left the hospital, when he first started his new life in Italy. As we had never mentioned his love affair with you, these revelations must have come as a great shock to him, of course.'

Robert Riley tapped another cigarette on his packet and glanced up at Venetia, his features appearing strained. 'He's hurt and he needs to deal with it. I'm not surprised he's unreachable there, but he knows you were a victim as much as he was. Still, this adds a heavy load to his already difficult situation, and as I've said, he needs to learn how to deal with it.'

'You're really a Machiavellian lot, playing God, meddling in other people's lives. No wonder the world is in such a mess... How can you live with yourselves?' Venetia was fuming as she paced up and down in front of him. 'So what was the exact plot?'

'I'm afraid I can't tell you more – you'll have to ask your father. I just wanted you to know that Gareth never dropped you as you'd thought, and that William has been haunted by what he did for the past decade.'

'But...'

'Talk to your father, Venetia. He's waiting for you in England.'

*   *   *

Venetia was suddenly jolted from her bitter thoughts by the creaking of brakes, as the train slowed to a halt, and the nasal voice of the stationmaster announced Chichester station. She got up and pulled her duffle bag down from the shelf above her seat. She had brought the bare minimum with her as she didn't intend staying long in England. Forty-eight hours at most – just as long as it took to have it out with her father. This would be a confrontation long past the expiry date.

There was a nip in the air as she stepped down onto the platform, and a thin, dispirited drizzle had just started, something the English somewhat romantically call 'April showers'. Bracing herself against the cold and sudden desolation, Venetia walked through a small open gateway and out into a lane. A silver-grey Rolls-Royce was drawn up outside the station building, and an elderly chauffeur in a smart grey uniform came to meet her.

'Welcome home, Miss Venetia,' he said, a broad smile lighting up his face as he rid her of her bag. 'Is that all?'

'Yes, Giles, thank you. Just a short trip this time, I'm afraid.'

Giles had been with her family as far back as Venetia could
remember. He had started off as a groom when Sir William was
a young man and had been promoted to driver when Venetia
was still at prep school. He opened the door of the car and
placed her bag in the boot. British summer time had started,
so although it was almost seven o'clock, it was still light; that
hour between daylight and darkness when it was still too light
for the happy glow of lamps, but with the outside world already
misting itself into the furry outlines of dusk.

The car turned in at the wrought-iron gates with the familiar
coat-of-arms engraved on them, and purred almost noiselessly
along the well-kept driveway of fir trees that stretched for almost
half a mile. Venetia shivered despite the heating in the vehicle.
Inwardly, she was seething with mixed emotions, her temper
simmering away in a grimly held silence, while she tried to prepare herself for perhaps the most important challenge that she
would ever have to face.

William Aston-Montagu was someone who was used to getting his own way; no doubt life as an army man had made him
so intransigent, she thought. Still, his overbearing ways had
alienated Venetia ever since she was a child, and her rebellious,
independent streak only served to infuriate him on many an
occasion. She didn't relish this meeting with her father, but she
knew that for her own peace of mind she needed to know all the
facts behind this gritty episode of her life. She must have it out
with him so that she could put it behind her but, however much
she tried to feel relaxed, she was feeling the opposite – so much
had happened in the last forty-eight hours that it was hard not
to feel shell-shocked.

Ping Lü's wise advice came back to her. She touched her talisman and reiterated it to herself as they approached the house.

*To be wronged is nothing unless you continue to remember it...
Crush the rose of anger so it may only leave its delicate
fragrance on your hands... Learn to forgive an evil deed so
you do not remain the victim of its consequences forever.*
She resolved instantly that whatever it cost her, she would
not use hurtful words.

Aston Hall was a Grade I-listed Jacobean property that had
been built to last. It stood in a spectacular setting, dominating
the surrounding countryside, its imposing red-brick façade
pierced by mullion windows with diamond-shaped panes of
glass, and a central portico sheltering stately, iron-studded oak
double doors. The austere rambling house was three storeys
high, with elaborate multi-curved Flemish gables, Tudor arches,
and barley-sugar twist chimneys typical of the Jacobean age.
It was framed on both sides by mature pink rhododendron
bushes, which helped to assuage its gloomy aspect. The place
was grand rather than handsome, stilted as opposed to comfortable, and Venetia had always hated it.

There were trees everywhere: poplars and willows and
deep evergreens, flowering shrubs and fountains. In the far-off
distance, beneath the house and overlooking the lake, a giant
magnolia on the lawn was in bloom, in the shade of which
Venetia had spent most of her summers reading.

In her mind's eye, Venetia could see the terraced garden at the
back of the house, which at this time of year was bright with
spring flowers: tulips, daffodils, zinnias and marigolds, seemingly
grown with careless grace between the winding paths; aubrietias
cascaded over the rocky walls in brilliantly hued profusion. She
much preferred those parts of the grounds which, because out of
the way, were less formal and so much more colourful.

The car came to a halt at the front of the house. Venetia
instinctively lifted her chin and braced her shoulders as

Giles opened the car door for her. The iron-studded oak doors opened as if by some automatic signal and Soames the butler appeared.

'Good evening, Miss Venetia. Welcome home, I hope you had a pleasant journey?'

'Good evening, Soames. Very pleasant, thank you.'

'Sir William is in his study. He said to let him know when you would be ready to join him for a glass of sherry in the drawing room. Dinner will be at eight o'clock, as usual.'

'Would you please tell Father that I'll join him at seven-thirty, thank you, Soames.'

The hall was grand, with a black and white marble floor. Its walls were painted the colour of old gold, the wide staircase that led off it to the upper floors thickly carpeted in leaf-green. Concealed electric lights flooded the interior with a soft glow; the hangings across the big landing window were dark green, slashed with gold. The only decoration was a round ebony table standing in the middle of the room with a great jar of arum lilies spilling out – cold, austere and beautiful.

More than ever, Venetia hated the place. Instinctively she compared it to Miraggio. Even though Aston Hall was far grander and more spectacular, with a museum-like quality about it, she couldn't wait to get back to the warmth of Italy. The grandfather clock in the hall boomed seven strokes as she made her way up to her bedroom.

The room was exactly as she had left it a year ago. Venetia took off her chic Parisian mackintosh and went to look out of the window. A milk-white mist lay across the lake and covered the lower part of the garden and grounds. Far beyond, on the opposite bank, the forest stretched like a black reef washed by silver foam. The sheer ethereal beauty of the scene made her catch her breath, yet there was an added poignancy in the very illusion of peace it created. For there was no peace in her heart, only an ongoing passion which burned like a flame. She was dismayed and almost frightened by the intensity of it.

She missed Paolo, she ached for him; she couldn't bear the pain of being without him, especially knowing that he was hurting after what he'd been told. It was as if she had been caught in a great tidal wave. Could he ever forgive? Would he ever forget? If she was irredeemably tainted by her family in his eyes, how could they possibly take up again where they had left off? A hand seemed to close upon her heart, squeezing and twisting it.

Judd and Paolo were one. Ping Lü had been right – the wise Chineseman had known all along. *All becoming is circular,* he'd said, with that enigmatic little smile so characteristic of him. Venetia found it hard to say what her feelings for Judd had been all these years. She would probably have denied that she loved him. Besides, how could she love him? She was hurt, broken. Yet all through those years her thoughts had almost always included recollections of some walk or talk with him. Though Paolo and Judd were one and the same, now she knew that it was Paolo she loved, the man who had suffered, and through this suffering he had acquired a sort of compassion, generosity and wisdom that, now she came to think of it, Judd had always lacked.

Venetia washed her face and combed her hair; she was not going to change. She was not there to entertain or to be entertained, but to find out the last gruesome details of her wretched love story.

A brooding silence hung over the house when she went down to meet her father. The only sounds she could hear were the beating of her own heart and the tick-tock of the grandfather clock.

The living room at Aston Hall was one of six reception rooms. It was a large room, almost square. Three of the walls were lined with mirrors, and between each of them, concealed lamps gave out a rosy, flattering glow. The fourth wall was occupied by paintings by Turner and Andrew Wyeth. The paintwork was all ivory, with polished oak floors, covered here and there with a few soft-toned rugs. There were heavy oak beams across the ceiling, and the doors and casement windows were also in dark wood. The Jacobean tapestry on the window seats, curtains and cushions made a perfect foil for the ancient carved furniture and the faint gleam of pewter. Two or three occasional tables and several French gilt chairs were grouped at one end of the room, while at the other end were two brown leather sofas set opposite each other with a Chinese red lacquer coffee table between them. A large stone fireplace housed crackling flames, and above the mantelpiece hung a huge nineteenth-century oil painting of Aston Hall, surrounded by its landscaped gardens.

When Venetia walked in, she didn't see her father immediately. He was sitting in the only armchair at the far end of the room, next to one of the windows, under the light of a standard lamp. Next to him was a small round table, and he was smoking his pipe.

'Hello, Father.'

He got up to greet her as she came towards him. A tall and once muscular man, with a hard but handsome face, Sir William Aston-Montagu was now more portly and balding, with thick, wispy eyebrows that were still quick to express his every mood.

'Ah, Venetia, my dear… You look tired.'

When she showed no intention of giving him an affectionate greeting, moving instead to stand casually by the old casement window, her father sat down again.

'Well, I haven't slept for over twenty-four hours.'

There was silence for a few moments while they seemed to measure each other.

'Yes…'

'I have you to thank for that, of course.' Venetia's voice was brittle.

'Come to give me the third degree, eh? Yes, I suppose I owe you an explanation.'

Venetia looked at her father in the shadowy light, her eyes ablaze with anger and unshed tears. 'I think you owe me much more than that, Father, don't you think?'

For a long moment nothing was said while Sir William drew on his pipe. His expression was unreadable but his eyes looked tired and old in a way they had never done before. 'Yes. You know, it wasn't intended to go wrong the way it did – he wasn't supposed to come to any harm.'

She hugged herself, gripping her arms tightly to stop her hands from shaking with anger. Her voice was cold and hard. 'That's beside the point. How could you bring yourself to interfere, and manipulate my life and that of Paolo's… I mean, Judd's, in this most contemptible way? Do you realise what you've done? Have you no conscience at all?'

'I can understand your fury, but at the time I thought I was doing the right thing by you.'

She stared at her father, torn between anger and a terrible sadness. 'I was in love with Judd, I was going to have his child, for heaven's sake – your grandchild.'

Sir William lifted his hands in a small gesture at her challenging tone, looking at her with his usual gruff and irritated expression, tinted with some discomfort.

'Yes, my dear… I know… it's all very regrettable, but I honestly thought that I was protecting you.' His eyes switched from her face to the flames flickering in the fireplace and he paused, as if choosing his words carefully, struggling with his pride. 'I recognise my error now, and for ten years I've been carrying my guilt. It's been a heavy burden ... I tried to help Judd as much as I could, without him knowing of course where the help came from. He's always thought that it was the government who provided him with this new life...'

Her amber eyes filled with contempt. 'You mean you tried to salve your conscience.'

Sir William's eyes hardened a little. 'Well, my dear, if you want to look at it that way, suit yourself,' he answered dryly, tapping the contents of his pipe into the ashtray on his table. 'But in some ways, your Judd is much better off as Paolo and...'

Venetia felt almost physically winded by the shock of his words. 'I can't believe what I'm hearing... How cynical can one get? You're completely immoral...'

'No, my dear, I'm realistic and practical,' he half snapped.

The young woman stared at her father, eyes blazing. 'Judd's totally lost his memory. Do you realise how dreadful it is to live with a vacuum in one's head... to lose the sense of who you really are?'

Sir William nodded. 'I imagine that it's pretty horrendous, but look on the bright side,' he said calmly. 'He knows he's been a hero who has rendered a great service to his country. He was given a whole new identity, with the means to create a good life for himself – which he has, I must admit, with great success.'

'Don't be such a hypocrite, Father! All that would have been acceptable if he hadn't been deliberately manipulated to take on such a dangerous mission in the first place. Your dear friend Robert Riley told me that you exploited his patriotism. You always knew about the insecurity he felt among his public-school peers.'

'You're right, of course, Venetia. I admit Robert recruited him for this job as a favour to me because I wanted him out of the way. That posting would have separated you long enough for... well, for one of you to sever the ties between you... and I admit that I intercepted the letters that you wrote to each other...'

'Letters? *My* letters to Judd?'

'Yes, your letters to Judd, which were blocked on arrival and the letters Judd wrote to you, which were seized before they left the barracks.'

'So Judd never knew that I was pregnant, he never knew I was pregnant?' Venetia repeated her words mechanically, as if she could scarcely grasp their import.

Sir William paused. 'No.'

As a drowning person is said to see his past life before his eyes, so Venetia seemed to see with piercing clarity all the days that she had spent waiting for Judd's letters, and relive the same disappointment when she'd come back from the postbox at the gate empty-handed. Suddenly everything seemed to fall into focus. There was no mystery about it any longer; Judd had loved her all along. Both of them had been manipulated by those who should have been the dearest to her.

Venetia sat down on the casement window seat, clenching the edge of the cushions with her fingers. Tears welled in her eyes.

'Oh, Father, how could you do such a hateful thing to your own flesh and blood?' she cried out, her voice choked. 'Just because... just because you didn't approve of Judd... because he didn't come from the same snobbish background as you do! How could you? How *could* you?' She raised her eyes, though she could barely look at her father. 'Did Mother know all this?'

Her father shifted in his chair. 'Yes, but your mother's loyalties lay with me. You should not blame her – she believed that I was right and that we were protecting you.'

'That's no excuse for such deviousness, and you know it. I hate you!' Venetia was trembling now, unable to contain her distress at the revelation of this betrayal on the part of both her parents.

'Well that, my child, is your prerogative.' His voice had dropped to a gravelly murmur as he picked up his pipe again.

'I'll never forgive you.'

'That saddens me, Venetia, but I can well understand your reaction. There are days when I can hardly forgive myself,' he muttered. Sir William gazed into the fire again and pulled a pouch of tobacco from his pocket, tamping it down into his pipe. 'After you lost the child, and I saw you lying there in that hospital, and Judd was also in hospital... well, I had time to think. I know you may find it difficult to believe, but all these years I've wanted to try and put things right somehow, and when we found out that you had accidentally met the boy again, it seemed the opportunity had offered itself.'

Venetia looked at her father properly for the first time that evening. Yes, he had certainly aged and for such a big, imposing man, he appeared smaller. She was shocked to realise that a sadness had slightly softened his once-proud features. All through her childhood, he had been so wrapped up in his work that he had shown her little interest; and as she had grown into a young woman, he had hardly given her a moment's consideration – apart from when they were arguing about what she should do with her life, of course. Despite the words that he struggled with now, her anger couldn't be swallowed in an instant; she was still unable to forgive all the misery he had caused Paolo and herself. Venetia lifted her chin resolutely.

'And interfering again, as Riley has, might have spoilt my life for the second time. I can't imagine that Paolo will forgive the evil that has touched his life. How can he look into my eyes after what you, my own father, have done to him?'

Sir William lifted his bristly eyebrows. 'I think you're selling him very short – Paolo is an intelligent man. His reaction was rather surprising. He was more upset for you than for himself. The first thing he said when he learnt the truth was: "Poor Venetia, how she must have suffered."' He gave a grunt that was nearly a laugh, and looked at his daughter wryly. 'He's really quite something, your Paolo! I think now that you've found each other again, and despite all these unfortunate events, you'll have your happy-ever-after, and I'll be able to go to my grave in peace. Your Nanny Horren often used to say: "*If two hearts are really destined to find each other, Fate will find a way of reuniting them.*" I never understood half of what that woman said, or what that meant – now I know. Good woman, Nanny Horren... You were obviously going to come together at the end, and after all that's happened, I'm grateful it's worked out that way.'

She glanced at him. 'I suppose you destroyed the letters?'

'No, I've kept both yours and Judd's in my safe all these years.' Sir William reached over to the small table next to his chair and picked up a thick white package. 'Here they are, unopened. You can do as you wish with them.'

Venetia looked up at her father, with that expression of amazement and scorn. She got up from the window seat and took them. 'A little bit late in the day, but I'll have them, thank you. At least you had the decency not to do away with them or pry – I'm sure Paolo will be as eager to read mine as much as I am to read his.' She found it difficult to keep the sarcasm from her voice and he frowned.

'Need you be so bitter? I'm sorry, Venetia, to have hurt you so badly. I don't blame you for hating me. Still, I do hope that one day you will find it in your heart to forgive me.'

Venetia looked down at the envelope, turning it over in her hands. She gave a quiet sigh. After everything that had happened, through her anger, she still wanted to believe that her father was truly sorry. 'I suppose I've already forgiven you deep down. After all, you're my father... but I could *never* subject Paolo to your presence. He's suffered enough and I really don't know how I will be able to look him in the eye. I'm so ashamed.'

William Aston-Montagu lifted himself out of his chair and moved towards his daughter. He put his hand on her arm.

'I will not impose myself upon you, but you must know that this house will always be open to you both – and to your children.'

She looked hard at his face. 'Thank you,' she whispered. Her expression stiffened again and she stepped away from him, rejecting his tentative sympathy, the short-lived moment of non-combat over.

Sir William stared at his daughter for one long moment. 'One last word of advice, though,' he said finally. 'It is not a good thing to look back. By all means give the letters to Paolo, but it wouldn't be healthy to rehash all that again. Now that you know what you needed to know, let sleeping dogs lie and be happy.'

Venetia smiled ruefully. 'On this occasion, you may be right...'

'Will you have dinner with me?'

'No, thank you – I'm very tired and I would be grateful if Soames or Jenny could bring a tray up to me. I'll be leaving first thing in the morning.'

Sir William gave a grim half-smile and nodded, as if unsurprised by his daughter's answer. 'I don't get much sleep nowadays – just a few hours a night. I'll be in my study if you would like to say goodbye.'

Venetia's face softened a little. She had never seen her father contrite. In the big room now he seemed half the man she had known.

'Yes, Father, of course. I'll come and see you before I go.'

*   *   *

Night was falling. Paolo was making steady progress as he headed up the winding road back to San Stefano. He glanced at his Rolex. It was getting late and he wanted to get a good night's sleep before he left for Venice in the morning. A subtle agitation still spread through every part of him, as each turn in the road brought him closer to Miraggio, where he could breathe again and pack his things. At least he wouldn't have to waste time tackling Antonio on his return, he mused. When he had rung Ernestina to tell her that he was on his way back, she had taken great satisfaction in telling him that the caretaker had already vacated his cottage and disappeared, taking his dog with him. It seemed that he knew what was coming to him and had thought better of facing the wrath of his employer.

Trees gave way to vineyards sloping away from the road as the car sped onwards beneath a darkening sky. Paolo glanced up at the emerging moon. He wondered what Venetia was doing at that moment, where she was, what she was feeling. Maybe she had left the city; she could be anywhere. All he knew was that he had to find her.

Venetia… despite the shock it had been to learn about the pernicious manipulation of which he had been a victim, Paolo felt a sort of relief. It was almost as if he had regained part of his identity… Venetia had been, and still was, the only love of his life. It had always been Venetia. Why wasn't he surprised? It all made such perfect sense now. From the moment he had set eyes on her on that misty evening in Venice, it was as if he had always known her.

He inhaled deeply, trying to control the agonising need for her that was cramping his body. The muscles around his mouth twitched with the strain of not being able to kiss her immediately, his arms ached with the urge to embrace her, every part of him needing her close. He wanted to hold her supple form against him and fill his lungs with the sweet fragrance of her hair... to touch the velvet silkiness of her skin. Only then would the restlessness that pervaded him subside, this lost and lonely feeling that took over his being every time he was parted from her.

He tried to think of other matters, ones that had been at the forefront of his mind ever since Robert Riley had told him the truth. He had greeted those revelations with mixed feelings. At first his heart had hit so hard against his ribs that his throat had closed, and breathing was impossible; he had thought for a moment that the shock was so great it would kill him. Then, after the impact of the first blow had subsided, incredulity, anger, revolt, hatred, but also love, and a sort of joy, had battled for supremacy in his tormented, confused mind. Riley was to meet Venetia and tell her everything; he would persuade her to then meet with her father in England. What would her reaction be? Would she forgive the lies and deceit of the last ten years? Would she forgive the lies *he* had been forced to tell her? Slowly, as rational thinking had come back, he had sought refuge at the monastery in Sardinia, where he had been before looking for help and counsel, and the only place he knew could help him again. Shock, and the fear of Venetia's response, had turned him deeply in on himself. Though it pained him as much as this new collapse of his reality, he couldn't bring himself to speak to her until he had found the right words to bring her back to him.

Although the thought of what Sir William Aston-Montagu had done to him, and to his own daughter, still twisted a knife in Paolo's gut, the acuteness of the initial anguish had passed, and he knew that the few days he had spent in retreat at the monastery had done him good. Talking about his anger and his hatred for the man had, in some ways, assuaged the pain and made him less embittered; and despite some resentment still remaining, he was conscious at last of a great peace and acceptance he hadn't felt since he had woken up in that hospital bed all those years ago.

Paolo remembered the monk to whom he had opened his heart: how he had listened patiently, attentively, his face as immobile as a carving in stone, his bony fingers clasped tranquilly as if in the habit of perpetual prayer, his blue eyes resting kind and steady on Paolo's troubled face.

The words of the tall bony man, with hawk-like features and a misleading harshness of tone, came back to him: 'Hate does not cure anything, my son, and it is not for us to sit in judgement on anyone. It is a thousand pities when a parent interferes to this extent, but you see, God in his extreme kindness doesn't leave anybody... life is not ruined so easily... and even if it hadn't come right in the end, as it has, we must forgive. God in His great kindness every day forgives each one of us. It is astonishingly easy to forgive when one understands the motive. I do not think that Venetia's parents' motives were as selfish as they seem, only mistaken.'

Paolo's hands gripped the steering wheel firmly as the road curved back and forth. Thoughts that had plagued him over the last few days returned. Would Venetia be able to trust him again? What if...? Cold sweat rose up on his spine at the thought that he might have lost her... Venetia, the love of his life.

The ancient walls of Miraggio came into view as Paolo rounded the bend. He put his foot down, punching the gas pedal, and the nervy car flew up the hill. In response, his muscles tensed and his pulse rate accelerated. He slowed the car to a crawl as he entered the tall gates and stopped opposite the front door. The glimmering windows of the big house cast their pale yellow light out on to the gravel. In the sky the moon was gleaming, bathing the place in its brightness.

He made his way to La Sirena without thinking. If he couldn't be with Venetia tonight, he wanted to walk through the cottage garden and surround himself with the echo of her presence.

As Paolo drew near the cottage, he saw a figure outlined against the melting dusky-violet of the evening sky. He felt the blood coursing through his veins and the heat building up inside him. For a brief moment he closed his eyes, as if to blink away the mirage.

But when he opened them again she was still there: Venetia, sitting on the slope, her back turned to him, looking out to sea.

The earth, the sea, the woman – his love – all lay transfixed in the flooding glow – the beauty of it pressed on him with crushing strength. The world seemed to spin gently, lost in the depths of utter silence, growing stranger and lovelier with each moment. Everything appeared hushed with ecstasy.

Paolo seemed to be lost in the picture as though standing outside himself in that still scene. His heart was beating heavily: she had come to him. For a moment he saw more clearly how she had always been with him; for years she had been there in the depths of him, lifegiving, but an unacknowledged echo of the past, an echo of a love so pure, so deep that it had survived even the annihilation of its memory. Paolo could not define what Venetia represented to him because it was something beyond and all around him.

An owl hooted twice uncertainly, intensifying the enfolding stillness. After a pause, a blurred answering call came from across the garden, and then the bird flew past on its heavy, shadowy flight, milky-white, almost noiseless. It startled Venetia and she turned, and then his eyes were fixed on hers.

For a moment, the silence deepened, and the darkness seemed to deepen too, becoming almost tangible.

Getting up almost as if in a dream, Venetia came to Paolo, her eyes shining with a myriad of emotions. Paolo wondered how people conveyed anything by speech as he watched her approach, himself unmoving. He knew that words would have served him perfectly well not so long ago, for other people, in another life; there are overtones and undertones of understanding which are caught by only those who have had the same experience… but the *words* themselves to express that sole and final espousal he felt for Venetia right now – how inadequate they would be. There was an exquisite silent intensity that hung in the air between them now.

So Paolo said no word as she came to him, but his eyes dwelt on her as she moved towards him in the silence with faltering steps. When she reached him, he gazed down wonderingly. Without speaking, he simply drew her close, holding her with his arms stretched right round her so that their bodies were pressed together. Looking at her, he felt as though she were no longer in herself: she was in him, and he was in her, their beings had become one. The struggle was over.

Paolo's eyes, once serious, impenetrable, and perhaps a little questioning in their depths, changed now, reflecting utter peace. Leaning forward, he bent and kissed her gently, on her forehead first, then on her parted lips. As they stood there close to each other, ringed by moonlight in La Sirena's garden above the sea, he could see her face, always newly mesmerising to him, become more captivating still – so tranquil was it. Then a cloud engulfed the moon, and dark breezes whipped up. It was as though they themselves were not permitted to look on their full delight in case it angered the gods, and so Paolo picked up Venetia and went into the cottage.

That night their lovemaking had an intimacy it had not had before. This new familiarity had nothing to do with the recent times they had made love. Their bodies suddenly seemed to remember things about each other that they hadn't expected. There was a sense of rightness, of coming home, that wrapped around them like a tender embrace.

Life would go on, that was the natural order of things, and there was much to heal in them both; but tonight grief, anger, regret all dimmed and faded to oblivion in the midst of their love.

'Oh, Paolo, I feel so happy I could die – right here, right now!' Venetia whispered as he held her still-trembling body against his, her eyes starry bright with love and hope and laughter.

'Don't talk of death, *tesoro mio* – we've been dead long enough. Tomorrow we shall begin to live.'

'Yes, tomorrow… what a lovely word… we'll have a whole life of tomorrows.'

They were a man and a woman in love. Hand in hand they would follow their silvery path and climb the steps to the moon; Paolo would cherish and protect her for as long as he lived, and Venetia would make a home for him, bear his children, and compensate for the years of misery he had been through. They belonged … nothing else mattered. Finally the echoes of their love had reached the gods, and life became clement because they had proved they deserved their happy ever after.

Night deepened as the moon disappeared, and the inky shadows enveloped their entwined bodies, but all they saw was the miracle of a new dawn in each other's eyes.

Q AND A
WITH HANNAH FIELDING

A Fine Romance

What are the ingredients of a perfect romance novel?
Escapism with a plausible plot, a little suspense, magnificent surroundings and characters that are real and compelling.

What makes the perfect hero?
Physique matters but charisma and strength of character are more important than looks, in my opinion. I like to see a balance of machismo and kindness, wit to add piquancy and, of course, passion, passion, passion! I love Mr Rochester in *Jane Eyre* because he's so human. I like a hero who is imperfect; that makes the story all the more vivid.

What makes the perfect heroine?
Beautiful, strong but still feminine, intelligent and passionate; a certain amount of innocence and a generosity in lovemaking. My favourite classic heroine is Jane Eyre: assertive but feminine, a passionate nature, a strong sense of her own self-worth and justice; and I admire her integrity and generosity of heart. All my heroines are to some extent naive where emotional experience is concerned (for example, Coral in *Burning Embers*): definitely an element that reflects my own naivety when I was young.

Why do you write romance?

I'm an incurable romantic – a passionate and imaginative dreamer, in love with the beautiful places that I visit on my travels. I write what comes from the heart: romance.

Inspirations

When and why did you start writing?

Stories and writing have always been part of my life. My grandmother was a published author of poetry and my father, a great raconteur, published a book about the history of our family.

My governess used to tell me the most fabulous tales and when I was seven, we came to an agreement: for every story she told me, I told her one in return. The rambling house in Alexandria, Egypt, where I grew up was built on a hill overlooking the Mediterranean. My bedroom commanded the most breathtaking views of the ever-changing sea, which made my imagination run wild. I would dream of princes that flew in from faraway lands on their magic carpets, princesses dressed in gowns made of sunrays and moonbeams, and dragons rising from the waves that crashed against the rocks underneath my windows. Later, at the convent school I went to, the French nuns who taught us sowed in me a love of words and of literature. When I was about fourteen, I wrote short romantic stories that I circulated in class, which made me very popular with my peers but less so with the nuns!

To quote Anaïs Nin: '*If you do not breathe through writing, if you do not cry out in writing, or sing in writing, then don't write.*' I do all that. Writing is my life.

Art, culture, food and fashion are key features in *The Echoes of Love* – how do you find that they help tell a story?

I try to convey every detail my imagination is conjuring up –

all the senses are involved, so that the reader can form a clear picture of the story's setting and understand the characters and their reactions. 'Write about what you know' and 'write from the heart' are my mottos.

My governess was half-Italian and half-French, and my daughter, Alexandra, to whom I have dedicated *The Echoes of Love*, teaches the history of Italian art all over Italy, so I had a lot of inside information for this book. Apart from that, I've travelled many times to Italy, and as background research, I cooked local Venetian and Tuscan dishes, listened to Italian music and watched classic Italian films. As for fashion... I've always been interested in fashion and jewellery, and I do enjoy describing what my heroine is wearing. Italian fashion – wonderful!

Do you believe in Fate?

To a certain extent I believe in Fate but, having said that, I also believe that you make your own destiny. '*Aide toi et le ciel t'aidera*' was a favourite saying of my governess: '*Help yourself and heaven will help you.*' I definitely believe there are people who have the gift of second sight. Besides, I'm a romantic and, for me, fortune tellers equal mystery and romance. That is why Fate and fortune tellers often feature in my novels in some way or another.

Do you always use exotic locations in your novels?

So far, yes, because that's what I know best and they are places that excite and inspire me. The warm nature of the people, their flamboyant customs and traditions, the vivid colours of their countryside, the lush tastes of their cuisine, the passion in their music and their language... all that helps me paint a rich and vibrant canvas in which to set my romantic plots; not to mention their dark, sultry, brooding heroes who will sweep my heroines off their feet with their passion and virile Mediterranean *savoir faire*!

If I had to choose the four most romantic places in the world they would be the Alhambra in Spain, which is an Arabian Nights palace, startling in its beauty and impact on the imagination; Oxford in England, where the city overflows with antiquity; Yellowstone National Park in the USA, for its breathtaking wide expanses left to nature's will; and Aswan in Egypt, where the desert night delivers infinity, eternity, beauty – all those grand emotions that inspire romance.

Nature is present almost like a separate character in your books – why is it so important to you?

I have always been a writer who pays keen attention to setting; to describing sights and sounds, smells, tastes and textures. Place holds such power to colour a story. All my books are borne of my travels; of poking around in back streets and cafes; meeting locals and exploring landscapes – and, of course, reading up extensively on cultures. My aim is to transport readers to places I've visited and loved. In a way, I'm sharing my happy experiences with the person who has done me the honour of reading my book.

For half the year, my home is in Kent, England, and for the other half I live in France, on the southern coast of Provence in the county of Var. At my French home, I see the most breathtaking sunrises and sunsets imaginable. Every time I sit on the verandah and watch nature play out its most magical show, I cannot fail to fall in love with the place, with the world, with the very notion of romance – and from there, the writing flows on to the page.

Your books are full of wonderful proverbs – do you have a favourite?

I have many favourite proverbs and quotes, but the one that has served me best is: '*If at first you don't succeed, try, try again.*'

My father used to tell me this every time I got frustrated that I couldn't do something or other. Now, when I am at my wits' end and about to give up on something, I hear his encouraging voice and it injects a whole new energy into me.

A Writer's Life

When and where do you write?

One way or another I am always writing – if I'm not actually writing, I'm thinking about it.

In France I write mainly in my room, overlooking the most fabulous view of the Mediterranean, but also in my gazebo. On a sunny day when there are not many crowds around I sometimes escape to one of my favourite places on the coast, sitting for hours dreaming and plotting, or in the many pavement cafes in nearby towns, where I can sip a *café latté* and people-watch to my heart's content. While the English countryside doesn't have the same intensity of heat or colour as the bay of St Tropez, my refuge and inspiration there is our oak-panelled library, where I write surrounded by the works of all my favourite authors, while a fire is roaring in the wood-burning stove and an almighty storm is howling outside.

Who is your favourite living writer?

My favourite writer is usually the one who wrote the latest book I've enjoyed! I read voraciously, and regularly post reviews on my website but here are a selection of writers and their books that I've particularly loved: Penelope Lively – *Oleander, Jacaranda*; Jennifer McVeigh – *The Fever Tree*; Paula McLain – *The Paris Wife*; Lynn Kerstan – *The Golden Leopard*; Meg Cabot – *Ransom My Heart*; Julia Gregson – *Jasmine Nights*; Santa Montefiore – *The Summer House*; Barbara Freethy – *Ryan's Return*.

Who is your favourite classic writer?
My real favourites are the French classic romantic authors of the nineteenth century, whose books I grew up with. I devoured them during my teens and still re-read my favourite stories and poems by Victor Hugo, Théophile Gautier, Balzac, Stendhal, Chateaubriand and Leconte de Lisle, to name just a few. A more contemporary writer, M. M. Kaye, author of *The Far Pavilions* and *Shadow of the Moon*, has also influenced my writing because I so enjoyed reading her highly descriptive books.

If you weren't a writer, what would you do?
I'd renovate rundown period cottages (which I did before I sat down to serious writing), or I'd be an antique dealer. I love rummaging in the *marchés aux puces* of various countries and learning about ancient civilisations.

Find out more at **www.hannahfielding.net**